*Also by A. A. Attanasio in New English Library paperback*

The Moon's Wife
Solis
Radix
The Dragon and the Unicorn
Arthor
The Last Legends of Earth

## About the author

A. A. Attanasio was born in Newark, New Jersey, in 1951. He is the author of such highly acclaimed novels as *Radix, Wyvern, The Last Legends of Earth* and *Kingdom of the Grail*. He lives with his wife and children in Hawaii.

# The Dark Shore

### A. A. Attanasio

**NEW ENGLISH LIBRARY**
Hodder and Stoughton

Copyright © 1996 by A. A. Attanasio

First published in Great Britain in 1996
by Hodder and Stoughton

First published in paperback in 1996 by
Hodder and Stoughton
A division of Hodder Headline PLC

A New English Library paperback

The right of A. A. Attanasio to be identified as the Author of
the Work has been asserted by him in accordance with the
Copyright, Designs and Patents Act 1988.

10 9 8 7 6 5 4 3 2 1

British Library Cataloguing in Publication Data
A CIP catalogue record for this book is available from the British Library.

ISBN 0 340 64947 X

Printed and bound in Great Britain by
Cox & Wyman Ltd, Reading, Berkshire

Hodder and Stoughton
A division of Hodder Headline PLC
338 Euston Road
London NW1 3BH

To Nick Austin
for helping me find my way
through the dark within
that is itself a light

I will give you the treasures of darkness.
*Isaiah* 45:3

## Acknowledgments

✦

I am indebted to John Bergin for his conceptual panache in helping me visualize Irth. He went with me on my journey as west as darkness and accompanied me across the immense open dream to the Dark Shore. This novel is better for his company.

# Contents

✦✦✦

Prelude: Death's Fences ................................................................ 1

## Part One: Irth

Cacodemons ...................................................................... 9
Dogbrick and Ripcat ........................................................... 35
I Gather the Darkness .......................................................... 63
One Day in the Calendar of Eyes ............................................ 91
Lord of the Nethermost ...................................................... 129
What Lives After ............................................................... 157
The Cloths of Heaven ......................................................... 187
Dark the Seed ................................................................... 215
A Maiden in the Fastness of Ogres ........................................ 241

## Part Two: The Abiding Star

Thief of Shadows ............................................................... 271
Three Blind Gods .............................................................. 299
Ladder of the Wind ............................................................ 329

The Star Fallen ................................................ 363
Strange Planet, Dying ...................................... 391
The Stars Under Our Feet ............................... 429
A Flesh of Dreaming ........................................ 461

*Appendices:*

Documents
*The Gibbet Scrolls* .......................................... 495
About *The Gibbet Scrolls* ............................... 499

the dominions of Irth

Saxar

Zul

the Qaf

Andére Crag

Keri

Malpais Highlands

the Falls of Mirdath

Old Sharn

Lake Apocalypse

Planet 520

Spiderlands

Mjoadrun

Dorzen

Ux

Elvre

Rainbow Forests of Bryse

Arwar Odawl

Drymarch

Sharna-Bambara

Floating Stone

Mere of Goblins

Cloths of Heaven

Palace of Abominations

the Reef Isles of Nhat

# Prelude:

## Death's Fences

---

The power of the witch is in her hair. The ones who killed her knew this. They cut off her long tresses, tied them into devil's shoelaces, and bound her hands and feet. Now she lies on her back, naked, still, her blank, insensate stare fixed on the night sky, the black of her pupils blown wide – and in them, the inverted reflections of the star-whorls, the spiral stairways we descend, bodies falling out of the lucent darkness of the heavens, ragged shards of starlight caught in our windy hair, both of us racing to her silently as light, quietly as pain.

But she is gone. The ones who killed her knew what they were doing, and now she is gone. She has left behind the form we labored so hard to build. It lies on the forest floor like a discarded garment.

When we bend close and listen, we can hear the shadow of her life, fading, yet singing. It breathes from within a deep inner dark. This is the shadow of death. Despondencies thicken.

Quickly, I step back. We must not listen too closely. We must not listen, or we will lose our souls before we find hers.

Where to look? Where else but in the world she occupied, in the forest. She is here somewhere.

You linger over her and will not budge. I warn you: The music in death's shadow has elements of awe and enormity that gleam with cold emotion, with violence. A wolf crying at its own echo. The soul is lost in these sounds. But you will not listen. You will not budge. So, I go alone to find her.

Even through the darkness, I can see the footprints of her killers in the leaf litter of the forest floor. They run westward, to where blunt hills surge. The tracks lead me through the comfortless dark, along corridors of walnut and oak, to the spine of a hill. From that crest, I gaze down upon a river and a town.

The silver horn of the moon discloses the serpent curves of water where the killers have taken the witch's soul, wanting to drown her. And there, in the slick water, her soul would have shriveled away – but for the town. The killers feared drowning her this close to their community. They feared releasing fetors, noxious vapors, near their families and so they carried her on. And by this fear, there is yet hope for her soul.

But here the killers leave no more tracks. They wade through the shallows, and I cannot see if they have gone up or downstream.

The mud of the bank quivers like frogskin as I kneel to lay my hands upon the water. I would know this river that jellies forth from the old life of the hills. Its satin-black length slides past the glittering lights of the town, and within its depthless mirror I feel all its names – Carrier of Shadows, Grassy Shoulders, Footsteps to the Wind. These are river names given by the aboriginal peoples whose tribes once dwelled here, names remembered by vague ghosts that still hover in these woods.

The wraiths of the forest gather on the embankment as I rub the water, feeling with me for the killers and the soul this river drowns. I rub the water and launch upon its stammering ripples the forest ghosts. Then, I wait as the specters drift into the darkness looking for the witch.

The town's wharf lanterns and dock lamps reflect in the river-bend like an angel's fiery arm that extends across a stretch of silence and hands me a cry. The ghosts carry back to me this whimper of exhausted pain – this shadow flicker of life from the witch.

That is all I require. By that slim cry, I feel my way toward her, upstream. I approach silently over the gravel bars, past the slow dismantling of willow banks and the spectral reflections of birch islands. Soon, I smell the fragrance of depleted rage. The killers have completed their work. Night spills around them with the dirty smells of the drowned soul. The evil red eyes of cigarettes and cigars pulse in the dark coves of the forest, where the killers smoke to cut the sour miasma of death.

Out of the foggy aura of the river, beneath the balding moon, I rise. The red eyes brighten and fall with shrieks and howls of despair. The killers believe I have come for them. But I have not. I do not pursue them as they scamper away under their fluttering moans. I have come for the soul, and I find her on the muddy bottom of the river, shivering, full of perplexity and pain beyond forgetting.

The killers have ruined her. Yet she lives. Within the glass sphere of her consciousness, new shapes swirl as though another form of life were possible. Of course, it is not. She is deformed. Never again will she fit into a form that could pass for human. Never again can she do our work for us here among autumn's brood and winter's whips. Never again will she dance for us under the spring moon or roll in the flowerdust of summer and chant happy songs before the long boiling twilights.

She is ruined. A part of her soul is dead. An animula already thrives off her necrosis. When I touch it, it feels like deep isolation. Sadly, I lower her back into the water, and she cries. Oh, she cries! And a great sense of distance opens in me. The force of her life swells with her cries, then dissolves and vanishes like wishes.

The essential shadow of her secrecy remains. The shadow of death. The very shadow that captivates you at her body now holds me fast in the sleek waters of the river where her soul has melted wholly away. An irrational feeling of enchantment grips me. It is desire, shining madly. It is the desire that speaks of our ancient life and the deep, sensual dark of the dreamer.

I cannot budge. The vacancies of her soul hold me here – vacancies filled with a dark music that speaks of her. The stream laps at my legs, urging me to walk along with it. But I will not budge. I will stay here for a long time, haunting this riverbank, just as you will linger in the woods where her body died, where you cannot remove your gaze from her face with its splattered blood welded in rays.

For a long time I will remain here listening to the floating echoes of her despair. I will wait for the killers to return to the scenes of their crime, wait for the hot taste of their blood to free me from my cold fascination with the soul's dark music.

And while I wait, the music speaks to me as though the soul were just a song someone played. Just a song. At the most remote end of receding, the soul's shadow is singing. I hear it in the shattered light of the river. I hear it in the stream's fluid shadows, in its soft black wind, and in the starlight breaking in waves along its currents, quietly as pain.

The clank of winter wakes me from my murderous trance. The sun is not yet up, and smoke rises from the frozen river in starspun veils.

I had become entranced watching things flow: autumn colors like a breathing fire, river currents, time . . .

The killers never returned. The cold sets me free from my trance of grief: Through a soul-land of snow and ice, I wander inside the death song of the witch—

Mist circles the white mountains. I return to her body, but it is gone. And you are gone, as well. The sun climbs through the icy trees in starbursts of frazzled light.

Looking for you, I climb back into the sky. Your large house above the clouds is empty, its blue walls blank as the sky around it. So is your alchemic laboratory between the stars. Its vast chambers are devoid of the retorts, alembics, distilling coils and furnaces that once preoccupied you.

You've gone back whence you came, back to the bright coast of first light, to a world inside the fiery origin of the universe. And you've taken all your alchemic gold, all the magical stuff you came

4

to my cold world to create – all save these few flakes.

They gleam darkly in my hand like the dust of sunset.

A great being of light such as yourself would consider these motes insignificant. You probably never even noticed them scattered so thinly on the floor. But to this cold creature, these traces of wonder are seeds of magic – raw power.

While I hold them, I live in two worlds at once. I experience the unimagined radiance of your fiery realm and yet remain a creature of darkness.

Striding through your lab's familiar astral hallways, walking into starry rooms filled with your absence, I determine to go back down. I will return to the forest, and I will plant these seeds of magic in the fertile ground of the Dark Shore.

In time, if I work the soil right, if I apply correctly the mysteries you have taught me, the power will grow. Then I will have the magic to follow you. I know where you will lead me. To the bright shore. To where you have taken the witch's spirit, away from its broken body and deformed soul. Back to its place in the light of creation.

Her name was Lara. She was a wild child when we found her. A forest child. We saved her from beasts and gave her power over all the forest.

A thin blue flame ran under her skin when she danced for us.

Like rain's most lovely pale daughter, like fog, she floated on the earth. Her grace healed all who needed her, and she served the ill and hungry as well as she served us. She used her magic so ingenuously and with such largeness of heart, I fell in love with her. You did, too – or so I thought. Wasn't it our love that had changed her from animal-child to beautiful cosmic dancer?

Since she has died, her fragrance is everywhere.

Nothing binds me to this earth now that she is gone. Nothing but the shackles of time, and I am working hard to break those.

It was my fault she died. You chose me among all others to help you. I was chosen because I was strong. I was supposed to be

strong enough to keep my people in line. You trusted me. Worse
– she trusted me.

I failed, because I miscalculated evil. I got so absorbed in my
love for Lara, I didn't see how she scared the others.

And she did scare them. The wind talks to the sky, the trees
talk to the wind, and she talked to the trees and told their secrets
to whoever asked. Talking to the unseen, collecting spider's milk
under the moon, singing people's pains back into their wounds,
she frightened them even as she worked so hard to help them.

I failed: I killed her with my love. I should have been more
detached. You, too, should have kept an eye on her. But you were
preoccupied with your alchemy, making your precious gold.

Yet, really, how could I have noticed that the others feared her
as much as they did when they feared me more? That was how
you wanted it, wasn't it? You wanted a strong man to help you
gather your alchemic ingredients and to keep the others at bay
while you plied your occult craft.

You worked like the wind. You came and you went.

Desire, dreams, and death. That's what the others saw in her. I
should have noticed sooner the obvious looks of fear in their faces
when they met her. I ignored the obvious, because I had become
used to seeing invisible things.

The sea grows old in its bed – but I have left that weary world
behind. I have cut through the shackles of time. I have climbed
higher than the sky.

The flakes of alchemic gold you left behind all those years ago
have grown powerful enough to transform me into a being like
yourself, a being of light. And now I'm sufficiently strong to leave
the Dark Shore and climb a ladder of stars into your luminous
world.

Lara's spirit guides me, and I feel no nostalgia for the cold reality
I leave behind. My grief grovels in weeds. I rise far above it, toward
fathoms of light. I soar into a new world beyond death's fences.

# PART ONE:

## IRTH

17  Among the dynasties of creation, first stands Irth.
    First out of the fiery Beginning. First into the
    abyss of dark and cold.

18  Irth is the original *place*. It lies at the very threshold
    of origin and is made from shadows cast in the
    morning of time by the earliest rays of Being.
    Perched between the nameless power of the
    Beginning and the unreckonable emptiness of the
    Gulf, Irth spins, weaving day and night, chance
    and fate.

                                        *— Origins* 2:17–18

*S*ilence listens.
     – The Gibbet Scrolls

## Cacodemons

❈━✠━❈

At the time of the Conquest, a loaf of bread in most dominions cost a newts-eye. Small as a child's pinky nail and lustrous black with vermilion and emerald razor lines, the hex gem known as newts-eye carried the smallest possible charge of Charm – just enough to keep a healthy person awake one night, or to heal a small wound, or to boil three cups of blue tea, or thread radiance through seven nights, or stir a wisp of breeze for several hours, or buy an excellent loaf of nutbread still steaming on the baker's palette.

And that was just how the waif Tywi spent her last newts-eye. She had kept this tiniest of hex gems in the heart pocket of her tinker's vest for luck. Twenty-seven days it had soaked in her body warmth while she looked for work among the factories and the shanty villages of smithies and tool-and-die shops.

She found no work. For most of those days, she lived out of trash bins. When she could abide the hunger no longer, she decided to spend her last newts-eye.

In the indigent desert dominion of Qaf, upon the barren seacoast realm of Zul, among the smoldering alchemic factories of the seacliff city of Saxar at a narrow, windowless bakery in

Amble-By Lane, she purchased a fragrant loaf of nutbread. It was either buy bread or use the Charm to cure her exhaustion and ward off sleep one more night. At least, she would not be hungry tonight when she fought drowsiness and the perils of dreaming.

The baker's son used the newts-eye as one of three to fill a point in the triangular husk of an arrowhead nut. That was the smallest amulet that could exist: three newts-eyes linked to a quoin. The quoin could be any small flat surface. The rich set their newts-eyes in gold. For the baker's son, the flat, three-cornered pod of a common arrowhead nut was sufficient, for he would be spending this amulet in the festal parade.

With a single quoin, one could dance, sing, and march all night and at dawn return refreshed to the factory line. The baker's son made a dozen to pay his merry way to morning as a parade dancer.

The amulet with Tywi's newts-eye went to a bouncer at a throb palace for admittance to the dance hall. The next day, the bouncer fit that quoin into a prism, a pyramid made from four quoins, and paid that and six other prisms to Whipcrow, a corrupt factory manager, for a better position on the assembly line.

Whipcrow gave those seven prisms and thirteen more to 100 Wheels, a security agent who guarded the warehouses the manager sometimes pilfered. 100 Wheels had a charmwright work the prisms into an elaborate shoulderguard amulet for the city master.

The city master, pleased with the gift, renewed 100 Wheels' work contract and, ever eager to curry favor with his own superiors, included the intricate amulet in his regular tribute to the realm's marquessa, Her Ladyship the Sorceress Altha. The marquessa's husband, Lord Hazar, patron of the arts, admired the amulet's clever assemblage of primitive prisms shaped into a modern shoulderguard. The quaint fact that some of the amulet's quoins consisted of nutshells culled from the street weeds of Saxar inspired him to offer the piece as an emblem of his remote realm to their powerful ally, the wizarduke and regent of all dominions, Lord Drev.

And so, the newts-eye of an impoverished, unemployed factory laborer found its way far to the south, to the opulently manicured Dominion of Ux and the floating capital city of Dorzen. Lord Drev initially ignored the shoulderguard and the other gifts that routinely appeared on the altar of the central court. Each day, the adepts swept the offerings away and extracted their Charm for the wizarduke's own talismans, and he thought it courteous to at least glance at them first.

In the mirror surface of the silver ingots stacked atop the altar, he glimpsed himself, tall and swarthy, with sable hair worn in loose coils over his neck and cropped close at his squared temples. His young, broad face held a quiet, almost stern reserve warmed only by deep eyes startlingly blue as a far sea. Despite his station as the most powerful man on Irth, he wore a simple brown work uniform with black piping. The only signs of his exalted position were the gold armorial star crests at his collar and a white leather amulet belt with full pouches and the crushed wrinkles of much use that girded his tight waist.

He stepped closer to the altar, glanced at the daily offerings that stood on display, swept his gaze around the empty court galleries and back to the gifts. Among the usual glitter of hex-gems and ingots charged with Charm sat a quaint shoulderguard fashioned from crude, handmade prisms.

He picked it up and, quite unexpectedly, heard a chime of longing, a mute echo of fate. Quickly, he returned the amulet to the altar and stood back, warily watching it perch on its reflection in the champagne marble.

As a child, when he had first learned to scry, he saw true love was only thinly possible for himself, and then solely with one woman, a commoner he would have to search to find. Many times in his life he had sensed her from afar, but never as clearly as he had with this primitive amulet. He knew then, some part of it had belonged to her.

He turned his back on the altar and cursed his sudden hopes: *Why now? Why now when love is well-nigh impossible!*

The rueful yearning he experienced when he held the shoulderguard struck him with the same vivid memory of destiny he had felt whenever he had contemplated love in his green years, not long ago. In that happy time, when Mevea his sister was alive and wore so affably their Brood's mantle as Duchess, to scry love with a common woman and contemplate a life of labor and family in a distant dominion seemed possible, if outrageous.

Since Mevea died, however, and the mantle had come to him, love of any kind was impossible. The Duke of Ux, like the Duchess before him and their mother before her, would rule for the benefit of the people, not for his own fulfillment. The love that possessed him was impersonal, vast and magnificent as all of Ux.

*Still*— If there was any chance of finding *her*, his dearest stranger . . .

Mevea had died a thousand days ago, and every one of those days, Drev had worked hard to fulfill her legacy. He had pushed himself to his limits to serve Ux as duke and all the dominions as regent. Perennial trade disputes had been successfully arbitrated and commerce flourished for the time being. Small wars had been fought and won to preserve the union of dominions, and he had personally taken the field at each battle, adamant to prove his mettle and his worthiness as Mevea's successor. Irth, once again, was as stable as it had been under his sister's care.

All at once, Drev knew that if he did not now pursue this hint of destiny that he felt within this humble newts-eye – if he did not track down his true love at this rare time of peace – he never would.

Using his considerable Charm to disguise himself, the wizarduke wove a skin of charmlight that put upon him the appearance of an indigent old man, aged as a storm-twisted tree. Then he used the newts-eye in the shoulderguard he had just received to fashion a seeker, an amulet that would lead him directly to the woman who wore his shadow of destiny.

The palm-sized seeker guided him north, and he flew by light cruiser across the blighted expanse of the Qaf to the kingdom of Zul and the cliff city of Saxar. Through the steep streets the newts-eye guided him into the factory district, past smoking refineries and clangorous foundries.

Never before in his 17,000 days had Lord Drev visited this industrial metropolis, and he was appalled at the poverty he witnessed among the steaming assembly plants. Here, where Irth's amulets were manufactured to carry Charm into the world, scores of charmless people cluttered the alleys, scavenging among the waste bins for scraps of hex-metal and witch-glass to sell for food.

At one such bin, in a lading yard strewn with fuming mounds of smelter's slag, the seeker pulsed three times in his palm and stopped, abruptly announcing he had found the owner of the newts-eye – the woman whom fate had chosen for him.

He lifted the lid of the trash bin and inside found among ribbons of scrap metal and shattered packing crates Tywi curled up asleep. She was a woman half his age, which explained why, when he was a child and first became aware of her, he had only been able to scry her in the future, for she had not yet been born at that time.

With her dirty brown hair cropped close against lice and her gamine face smudged and streaked with soot, she offered no immediate physical appeal to Drev. *Yet – she is the one*, he realized and looked upon her rag-garbed body, her skinny bruised arms and the scabs on her knees with gentle regard.

'Hey, old coot!' A belligerent voice shouted from behind.

Drev turned and faced several young scavengers striding toward him with planks of wood in their hands and malicious scowls on their bent faces.

'You're in the wrong alley, coot.' The scavengers closed in, waving their clubs threateningly. 'What's that you got in your hand, old man?'

Drev pocketed the seeker and showed aged, gnarled hands.

The scavengers surrounded him, plucked at his gray, torn traveler's mantle and poked him with their wood sticks. One reached into his pocket and came out with the gold disc set with hex-gems and Tywi's newts-eye. 'Look at this! You found a real treasure, coot!'

Before he could reply, a voice piped up from over his shoulder. 'Give it back, boys.'

The lid of the trash bin banged open, and Tywi rolled out and stood at the old man's side.

'Forget it, Tywi,' the scavenger holding the seeker declared. 'Look at this thing! It's a *whole* amulet. It must be worth dozens of prisms.'

'Give it back,' Tywi insisted. 'He's just an old man. He needs it more than we do.'

'Squat on that, sister,' the scavenger said with a surly frown and backed away. 'The coot's already spent his life. We got to think of ourselves.'

Tywi advanced and held out her hand. 'Give it back, stoodle – or I'll sic Dogbrick on you. I swear it.'

A look of fright crossed the scavengers' faces. 'Hey, come on, Tywi. We're just looking out for ourselves here. Why you want to make that kind of trouble for us?'

'Give it back.'

The scavengers looked at each other trepidatiously and then passed the seeker to Tywi.

'Here, old man,' she said and pressed the seeker into his bony hand. 'Take your amulet and get where you belong.'

Drev stared into her face, gazing past the grime and fever sores to memorize the waif's rabbity features. She was not unattractive, only toughened by her streetlife. Her hard expression startled him with what it revealed of a life without possession, where all was drift. He wanted to speak to her, but she slapped his shoulder in friendly farewell and strode away with the charmless young men who had woken her.

'Come on,' she beckoned the others. 'Let's find our own Charm.'

The wizarduke started to pursue her across the lading yard as she skipped ahead to lead the others away from the old man, but before he could move, a chime sounded in his skull. It was a piercing alarm sound he had not heard since his last battle, several hundred days ago. He gave an exasperated groan. His first thought was that another insurrection was under way, and that could not wait for the fulfillment of his personal whims.

Quickly, he reached under his skin of light and used his glory belt to set upon the retreating Tywi an Eye of Protection. The Charm he focused upon her would last only a season and she herself would never know she carried it, yet for its duration the invisible Eye would give her minimal protection. At least, for the time being, she would not float away on the nocturnal tides that snatched the charmless when they slept.

He watched Tywi disappear with her cohorts into an alley, then reluctantly shed his skin of light and used his amulet belt to summon a light cruiser. Only after the insectile shadow of the cruiser fell over him and he clambered up the drop-ladder did he learn what summoned him. Not insurrection or the small riots that flared up occasionally in the factory districts. No, this time, a new, unprecedented terror stalked Irth. The captain of the cruiser had far-see crystals to show him of a hamlet torn to pieces as if by a windstorm – but no windstorm would have disemboweled every citizen, man, woman and child alike.

Neither the captain nor any of the crew had even the slightest notion what evil could have caused such massive destruction. They flew the wizarduke directly to the grasslands of Sharna-Bambara and the site of the atrocity. And there he viewed for himself the distinctive mudprints of sizable claws.

On his return to Dorzen, more news arrived of slaughtered villages and massacred travelers in Sharna-Bambara. Whatever curiosity about Tywi he may have had vanished under an avalanche of terrifying reports depicting monsters falling out of the night sky above the grasslands and attacking everything living. The few rare survivors spoke of demonic creatures of abominable ferocity greater than Irth had ever witnessed before.

The wizarduke dispatched squads of his Falcon Guard to patrol Sharna-Bambara and report back to him. When three of those squads were butchered, he gave in to his advisors and, for the first time in his family's history, hired a master from the Brood of Assassins, an expert on murder, to find out what was going on.

By then, the first far-see crystal images of the massacred Falcon Guard had been received. What they showed was unbelievable – horrendous serpentine creatures with tentacles and talons, unreal things of hideous proportions. *Cacodemons*, the wizarduke realized, though he was loath to believe it. Yet he could not deny the fact finally: They were the evil beasts of children's fright stories, come vividly alive.

Days lapsed, and Drev felt helpless as the bloody reports of destruction kept coming in. He strove to keep this black news secret, to avoid all-out panic and the collapse of the union. This was possible only because the destroyed villages were in remote regions of the realm. Concealing everything, he attended court functions and fulfilled his responsibilities as regent with his usual aplomb.

Only when alone in his vaulted court did he frown deeply and not bother to hide his worry. The Brood of Dorzen – all the hundreds of kinfolk who ruled Ux and who looked to him for leadership – were at grave risk. They were, in fact, in greater jeopardy now than at any time since his great-grandfather, the famous One-Eyed Duke, who was their common ancestor, waged war with the Fierce Realms to unite the Seven Dominions.

Just days ago life had been sweet enough for him to entertain amorous thoughts – and now, scores of cacodemons were falling out of the night. Such monsters had never before trespassed Irth, and everyone but the most charmed and knowledgeable wizards believed still they were imaginary beasts. Night after night, they landed in the grasslands of Sharna-Bambara and ravaged the lush farms and ancient villages with rabid abandon. But the most dread secret of all was that no one could thwart their savagery, because Charm was useless against them.

In the central court, Lord Drev erected a lifesize simulacrum of a cacodemon. No two demons looked alike. Many were limbless and tentacle-coiled. But he had selected an image of a more humanoid type. Because it did look eerily like a man, he thought he could take its measure with a close visual inspection.

It stood a full head taller than himself, a crocodilian hulk, greenblack and viperously human, with robust limbs, hook-taloned hands and feet, and a slitherous spine serrated to a lash of tail. A skull-fixed grin of fangs hung beneath an eel's embryonic brow, where tiny, black hypnotic eyes tightened their diamonds to a wrathful glint.

Lord Drev looked away. Folds and creases in the thick torso disclosed other faces, tortured and enraged visages embedded in an underbelly of scaly seams.

Disgust churned in him, and he waved away the abomination. It vanished at once, and where it had loomed, a shaft of clear radiance shimmered wetter than water.

For a long time, he stood gazing into the pellucid light, afraid to think, knowing that thoughts could only lead to further terror and panic.

Then, an urgent voice roused him: 'Sire – I have news.'

The wizarduke motioned to the dark alcoves, admitting the vigorous, familiar figure of Nette, the weapons master he had recently retained from the Brood of Assassins. The Dominion of Ux had never before employed these dread mercenaries and, indeed, over the generations had fought them many times among the ranks of every rival. But then, never before had cacodemons dropped from the night sky.

Nette advanced energetically – a short, mobile woman folding back the cowl of her black utility uniform, revealing a square face with a bronzed, burnished complexion. She advanced into the shaft of clear light at the center of the court and bleached to a shadow figure.

Standing perfectly still while the gemlight searched her for arms and poisons a seventh time since she had entered Dorzen, the weapons master squirmed inside to share her devastating news with the mighty wizarduke. Though she had been hired by Leboc, the duke-regent's marshal, and never before met young Drev, she was inclined to dislike this lord who had come to power by default, and, as with all other Assassins, she had little respect for his brood who had spurned the services of the Assassins all these generations. *Until now, when suddenly the nightmare has found you and Charm no longer works! Proud Drev, you are moments from your fall.*

She gloated and knelt on one knee before the wizarduke. Then, head lowered, she blanked her thoughts, expecting him to read directly from her brain the information he needed.

'Rise, Nette, and speak,' the duke said quietly, with a comradely intimacy she had been trained to disregard. But without her amulets, she found it difficult to repress her surprise and sudden admiration for any ruler willing to hear the truth to his face.

She stood up and stared at him, noting the tiny tics of fear at the corners of his handsome features. She realized then that he was not using Charm to sedate himself. The soft warmth of his voice was an act of self-mastery.

*He is not the craven weakling I expected*, she thought, and her stomach winced now to have to tell him her sinister news.

'What I have to say is meant for your reply alone,' she warned him, increasing the pressure of her stare until she was certain he understood.

'I have no secrets on this matter from my Brood.' He half-turned to his left, toward the red shadows of a gallery where family members attended, and he exposed sadness in his long profile. 'We must all know the truth. That is why I had Leboc hire you. Now speak, and let all in Dorzen and Ux hear.'

The weapons master canted her head warily and warned him again, 'The Dark Lord has said that this message is for you alone.'

Lord Drev stepped down from the altar stage and beckoned for her to exit the gemlight and join him on the marble stairs. 'You have met with him, then?' he asked with barely restrained eagerness. 'The lord of the cacodemons?'

'Oh, yes,' she said, amazed to be released so casually from the cage of light. 'I have met with the Dark Lord, master of the cacodemons.'

'And?' The duke took her arm, escorted her to the stairs and made her sit on the steps beside him like an old chum. No false pride hid his deep consternation. 'Tell me everything.'

She met the duke's earnest stare with cold appraisal, yet behind the mask of her conditioning, she began to like this hapless man and searched for some way to soften the blow of what she had to say.

'I bear this message for you only,' she warned him a third time, as she had been taught. 'Read it first and then decide if you would have this spoken to all of Irth.'

Drev puffed out his cheeks and held his hands emptily before him, showing that he had no choice. 'I am Duke Dorzen Drev, wizard of Hoverness, sovereign of Ux and regent on the Council of Seven and One. How dare I conduct secret negotiations with monsters? No, Nette. The ghosts at this altar would never let me betray my people's trust. Say aloud what the Lord of the Cacodemons would have me know.'

'Very well, sire.' The assassin watched him through the shaded slits of her recessed eyes, attentive as a boxer. 'The Dark Lord would have you know that he is not a monster, not a cacodemon, nor an invader from another world, as are his troops. He claims to be different. He says he is a man of Irth, one of many cast into the Gulf by you, and he has returned to seek vengeance.'

'Nonsense.' Lord Drev huffed a laugh. 'I won't be duped this way. No one returns from the Gulf.'

Nette's eyeslits widened. 'This one has returned, my lord.'

'How do you know?'

'I am Nette, weapons master from the Brood of Assassins, adept of illusion and minister of lies. How dare I not know the truth when I see it?'

He smiled sadly at her gentle mockery, and she liked him all the more.

She had to employ internal arts to continue without emotion, her voice dry and serious: 'No, sire. The ghosts of the Brood of Assassins would never allow me to betray your trust. You have hired me to intermediate with the Dark Lord. I have, and I can assure you that he is real. He is all that he claims to be.'

The duke gripped her arm as she spoke and felt the veracity of her words; then, he pressed closer, clutching her arm like a doddering grandmother reaching for understanding. 'How can he have returned from the Gulf? The abyss falls away forever.'

'Not forever, sire,' she whispered the obvious. 'There is the Dark Shore.'

He shook his head stiffly. 'Myth.'

'Then it must be myth that devastates Sharna-Bambara at this hour.' She waited until he raised his young careworn face. 'You have seen the reports. Hundreds have already died, savagely ripped apart.'

He let her go abruptly and stood up. 'The cacodemons are real enough. I do not doubt that any more. But they are some wizard's evocation gone rogue.'

'Sire, you are ignoring facts.' She followed him up the wide steps toward the altar of golden stone. 'No wizard has ever evoked more than three spirits at one time. There are already over a score of cacodemons, and others fall out of the sky each night. You would need a gang of wizards working full time. And even then, all their destructive spirits would scatter like mist before our Charm.'

The duke stopped and leveled a penetrating stare. 'You are certain that there is no way to fight these creatures with Charm?'

'They are not of Irth, sire.' She stepped up alongside him. 'Charm has no effect on them whatsoever.'

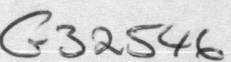

'Yet they are physical beings, Nette. They tear down buildings and slaughter people.'

'Yes, they are very real, but they come from a different, colder level of reality.' She lowered her voice sullenly. 'Every test I conducted indicated that the cacodemons and their Lord are impervious to Charm.'

'You just said that the Lord of the Cacodemons is a man from Irth. Surely, our Charm can seize him?'

'The cacodemons protect him. He is ever in their shadow – even when they appear to be nowhere near him. He is invincible.'

'No assembled creature is invincible,' the duke scoffed. 'You, an assassin, should know this.' He clasped his hands behind his back and paced slowly around the altar. 'There must be a way to fight them.'

'I could find no weakness susceptible to our amulets. The Dark Lord may once have come from Irth, but he is no longer of Irth.'

'Yet he has returned – if we are to believe him – from the Gulf itself to seek vengeance upon me.' He stopped, framed by the ingots heaped atop the altar, 'Who is he?'

'He says you know him well. He carried the sword of Taran against you—'

Lord Drev jolted as if struck. 'Wrat!' *Of course! If any of the damned are to return, it would be him*, he thought, for that renegade had been crazy, lit madly from within, a hollowed gourd of a man shining with evil intelligence.

'He calls himself now by his war name, Hu'dreVra,' Nette said cautiously before the duke's silent fury.

'He killed my sister!'

She moved toward him, but he stopped her with a gnashed hiss.

'My lord—' She acquiesced and stepped back, thinking, *Here stands the wealthiest man in the world – and yet he cannot buy his way free of this nightmare.*

The duke teetered between a chasm of grief and a whirlwind of rage. To control himself, he closed his eyes and turned inward.

He silenced his anger by opening himself to an ocean of emptiness wider than planets.

In the thousand nights since Mevea had died, Drev had often sat for hours before the telescope panels in the ceiling, watching islands of stars adrift in the black vastness. Recently, he no longer needed to see the glimmering darkness. He could feel that cold and secret sea within him, and he immersed himself there.

Once the frosty ethers absorbed his rage, he stepped back from the gulch of sorrow within him, faced Nette and spoke strongly, 'Weapons master, do you confirm that the Dark Lord is the renegade leader Wrat?'

The square block of her head gave a fateful nod. 'Yes.'

*Damn!* The duke had thrown Wrat into the abyss with his own hands. Every day since, he had vividly cherished the image of the scrawny upstart with his screaming weasel-face dwindling terrified on the riptide darkness into the abyss. That horror had been poor balm for his wounded heart, yet that was all he had to counter the gruesome memory of his sister's death. Here, in this central court, Wrat had impaled her on the sword Taran.

With his emotions in check, the duke saw clearly that if Wrat had truly returned from the Gulf, then he had come back as a god. *No wonder none of my attempts to scry or far-see the so-called Dark Lord have revealed him. He has become immune to Charm!*

'Sire—' The weapons master dared disturb the duke's thoughts. 'There is more.'

'Yes, I know.' He passed her a weary, resigned look, a thin mask over his seething anger. 'The madman's demands. What are they?'

The weapons master answered flatly, 'At dawn in Elvre, the Dark Lord will descend upon Arwar Odawl and destroy it.'

The wizardduke held his anger in check and received this news impassively. He knew what Wrat was doing: Arwar Odawl was the smallest of the realms. He would cut the weakest from the herd to terrorize the others.

'And his demands?'

'No demands, sire. Arwar Odawl will be attacked at dawn by cacodemons and destroyed. The Dark Lord intends to show that his cacodemons can devastate more than just villages and hamlets. Hu'dre Vra will demonstrate his might to all of Irth by reducing a floating city to ruins.'

The duke glared, incredulous. 'He *is* mad!'

'Yes, I believe you are right,' Nette replied ruefully. 'His psychopathic traits are extensive: Delusions of self-reference have convinced him that all creation exists to serve him. And he entirely lacks conscience. People are things to him, sire.'

The wizardduke spoke bitterly. 'What is to be done with this madman, Nette?'

The weapons master shook her head slowly and direly. 'Unless you surrender to him, sire, the Dark Lord threatens to savage every dominion on Irth and spare none his wrath.'

'So he means to turn the whole world against me?' He laughed without sound at the cruel obviousness of Wrat's stratagem. 'Do you believe that if I give myself to him he will spare the other dominions?'

Nette answered crisply, 'No.'

The young duke frowned at this confirmation of what he already knew. 'Thank you, Nette.'

'My lord, will there be a reply?'

'No.' He faced away from her and began pacing again. 'No reply. You have done a good job. I will see you receive a bonus with your discharge fee.'

Nette's jaw jerked up in a gesture of obvious surprise. 'It would be prudent to retain my services, sire. Now that there is a veritable price on your head, you will need a worthy weapons master.'

Drev paused and glanced over his shoulder with a wry smile. 'If all you say is true, then no number of weapons masters can protect me when the cacodemons come. From all others, my glory belt will guard me well enough. You may go now, Nette.'

'Thank you, sir,' she acknowledged tersely, then added with more warmth, 'and glad fortune be yours.' She received her dismissal with an unexpected tinge of regret. Despite her prejudice, she had come to respect this sad and desperate duke, because he refused to act out of sadness or desperation and faced his doom gracefully.

Once Nette departed, the wizarduke pointed to the groined ceiling, and the dark alcoves lit up in a wide rainbow circle of breathing light. 'Send this last conversation with weapons master Nette to every city in every dominion on Irth,' he commanded, and the colors began to parade clockwise through the alcoves. 'Also, alert the Council of Seven and One at once and call an immediate emergency session!'

Among the red shadows of his brood's gallery, he watched the agitated movements of his family: Mevea's children, two salamander skinny boys, both under five thousand days old; his cunningly ambitious brother-in-law, Baronet Fakel, and the baronet's new wife, the silent, veiled witch dancer, Lady Von; and all their flamboyant entourage of astrosophers, animal servants, and garish hangers-on.

With the revelation that the wizarduke had become the Dark Lord's target, the people in the gallery began scrambling to distance themselves from him, and he had no need for the gate that kept them from getting closer. But he kept the invisible shield in place. He did not want even the appearance of favoring his personal interest or his family's in the hard decisions to come.

The alcoves darkened, and the wet shaft of gemlight at the center of the court widened to a glass table at which sat seven leaders, one from each of the other dominions: They occupied antechambers at palace cities in their own realms, yet the Gemstar that Drev's grandmother had placed above Irth enabled them to hold conference as if at one site.

The four sorceresses and three wizards did not hide their dismay as they had at earlier meetings, when there was yet ignorance enough to doubt the Dark Lord's threats. The mages wore frantic expressions. They had watched Nette's report.

'Arwar Odawl stands at full alert,' declared the lord of that capital in Elvre, the aristocratic margrave, Keon of Odawl. He rose, quivering with indignation, his amulet tabard rattling. 'I call upon the Council to send defenders at once to stand with us against the Dark Lord.'

The Council agreed unanimously – though that did not ease Margrave Keon, for he sat stiffly, the fine, disdainful features of his patrician face locked in furious determination.

In that stony defiance, the wizardduke witnessed the triumph of the Dark Lord. No matter the Council's resolve to fight, they stood defenseless before the cacodemons. Earl Mac of Sharna-Bambara reminded them of that. He described further atrocities in his dominion, where the cacodemons continued to plunge out of the night sky. Orchard valleys had been ripped up by the roots, highways broken into cobbles, and whole villages butchered by the slaverous creatures.

'You must hide!' Ladyship Rica urged. She and the other Council members had known Drev since he was born. Rica the Conjurer from the Reef Isles of Nhat had been his mother's strongest ally and his sister's godmother. She wanted him to live, as did Ladyship Altha, the powerful sorceress of Zul.

But others delighted in his horror, especially his family's enemies, the enigmatically beautiful witch queen Thylia from the Malpais Highlands and the wrinkled empty skin that hung from a stick and spoke with a blue tongue of flame in a shriveled face of green fungus, the warlock Ralli-Faj.

'Yes-s-s!' the warlock's tongue sizzled in his mummified face. 'Hide! S-step down! Resign the regency.'

Lyna, the stout enchantress from the Falls of Mirdath, rose next and spoke with her usual serenity. 'Ralli-Faj is correct, Lord Regent, though for the wrong reasons, of course. Your power should not devolve to your enemies, yet you must step down immediately, because your history with the Dark Lord endangers the entire Council.'

'S–step down!'

Lord Drev flared a hot look at the warlock, then removed the glory belt of white crushed leather.

'None has scryed this.' He spoke with deliberate lack of emphasis, suppressing his welter of emotions so none would later say he acted in panic. 'This is an unforeseen act – a pivot of history. Let it be known, I act for the benefit of all.'

He passed a sober, steady look among the other members, held up the belt with its bulging pouches of talismanic power, and announced, 'I am no longer regent.'

Lyna congratulated him with an awed nod, her tiny eyes, like the eyes of the others, fixed on the glory belt in his white-knuckled grasp. 'Council rules require you to choose a successor from our bench to serve out the remainder of your regency. What is the remaining term, Thylia?'

'11,269 days,' the witch queen answered and displayed the recording abacus.

A fractured laugh erupted from Earl Mac, the bald wizard from Sharna-Bambara, and, despite his gruff manner, his tattooed face buckled and sparkled with tears. 'Forget the abacus. There's nothing more to record. This is the Last Day! The regency is over. The Dark Lord has come to walk on our necks!'

'No!' Margrave Keon of Odawl shouted. 'We must fight!'

'With what?' Thylia queried, puzzled at the stubborn ignorance of the others. 'Charm is ineffective. Will you fight with sticks and stones?'

'S–step down!'

Lord Drev walked the length of the bench, holding the heavy belt before him. He had long ago decided who would get the glory belt if he had to abdicate. He stopped before Ladyship Rica. 'You were the staunchest ally of my mother and my sister. You are worthy to fulfill my term.' He held the white belt in both hands doubled over, its pouches jigsawed together to form the falcon seal talisman, the most potent amulet on Irth.

'The dire threat from Wrat the Scavenger against our most

venerable and vulnerable of realms requires me to defeat the choice of my own heart, however, and to pass the falcon seal to that one of us who needs its power most – the noble Keon, margrave of Odawl.'

The haughty margrave gasped when his name sounded and rocked back in his seat as the falcon seal, emblem of the Abiding Star, Source of All, came through the sheets of gemlight toward him.

'Will you stand apart and uphold the Council of Seven and One?' Lord Drev spoke the ritual words, transferring the ultimate authority of the regency to the startled margrave.

Lord Keon, silent, stunned, leaned forward, arms straight, blue knuckles on the tabletop. He peered into Lord Drev's pale eyes and a silent knowing passed between them. They both understood that this grand gesture of hope was ultimately hollow unless some other weapon than Charm could be found to stop the cacodemons.

The margrave straightened proudly before the inevitable and spoke the traditional assent with conviction: 'I will stand apart. I, Keon, Margrave of Odawl, will stand apart as regent and uphold all the rulings of the Council of Seven and One.'

The wizarduke placed the falcon seal amulet on the glass table, before wide-eyed Keon, and stepped back out of the gemlight.

In turn, the others pronounced their fealty oaths, and Lord Keon opened the falcon seal and donned the glory belt. Less than a day remained before dawn in Elvre and the threatened attack of the cacodemons; so, the new Lord Regent waived all further ceremony and, with a glittering look of gratitude to his predecessor, closed the session.

The glass table with the seven sorcerers and witches vanished, and Lord Drev stood alone, ringing with emptiness. *I have given up everything*

He pointed to the gemstone at the canopy of the court's central vault and made a fist. That dulled the gem and shut out the incoming calls he expected from the allies who would want to console and the foes eager to taunt.

With a wave, he opaqued the gallery and assured himself seclusion even from his family, though no one there would want to see him now. Baronet Fakel and Lady Von were surely on their way out of Dorzen with his young nephews, intent on getting as far as possible from him and the vengeful Dark Lord.

And there was no slip nor sleight in the new regent, Lord Keon, failing to summon him to Arwar Odawl to stand at his side in the coming dawn battle. He had become a pariah. In their hearts, and even in his own, responsibility for the arrival of the cacodemons lay with him, for he had been the one who had defeated Wrat the Scavenger and did not slay him but threw him to the Gulf.

The young wizarduke climbed the stairs to the altar and touched a long, thin amethyst panel set in the pedestal. The panel slid out as a drawer, baize-cushioned and bearing a silvergold sword, a black scabbard, and a red belt.

He took the sword by its metal haft, which was of one piece with the blade, and the silvergold shaped itself to his grip and widened its guard to protect his wrist. The strength of its Charm had not diminished in the thousand days that it had sat inert. It changed the light of air around it and made his arm feel bold.

Gazing into its sensuous bright lines, he could hardly believe such loveliness could surrender to horror. Yet, this blade had killed Mevea – and hundreds of others. Legend said it had been forged in Hellgate by the infamous blind smith Tars Kulkan, who first learned to capture Charm with metal and used that knowledge to make weapons.

It was called the sword Taran, because the Liberator, the tailor Taran, had in the midst of battle plucked it from the dead hand of his master and turned the tide by slaying three kings that day. Whole realms fell to this sword long ago, and the tailor became a lord. Over time his sword was lost, only to be found tens of thousands of days later by a junk scavenger named Wrat.

Lord Drev sheathed the weapon. This was no time for moody contemplations of the past. Wrat was coming again.

*Hu'dre Vra! The Dark Lord!* The wizarduke guffawed at the puerility of his enemy – and his laugh in the hollow chamber echoed back at him ominously.

Already, he had lost his sister and now his very place in the brood to that weasel-faced scavenger. The Dark Lord would come next for his life.

To stand and fight was hopeless, this he knew with certainty. As the target of evil, he owed it to the others to lead Hu'dre Vra away.

*Rica of course is right.* Drev reviewed his decision as he strapped Taran over his brown work uniform. *I must hide until I find my chance to strike.*

He removed the gold armorial star crests from his collar and laid them on the altar. At last stripped of all talismanic power save the sword paid for by his sister's blood, he was ready to begin to find his own way back to Dorzen, back to this very court and this altar of dominion.

Cold fear gripped him, locked him into the dread realization that there was really no hope of return. He was going to his death. Not that he could scry his doom. Not yet.

With his hand firmly on the sword's hilt, he had the Charm and skill to see he would not die this day. The near future undulated like a heat mirage before him, hazy, full of shimmery hues and sunshine – undimmed, as yet, by the shadow of death.

*Life is hope,* Drev counseled himself, trying to thaw the frigid certainty that he was doomed. *No matter the odds, we cannot panic. Else then, Wrat wins by default, without even a fight. I will not have that.*

The cramp of dread in his heart did not relent.

He dismissed the liquid glimpse of the future, and his gaze returned to the altar. None of the treasure piled here belonged any longer to him. None of it ever had. He had always used the offerings for Dorzen and Ux, and he felt proud that he could simply turn his back on his office at a moment's notice like this and know that he left behind no troubles for the clerks of the new leader.

29

*If there is a new leader*, his fright scolded him.

But then his gaze fell on the amulet with the newts-eye from Saxar. He picked it up and heard again the chime of longing for a future where love was possible.

And the newts-eye that the factory waif Tywi had spent for a loaf of nutbread became a pivot of destiny, a wedge of faith that struck like an ax the paralyzing ice of hopelessness and indecision.

*Why not go to her again, wherever she is now?* Drev pondered. At the mere thought of such a foolish notion, he scowled at himself, plucked the amulet from the altar and fitted it into his shoulder pocket. As its faint charmlight suffused and dimmed away within the radiance of his own Charm, he stopped and thought again. *Dangerous possibility*, he knew. *Yet why not? What is left to lose at this point?* With what time was left him, he might yet disclose for himself why fate had bound her to him and in so lowly a station.

*Fate*, the wizarduke quoted from sacred text, *is the pattern within the radiance of the Abiding Star and our lives the screen upon which it is projected.*

Though he was a moral man of stringent principles and pride, he was not a holy man. He had been trained in the Lazor lineage of pragmatic wizardry, and he thoroughly comprehended the mechanics of hex-gems and amulets. The enigma of Charm and the awesome reality of the Abiding Star that rose and set each day had always been too vast to contemplate in his hectic life at court. Yet, here at this threshold of a dangerous new life, reciting these passages that he had first learned in temple at his mother's side gave him comfort.

*Why not fulfill this scry from my green days?* he asked himself from this pivot, this clarity that balanced hopelessness against faith. *Why not trust that fate is faith?*

For a moment, he hesitated at the thought that in seeking her out, he would be putting her in danger. *But is not everyone in danger, always?* he reasoned. *Merely to be alive is to be at venture to extinction at any moment. And perhaps I can actually do something to help her, protect her somehow.*

He determined then to go to her once more. He would use again the faint aura of her within the newts-eye to track her down. If he could find her – and if she would have him without any Charm but his sword and this one amulet – then what?

*Fate will decide.*

He called for a standard issue traveler's cloak and a provision sack fully appointed for a trooper in the wilds. The marshal from the Falcon Guard who delivered the items knew well what his lord intended, and his eyes sparkled. He had served beside him since Mevea's death.

'You cannot go alone, my lord.' The marshal's red whiskers fanned along his jawline as he cast an unhappy and disappointed look at the darkened court.

'There is no other way, Leboc.' The wizarduke adjusted the harness straps of the pack and slung it over his shoulder in counterbalance to his sword.

'Lord regent—' the dismayed man blurted before he caught himself. 'My duke, you will fare better with a personal guard.'

Drev scowled. 'No. Together, we will simply be a bigger target.' He could see that getting out of Dorzen was not going to be easy unless he abandoned farewells. He threw the blue cloak over his shoulder and turned away from the old soldier. 'As your slip of tongue implies, dear friend, you and the Guard still think of me as regent. But I am not. Your place now is with the new regent.'

'The Falcon Guard will deploy at Lord Keon's command,' the marshal stated curtly as he followed the duke into the mosaic tile corridor that led to the gardens. 'We have already received readiness orders to move out. By evening, those of us who remain will leave for Arwar Odawl.'

The duke stopped abruptly and spun about. 'What do you mean, *remain*, Leboc? Desertion from the Guard is still punishable by death.'

The marshal stroked his grand whiskers nervously. 'At term's end, all Guard commissions are released.'

Lord Drev glared, appalled at this man he thought he knew. 'This is not term's end, marshal. This is a transfer. You and the other guards are still bound to obey the regent.'

'We will stall with legal motions.' His round, ruddy face bore no cunning, only determination. 'We can easily tie the Guard down until after tomorrow. If that surly Wrat makes good upon his threat and destroys Arwar Odawl, the legal charge will be moot, and we will live on as avengers.'

*Madness!* the wizarduke thought and stared aghast at this ugly man made handsome by scars, the compact warrior who had fought in the field beside him and always bravely. *Leboc – staunch Leboc – is talking treason! Anarchy has come!*

'I see the fear in your face, my lord.' The marshal leaned confidentially closer. 'We understand. The Guard are also aware of the reports from Sharna-Bambara. We all know what we're up against – at your side or on our own.' Pain pinched the corners of his avid yellow eyes, and the gruesome man suddenly appeared about to cry. 'When the new regent is dead in the ruins of his city, the avengers will come for you to lead them. And will you then raise the sword of Taran against the Dark Lord?'

Gently, Lord Drev pushed him away and said as tenderly as he could, 'Go, Leboc. I am no longer your commander – or I would hold you for treason.'

A hurt disappointment glanced off the aged warrior's face, and he stepped back and swung a despairing look down the corridor to the wide open doors of the central court. Several officers of the Falcon Guard had appeared there with a squad of anxious troopers.

'Farewell, Leboc.' The duke saluted his comrade formally and held his gaze, appealing to his sense of duty. 'Please, serve me this last time and see that no one impedes my departure.'

Brow furrowed, Leboc watched the wizarduke march past him, and he sputtered, 'You're not leaving now, are you? Just like this?'

The metal doors to the gardens banged open, and the wizarduke was gone, into the hedge maze he knew from childhood, with its arboreal tunnels and secret portals that led down, out of the city.

'What will I tell the others?' the marshal called into the violet and silver shrubbery. 'Where will I say you have gone?'

'Say whatever you will,' Drev's voice lifted out of the balmy garden. 'Tell them, I belong now to fate.'

## Dogbrick and Ripcat

◆━✦━◆

A crimson scent of danger cut through the stink from the factories of Saxar. Dogbrick stopped suddenly on the steep slope of Smelters Alley and swung his long head sideways, swiping direction from the perilous smell.

It wafted upward from where the alley opened into a maze of tinker shacks. He recognized the acrid hue of the scent, the clove-tanged bitterness of 100 Wheels, nemesis of all who lacked Charm. 100 Wheels the pitiless, faceless as a surgeon, prowling the crooked streets for the desperate, the survivors living without amulets. 100 Wheels the Charmed, the murderous security agent hired by the factories to break thieves such as Dogbrick.

Up from the smoldering well of the alley, 100 Wheels approached.

To calm himself, Dogbrick drew a deeper breath of the fetid air and nearly choked on the acid fumes from the smelters. The tight alley held more than a score of foundries, their round walls scorched over millennia to volcanic glass, bulging blue as eggplants. Any one of them could be involved in the lucrative smuggler's trade. Perhaps 100 Wheels was not coming for him.

This infernal district minted most of the world's useful

amulets, and Dogbrick expected factory agents to abound. Feigning nonchalance, the thief paused before the convex wall of a smelter's shop and pretended to regard his broad reflection. Briefly, he admired himself, pleased that the tawny locks of his mane and beard did not appear lanky in the grisly heat from the foundries but rather swerved proudly over his ponderous shoulders and stout chest.

100 Wheels appeared at the bottom of the hill, her lissome quicksilver shape making the cobbles at her feet gleam. Rusty pink hair floated around her like hot, drifting ash, and long, devilish, wicked eyes in the silver dish of her face brightened like embers.

Dogbrick watched her reflection in the heat-tarnished wall of the smelter's shop. The agent ascended the alley with her head slung forward intently, her slinky form seeming to expand muscularly with each step.

The thief saw she was coming for him. Casually, with his back turned, as if still oblivious of her, he edged away from the foundry to continue his stroll. Then, as he stepped from the kerb, he bolted. Large frame filling the narrow passage so tightly shop fumes and vent steam danced after him, he barreled up the alley. He had no hope of escaping 100 Wheels – nor had he any need to escape, for on this lucky morning he had nothing to hide.

Dogbrick had been on his way to get information from a factory spy about what was worth stealing tonight, and he had in his possession at this time nothing illicit. Yet he ran with all his might. He wanted to see how far he could get before the fabled 100 Wheels boxed him. Such information would prove useful on the crucial day when she did come for him while he was delivering. Then he would know how long he had to lose his loot.

Bursting from the alley, fang-glints and leather cloak of clattering amulets a windblur, the thief startled two smiths lugging an ingot between them. The metal clanged on the flagstones, and the workers threw themselves to the gutter under the bestial shadow of the leaping man.

Not sparing an instant to look back, Dogbrick crossed an empty lading yard and jumped down a dingy stone rampway. The chute dropped him into a puddled lane behind the charm-wrights' shops. Three lizardwings startled from among refuse drums when he thundered past and whirred in the air after him like pieces torn from his shadow.

The crimson scent of musty cloves sharpened, and Dogbrick dashed to the end of the lane and vaulted the pronged iron fence that blocked the precipice. He plunged, arms outspread, cloak billowing.

Though he could see nothing through the factory smoke swirling in the air, he knew precisely where his blind fall would take him. Like every thief in this cliff-city, he was adept at leaping from one level to the next to elude capture, and he always knew where the nearest jump street could be found.

The dense smog shredded, a jolt of cold salty air stunned his lungs, and the city's improbable vista loomed before him as he fell into the clear sky.

Saxar gleamed like black mica, its tiers of smoldering factories and tilted streets hewn into the raw rock of titanic seacliffs. Far below this fuming hive, the Ocean surged, its silver tusks flashing in the morning glare.

Dogbrick threw his head back to view the city's heights and glimpsed the black dirigibles from the south. Three of the ornately festooned trade vessels hovered near the sky bund with its massive trestles, far upwind of the sulfurous smoke.

Farther yet, suspended deep within the cobalt fathoms of the sky, the worlds of Nemora and Hellgate hung like chunks of transparent crystal. Beauty and grace possessed him for one glorious instant. Then, the orange mist from the numerous spires and minarets of factory flues received him once more into its sour fog.

Dogbrick met the gutterstone of Amble-By Lane with legs bent and recoiled easily over the rusty railing on to the pavement. Winded from his sprint, he hurried gasping downhill, hoping to lose himself in the furnace smoke pouring through the cramped byways among the refineries.

His hands under his cloak began nimbly closing amulets, wanting to make himself less conspicuous in the alchemic haze. The shaft of blue daylight that had been fitfully glinting overhead vanished, and snaky coils of smog tightened around him. He continued running past blistered metal doorways and open hangars gusty with sparks and the clangor of metal finding new shapes.

The slanted lanes of jammed buildings seemed deserted except for an occasional apprentice running errands. But Dogbrick spied where the grim denizens watched – children squatting under mossgrown piers and in the rancid shadows of gargoyled cargo bays. The older ones, the longest survivors, did not show themselves at all. Yet he was aware they watched, too – from the guttergrates and sewerlids.

These oblique streets of sooty stone held no secrets from Dogbrick, because he had grown up in this blighted precinct. Orphaned at an early age, he lived wild in the burnt warrens behind the factories, catching his food in the weed lots and the slag yards, sometimes stealing it from windowsills or bird-feeders of homes on the bluffs where the factory workers lived. All his life, he had been running the angular alleys and hobbled stairs of dripping stone that plumbed this vertical city.

Even without the giddy strength of his amulets to brighten his step and boost his leaps, he moved swiftly and smoothly among the refinery district's mongrel paths. Under a colossal skyline of retorts and alembics, he scampered along pipes, dropped to a drainage culvert, and hurtled down traces of withered sumac between corrugated warehouses. Though he no longer sensed 100 Wheels, the thief pushed himself until his muscles felt molten and his legs staggered.

He stopped with his hands on his knees in the mouth of Peek Alley at the corner of Everyland Street. Farther up, above the clouds of factory exhaust, Everyland opened to an opulent boulevard flanked with stately spark trees and the onyx estates of the wealthy.

As a young child, he used to think that Charm from above trickled down with the pavement seepings, and he had spent a lot of time on the rheumy end of this street splashing in the green puddles. Later, orphaned and bereft, when the nether dank became unbearable, he began prowling the skullcolored buildings of the district, looking for open offices he could plunder. In the cavernous market halls, he stole unrefined ore by the pouchful, bags of conjure-wire snippings, hex-metal shavings and shards of broken witch glass, anything that he could sell later to the charmwrights. They were glad to get these materials at a fraction of cost, and by this bold thievery he survived.

Dogbrick blew off these unhappy memories with a heavy sigh and straightened, looking for 100 Wheels. Her scent of burnt cloves had disappeared. Only a few drab workers from the office buildings flitted through the noxious steam and gusts of rubbish drifting up the street, and no one with much Charm was anywhere in view. He was surprised to have gotten away, and he wondered if he had been mistaken about the security agent coming for him.

Hope flared briefly, then guttered with the first glimpse of liquid light at the edge of his vision. Torn tinsel gleamed from the opal mistings inside Peek Alley and more silver shadows flickered among the vapors rolling up Everyland Street. Wherever he looked, a chrome figure shimmered in the haze. 100 Wheels closed in from all sides!

'I've warned two smugglers and a yegg in the time you've been running,' she scolded in a hot voice that came from every direction. 'Stay – and listen to what I have to say. If I'd wanted to box you, you'd never have gotten out of Smelters Alley.'

By lack of scent, Dogbrick knew she approached from downwind, and he ignored the apparitions that cast no odor. He settled on a fluid platinum shadow running against the amber smoke of Peek Alley. In a dramatic and mockingly brash gesture of submission, he removed his amulet harness and his mantle, held them at arm's length, and dropped them into the alley.

'Nemesis of the Hopeless!' he brayed, thick arms extended, exposing his blond underbelly. 'I stand defenseless before you! I have nothing to hide.'

'You always have something to hide, Dogbrick,' 100 Wheels chided from behind and laughed hideously to see the stiff hackles bristle across his wolfpelt shoulders. The sudden stink of her walloped his sinuses, and the luminous figure pressing through the mist of Peek Alley vanished.

Dogbrick spun around to face long red eyes in a visage empty as a mirror.

'You're a parasite,' 100 Wheels spoke from so close he could see through the radiance of her Charm to the vizard of a peeled skull, its empty eye-grots spitting flames. 'You have to hide to survive.'

With a yelp, Dogbrick leaped back a pace, stumbled on his dropped harness and mantle, and crashed to the pavement.

100 Wheels shook her head and stepped into the alley. Her radiance lifted rainbows from the black smoketarred walls. 'Sit – and listen, Dogbrick. I can't squander any more time on you. There are many others I've yet to track down. The factories have sent me to warn you all, every thief and smuggler in the city. Arwar Odawl has fallen this day.'

Dogbrick rubbed his head where the kerb had kissed him and blinked perplexed, finding little to remember of Arwar Odawl. It was a tiny kingdom far to the south. He knew of it only because of its famous brandy of the same name – and also, of course, because it was renowned as the oldest city on Irth.

'For over two million days,' the shining woman said, 'the Brood of Odawl have ruled Elvre unmolested, protected by their most venerable Charm.' She bowed closer, and her hair diffused the space around her bright as fire. 'Now that Brood is broken.'

Dogbrick could not imagine why she had run him down to tell him this. *Mists rise and kingdoms fall* . . . So went that most famous of ballads from the *Songs of Truth*. But he did not want to annoy her, so he did not hum the tune but rather feigned interest and asked, 'What warlord has taken Arwar Odawl?'

'No warlord.' She gazed flatly at him, and he saw his bewildered expression in the pan of her face and shut his mouth.

'You said the city fell.' He hooded his eyes with incomprehension.

'Yes.'

'You can't mean—?'

100 Wheels hung her head, and her pink hair drizzled over her shoulders. 'A terrible thing has come upon our world this day. Arwar Odawl has fallen into the jungles of Elvre.'

'Into the jungles . . .' Dogbrick's mind reeled at the thought of a floating city cast to the ground. Thousands lived in that city! If the factory agent were not herself telling him this, he would never believe it. Numbly, he groped to understand. 'The entire city?'

'Utterly destroyed this day.'

'How?'

100 Wheels raised her silver face through her powdery hair, and her long, devilish eyes gazed unblinking. 'By cacodemons.'

'Caco—' Dogbrick shook his head with such violent disbelief his curly tresses fanned. 'Only children believe in cacodemons.'

'The Dark Lord has come from the Gulf,' the agent continued solemnly. 'From the Shore of Night – and he commands a host of cacodemons. Today he has struck Arwar Odawl from the cloud paths. In the days ahead, he will advance upon the other dominions and their cities. I have come to warn you of this, Dogbrick – and to ask: Will you stand with us against this enemy?'

'Stand with you?' Dogbrick sat up taller. 'Are you summoning *me* to arms?'

'All of Irth must unite against this threat.' 100 Wheels extended her open hand, and Dogbrick rose to his feet, lifted by a balmy force so quiet it nearly felt like his own volition. He marveled at the luxurious Charm the factories commanded and listened astonished to what their agent spoke: 'I have been sent to recruit fighters from Saxar. You ran well just now, Dogbrick. You have the agility and the physical might to make an imposing warrior. Will you join our ranks and fight to save our city?'

'Fight?' The thief gestured at his harness of battered amulets lying crumpled at his feet. 'Nemesis, do you think if I had Charm enough to fight I would seek my destiny as a thief?'

'You do not understand.' The long red eyes flared impatiently. 'The dominions need warriors, people who can fight with their hands and their wits. We need street fighters – like yourself.'

'Alley brawls are necessary down here,' he said, gesturing to the pitted bricks blackened with caked slurry, 'but up there? Charm would squash us.'

'Charm is useless against the Dark Lord or his cacodemons.' 100 Wheels said this softly, unwilling to be overheard by the empty streets, yet her words clanged loudly in the thief's brain.

'No Charm?' He tugged at his handsome beard, trying to comprehend this.

100 Wheels abruptly turned away and strode out of the alley. 'I have no time for your befuddlement, Dogbrick. If you will fight against the Dark Lord, come to the Millgates tomorrow at noon. There, you will be trained with the others.'

Erased by mist, the silvery woman seemed to dissolve with the smoke galloping up Everyland. Only a faint bitterness of cloves and her harsh voice lingered:

'If you do not come, then life is over for you. Until the Dark Lord is defeated, Charm has no value. No matter how many amulets you steal, they will be only so much stone and metal when the cacodemons come to devour us.'

Her voice and her dangerous scent drifted away.

'Wait!' Dogbrick called into the wind. 'Who is this Dark Lord?'

Passers-by glared at him from their dingy sunshafts as they hurried to and from the market halls in the skullgray buildings. Seeing him in this caustic air without a cloak and ranting, they thought he was a drunk survivor, and he was lucky no one tried to spike him.

He picked up his mantle and harness and put them on. The reek from the factories dimmed and the air brightened around him with every amulet he opened.

He wore thirteen. Seven were power wands: amber-black rods, each long as a hand and thick as two fingers. Even with his brawn, he possessed the stamina to unsheathe only five wands at one time, but he kept the other two as reserves.

The power wands formed the brace of his harness and fitted snugly across the hull of his chest: A central wand lay in the groove of his sternum and the other six pressed three on a side against his ribs, positioned to infuse power directly to his vital organs.

Two niello eye charms clasped the harness as shoulder cusps like epaulets. The ebony lozenges projected Charm into the surroundings, disabling all projectiles directed at him, including toxic fumes. The hex-circuitry within them also allowed him to feel around corners and into darkened stairwells.

Under his beard, three rat-star gems studded the neckstrap of his harness, directing a nimble energy into his brain and quickening his wits. The moment he unhooded them, they began squealing with the grotesque implications of 100 Wheels' message: A Charmless world beset by cacodemons!

*The world is ending!*

He put a hand under his beard and lidded two of the gems. That softened his anguish, and he gained sufficient composure to peer out of the alley at the sparse traffic on Everyland. Far across the foggy Market Plaza, in the vaulted colonnades of the auction arcade, business appeared robust. No one in that radiant arena seemed aware that a dominion had been destroyed – let alone that cacodemons had suddenly become real and Charm offered no defense.

Out of the mist on Everyland, drays floated up with rangy stevedores hanging from the sides. Dogbrick knew what lay beneath the chainmesh tarps covering the drays: Fetish marl quarried from the glacial geodes of the Edge, a lithified silt congested with hex-gems.

Boots sparked on the cobblestones as the workers struggled to guide the buoyant carts to their berths. There, the drays released their mineral cargo in sparkling avalanches of gem dust. Appraisers and buyers from the factories emerged from the skullgray buildings and mingled with the dealers and the charmwrights. While they haggled, security agents and thieves lurked among the dunes of alchemic marl that sat in the market alcoves like heaps of dirty sunset.

Dogbrick weighed the possibility that 100 Wheels had deceived him. Perhaps this was her perverse way of mocking him, of venting her frustration at not being able to legally seize him. He snorted a laugh at himself and turned away from the luminous vapors of Everyland Street.

But as he strode down Peek Alley with his sunshaft dazzling off the glaziers' round windows and crystal curtains, he did not believe 100 Wheels had lied. Rat-star gems, even ones as cheap and unreliable as his, could easily see through a deception that huge.

*No*, Dogbrick spoke to himself, *100 Wheels did not lie. The world is ending!*

He groped in the capacious pockets of his cloak for his thirteenth amulet, perhaps his most important one – a seeker. Like all seekers, its starshape woven of gold filaments encased a homing bauble minted to locate the person whose lock of hair it clasped. The tuft of white hair in this seeker belonged to Dogbrick's partner and was rigged to dissolve itself if anyone but Dogbrick opened it.

The thief found the seeker in his collar pouch but did not open it. His partner slept by day. That was just one of his strange traits – that he slept. Only the poorest people, those with no Charm, suffered the risks of sleep. Yet Dogbrick's partner *sought* sleep. If Dogbrick woke him because of a ruse, he might slash into one of his silent rages.

Dogbrick released the seeker and decided not to disturb his partner but instead meet with the factory spy and seek confirmation. He exited Peek Alley at a drain ramp, dropped on to Merchants Boulevard and rode the city trolley uptown, back to Smelters Alley.

Hurrying because he was late, he bolted frantically among the steaming tinker shacks, twice missing the obscure sunken postern crusted in rime. No more than a stained hole in the ground, it led through a dank tunnel of weeping stone to the gusty cliff-stairway called Devil's Wynd.

Dogbrick quickly descended the treacherous switchbacks as fast as he could leap and still watch his step on the timeworn cobbles of the narrow stairs. If he fell, he would plunge through veils of smog a long way to the heaving waters hidden below. Despite this immediate danger, the burly man could not keep his mind from the appalling revelation: *Charm does not work upon it!*

The weight of that thought stopped his descent. Huffing anxiously, he turned sideways and pressed his back to the pocked wall of rock. His fingers fumbled at the neckstrap under his beard, adjusting the rat-stars to meet his implacable dread. Yet that did little good. Acid mist enclosed him even through his sunshaft, and the burning fetor of the Devil's Wynd that had always before hurried him along went unnoticed as he tried to see a way past his horror.

*Ruder fear no man could bear!* He dug his blunt fingers into the wall's powdery rock and dizzied a moment before the enormity of what he had so recently learned. *Without the hope of Charm, why am I here in this stink? My mistress is hope! Without her, I should be frolicking at* The Wise Fish *for what last pleasures can yet be disclosed before the cacodemons come!*

'Dogbrick!' a thin voice pierced the opaque fumes. 'Is that you I hear whining?'

'Whipcrow—' Dogbrick called upward, surprised.

'You're late. It's well past midmorn.'

'Am I at the eleventh?' Dogbrick asked, squinting to see the narrow, black figure of Whipcrow emerge above him.

'You ran past me at that bend. This is twelve.' Whipcrow sat so that his tight face, narrow as an ax, fell eyelevel to the big man's hairy browledge. 'I thought 100 Wheels had you by the tail. But nobody's behind you. What's wrong?'

'I lost count.'

'So—' Whipcrow twitched impatiently. 'What's wrong?'

Dogbrick could no longer restrain his fright, and he blurted, 'I just found out – that's why I'm late. I just found out!'

Whipcrow's swarthy features widened with shared awe. 'Me, too! Crabhat boxed me on my way here. You heard, then? Arwar Odawl—'

'Fallen into the jungles of Elvre!'

'Yes! So Crabhat said. Where did he find you?'

'100 Wheels found me, in Smelters Alley. Ran her all the way to Everyland.'

A mocking grin of disbelief crossed Whipcrow's unhappy face. 'Save your bragging for the Dark Lord.'

'I think it is a ruse, Clever Crow.' Dogbrick nodded knowingly, glad that someone else had also heard this outrageous tale. 'I think this Dark Lord and his cacodemons are a ploy by the surgeons to unnerve those who have eluded them and mocked their authority.'

Whipcrow's frown deepened. 'And so we will gather at the Millgates to be trained and instead be herded away to the tide pools, eh?'

'Perhaps.' Dogbrick brushed back his mane defiantly. 'I say we ignore this malign thing and disobey those who would thwart us with fear.'

'Ignore it?' Whipcrow lifted one sketchy eyebrow. 'So, you'll still do business?'

'Why else would I be here in this stink?' Dogbrick asked sarcastically. 'What do you know?'

'I know where you can pick up as much trance wrap as a man can carry.' Whipcrow's tiny eyes tightened at the corners, and he added, 'None of it is marked! That's what's so precious, so very precious. None of it can be traced. It's all yours – if you can handle shriekers.'

'How many?'

'Many. Whoever goes in will have to dance to get out.'

Dogbrick budged Whipcrow aside with one thick finger and climbed past him. 'Call me when you have some real work, Crow. No more dancing.'

Whipcrow clenched a fistful of the thief's cloak and pulled himself upright. 'This is real, Brick. If you can move as fast as you did on the scarab job, the trance wrap's yours. It's the same as the last time. The shriekers are gang-rotated, and I know the pattern and the timetable. If you're fast, you won't see a shrieker until the exit gate. Then just dance the way you did last time and you're out. What'd you get for that scarab? You paid me a wand for that – so you probably got three for yourself. Ha! For the same risk, we can share a fortune.'

'Share?' Dogbrick glared. 'You'll get your quarter.'

'Half this time,' the gaunt man insisted, gray expression cold as rain. 'An opportunity like this won't happen again for me.'

'Especially if there *is* a Dark Lord.'

Whipcrow released Dogbrick's cloak and stepped back, and the wind lifted his sticky black hair like feathers. 'I fear that, Brick. Oh yes, but then the wrap will be even more valuable, won't it? Everyone will want to forget their misery. So, either way, we are rich.'

Dogbrick bent closer. 'Tell me what you know, and if I succeed, you will get a third. After all, if I fail, it is I who must pay with my life.'

Whipcrow conceded with a weary nod. 'But first, you must agree to pay me my third even if the Dark Lord himself comes to Saxar.'

'He had best stoop swiftly to our cliffs,' Dogbrick assured him with a thick grin, 'for if what you know and tell me is true, you will be paid by morning.'

'So, tomorrow midmorn, then. We will meet on Mirage Climb—'

Dogbrick nodded with understanding. 'The willow park above the Millgates.'

'Yes, we can look down from there on the grounds where the factories will gather their army.' His blue lips curled mockingly. 'I would see who the surgeons lure to their ranks.'

'Good.' Dogbrick's smile vanished in his beard. 'Now tell me what you know.'

Whipcrow beckoned the thief closer to the corroded wall and told him everything with a direct intensity that lost not a word to the rasping wind. He had Dogbrick repeat back to him what he had heard before he sealed the agreement with the dim smile of a man who has just surrendered the authorship of his future to another – the soft despair of those who must wait.

'Mirage Climb well before noon tomorrow,' the spy confirmed a last time before he flew up the worn steps into the smoky attic of Devil's Wynd.

Dogbrick saluted him jubilantly, then bounded down the smooth stairs, giddy with the bargain he had struck. *Two-thirds of all the trance wrap a man can carry!* He had only to convince his partner to take the risk.

The scarab job had nearly killed the strange fellow, and they had both sworn off dangerous ventures. But this was an extraordinary prize, a genuine oath-breaker, and Dogbrick hummed with eagerness to talk business. He opened his partner's seeker and spoke aloud his name to activate it: 'Ripcat!'

The golden star directed him by emitting a cool current, an invisible and silent guide who confidently led him to the nearest exit. Emerging from the wynd through a nitre-toothed tunnel, the thief climbed into the brash glare and noise of a weaver's bazaar.

Talismanic tapestries hung on scaffolds. Thousands of flamboyant panels crowded the sunny plaza and climbed the radiant boulevards beyond. Each tapestry had been woven with filaments of trance wrap so that the illustrations they depicted lived for those who pumped Charm into the fabric.

Crowds milled about, many chanting passages from their favorite panels and dancing the vigorous weaver's jig. Seeking Ripcat through this confusion would take longer than waiting until twilight when the odd man came out of hiding. Dogbrick closed the star amulet and returned it to his collar pouch.

Hellgate had vanished in the radiance of noon, and only Nemora's crystal skull marred the azure void above Saxar. Devil's Wynd had carried him across town, outside the gloom of the refineries and mills. Like a giant's fleece, sooty and tawed, industrial smoke stood massively to the east.

The weavers' urgent cymbals beckoned, and he considered whiling away the hours here, enjoying this magic. After all, the trance wrap he would steal that night made this bazaar possible. Without it, there would be no weavers, and by this time tomorrow, he would never have to pay for trance again. *Blissful irony*, he exulted, before a deeper irony jinxed his pleasure, *especially if there is a Dark Lord.*

Until he knew the truth of 100 Wheels' warning, his old joys could not offer him their familiar zest. He retreated from the immense bazaar and caught a city trolley going to the seacoves. For most of the ride along Fiddler Street, the spicy carnival fragrance of the weavers clung to him, and he prayed 100 Wheels had lied. He didn't want cacodemons ripping apart the tapestries. He wanted to know again the stupendous abandon of talismanic rapture.

If all Charm became worthless, then his whole life, everything he had struggled to possess with his thievery, lost value. All his risks and hard work had been in vain.

Anger swarmed from that thought, and he opened a window to clear his head of the bazaar's perfume, the scent of mirage. A headlong stream of sea wind gushed into the hollows of his body and fit him to the world again.

In the burning air of the factory district, impacted with

childhood sorrows and stalked by the surgeons, Dogbrick detached and grew strange to himself. The brisk air restored his happy hopes. Watching Fiddler Street's lean, pastel houses float by, he could not imagine cacodemons trampling their blossom terraces or disturbing their serene spiral balconies and floral turrets.

By the time the Ocean rose into view, the thief had convinced himself that Saxar would never be invaded. The refinery town clung to titanic cliffs at the most remote and desolate extreme of the Qaf, an epic desert swarming with gruesome terrors. No military force had ever amassed enough Charm to cross that unruly wasteland.

Nor could any sizable force approach unseen from the Ocean, because the Edge cut close to the horizon at this latitude and whole armies could easily fall off the world and into the sky's cold abyss with one charmed shift of the wind.

The other passengers on the city carriage – charmwrights in suede aprons, a witch silent within her veils, and a mentor talking history with her two young neophytes – sat well apart from the scruffy troglodyte whose pugnacious features carried a dim and uneasy smile. He took no offense. In fact, this close to winning his fortune, he felt benign to the whole world, and the presence of the other passengers graced him. They made him feel like a citizen, instead of the thief he was, and he nodded amicably to each of them as they came and went.

Dogbrick rode to the end of the line, following Fiddler down through the talus hills of rubble neighborhoods that sprawled across the steppes. The sight of the blackstone piles stained with cliffbottom seepings filled him with shame, for he had ineptly plundered many of these meager households while learning his trade. When he was wealthy, he would pay restitution. He had promised himself that for years, and at last tomorrow he would have that proud chance.

Fiddler dwindled to a sandy trace meandering through dune towns and driftwood villages transient as their sand moorings.

Gull shrieks and spindrift stung the crisp breeze, and he hummed a jaunty tune, alone finally in the floating carriage.

On tidal flats shining bright as beaten silver, the track widened again to an avenue of mariners' shops. He leaped out before the carriage began its swivel around the turnpole and landed in a splash of sand.

With a frisky stride, he crossed Ocean Avenue and marched along the mossy tidewall, saluting the marina workers and drydock hands who sometimes did business with him.

His destination was *The Wise Fish*, a lantern-hung den where sail menders and talisman braiders ate together at the open grill. The owner, a former thief, provided a discreet place to do business and get a decent meal. Dogbrick liked its location at the far end of the longest pier, where it commanded a view of all Saxar.

To avoid the long walk down the pier and inevitable encounters with people who owed him or wanted to do business, he climbed down from the tidewall and waded through the shallows. Seahorses shed bright peels of color through the crystal-lit water, and periwinkles swirled up in his wake.

At the pier, he climbed the notch ladder to the wooden catwalk connecting the pilings and made his way among the busy seiners in their blue slickers and red gloves. Only two owed him, and he settled quickly with them, arranging for deliveries of mollusks to the den in the coming days.

The world functioned so familiarly that the thought of cacodemons once more seemed childish, and the hope of impending fortune ripened his swollen heart. With waves swirling in a havoc of foam under him, he climbed shrouds to the hatch in the floor of *The Wise Fish* and knocked.

His rhythmic code slid the bolt at once, but the hatch opened on darkness and silence. Warily, he ascended into a gloomy chamber hung with reeved ropes, nets and marine skeletons. Lanterns stared blindly, and the socket of a room, with its cracked mead table and wobbly benches, looked pitifully small and empty.

The dozen people sitting in the window bay staring morosely out to sea looked ghostly, wavering in the aqueous shadows like phantoms.

They knew.

Dogbrick's hackles flurried, and with one glance at him, they saw that he knew and returned to their vapid staring.

The racket from the Ocean crowded the room with its timeless din even after Dogbrick pulled the hatch shut behind him. Someone had draped a kelp shroud over the sibyl's cage, and without her silken mesmermurs the den had no Charm. It appeared for what it was, little more than a lean-to at the end of a pier. Even the grill was cold.

Dogbrick sought out Wise Fish herself and found her huddled with the others in the bay. She sat with her back to a vintage keg of blue beer, her pupils blown wide, stenciled with windowlight, cloud ranges and the deep horizon.

'Arwar Odawl—' she whispered when he loomed into view, her best customer, her finest student. 'An age ends.' She shrugged her eyebrows with hapless regret. 'And all our Charm cannot save us.' Without the candy glare of the lanterns, her glossy skin looked bloodless, and the chill glint of her brow revealed skull.

Dogbrick regarded the others. They were all drunk, and they glowered darkly with the truth they shared. He knew every one of them. Most were thieves, several others survivors, the rest scavengers – a telling selection from the murky cellar of Saxar. These hardened folks could not easily have been fooled, yet he dared offer hope against their gloom, 'Perhaps this is a ruse of the surgeons . . .'

Everyone glowered, and he shut up. One of the thieves handed him a flagon of blue beer, and a place was made for him on the windowbench. He sat and sipped the yeasty foam, waiting for someone to speak. Numb within a widening fear, he flung his attention out the window, to the drapes of black seacliffs starry with the afternoon light caught in the glass of the city.

Presently, one of the scavengers explained how she had found out about the Dark Lord from the night trawlers, the nocturnal crews that gather Charm by sending their giant kites climbing the strong ebb winds. From the cope of heaven, their crystal eyes not only reflect Charm from the Abiding Star, they also overpeer the world. The shocked night trawlers showed the scavengers images in their far-see crystals of Arwar Odawl burning in the jungle.

The survivors learned about the Dark Lord, his cacodemons, and their destruction of the oldest realm on Irth through a far more primitive medium – carrier slinks. Possessing no Charm, survivors depended on aboriginal skills from long before the advent of amulets, and they used animal carriers to stay in contact with survivors in other cities. Confirmation from them that all of what 100 Wheels had said was true forced Dogbrick to accept the grim reality of the Dark Lord.

He swigged deeply of the blue beer in dread honor of the new, omnipotent warlord and spent the remainder of that day in silence with the others, watching Saxar come alert to the horror. The afternoon wave of black dirigibles brought the first direct news from the south. Soon after, the temple chimes began, and the factory flues stopped smoking early.

Watching the fumes clear away in broad daylight and reveal the oxide-seared streets and roasted buildings of the factory ranges inspired awful fear, and most of the onlookers in the den left at once, called away to do whatever outlandish tasks remained to them in this end time.

Dogbrick lingered. His partner knew where to find him if the city alarms woke him early. And if he slept through this, all the better, the thief reasoned, for there was yet a fortune to be seized – if they dared.

He helped himself to another flagon of blue beer and saluted Wise Fish. She sat motionless, entranced by the eerie sight of Saxar naked. Cancerous colors blistered the cliff slopes of the manufacturing districts and exposed a charred labyrinth, a torched nest of sinister furnaces, vats livid as cankers, and distillers coiled among themselves like burnished black vipers.

The streets teemed as workers scattered to their homes, and Dogbrick amused himself for a while peering through the den's spy glass at their desperate flights. *Where do they think they are fleeing?*

'To love,' he answered himself aloud, and Wise Fish flinched from her stupor.

'Arwar Odawl—' she moaned.

'The citizens flee before the Dark Lord into the arms of their loved ones,' Dogbrick said, watching skilled charmwrights and common laborers alike hurrying through the baked streets to the trolley stations. 'What does this reveal to us of human nature, Wise Fish? Is evil good because it drives us to love?'

Wise Fish struggled to press a sharpeye amulet to her sweaty brow. At its touch, a torpid smile lifted through her slow as an anchor and hauled alertness into her eyes from a long way down. 'You are a selfish and conniving schemer, Dogbrick. You only pretend interest in humanity. All you truly care about is yourself. I want no more of your greedy company. Go away.'

Dogbrick lowered the spy glass with a scowl of disbelief. 'You're drunk.'

With the sharpeye pressed hard to her brow, she repeated, 'Go away.'

The thief put down the spy glass and met her vehement gaze with a relaxed expression of understanding. 'Of course, you're in shock. I'll leave.'

'Don't come back.'

Dogbrick's ears pulled back at her harsh tone, a cutting voice he had never heard from her before. 'What do you mean?' he protested and knelt before her. 'I'm your best customer. And you still haven't taught me everything you know about the business.'

She made a disgusted look with such violence she nearly dropped the sharpeye. Her head bobbed forward, eyes whiteballed, and the thief stopped her with one finger. The touch startled her alert, and she relied again on the glistening sharpeye to defeat the blue beer's languor. When she could speak again, she said sharply, 'Forget the business, Dogbrick. There is no more business. There is no more world.'

'Well,' he agreed, gazing softly at his mentor, 'the world may have ended, but we go on.'

The old woman blew a long, exasperated sigh. 'Without Charm? I'm not living my old age as an aborigine. I'm no survivor.'

'Fish,' he cajoled, 'I thought you were wise. Every world needs thieves and a good grill. We'll thrive.'

She sank back with despair at his ignorance and spoke spitefully, 'The Dark Lord has not come to Irth to rule, you muttwit. He is here to destroy.'

He gestured widely, trying to encompass her in his warmth. He had never seen her this way, and it frightened him to the core. 'He can't destroy the whole world, Fish.'

She pulled away the sharpeye and closed her green lids, shaking her head remorselessly.

Dogbrick took her hand and held it and the sharpeye to her forehead. 'How do you know this, Wise Fish? I heard nothing of this from 100 Wheels.'

She shoved him away. 'You will if you go to the Millgates tomorrow. By then, the sorceress Altha and her pet Hazar will disclose all to Saxar.'

Dogbrick squatted before her with a narrow countenance, remembering that Wise Fish had a granddaughter and a niece both well placed in the polar palace of Zul and privy to the whims of the peers, the rulers of the dominion. 'What do the peers know?'

'What would they not know?' She conveyed her disdain with a snarl. 'They have all the Charm. For what that's worth to them now.'

Dogbrick leaned closer to the black bores of his teacher's eyes. 'Who is this Dark Lord, Wise Fish?'

'Death himself.'

He pulled back, scalded by the venom of her voice. 'What do you mean?'

She pulled him near again, lifted his woolly earflap, and whispered with hot fright, 'He is from the Dark Shore.'

Dogbrick stood. 'How can that be?'

'We'll need a lot more rat-stars than we have now to know that, muttwit. So just shut up and go away.'

The thief bent and lowered Wise Fish's arm so that her hands lay on her smudged gown. Her head rocked back, and he fit a towel from the grill under her neck so she rested more comfortably. Then, he plucked the sharpeye from her grasp. He admired the amulet's milkstone orb in a setting of tiny scarlet djinn-knots and decided to keep it.

She had never called him a mutt before. She had always treated him as a man. The word had stung both times, two slicing lashes that cut him to numbness. But he forgave immediately. This was Wise Fish, the woman who had lured him from the warrens and sheltered him. The shock had broken her, or else she would not treat him this harshly. She never had before. Yet, even with her harshness she taught him, and her last lesson was the limits of love. He would keep her sharpeye as a reminder.

The rest of the afternoon, he sat in the bay window and watched the fleet come in early, an event unprecedented in Saxar's history. The colorful vessels in the Ocean each day unfurled huge talismans designed to capture the radiance of the Abiding Star. The numerous amulets that continually changed hands and sustained the city were minted from the Charm harvested by these ships. Many citizens would suffer in the days to come from the drought of these few hours.

But Dogbrick determined not to be among them. The world had ended – but he would go on. He would defy despair. His own teacher had named him a mutt with her last words to him. To honor her, he would go beyond all that she had taught, and he would prove himself a man.

In the last yellow hour of the day, he flicked a farewell to the yegg and the survivors who were trying to light the grill but did not look at Wise Fish. Their goodbye was already wide enough for him, and he was afraid she would call him that name again. He did, however, pause before the sibyl's draped cage.

With a flourish, he removed the magenta shade of dried kelp and set the gold sphere of the cage spinning wildly. Amidst a thrashing of crimson and green feathers, shrieks clawed at him, like rough, shrill sketches of dying.

The sibyl showed its tongue of fire, and Dogbrick laughed to watch its gaudy feathers quivering over its marbly nakedness. The color of the wings bronzed with anger.

Dogbrick seized the cage and stopped its spinning. 'Tell me true, sibyl – am I man or am I dog?'

The sibyl spit blue sparks, then whistled, '*How you die decides that!*'

Dogbrick laughed to hear once again his destiny spoken aloud. 'Mark that, Fish! The sibyl cannot lie. I am a man, for I will not die like a dog. I am my own master!' He kicked open the hatch and descended quickly before his mentor or the sibyl could reply.

The ebb-swirl churned below, violent as the emotions twisting inside him. He dropped on to the catwalk. The seiners had run off at the sound of the first alarm, and he stepped over lank coils of rope and twists of net dropped in panic. Bleats of ship horns announced the last of the fleet entering the marina; otherwise, the alert had passed and a shrill chorus of gulls rose above the thudding surf.

He took out his seeker, opened it, and called, 'Ripcat!'

A chill current guided him along the catwalk on the underside of the pier to the tidewall. The beach was empty, except for the scavengers, who had to work or starve. The streets, also, stood vacant, and he had no trouble finding a city carriage. Three stood unoccupied at the turnpole.

He rode up Fiddler Street, past the plaza where he had emerged from Devil's Wynd. The bazaar was gone, scaffolds and tapestries removed. The cool directional breeze led him out of the carriage and across the plaza among the afternoon's long shadows. In the distance, the cliffwalls usually hidden by factory smoke revealed their brown, lacy erosion like giant diseased lungs.

A troupe of religious singers rode the crosstown city carriage with him. They kept to themselves, droning softly, though he stared right at them with his baleful, bonehooded eyes and smiled. He wanted them to acknowledge his humanity and so he tried to keep his black lips closed over his orange teeth.

Before he could introduce himself, the ether trail left the carriage. He stepped into Cold Niobe Plaza at the crest of Everyland Street, under the imposing dragoncoils of the marmoreal arch. Pausing at the kerb, he peered straight down Everyland into the pit of an extinguished hell. Silverblack temples jammed the crater, the storage domes and chimney-steeples of refineries, casting spidery shadows over the tarnished alleys where Dogbrick had grown up.

For a moment, he stood entranced by the craggy buildings baked to an iridescent enamel. He had never before seen his neighborhood in direct light, and he traced with his ardent gaze the familiar places of his youth in all their colors of ash.

'I have not risen this high to fall again so low,' he spoke aloud to the depths, and his words sounded dreadfully frail among their echoes.

Eagerly, he followed the seeker to a city carriage and traveled up Everyland. He wondered how his partner would respond to the coming of the Dark Lord. Ripcat was unpredictable in all things but one – virtue. He was the only honest thief on Irth. He gave away everything he stole and kept only enough Charm to protect himself while he slept.

The carriage sailed through cloistered spark trees, and the perfumed air sparkled. Dogbrick gazed at the opulent onyx estates set in the deepening shade of hedge ranks and treecrowns and saw no human figure. Everyone was watching their crystals this evening. Dogbrick snorted at the image of turtle-jowled Lord Hazar and her portly Ladyship Altha reassuring Saxar from their arctic citadel.

Blinding rays of horizontal daylight illuminated the park at the crest of Everyland, where the carriage reached its turnpole. Dogbrick dismounted and stared east, into the purple sea and approaching night. Flares of color ignited from the pools, linns and water gardens in the wide estates below.

Dogbrick wanted to walk down the park slopes to the viewing platform and survey the naked city, but the chill breeze in his hand blew the other way. Squinting into the hot light, he climbed a cinder path through a grove of jigsaw trees to a riven and mossy bluff. Stone steps curved upward toward the summit's faceted boulders and wild twists of cypress.

The seeker stopped at a high ledge of baked guano, white and slick as enamel. Beyond, the welded land sloped gradually downward into the ancient volcanic plains of the Qaf. On the bright, laminar horizons of sunset, mesas and plateaus stood like distant vermilion kingdoms.

Dogbrick turned a slow circle, looking for his partner. Twilight shone less spectacularly than when the factories ran till nightfall. Apricot haze filled the clear sky, and it was easy to see that the cypress grove below was empty. The wind wafted out of there medallioned with scents of birds and sap resins but there were no people among the sepia-faced trees.

The thief sensed no one nearby. This was a typical haunt for his strange partner, remote and yet exposed. *Is he invisible?* Dogbrick's hackles quivered under his cloak and lifted his shoulders in an involuntary shrug. 'Ripcat—'

The nine gates of twilight opened, and the scalloped colors crowned the point in the desert where the Abiding Star set. There the horizon glowed like a hot edge of nicked razor. The thief could see for miles to distant sandfins and gypsum reefs burning hot as fallen stars. No one was out there.

Festal lights glimmered in Saxar, far fewer than usual, but sufficient to outline the city's chief arteries. Flares followed the fractal coastline, illuminating the scavengers' advance as they followed the tide out.

Dogbrick watched in fascination the luminous workers toiling to keep up with the retreating tide. The Dark Lord had come to destroy Irth, and still the work gangs searched avidly through the Ocean's droppings, rummaging among the debris of wrecked coral and mussel beds for the rare, invaluable jetsam and flotsam of far-off kingdoms – spilled cargo, lost spoils of war, uncovered treasures of far-gone ages, some even from other worlds, cast adrift in the terrible clashes of mages and sorcerers.

The tide pickings would become spectacular in the coming nights as the jungle rivers washed through Elvre and the wide scattered ruins of Arwar Odawl. But on this first night of the horror, there was only just enough activity on the tidal flats to make out the seacove where Wise Fish sat in her stupefied gloom.

Dogbrick huffed again at the thought of her. She had betrayed him to fear and called him a mutt. That hurt, because she was the one who had shown him how to believe in himself as something more than a beast – as a man, able enough in body and wit to climb the heights.

*Heights are also depths*, he quoted from Gibbet scripture and lifted his stare out of the cliff city to the wide tracts of wasteland. Wise Fish never learned that truth. She only knew how to climb. But then, she had never been to the Qaf. Out there in the imponderable wilderness, Dogbrick had walked the floor of creation, searching for the mettle to become a man. He came back with singed fur, a blistered snout – and his partner Ripcat.

Dogbrick had found him wandering out of the Qaf staggering blind with heatstroke. That had been nearly five hundred days ago. Since then, the partnership that had found them charmless had won them more amulets than they could use. If the Charm in amulets could have been preserved, he and Ripcat would have stopped thieving after their first ten days. But amulets wore down and the fate of the charmless was bleak as the Qaf.

'Ripcat – are you out there?' Dogbrick called into the maroon shadows of night. A treasure of trance wrap awaited their attention. 'Ripcat—'

Overhead, stars, planets, and cometary globules clustered. Cold trampled across the hot gravel beds with a crackling of sparks, and the thief pulled his cloak tighter. He restrained himself from calling again. The seeker had led him here, and he would wait. Ripcat had to be close, even if he could not be seen.

He closed his eyes and tasted the sage breezes.

Nothing.

Then, he stopped breathing and listened through his beating pulse to the glittering night. And he heard again nothing, nothing at all of man. But he did remember another line from The Gibbet Scrolls. It swam up out of memory and fixed him more securely to the moment: *Silence listens.*

When Dogbrick opened his eyes, Ripcat stood before him, fur glossed blue by starlight. The wind tufted his shoulders yet he wore, as usual, only trousers and ankle boots, proudly displaying his taut human torso.

'Cat!' Dogbrick jumped to his feet. 'I am stupendously happy to see you. I had hoped to find you earlier – to tell you as soon as I found out – but Cold Niobe was clogged with a weaver's bazaar.'

Ripcat climbed the bluff, slow and adroit, using ascent to stretch his muscles. He had been curled asleep under the ledge where Dogbrick stood, until the cold woke him.

A gust of dark laughter shook Dogbrick. 'You have no idea what's happened, do you?'

Ripcat's curved eyes watched him curiously, and Dogbrick laughed again.

'Come! You must see to believe.' He led his partner through the cypress grove and down the cinder path among the jigsaw trees to the park's viewing platform. Even before the city came into sight, Ripcat sensed an astounding change. The smell of the Ocean met him stronger than usual, untainted by the grimy carnival fumes from Saxar.

With a bound, Ripcat was at the timber railing and leaning far out, peering down at the shadowy cliffs for the city immersed in the night. Apart from the scavengers' torchlights across the tidal flats, Saxar looked dark. A sparse scattering of festal lamps flickered on the main avenues, too dim to ward off the night.

Ripcat spun about, green eyes sharp with surprise, and perched on the rail facing Dogbrick. He waited to hear what had become of the fire festivals and lantern ceremonies that flowed every night through the streets incandescent as magma.

Dogbrick suppressed another black laugh. His partner's chiseled head, with its short, dense fur gnarled with scars and lumps, looked funny gawping, as if it had inadvertently slouched forward under the weight of its heavy slung-jaw and big eyes.

'The world has collapsed,' Dogbrick declared and clutched at his bounding beard in fright. 'While you slept, dreamy Cat, everything has changed!' The large thief stepped closer and spoke with hushed intensity and a crazed glint in his merry eyes. 'You could think of yourself as the Dreamer, who took a nap in one world and woke in another. Maybe you should return to sleep.'

Ripcat sat back and watched him like cool green grass.

'Forgive me,' Dogbrick conceded. He gripped his brow between thumb and forefinger, and his voice broke into another brittle laugh. 'I'm giddy. The world has become very dangerous, my friend. And I must laugh or go mad with fright.'

With the blind city to vouch for him, Dogbrick told Ripcat what had transpired that day. His partner listened zealously. And after the story was told, the rapt listener sat ruminating a long moment, pug-head bowed; then, he slinked over the railing and down the cliff. Nimble as a shadow, he vanished into the night on venturesome paths among the wild rocks and brush of the precipice.

'Hey!' Dogbrick called after, clutching the railing to lean farther out.

Ripcat looked up, tinfoil eyes agleam in the darkness.

'Where are you going?' the big thief asked, gruff with surprise.

The eyeglints jerked away, and an indigo whisper came back and colored the darkness, barely audible, yet pitched perfectly for his ears and understanding, 'To the dance.'

# 1 Gather the Darkness

✦✦✦

Romut squatted on a knoll overlooking the sea, looking much like a big toadstool in the dirty light of dusk. Half-man, half-gnome, he glared at the world through a permanent scowl of bone-hooded eyes lidded and squinty as a man's but with orbs that were wholly black, gleaming bituminously, holding the dark plains before him in a gnome's night-piercing vision. He searched for ogres, the masters of this misty land.

Among the fumes blowing off the waves in the stiff maritime breeze, Romut spied the first crew of scavengers slogging among the dunes, laboriously dragging their hooks and nets. They would be expecting him to join them soon, but he was in no hurry. A thousand nights he had toiled among them and he knew well how long he could linger before the ogres would arrive to oversee their work.

He drew a leaf of langor-weed from a pocket of his tattered vest and rolled it with one stubby-fingered hand while he fumbled in another pocket for his flint pebbles. With the tightly curled leaf between his thick, blistered lips, he clacked the blue pebbles expertly between his fingers and caught the first spark with a sharp intake of breath. The langor-weed flared briefly and cast livid shadows across his ponderous features.

After the first keen burn in his throat, the acrid smoke filled the hollows of his body with mercies of ease and a thin joy, and he regarded the bogland below with a softer mien. Twilight rain hung in harps over the distant gloomy islets. Beyond them, the last scarlet chords of the day darkened toward purple and kindled the sea-mist to a sepia smudge against which the shivery shrubs atop knolls and dunes stood like scorched lace.

Romut let the weed's soft euphoria carry his memory back to a grander time in his life, a thousand twilights earlier when he had, for a glorious moment of his tedious life, known true power. Then, he had worn a skin of light shaped to make him look tall and manly. And though the others of the Bold Ones had laughed at him for his vanity, he was the only one of them to survive. All the other so-called Bold Ones who gathered under the sword of Taran to serve Wrat were cast squealing like runtlings into the abyss by the mighty wizarduke Lord Drev. Romut alone survived by shedding his skin of light and fleeing to this foreboding place of mist-magic and bog giants – the Reef Isles of Nhat.

A dark laugh smoked from his chest at the thought that he had escaped the abyss for *this*. Every night since the terrible fall of the Bold Ones, he had pondered ruefully if it would have been better for him to have fallen away from Irth entirely rather than to cower here under the glaring scrutiny of the ogres, who worked their scavengers like beasts.

Again, Romut peered into the misty night for the arrival of the overlords. He wanted to dwell further on his splendid past, for those famous memories gave him the strength to hoist the dredging hooks and trawl the nets that raked the star-bossed shallows for the treasure the tide had forsaken. Yet he dare not arrive late on the tidal flats. Ogres detested gnomes, and they sought every excuse to torment him for his gnomish blood. He did not ever again want to hang from his heels above a viper-wasps' hive stung so full of toxin his eyes sealed shut and breath squeaked through his hot, swollen throat and sizzled in his crispy lungs.

He stood up at that grisly memory and stretched till his bones popped. With his hands atop his bald, warty head and the rolled weed dangling from his protuberant lower lip, he watched the last bruise of day heal into a horizon of pinwheel stars. Unlike all the other pitiable scavengers he saw milling below on the tidal flats, waiting for the bosses to come and direct them, he had wielded power once himself. He had known what it was to be feared. And so since then he had been careful not to forget, careful to remember that he had once been far more than what any of these others dared dream they could be.

'Romut—' a sourceless voice called.

The gnomish man sucked harder on his burning leaf and peered about with his black, scowling eyes. 'Who calls?' he growled.

The starlight developed a vast face in the cryptic mists floating up the knoll. Sick with abrupt fear, Romut dropped the langorweed from his mouth and backed away two stiff, jolting steps. He thought a bog giant's face had reared up from the marsh below, the countenance was so huge, swollen and mossy. But then, he saw that the visage was disembodied, an apparition composed of pale green swampgas. The misshapen features in the blue starlight leered with menace.

'What do you want of me, phantom?' Romut challenged. 'Who sent you?'

'One you know and yet know not,' the spirit spoke as it slid closer.

'Who are you?'

'What you say.'

'You are a shade,' Romut declared, certain that his night-vision did not deceive him. 'Whose Charm sends you here?'

'The very one who calls me back, now that you have been found!' The incandescent face beswirled to molten vapors and vanished in the wind.

A shiver jumped through his tense muscles and made his bones clop. 'What deviltry is this?' He voiced his fright aloud. 'This is not ogres' work. Those brutes have no Charm at all.

Then who? Who do I know and yet know not?'

No answer accompanied the flitting bats that blurred overhead, and Romut stomped angrily on the fallen butt of langor-weed, wanting to believe he had suffered an arrant vision induced by rancid smoke.

'Prepare to be taken!' the specter's voice interceded, and the squat man heaved about, lurching with fright.

'Who speaks?' he cried to the clouds of stars.

Silence received into its ultimate enormity the dull thunder of surf and the dim twitter of bats.

'Take me then!' Romut bawled to the night and strode down the knoll, churning with fear and undirected rage. An apparition such as he had witnessed required more Charm than any mortal being he knew could muster. *Unless it be the wizarduke*, he thought with a spasm of fright. Lord Drev had sworn to avenge the death of his sister, Lady Mevea, upon every wretched champion of the Bold Ones. *Has he found me out at last?*

Romut hurried through the marsh mist, so distraught that often he splashed off the trail into mudspits. By the time he staggered onto the quaking sand of the tidal flats with their luminous and blurred reflections of the heavens, mud plastered his leggings and gobs of mire hung like putty on his large and hideous face.

The other crew workers, humans all, peered curiously at him, but none dared query him. Though he was half their height, he was generally avoided for his rageful temper and gnomish strength. He intimidated the other scavengers, and none pitied him when the ogres flogged him with medusa cords or hung him upside-down over the droning, fire-poked hives.

These bitter memories scattered at the approach of the ogres, and he stood head bowed among the others, awaiting that night's commands.

The ogres, with their powerful bodies and small, sooty faces, strode the line of scavengers, bellowing orders. A pall of burnt vomit accompanied them, the sour perfume of ogres. Their fleecy manes shook with the enormity of their voices. Legs thick as tree trunks sunk them past their ankles into the wet sand, yet they moved with eerie agility. The massive excess of their shoulders and muscle-cumbered arms seemed to hover as though the huge might of invisible wings unfolded behind them.

Unshod and naked but for shaggy kilts dark and matted with smeared gore, the ogres looked primitive, though they possessed minds even more nimble than their quick bulks. They were renowned throughout Irth as supreme tacticians, and every army coveted their counsel. But ogres kept wholly to themselves. They despised Charm and preferred to live by the timeless and aboriginal traditions of their ancestors. Supreme opportunists, they had swarmed into the Reef Isles of Nhat a thousand days earlier, after the wizarduke Lord Drev had broken the Bold Ones, who had originated in this knolly land. Since seizing this swampy coast and all its many islets, they had enslaved what remained of the human population to serve as scavengers, and they used what valuables could be dredged from the shallows to trade for what they most coveted: Rare dew-wine from the grasslands of Sharna-Bambara.

'Dig dunes!' an ogre shouted and pointed out three scavengers, who immediately dashed off to probe the slipfaces that had been scalloped at high tide.

'Drag foreshore!' another ogre yelled and dispatched others to pull their nets through the slimy, weed-tangled tide-margins.

'Rake shoals!' The order fell upon the workers laboring beside Romut, and they splashed across the pools, rakes held above their heads for balance.

'You, gnome!' An ogre thrust at him a grin like a grimace. 'Net waves! Go!'

Romut dared not hesitate, though the chore assigned him was the most dangerous. He seized a bale of net and hauled it into the shallows. The ogres enjoyed sending the shortest scavengers toward the deepest water, where the threats of striker-eels and rip-currents were greatest.

Underbreath, the gnomish man cursed the foul-smelling overlords and marched doggedly toward the distant breakers. Unlike, the coastline elsewhere on Irth, here among the Reef Isles of Nhat the Ocean rose and fell serenely, because over the aeons the world's three largest rivers had silted wide littoral plains. Even so, Romut soon found himself chest-deep in water.

Ahead of him, the retreating tide broke in luminous waves and filled the air with its spume. Numerous small islands cluttered the horizon. On most of them, ogres dominated other scavengers, and Romut could see occasional glints of starlight off their rakes and net-weights.

In a cove of the largest island, a dragon wallowed. Its wings flame-flickered under the night sky. Like lightning, its scaly length flashed as it rolled with pleasure in the surf. Its meat-hook talons flexed against the heavens, and the crystals of its eyes glared from under granite brows. Then, without warning, it spun about and heaved toward outer space, its sharp silhouette a smashed outline in the night's starry window as it hovered almost motionless.

Something had frightened it. Romut gazed around as the foaming water sluiced about him and looked again for the huge face of green gas. But he saw nothing unusual, just scavengers turning the slick sand with their long rakes and trawling the shallows while the ogres built their driftwood fires. Of course, the familiar scene offered little assurance. A dragon's senses far exceeded all other creatures', and it had sensed something frightening.

*Lord Drev* . . . The fear of the wizarduke's revenge returned to Romut. *Yet how? How could he have found me? He and all others this side of the Gulf know nothing of my true form. They seek an illusion – if they seek me at all.*

When he looked upward again, the dragon was gone.

Romut returned to his work. He dared not give the ogres any excuse at all to punish him, knowing they relished his suffering. Only his usefulness as a laborer spared him their sadistic glee. His gnomish strength enabled him to perform the work of two men, and the ogres took advantage of that. He labored alone at the tide's retreating edge, using his large bare feet and stout legs to resist the undertow and relying on his luck to spare him the lethal bite of striker-eels.

Romut's luck was both his jubilance and terror. It had made his twelve thousand days on Irth possible – and it had delivered him into abject poverty, snatched him from that, and hurled him back again. He had been born not far from this swampy coast, in a mire where his human mother had been exiled after her rape by a gnome. She had died birthing him, ripped apart by his huge head and with neither midwife nor Charm to save her. That had been the terror of his luck. And as luck would have it, a scavenger found him strangling on his birthcord and saved him to work the tidal flats. That grim luck owned him for the first ten thousand days of his life. It owned him then as it owned him again at this ogreish time. And in the time between, it had led to Wrat, the scavenger who had found the sword of Taran, and for one brief and glorious interval, Romut's luck had touched him with power.

Hurling the net-weights athwart the churning waves and bending his stout body to drag the seine through the surf, he fetched his mind back to those gratifying days when he wore the skin of light and wielded Charm. He remembered with delight the women he had taken for his own, their protests stitching his desire tighter to his will. With joy, he recalled the men who dared defy him and how he deftly painted every one of them in the garish paints of their own blood, killing each one slowly in a tireless, insatiable, and savage amazement at their suffering. These memories gave him strength, even against the turn of luck that had stripped him of his skin of light, of his Charm, and had returned him here, to serve ogres.

He had forgotten entirely the green mask of mist and the startled dragon when the first horrified bellow sounded from the shore. That cry inspired terror in all who heard it, because it was an ogre's wail.

Perched atop a dune above the strand where the ogres' fires blazed, an ominous figure hulked. Romut could not see it clearly from where he stood in the crashing surf, yet he could tell from the agitation among the ogres and the outright panic of the scavengers on the shoreline that whatever had alighted there was terrible.

Inspired by the fear of the others, Romut crouched in the waves and watched as the ogres fled down the beach. There they stopped, their panic stymied by the appearance of other figures atop the dunes, each as large and menacing as the first.

Awestruck, Romut watched as the ogres collapsed to their knees in utter submission.

Sick with sudden dread, the gnomish man backed deeper into the withdrawing tide and felt the tug of undercurrent loosen his toehold on the sandy bottom. If he surrendered to the sea, he would either be swept away to be devoured by eels or flung, like all the other Bold Ones, into the Gulf – unless his jubilant luck asserted itself and he managed to swim against the tide to one of the many islets.

He chose not to gamble just yet with his life and pulled away from the tide's grip. He wanted to see what were these creatures that broke the aggression of ogres by their mere appearance.

Two scavengers came splashing toward him, eager to throw themselves into the Ocean. 'Cacodemons!' one cried to him hysterically, as in warning.

*Cacodemons?* Romut puzzled at this. As a child, he had heard fright tales of such creatures, but he knew well enough, now that he was grown, that they were not real. Keeping to himself and spending as little time as possible with the other scavengers since fleeing the wrath of Lord Drev, he had not yet heard the terrifying news of cacodemons falling out of the night and into the fields of Sharna-Bambara.

Amazed, he saw the two scavengers surrender themselves to the riptide and watched in bewilderment as their bobbing heads and flailing arms slowly dwindled toward the horizon.

This display of hopeless struggle against the tide determined him to abandon any thought of swimming to another isle. He lay flat and rode the rushing foam toward the shore. As he neared, the cacodemons came more clearly into view.

Tall as the ogres, they had a reptilian sleekness, with stark bones jutting under the husk of their malevolent faces. Violent fangs meshed in their hooked jaws, and – most horrible of all – their bellies carried within them other faces, horrid features displaying clamped grins of meshed teeth and spidery, tar-drop eyes full of evil intent.

Seeing this abomination, Romut believed at once he possessed the strength to swim against the legendary current and find sanctuary on one of the reef isles. Quickly, he turned and waded back into the waves. But the cacodemons had already spotted him.

Whimpering, he fought the anguish of terror to fill his lungs, then dove under the waves and pulled himself along the sandy bottom into deeper water. Until the breath in him burned so hot it began to char his mind, he stayed underwater. When at last he burst up for air, he found that he had swum under the wavebreak and into the implacable grip of the outbound current.

He rolled on to his back and gazed shoreward. And what he saw poured cold through his veins: The cacodemons had risen into the night and carried themselves through the air as an abhorrent flock black and mute as soot, all gliding hard upon him.

With a yelp, he plunged underwater but had no breath to stay. As he came up again, the cacodemons floated directly above him, near enough for him to see clearly even in the dark the black beads of their hides, the wet rodent teeth in the creased faces of their underbellies, and the horrid smiles of their eel-browed heads.

He tried to go under again, but talons pierced his vest and hoisted him up out of the water. The vest tore, and he plunged again into the sea. An instant later, claws pincered the muscles of his chest, stabbed through his flesh, and hooked under his collarbone. He rose flaring a scream that withered to squeals as the underbelly faces gnashed their maws to chew at him.

The claws held him just out of the snapping reach of the hungry faces, and his squeals singsonged pain and terror.

Hung like a snatched trout, he gawped at the nightland below spinning away. The marshes with their ragged mists retreated, and the boggy shoreline where he had grown up a slave to the tides and where he had slaved again for the ogres vanished below clouds. By that he knew the cacodemons were carrying him inland, toward the highlands. He assumed that there, in some bone-strewn aerie, they would devour him.

A cold laugh shuddered from beyond the wingless demons, and Romut moaned painfully to behold again the green face of mist, smaller, streaking like a comet beside him. Its bald, baleful visage wrinkled with malignant mirth: 'Romut, you are taken! Now prepare to meet the Dark Lord! Ready yourself to submit before Hu'dre Vra!'

Romut bawled hysterically. His body buckled and came within reach of the slaverous faces in the whittle-ribbed torso of the cacodemon that held him. Rat-teeth gnawed at his abdomen, and he jerked away in pain, leaving rags of his flesh in the chewing mouths.

Simpering in terror, Romut hung bleeding from the talons' steely grasp and gazed up into the gnashing faces crazed to bite into him again. The gaseous face blurring beside him spun with cruel laughter, then pulled closer and cackled poisonously, 'And now, Romut, you will wear death's shadow!'

The talons pulled him upward into the hungry faces, and their frantic jaws bit deeply into his body. Pain cut mortally. Blood sprayed and gurgled in his throat, stoppering his mad cries, drowning him in his own desperate suffering.

The talons unclasped, and Romut fell. Spinning blood through the dark air, he plummeted, entrails unraveling above him. Impact shattered the bone-chain of his spine and the plates of his skull, and he lay in a quivering pool of torment, staring helplessly up at the circling cacodemons blotting the stars.

Darkness wrinkled closer. Pain chilled colder. Death narrowed in.

At the very brink of unconsciousness, a huge shadow loomed over him.

'Romut!' The voice pounded him, and his smashed and ripped body jumped with hotter pain. 'Romut be whole!'

Suffering blew away like smoke in a stiff wind, and the spilled juices of his body, the smashed porcelain of his bones, the torn silk of his flesh fitted together, once again intact. He sat up effortlessly, his breath clear and easy, vision shiny and new minted, all agony gone as though his death throes had been a mere delusion.

The sinister, hulking figure before him wore jagged blades of black armor enameled with starfire. The phantasmagoria of its spiked helmet cowled like a cobra's hood, fanning out from a viper's grinning visage and a baleen of needle-thin teeth. Deep within its hooded sockets, hot eyes slanted.

'Romut—' A voice of void and darkness spoke. 'I am the countenance of death. I am the indifference of life. Hu'dreVra is my name.'

'Oh, great lord!' Romut whimpered.

'Silence!' Hu'dre Vra roared, and the space around him cracked into broken pieces of lightning. 'I am full master here. None may speak before me without my sufferance. Now – die!'

Like a bursting pod, Romut's torso split, and his viscera bloomed with smiting pain. Blood smoked like ink into the air around him, coloring the shape of his screams. Blackness touched him hard between the eyes, and he collapsed swathed in the chill coils of death.

'Now rise, Romut,' the great voice spoke again. 'Rise and be whole once more! The Dark Lord commands!'

Bloodsmoke swirled tightly around Romut, pouring back into his ruptured body. Lightnings doodled his flesh, stitching his wounds together. Suddenly he was intact and sitting up, gazing fearfully at the shining blackness, the serrated and glossy darkness of Hu'dre Vra.

With trembling hands, Romut covered his face and cowered before the giant figure.

'Now you see, little person,' Hu'dre Vra's enormous voice spoke, 'all life on Irth is at venture before me. By whim alone, I rule.'

Romut lay silent and shuddering.

'I can destroy you and restore you a thousand more times,' the thunderous voice said. 'Hu'dre Vra can find you wherever you go. No place is hidden from the Dark Lord.'

Green gas seeped through Romut's tight fingers and scalded his eyes with a frightful apparition of the mask that had first sought him out and had escorted him here.

'Do you understand?' The green mask spoke with its master's voice.

Romut whimpered and nodded his head vigorously.

'Speak!'

'Yes, Lord! Yes, I understand. Oh, yes, I understand!'

'Pain is my servant,' Hu'dre Vra said. 'Look at me, little man.'

Romut lifted his woeful face.

The mask of green gas shredded as the titanic black form stepped closer. 'Torment obeys me. Death obeys me. All life is mine to mangle and reshape as I please. Do you believe me, Romut?'

'Yes, Lord.'

'And will you obey me in all things?'

'Oh yes, Lord. Oh yes!'

The serpent grin of the black lacquered mask seemed to widen. Hu'dre Vra drew an ebony spike from the brassard of his saw-toothed armor. Deftly, he dropped the curved spike into the ground between Romut's knees. 'Take it.'

Romut grasped the cold metal in shivering hands, and it slid from the ground with a rasping sound.

'Now, Romut – pierce yourself through the heart.'

Romut gawped with fright at the stupendous being of darkness. 'Do it!

Squinting shut his eyes and grimacing so broadly that he showed his molars, Romut swung the sharp spike directly at his breast. When the icy tip bit his flesh, he balked. A dry sibilance of snakes coiling electrified the air, and Romut found the strength to drive the spike hard into his chest.

Pain flared. Its enormity convulsed him. And every involuntary twist of his body stabbed him yet again. Cut horribly, he wanted only to die. But death would not come. The monstrous presence of the Dark Lord kept him alive and suffering.

The torture lasted an abominable eternity, macerating him to a froth of bonemeal and body-glue. Madness seethed in him, and his mind bleared toward the mica-glitter of mute mineral matter.

'Be whole!' the Dark Lord commanded.

Instantly, the suffering ended. No stain of it remained.

'You hesitated to pierce your heart,' Hu'dre Vra said, 'and so I gave you suffering. When next I command you, obey at once. Do you understand me, Romut?'

'Yes, yes! I understand you, my Lord.' The gnomish man pressed his bulbous head to the ground and swore, 'I will obey you in all things without hesitation.'

'Good. Now rise.'

Romut flung himself upright.

'Rise!' Hu'dre Vra insisted – and they rose into the night sky.

Vapor trails of stars swirled motionless overhead as the two figures glided down the wind toward the shining, tide-hammered shallows of the Ocean. Light as spindrift, they alighted on the shoals. The redolence of seawrack and algal mats swelled about them with the breathing of the surf.

The Dark Lord swept a gaze across the empty strand. The ogres and other scavengers had vanished into the dunes. 'You know well this place, do you not, Romut?'

Romut lowered his head and spoke humbly, 'Yes, Lord. I have lived here my whole life.'

'Your life entire?' Hu'dre Vra asked with a skeptical tilt to his flared helmet.

'Uh, almost entire, my Lord.' Romut's mind raced, wild to determine what this powerful being sought from him. *Dare I tell the truth? How can I not? He must know everything about me – or can find what he wants easily enough. Is he the wizardduke's minion? Then, my luck is truly terrible. He has already killed me three times!* Horror bleached all further thought, and he answered mechanically, 'I left these tidal flats for a spell – with the Bold Ones.'

'I know of the Bold Ones,' Hu'dre Vra said, and Romut heard no malice in his huge voice. 'You served their leader, yes?'

Romut kept his head low. 'I did, my Lord. Yes. I will not deny it. I served him with all the others.'

'Tell me of him.'

'Wrat?' Romut peeked upward, saw the hot eyes fixed upon him, and spoke freely, afraid to withhold anything from that burning gaze. 'Wrat and I knew each other since we were runts, my Lord. We scavenged together. Just he and I. The others, they detested me, for I am ugly. Half gnome, you see.' He gestured at his squat, wart-knobbed shape. 'But he – Wrat, that is – he detested me, too – but he saw the usefulness of my strength. I've twice the physical strength of the strongest man, you know. And so he abided me, Wrat did, even sometimes defended me against the others. And I helped him pull the hooks and nets faster and longer than any other. It was I and none other who dredged the coral grotto and budged the boulders that revealed the sword of Taran. It was I. But he seized it and used it to unite the Bold Ones.'

'And did you begrudge him ownership of the sword?' the cavernous voice asked.

Romut shrugged off the futility of lying and said what he believed, 'At first, I did. It was I who uncovered it. It was I. But it was he knew best how to use it. Or so it seemed at the time.'

'Explain yourself.'

Romut splayed his stubby fingers over his thick chest. 'I – well, I would have kept the sword for myself surely. I would have used its Charm to better myself alone. That is my nature. Why should I have shared it? I am an outcast by birth. A grotesque. I would have kept that sword and used it for what good I could have for my own self. But Wrat—' A harsh laugh sparked in him. 'Wrat had a vision. He thought to use the sword Taran to unite all the scavengers in the Reef Isles of Nhat. "Why?" asked I bitterly. I who had turned the boulder, for none other had the strength to do it. "Why share it all?" And clever Wrat made clear that if we kept the sword for ourselves, its Charm would buy us small pleasures. But if we used it to rouse the many, to storm heaven as he put it, we could have the greatest pleasures, the joys of the Peers. We could be Peers ourselves! Yes, Wrat was a man of vision. A greedy, arrogant man with a vision. He wanted to raise us all – all of the lowest, most mean denizens of Irth – raise us to the very heights of Irth. To the heights! He promised us glory. He promised us we would make our own place among the Peers. He used the sword Taran for us all. Yet, it never left his hand. Not once. And we served him proudly. Until the end.'

'I know of the end,' the Dark Lord spoke mordantly. 'The wizarduke Lord Drev defeated Wrat and cast him and the Bold Ones into the Gulf. How came you to be spared that terrible fate, Romut?'

'My Lord—' Romut slumped with shame. He knew it was futile to lie before the Dark Lord, and he confessed openly, 'I hid. I disguised myself as myself. The wizarduke sought a man, for that was the guise I wore as a Bold One. When the others fell, I saw my chance to escape. I was craven. I admit it. I was a coward, and I fled and shed my skin of light. I became again the despicable thing you see before you now. I became again a gnomish man. The others were cast into the Gulf and I fled here, to these miserable flats where I began, where I thought the wizarduke would think last to search.'

'And Wrat?' Hu'dre Vra asked with the voice of a thunderhead.

'What of him? Do you not despise him for leading you and the others to ignominious defeat?'

'Despise him?' Romut lifted his stonejawed face defiantly. He had confessed his cowardice; he would not hide his pride. 'My Lord, what glory I have known in this life was his gift. In my skin of light, I took women, I slayed men. I knew power. I regret only that my arrogant master had not been more subtle. We were too bold.'

The Dark Lord's eyes sharpened like star flames. 'But if you had kept the sword Taran for your own, Romut, you would have known a life of comfort.'

'Perhaps.' *What does this monster want of me? Why does he toy with me like this?* 'My Lord, people despise me for being a gnome. Gnomes despise me for being a man. All would have coveted my sword. What comfort could I truly have hoarded for myself? No, my Lord. Wrat, for all his arrogance, was right to use the sword to uplift the lowliest. We stormed heaven. We failed.' Romut lifted his arms to his sides, exposing all of himself. 'If you are the wizarduke's ally and have seized me to wreak his vengeance, then I am doomed. But with the power you have shown me, how could I have told you other than the truth?'

'The truth you speak has not doomed you, Romut,' Hu'dre Vra spoke with reverberant intimacy. 'I am no ally of the wizarduke. I am his most dire enemy returned to bring vengeance down upon *him*. You know me well. Will you speak my name?'

'Know you, Lord?' Romut frowned with incomprehension and fright. 'You are Hu'dre Vra—'

'Such is my mask, Romut. But surely you cannot have forgotten me, the *arrogant* one who first led you from this place.'

Amazement clashed with disbelief in Romut, and dizziness spun through him at the outlandish possibility disclosing itself. 'Wrat?'

'The same!' Hu'dre Vra bellowed. 'Behold!'

The plates of black, saurian armor whirled away like a startled flock of black birds, and in the place where the titanic Dark Lord had towered there stood the small, lank-haired, weasel-featured familiarity of Wrat.

Romut fell to his knees in the sand. 'Are . . . are you some devil's illusion of my old friend?'

'Old friend, am I?' Wrat snickered coldly, his lean face squinting with contempt. He motioned with his pale, thin hands at his skinny body garbed in the coarse hempen tunic of a scavenger. 'I'm a greedy, arrogant man. You know it. So you named me.'

A cold wind circled Romut, and his head became curiously clear. 'Slay me now then, Dark Lord. Torment me no more.'

'I've killed you three times already,' Wrat said, annoyed, and turned away to view the distant Ocean with its combers smoldering on the far horizon. Nearby, tidepools reflected starfroth bright as cauldrons among the salt grass. 'This is where we began, old friend. This is the same damnable place. Hasn't changed at all. The stink of searot and that mad pounding. It was the pounding I hated the most. Never ever stops, does it? Damn waves just keep on pounding, forever. Used to think I'd go mad. Guess I did go mad. Made me greedy to get the hell out of here – and arrogant enough to believe I could take you all with me. Hey, remember how a good night's work meant finding some beat-up girder or some rusted sheets of dented plating? Scrap metal was a treasure! Ha! It was lugging in the dead rotted things I hated. Eight newts-eyes we got for every fifty kilos of dragon bones. Oof! Those slimy, tarry things stunk so bad we had to stuff seaweed in our noses. But that's what the alchemists and gallipots wanted, right? They wanted everything ugly and stinking in this stinking sea. Twelve newts-eyes we got for every stinking basilisk's bladder – the only part of the beast the flukes won't eat, it's so deadly foul. Puncture that thing you go blind from the fumes. You remember Skull Face. That's how he got that way.'

Tears stood in Romut's black eyes. 'It *is* you! Wrat! How?'

'How?' Wrat turned about and his pointy face grinned with malice. 'Murder, old friend. Murder. I killed them all. Grapes.

The Dog Dim. Rett. Skull Face. Little Luc. Chetto. And Piper. Oh yes – I killed sweet Piper, too. Murdered them all. You alone remain of the Bold Ones, Romut. You alone.'

Romut groped with his big hands where he knelt in the shining sand, trying to grasp the empty air. 'I don't understand.'

'That is why you are alive, old friend,' Wrat sneered wickedly. 'If you had fallen into the Gulf with the rest of us then you, too, would have landed on that nameless planet in the void, that cold world where we found the cacodemons. Unless, of course, you broke your neck in the fall like Harrow, Pinch, and Silly. They never saw the demons. They never had a chance to see that we were gods in that world. Gods! We could do anything there. We were hot beings in a cold world. We could do anything! The cacodemons obeyed us. They showed us the power place in their world, built by magicians in their world long ago. Magicians long dead or gone. They thought we were the magicians come back. And they opened the power place to us and revealed the first rung on the energy ladder that climbs back up through the Gulf to here. And we learned how to climb it. And we learned that with the cacodemons, with these monsters from the cold, we could be as gods here on Irth. Charm could not touch us. And the demons would do anything we wanted. Anything! They don't think. Not like us. They just obey. But I saw right away that Irth needed only one god. And so, I killed the others. I murdered each one of them. And I came back alone.'

Romut's glassy black eyes blinked, and he ran fretful hands over his bald and warty head.

Wrat recited slowly, 'Rett. Pinch. Grapes. Skull Face. Silly. Little Luc. Chetto. The Dog Dim. Harrow. And Piper. All the Bold Ones – save you and me. All dead. Save you and me.'

The Ocean talked from far off across the shining flats where the tide retreated, and Romut blinked hard again. He saw Wrat before him, smiling his malignant smile with half his small mouth.

'Get up, Romut!' Wrat boomed in a voice larger than his

spindling body could hold. From out of the dune shadows, dreadful shapes slouched, cutting from the night the barbed outlines of lizard men, bigger than men. Raspy breaths hissed. On every dunecrest and in all the sandy saddles between, cacodemons rose up, awaiting the command of their master.

Romut stood slowly, afraid to startle the enormous lizard men.

'Let us behold what we have wrought!' Wrat bellowed, and his scraggly body swelled to a bizarre extreme of beetle-black carapace shivering with caught starlight among its hooked plates and spiked edges. 'Let us fly!'

Romut cried out as magnetic wind swirled him upward into the black, depthless night. On all sides, the ghastly cacodemons soared. The Dark Lord hovered closest, obsidian apparition of death itself.

The gnomish man looked away, afraid to meet the stare of fire in Hu'dreVra's cowled mask. Below, the Reef Isles of Nhat ringed in surf drifted by. Cloud tatters obscured the view as they crossed river bogland. Where the vapors tattered, dark arteries branched among a wilderness of swamp darkness laced with pale mists. This was the Mere of Goblins, and Romut was glad for the wind-feathered clouds that hid almost wholly from view the demonic flashes of star-cobbled pools, linns, lakes, and tarns where dragons went to die and their huge carcasses floated upon the waters phosphorescent with the thrivings of giant centipedes and firesnakes.

Land fell away, and they sailed above the valleys of the sea toward a wrist of morning twilight. Romut stretched out his arms and legs, a flying human star. Eyes wind-teased and bleary in the bright dawn, he looked with amazement at the Dark Lord and his company of cacodemons. They hung against the pink clouds like black pieces of nightmare flung into the face of a new day.

Elvre eventually lifted its ocean limestone shores and jungle tassels above the horizon. By then, morning shone brilliantly through cloud plateaus, and a nether realm of enormous, strangled chasms of green passed beneath. Silver threads of waterfalls outlined jade cliffs and fed sprawling, branching rivers. In the midst of this wild verdure loomed a scorched mountain seeping vile subterranean fumes, the ground all around it rayed with burned streaks of impact.

This was Arwar Odawl. Cratered deep in the rank vegetation, the heaped ruins of the fallen city leaked brimstone vapors, and a sulfur halo hung above the crash site. Among the charred debris, carrion dogs prowled and crows flitted like black thoughts, feeding off the trapped dead that were too heavily weighted by rubble to ascend with the nocturnal tide.

They alighted on a skewed width of spalled pavement near the summit where motes drifted and spun in the yellow smoke. Romut gagged in the putrid stench, and the Dark Lord laughed like thunder.

'It's the smell of revenge, Romut. The stink of dead enemies!'

Hu'dreVra surveyed the devastation from his high vantage, his hook-plated arms outspread as if to embrace the whole steaming pyre in a pincered grip.

Romut swatted at the searing haze of flies and looked around nervously at the army of cacodemons perched on the baked and blistered girders and slabs. Their tiny bead-like eyes offered no hint of sapience, yet their fluidly nimble movements and alert, poised postures suggested predatory intelligence.

'I will smash all of Irth,' Hu'dre Vra declared, 'before I deign to build it again in my own image. Every one of the Peers shall suffer, for they all stood against us – did they not, Romut?'

'All,' Romut agreed, fighting back nausea. 'All led by their regent, the wizarduke, Lord Drev.'

'Oh, he shall suffer the most,' the Dark Lord promised. 'He will die many deaths before I relinquish him to oblivion. That I swear!'

Romut shuddered at the wrathful memories of his own deathly sufferings in the shadow of Hu'dreVra, and he went down on one knee and vomited strings of bile.

Hu'dreVra ignored him and summoned two of his cacodemons.

They were identically marked by maroon stains – splash marks, one about the right coal-chip eye, the other the left – branded by acid stains from the abominable magic the Dark Lord had worked to instill them with human voices.

'Ys-o.' The cacodemon with the marked right eye announced its name and stood below its lord on a jut of broken pipe.

'Ss-o.' The other spoke its name and uplifted in its clawed grip a severed head with blind blue eyes and a death-snarl locked in a rictus of agony.

'Ah, Lord Keon,' Hu'dre Vra recognized. 'Margrave of Arwar Odawl. How dead you look!' He laughed with proud and mordant humor. 'Now my vengeance is begun with the complete destruction of Irth's oldest brood.'

'Not complete,' Ys-o said in its smoky voice.

'The margrave's children yet live,' Ss-o added.

'No!'

'Yes,' Ss-o affirmed.

Hu'dre Vra hissed ragefully and struck from Ss-o's grip the lopped head, sending it bouncing down the tiers of the mangled city into the plutonic mists. 'Who are these fugitives of my justice? And where? Where are they?'

Ys-o gathered the sour fumes, and between the tines of its claws the mist thickened to a pleural fluid that dripped into the shape of a young, orange-haired, freckled woman of lean stature and blunt features. 'Jyoti.' The cacodemon spoke her name.

At her side appeared her younger brother, a diminutive lad with the henna hair and squared features of the Odawls. 'Poch.'

'Where are they?' the Dark Lord asked with inflamed annoyance.

'Not here.' The cacodemons spoke in unison.

'Not here!' Hu'dre Vra's eyes pulsed hot as gouts of lava. 'Find them! Now! Bring their heads to me. Go!'

The two cacodemons erupted into the sky.

'Bestial idiots!' Hu'dre Vra said through gnashed teeth. 'No one will brag they escaped the wrath of the Dark Lord. No one!'

A magnetic vortex flung Romut upward, and Hu'dre Vra soared after him. After one more slow circuit of the cataclysm that was Arwar Odawl, the Dark Lord moved away with his flock of cacodemons and Romut in tow, arrowing westward through the blue sky, faster than the Abiding Star.

Dazed by the wind, Romut curled upon himself and crossed his arms over his head. He watched Irth pass under his elbows, the tumultuous jungles of Elvre, riotous and vast. Crossing noon's blue meridian, he watched the dense wilderness give way first to chaparral and then the gauzy, cotton woods of the Spiderlands, full of confused updrafts and thermal towers of silver clouds. Such beauty belied the horrors that lurked below among the gossamer-spun shrubs.

The span of the afternoon carried them across the enormous prismatic tracts of the Rainbow Forests of Bryse. Jeweled sprays of brilliant branches reached from the spectral treetops, and glittering horizons stained the sky with colorful coronas.

Late in the day, the chromatic undergrowth fell away before a topaz sea dazzling in the Abiding Star's long shafts. Ahead lay the river-gorge dominion of Ux. Its capital city, Dorzen, floated in a panoply of cumulus above finger valleys of lush cloud forests and rock canyons layered in the pastels of time.

The city's high bastions, with their crystal-domed belvederes and curves of hanging sidewalks, etched its famous skyline against the pink twilight when the Dark Lord arrived with his entourage of cacodemons. No one resisted. Not a single shot was fired from the tiered balconies or rooftop magnolia gardens.

Two representatives of the Council of Seven and One waited under hovering globe lanterns on the terraced lawn beneath the city's towering sky-gate. The manicured park beneath the titanic arch of serpentine marble stood empty of all other presences save a flock of white peacocks that fled with the arrival of the cacodemons, who landed in prowling gangs among the surrounding willow groves and grass shelves.

The two representatives, Baronet Fakel and Lady Von, bowed

humbly as Hu'dre Vra alighted on the sward before them. The towering presence in spiked ebony shell armor and cobra-cowl helmet motioned to one of his cacodemons, and the slitherous creature flew toward the city. Then, the Dark Lord's luminous adder eyes touched upon the two who stood before him, acknowledging their presence.

'In the name of the Council of Seven and One,' Baronet Fakel spoke, his dark, handsome features composed, his voice strong, bolstered by the power wands under his crimson robes, 'we welcome you to Dorzen.'

Lady Von, his wisp of a wife, parted the gray veils of her witch dancer's headdress, revealing a pretty visage of sullen furtiveness, and added, 'All of Ux bows to you.'

'Then Ux shall be spared the fate of Arwar Odawl!' The Dark Lord's voice caromed among the city's glittering spires, and the attractive features of the two before him visibly relaxed. 'But what of the Council of Seven and One? What of Irth? Does Irth bow to me?'

'All Irth bows before you,' Baronet Fakel immediately asserted and lowered his head abjectly.

'Show me,' the Dark Lord commanded. He gestured at the gargantuan sky gate, atop which perched several cacodemons. 'This is one of the largest amulets in the world. Use it now to summon before me the Council of Seven and One.'

Baronet Fakel glanced at his wife in a fluster of surprise, and she nodded just perceptibly. 'Certainly, my lord,' he agreed and fumbled beneath his robe to produce one of the power wands strapped to his torso. He gestured at the pedestal embossed with coiled abstract motifs and nothing happened.

Hu'dre Vra crossed his arms. 'I see you are unfamiliar with the use of this, the largest amulet in the world.'

Lady Von nodded to the other pedestal with its design of interlocking rings, and when he pointed the wand at that, a shaft of pearl light descended from the apex of the arch and swirled aquatically in the space between the conqueror and his subjects.

'Forgive me, my Lord,' Fakel said with glum contrition. 'I have never before used the sky gate.'

'Of course not,' Hu'dre Vra said. 'That is a privilege that belongs to the wizarduke. So, where is Lord Drev?'

'He has fled, my Lord,' Fakel admitted. 'He fears your wrath.'

A sharp laugh cut across the night. 'He fears my wrath! And you do not, Baronet?'

'I fear you, my Lord.' Baronet Fakel mumbled to his eelskin boots. 'All Irth fears you.'

'Do you fear me more than you despise me?'

'I do not despise you.'

'You lie!' The Dark Lord's shout startled nightbirds from the distant treeline. 'I killed your first wife, Mevea, the wizarduke's sister. I skewered her on the sword Taran. The mother of your children spilled her life's blood under my hand. And you do not despise me?'

Baronet Fakel's mouth worked soundlessly, and his eyes moved wildly in their sockets.

'It is not possible to despise what is greater than us,' Lady Von spoke for her husband. 'Our fear and awe overwhelm all other emotion.'

Another laugh crackled from the black mask's needletoothed baleen. 'You have a sweet mouth, Lady Von. I will reward you for that shortly.' The cruel countenance glared at Baronet Fakel. 'Give her the power wand.'

Fakel complied and stared with dismay at the Dark Lord.

'Oh my! Look there, Baronet—' Hu'dre Vra extended a plated arm toward the night sky. Against the lucent starswirls flew the cacodemon he had dispatched earlier into the city. In its claws, two children dangled, legs kicking, arms swirling, their alarmed cries faint squeaks in the distance. 'There go the two boys Mevea dropped into this world for you. I think you should join them on their dark journey to hell, don't you? You are, after all, their father. Farewell, Baronet.'

Fakel backed away, both arms outstretched in horror. A

cacodemon broke from the pack behind the Dark Lord and slouched toward the terrified Baronet. Barking with fright, Fakel turned and ran two paces before claws seized his robes and hoisted him mewling into the night sky.

'Now, my dear,' Hu'dre Vra addressed Lady Von, 'summon for me the Council of Seven and One that I may hear for myself their capitulation.'

Lady Von glanced briefly at her husband's frantic writhings in the cacodemon's grasp as he diminished into obscure heights. Then, she waved the power wand at the shaft of pearl light and commanded, 'Convene the Council!'

The wet shaft of gemlight widened to a glass table at which sat two mages and six vacant blue chairs.

Hu'dre Vra put out his hand, and a cacodemon approached from the pack behind him and handed over a sturdy belt of white crushed leather. The Dark Lord fitted together the hefty pouches of the belt to form the falcon seal talisman. He held the emblem before the glass table in two outstretched arms. 'This is the most potent amulet on Irth,' he declared. 'It is the glory belt worn by the regent of the Council of Seven and One. And I took it from the corpse of the Margrave Keon in the ruins of Arwar Odawl. And so, he is absent tonight from our historic gathering.'

The Dark Lord paced before the table, presenting the glory belt to each seat. 'Earl Mac of Sharna-Bambara – a prominent wizard,' he announced before the first of the empty chairs. 'He has refused to submit to my rule. But he has also already been found, cowering in the sanctuary of Umber Moss, a holy place that offered him no escape from my wrath. At this moment, he suffers his fourth death in my Palace of Abominations. And he will die many more times before I surrender him to oblivion.'

'Ladyship Rica.' Hu'dre Vra spoke before the next vacant chair and jangled the glory belt in the gemlight. 'Conjurer from the Reef Isles of Nhat – the dominion of my origin. Absent!' He shook the talisman in his fist and rocked his black countenance side to side, like a bull mesmerized with rage. 'Find her and bring her to me for punishment – for none shall defy me and live, except in torment.'

A flock of cacodemons peeled away from the throng behind the Dark Lord and shot into the starry night.

At the next empty seat, he swung the glory belt like a noose. 'Ladyship Altha, sorceress of Zul. She and her husband Lord Hazar foolishly believe they can elude me. Track them down for the demented creatures that they are and deliver them to me for a punishment that will exalt death to a mercy.'

A tall ash-blonde woman, dark-eyed, with a rapturous face of patrician hauteur sat at the glass table, her witch veils folded in her hands. At the approach of the Dark Lord, she bent forward with elegant deference and spoke in a voice of indigo velvet, 'My Lord, I am yours entirely to command.'

'Ladyship Thylia,' Hu'dre Vra said in a tone of naked appreciation, 'witch queen of the Malpais Highlands. Your deference to me and to my mastery of Irth has won you preference in my eyes. You shall be my consort – queen of all Irth.'

'My Lord!' She looked up with surprised joy. 'I will live to serve you.'

'Of course. And you will live long and know every pleasure, every fulfillment that the human heart may hold.' He nodded with satisfaction. 'I shall come to you soon in your mountain fastness of Andezé crag. Await me.'

Beside the Queen of Irth, the Dark Lord paused before another vacancy and shook the falcon seal talisman vehemently. 'Lyna – enchantress from the Falls of Mirdath. Your absence condemns you! Find the fat woman and bring her to me that she may taste my wrath and know true bitterness.'

More cacodemons spurted into the heavens and vanished.

In the next chair, a stick stood propped against the glass table, and from it dangled a leathery skin. Limp rags of boneless arms draped the tabletop. A flaccid mask of human flesh empty of eyes, devoid of teeth, hung from the stick. In the gaping mouthhole, a blue flame danced. 'Hu'dre Vra,' a sibilant voice greeted. 'Dark Lord of Irth – I offer you my complete and devoted obedience.'

'And I accept, Ralli-Faj, warlock of the Spiderlands.' Hu'dre Vra stood squarely before the human husk. 'A wise man knows his master. Your wisdom has earned you the privilege of serving me as my personal weapons master. You shall go at once to the Reef Isles of Nhat and supervise there the completion of my Palace of Abominations, of which you shall be steward. The cacodemons shall obey you as they do me.'

In front of the last chair, the Dark Lord spoke, 'This is the empty seat of the wizarduke, Lord Drev. His absence bespeaks his cowardice. Find him and bring him to the Palace of Abominations, where his suffering will stain eternity!'

A drove of cacodemons rocketed upward, blotching the brilliant night.

Hu'dre Vra shook the glory belt over his upturned head. 'This is the mightiest amulet on Irth – and it cannot touch me or my hosts! For it is the gathered light of the Abiding Star – and I have found my strength far from the light of Charm, in the cold worlds hung in the void. I defy the light and all its Charm. For I am the Dark Lord, and I gather the darkness!'

Shouting that last word, Hu'dre Vra ripped apart the falcon seal talisman, and a spray of green fire showered over him. Tendons of lightning thrummed from his hands upward to the arc of the sky gate. And with a brittle roar, the gemlight and the glass table it illuminated vanished in a glare of voltaic fire. In the ensuing silence and deeper darkness, the sparkling ash of the incinerated glory belt trickled from the Dark Lord's clenched fists like diamond dust.

Lady Von lay on the ground with her face pressed into the grass, visibly quaking.

'Rise, Lady Von,' Hu'dre Vra commanded with vibrant resonance. 'Rise and receive the reward I promised you.'

The small woman pushed nervously to her feet.

With one wag of his finger, the Dark Lord beckoned forward

from the crowd of cacodemons the gnomish dwarf Romut. 'Lady Von, this is your new husband. Fulfill his every whim. And in return, I give you my countenance. At Romut's side, you shall rule Dorzen and all of Ux.'

Lady Von shuddered, eyes agape at the sight of the squat, warty man. Then, reluctantly, she complied with a curtsy that nearly dropped her again to the ground.

'Romut—' Hu'dre Vra spoke proudly and with sinister glee. 'You shall take for your own what was once the wizardduke's. And here, with the Lady Von, you will reign in my name. You will reign and be happy – happy at last for our defeat as Bold Ones, happy for our return, happy at last to destroy what once destroyed us!'

## One Day in the Calendar of Eyes

❖━❖

Billowed flames of stars filled the tall windows of the sanctuary's great hall. Incense tapers on each of the broad sills sent thin tendrils of smoke straight up into the fiery night, undisturbed by any breeze. The sages, who had finished their nocturnal meditations at the altars under the giant windows, retreated from the vaulted hall in single file, a crepitant line of swishing silver robes.

From his high vantage on one of the many tiered balconies overlooking the great hall, the sorcerer Caval watched the sages file through the mammoth arched portals and, like a trickle of smoke, disappear into the dark colonnade beyond. The sorcerer sighed. As a young man, he had wanted to worship in these grand corridors. He had wanted to be a sage. But his birthright had forbidden him that ambition. Only a sigh remained of a lifetime's yearning.

Caval, tall and robust, wore his bright red hair cropped close to his square head and his orange whiskers precisely trimmed to outline the sharp angle of his long jaw and the stern contours of his hard mouth. Garbed in bright tinsel and blue gauze windings as if for a funeral ascension, he gripped the balcony's prism-glass balustrade and surveyed the colossal hall for a last time. Soon,

Irth would turn to face the Abiding Star, and he would depart this world of form and appearances. Then, the lost ambitions of his youth, the history of social attainments and personal failures that was his life, and all the struggles of his brutal past would vanish. Forever.

'Nostalgic, Caval?' A wispy voice lilted out of a dark gallery alcove, and a tiny man haloed with a shock of shiny blue-black hair and dense beard emerged on to the balcony. 'It is not yet too late to join the sages. The Abiding Star abides.'

'Master Ah!' Caval turned from the balustrade and bowed so deeply before the sanctuary's adept that he showed the back of his bristle-cropped head. Though he displayed no sign of advanced age, the adept was well known to be the oldest man on Irth. The sorcerer replied in a tone of hushed reverence, 'I but pause to honor those who honor the celestial secrets.'

'Then stay, Caval.' The adept dressed in the manner of a common maintenance worker, with a utilitarian jumpsuit of neutral gray and black cloth slippers. He casually leaned an elbow on the balcony railing, which came to his shoulder's height, and looked up with admiration at the large man. 'Stay and honor those celestial secrets with us. You have been here only a short while. We have barely gotten to know you. Stay.'

'No.' Caval declined with a curt shake of his head. 'That would be graceless of me.'

'True,' the adept agreed, raising his thickly tufted eyebrows. 'You have accrued enough Charm to climb the Calendar of Eyes. The others would indeed find such reluctance graceless. But then, none among them has suffered the risks that you have endured to possess Charm in such bounty.' His eyebrows lowered and knitted to a fierce stare of command. 'Stay, Caval, and give them cause for wonder.'

'Wonder, Master Ah, or envy?'

The adept's stare relented to a soft smile, and he answered in his small voice, 'Are they not the same? What is it that evokes wonder in us but the desire to apprehend what cannot be grasped. Consider then, wonder is but a higher octave of envy.'

'Master, your wisdom humbles me.'

'That a man with the enormous Charm you possess can know humility fills *me* with wonder!' The adept laughed in frail gusts and pressed his back against the balustrade. 'That is why I wish you would stay among us a while longer.'

'I did not get my Charm through wisdom, Master – as well you know. It would be gracelessly brazen of me to pretend otherwise.'

'True, again, Caval. You are a sorcerer – but a sorcerer who knows humility and respects wisdom. You are a rare one. I will be saddened to see you gone from our midst.'

'If I were merely a sorcerer, Master, I would be tempted to stay and pursue wisdom with you and the sages. But I am a sorcerer from the Brood of Assassins – and a former weapons master at that! I gained my Charm by deeds of war and intrigue. You know all this, of course. Yet I say this now for my sake, for I dare not forget it. Charm is too easily lost. And the more Charm one possesses, the more easily it slips away. If I lose what Charm I have, Charm I have won through the suffering of others, I know I will lack the wisdom to remain humble. In fact, I know I would go mad remembering all the blood that has been spilled for me to have come this far. It is best, then, that I take the Charm I have and use it now, while I still have it, to climb the Calendar of Eyes, enter the caudal trance, and become one with the Abiding Star.'

The adept pushed away from the railing and gazed earnestly at the sorcerer. 'What you propose is worthy, Caval. In this world of form, Charm is hard won and easily spent. All of us, myself included, stand in wide wonder before your strength. You have the Charm to climb the Calendar of Eyes, where few among us have gone. It matters not how you won your Charm. That you have the wisdom to use it to return to the Abiding Star is proof enough that you are worthy. Most anyone else would use such wealth to make a comfortable place for themselves on Irth. A true man of spirit, you desire the Beginning, the source of all creation. I will say no more to dissuade you.' He bowed and backed away.

'Go now. Irth turns. The portal to the Beginning will soon open.'

Caval returned the adept's bow. 'Farewell, Master Ah.'

'Farewell, Sorcerer Caval.' His thin voice sounded without echo from the depths of the gallery. When the sorcerer looked up, the tiny, vivid man was gone.

Caval pondered what the adept had said and turned to face again the enormous windows lining the great hall. He saw that the sky had brightened. The fishnet of stars hung in blue darkness. *Perhaps I should wait another day or so and be certain I am done with this world.*

That thought sounded hollow. He knew well enough he was done with Irth. For over 45,000 days, he had worn this body. In that time, he had fulfilled all the disciplines, internal arts, and martial skills within the Brood of Assassins, and he had mastered sorcery and attained to the perilous rank of weapons master for the most venerable family on Irth. Every enemy that had risen against him and his masters, he had defeated. And all along, he had wanted none of it. All along, he had desired only to study as a sage and to earn enough Charm through the ways of wisdom to climb the Calendar of Eyes and pass through the radiant portal of the Abiding Star to the Beginning.

Gazing down at the empty hall of altars and meditation mats illuminated by moted rays from floating lanterns, he wished he could have attained his Charm in this hallowed place. But then, most certainly, he would still be a sage, for not even Master Ah had yet acquired sufficient Charm to leave this sanctuary and climb the virtually airless and deathly cold slopes to the Calendar of Eyes.

Caval nodded with satisfaction. The adept, he knew, was right. It mattered not how he had acquired his Charm. The power was his at last. He had satisfied all his allegiances. The Charm was legitimately his, to do with as he pleased. And it pleased him mightily to turn his back on this cruel world and to return to the formless, to the source of form, to the light that shone from the Beginning.

Confident of his decision, Caval pushed away from the balustrade and exited the balcony. He marched down a stone corridor that led toward massive bronze doors pocked with corrosion and stained by time. Tens of thousands of days had passed since anyone had possessed the Charm to open this huge pylon.

With a simple gesture, he flung the metal doors wide, and they screamed as they opened and sent loud echoes tumbling over each other down the corridor and into all the catacombed alcoves and tiered galleries of the great hall. Throughout the sanctuary, wonder ignited the hearts of every sage.

Beyond the pylon, musty darkness waited. Caval snapped his fingers, and the air around him glowed with a turquoise light that illuminated nitre-crusted walls – and an airlock. He gestured again and spent another tiny fraction of his Charm to shut the immense doors behind him. The clangor sounded dimly through the thick portals and shook the stones, pouring thin streams of powdered rock from the remote ceiling.

The sorcerer pressed his large body against the wheel of the airlock, and as it turned, the valve opened its seal with a sharp hiss, and the stale air sucked away. Cold bit into him briefly, before his Charm swirled warmth outward to protect him. He pulled the airlock open and stepped through.

On the other side, he found himself outside the sanctuary in the violet darkness where starlight chiseled a rocky horizon from shadow. Redstone walls – brown in the pre-dawn gloom – rose high above the mousehole that had released him. No one stood on the battlements under the starry fumes and the bright banners of stratospheric clouds. He departed the ancient sanctuary without witnesses and climbed a gravel incline blotched with phosphorescent frost.

Shielded by Charm, the sorcerer mounted the rocky slope toward a snow peak that glowed amber in morning light. That mountain was the Calendar of Eyes. At its terraced summit, vision extended across time and one could see ahead to the furthest ranges of creation – or backward to the source, to the Beginning.

Already, even at this height, time appeared layered. Glancing behind, Caval glimpsed the temporal mosaic of the sanctuary: an empty stone field with the ghostly overlay of scaffolded walls and the finished sanctuary itself maroon as a scab that peeled away to reveal again the rubble of an empty field and, at its center, a husk of ruins.

He concentrated on climbing. The bare scree crunched under his boots, and the tinsel and gauze windings snapped their tiny flags in the stiff wind pouring from the heights. Red sunlight blared from the crest.

Fearing he would arrive late, the sorcerer used his Charm to bound up the steep slope at such speed that glazed pebbles shot into the air behind him and dazzled with reflected sunbeams as they crossed the edge of darkness into the bright air. In moments, he traversed a treeless waste and churned through the blue snow drifts surrounding the powerful crag of the summit.

On a rampart above an icy cornice, he reached an open court of crystal flagstones surrounded by mighty rock formations. This was the platform where he would greet the Abiding Star and become pure light. He stopped and turned about to look back the way he had come.

His tracks were dark sockets in the wind-whirled snow of the nearby drifts. Farther down, the dim path of his climb lost itself in the gray gravel. The sanctuary appeared like a distant brown smear, small and insignificant on the cold rock face, barely visible among the shadows of the mountains. For as far as he could see, no lifeform exposed itself.

The lavender sky carried only a handful of sharp, silver stars. Low on the horizon of snow ridges, two worlds floated – Hellgate and Nemora, precarious smudges in the glare of the coming dawn. Ruddy light crept down the hanging rocks above him and would soon bring the Abiding Star into view.

Transfixed by the shine of glare ice at the peak, Caval stood motionless. These were the last moments of his mortal life. Soon he would abandon form entirely. He could not imagine what lay ahead of him, except that he knew he would be replete, whole in a way that was impossible in this world of physical limits and uncertainties.

'Here I am!' he exulted aloud. 'Here I am – in the Calendar of Eyes!'

The Charm he had struggled his long life to gather to himself and to master served him well. The cold wind and rare atmosphere caused him no discomfort. Never before had he fitted his body so well, painless and vibrant with health in these final moments before he would doff the flesh forever.

High cirrus cast metallic radiance across the blue sky, and the sorcerer opened his arms and turned a slow circle on the crystal flagstones, face uplifted to the void. So strong was the moment that he decided to gaze upon the many moments of his own past that had gathered upon themselves to carry him here, to his fulfillment.

With a beatific grin, he strode across the open court to a gap between two titanic boulders. From there, he could peer southeast toward the region where he had lived his days on Irth. Across the spare, silent distances of the wasteland, he unfurled his Charm.

As before, when he first glanced back at the sanctuary, time stratified. The mountainside's soaring rocks shifted under a blur of seasons – blizzards of past winters wavered in and out of sight between the shining blue days of lost summers. But he had no interest in the redundant cycles of elements among these high peaks, and he willed his vision to cross the still universe of ice and shale to the distant lowlands where once he had lived.

Whirlpool radiance opened a peephole. He peered into the swirling brightness and saw the shaggy cypresses and the viscous swamplight of Elvre, the jungle dominion where he had served the Brood of Odawl as weapons master. Scrim of moss and lianas parted and revealed a smoldering mountain.

Caval gasped. What he beheld was not a mountain but – a city! Slowly, unbelieving, he recognized twisted shapes as buildings collapsed into bubbling eddies of melted metal and rock. Broken avenues and upended pavements lay heaped in a turmoil of jetting flames and churning smoke. And everywhere, strewn bodies and torn limbs charred in the vast pyre.

The sorcerer tried to pull his vision backward, thinking that he had inadvertently budged into the future. He thought he was seeing some apocalypse-to-come, the same way he had glimpsed the ruins of the sanctuary further ahead in time. But his perception remained locked on the fiery debris.

'Arwar Odawl!' he cried out, identifying with certainty the toppled façades of buildings he knew too well.

Shock banged painfully in his chest, bruising his heart. Arwar Odawl had been the oldest and most picturesque of all the floating cities of Irth. He had lived most of his life there, and this silent mirage of horror scalded his soul.

A loud cry of horror cut through him. The unfathomed depths of the collapsed city hid from view thousands interred in flame and crushed stone. He could behold no more, and he spun away, hands slapped to his eyes.

*How can this be?* he demanded of his memory. When he had left Arwar Odawl, 843 days ago, the city had been secure and his successors competent. *What has happened?*

Caval slumped to the flagstones, and he sat crosslegged, head hung, dazed. His Charm wavered and left him shivering against the icy crystals. Gray eyes stormlit, he stared blankly, remembering the whole of his life in that beautiful city.

The margrave Keon had hired Caval directly from the Brood of Assassins when the sorcerer was untried, a callow sorcerer not yet 10,000 days old. A meticulous worker, he had proved capable, and for the next 35,000 days he had served the kindly and noble margrave as weapons master, creatively outwitting the enemies of Odawl so effectively that the old Peer knew nothing of strife during Caval's tenure.

Tears began to flow unhindered down his face, and he pressed his palms to his eyes and reviewed in his mind the enemies who could have done this.

Angrily, he rose and swiped the tears from his face. What did it matter who among the rival Peers had slain his former master and the people they had been sworn to protect?

*Arwar Odawl is fallen.*

The light went out in his body. All strength fled. Even his Charm wobbled against the buffeting cold. He knew if he let grief lead him, he would lose more of his Charm and then it would be nigh impossible to enter the caudal trance and become one again with the Abiding Star.

*Arwar Odawl is fallen* . . . He shook his whole body, trying to free it from the numbing shock of this truth. *Another form returned to the formless.*

But the lives – the people he knew . . . The inescapable horror defeated every attempt to free himself from grief and outrage.

Caval dared to open again the whirlpool tunnel of sight to Elvre. He had to be certain that he had not deceived himself. No word had reached the sanctuary of such a cataclysm. But that meant nothing. The sages would be the last to know, there in their most remote mountain fastness, cultivating indifference to history and all its multifarious forms.

His heart beat him again as he faced once more the mangled heap of the destroyed city. From over his shoulder, beams of daylight pared away the last of the nightshadows, and he cried aloud once more. He did not want to see this.

He dispelled the visionary vortex and turned away heavily. The white luminosity of the Abiding Star summoned him to the Beginning. Yet, after what he had seen, how could he go? Arwar Odawl needed him . . .

*Arwar Odawl is no more!*

Voices unfurled in the blinding new day. Young voices.

'Caval!'

Clouds loomed over the glittering snow peaks. Only his tracks marred the snowy ascent to the open court of crystal flagstones and ponderous rocks where he paced grief-struck. Ice slivers glimmered among the gravel beds far down the mountain. But no figures appeared.

'Caval! We need you! Where are you?'

The sky that enclosed the majestic prospect of mountains was a huge cave of winds. The tumbling clouds seemed to carry the voices to him from every direction in this cavernous space.

'Caval!'

Distant snowfields echoed his name.

'Who intrudes?' he asked, already knowing the answer. He knew these voices. He had heard them so often before in his former life, when Arwar Odawl drifted free above the mist-torn jungles of Elvre.

Once he identified them, the voices stopped. In the dark silences within, they continued their calling – pleas from the heirs of his former master, the two beloved children of the margrave Keon.

'Jyoti! Poch!' the sorcerer called aloud, though he knew they could not hear him. He had heard them only because he had used his Charm to open an astral window to Elvre. He called to them, because to hear their voices through the reach of his Charm meant that they were alive.

*Is it possible?* Hope flared in him that the unspoken voice of his master would call out next. *Is it possible the Peers have been spared?*

Concentrating, he stared down at the crystal flagstones where prints of snow left by his boots dissolved in the day's brilliance.

'Margrave!' he called out and squeezed his eyes shut, wanting to hear a reply.

When he finally dared to summon his Charm again, he heard once more the children calling him.

'Caval! We need you! Arwar Odawl is fallen! We alone have survived . . .'

His eyes snapped open, and the hot fire of the day branded his retinas and hurt his face.

*Keon is dead*, he realized. *Somehow the children have escaped this doom*.

He remembered their bright eyes of green rimmed in blue, their similar complexions freckling their pallid faces beneath golden-brown hair.

Daybreak heat lifted a soft energy from the flagstones and a subtle scent of warmed soil. That was to be the cue that initiated his caudal trance. If he wanted, he could still use these signals to trigger the trance.

Instead, he stood taller and slowly raised his face toward the cold breath from the mountaintops. Though he had no desire to return to the difficult and dangerous life below, he had been summoned by ones he could not refuse. The children of his former master needed him.

*Wait*— The heat of the day restored his charm to its full potency and gave him a new prospect to wish for. He would exploit his vantage from the Calendar of Eyes to see their future. Perhaps they would not need him after all. Perhaps the future would disclose something better than what he feared.

He watched prodigal clouds overflowing with daylight and freedom. Using his Charm, he projected his awareness into them with omen force.

Like a dream, mildness swelled in him, erasing all signs of the sorrow and fury that had possessed him. Charm opened the veils of time and obeyed his suggestions.

The woozy light of the clouds folded into shapes he recognized and forms he did not. He saw the margrave's children.

*Jyoti*— She had been 6,000 days old when he had retired, a young woman. Even then, though, she had displayed formidable martial skills. Her grandfather, the venerable warrior, Phaz, had trained her from childhood in the ancient fighting techniques, the acrobatic exercises from the far-gone times before Charm, when survival depended upon using the body as a weapon.

Not far in the future, her lissome body lay broken beside her brother's – *Poch*. He had been a frail child in Caval's time. Large eyes, diminutive and clumsy body – the very reason Phaz had favored the boy's older sister. On a nearby bend in the timestream, he lay dead, ribcage flayed open under the claws of a – *what?*

Caval squinted into the time glare, not believing what he saw.

*A cacodemon?*

He incredulously identified the creature crouched over the dead bodies of the margrave's children by its eel-lobed brow, its tiny, tar-drop eyes, and hulking saurian frame with horrid abdominal snouts of gnashing fangs. It was the monster of legend feared by all Irth children.

*How can that be?*

The dazzling grasp of the future loosened before his astonishment, and he had to concentrate sternly to restore its clarity.

The ripped-open bodies of Jyoti and Poch lay lifeless beneath the razorous claws of a cacodemon. Staring into its spider-bead eyes, the sorcerer perceived the others – the flocks of cacodemons that stampeded the future. He watched them falling out of the night sky, blotting the stars with their gruesome silhouettes. Hundreds of them dropping out of the darkness, swarming vehemently.

*How?*

The future scorched with all the destined acts of the cacodemons. Like storm clouds, they assailed the floating cities, and flames burst from the tabernacles housing the hover charms that kept the cities in the air. Streaking smoke, the cities plummeted. Dorzen – Bryse – Mirdath – Sharna – Keri – all fell to Irth with explosive impact.

*No!*

The sorcerer's gaunt cheeks glistened with tears. What he saw he knew was implacable.

*Unless . . .*

He pulled his vision of the future back to the slain bodies of Jyoti and Poch under the bloody claws of the cacodemon. The sapience of the monster struck him. By that he knew that the source of this taloned beast, with its heavy jaw ajar and its evil faces squashed among the creases of its belly, was human.

It was not a creature of Irth. It had fallen out of the Gulf from some distant cold world. But the sorcerer knew that bodies never fell to Irth – they fell *from* Irth. The Abiding Star pushed all forms into the Gulf and drew nothing at all to itself. And so, he knew that this beast smeared with grease from the carcasses of the margrave's children had been summoned.

*Who?* he demanded of his Charm. *Show me who has dared such atrocity!*

The cloud of future-knowing shifted and took the form of a weasel-faced man with shrill eyes and lanky, gummy pale hair.

*Wrat!* Caval fitted a name to that scrawny man, recalled from a small but virulent uprising of scavengers that the wizarduke Lord Drev had suppressed.

Away down the sky, where the clouds boiled above the ice ranges, the future came clear. Wrat, usurper of the sword Taran, had by some mysterious magic returned from the Gulf that had swallowed all the dead and whole armies of the living – and he had come back with a swarm of rabid cacodemons under his ruthless command.

Cloud banks revealed the future as a monument of abomination. Wrat would destroy every one of the floating cities and slaughter all the Peers, sating his lust for revenge inspired by the wizarduke who had defeated and humiliated him. Civilization would be smashed, and all who survived would be forced to live as animals again in the primitive conditions that had existed on Irth before people learned to make amulets and harness Charm.

'Jyoti and Poch are not yet dead,' he reminded himself forcefully and turned his back on the cloudshapes of the future. 'The future is a dream that must grow to actuality. It can yet be pruned and shaped. Nothing is certain. All is possible.'

*All?* his reason questioned.

'Nearly all—' he conceded and wondered if it was already too late to save those who called out for him.

The sorcerer stood with his back to a rock outcrop and faced the rising brilliance of the Abiding Star. What he wanted was formless. The Beginning. The source of all forms. Yet fate had dropped what he wanted down his life. The formlessness that was to be his reward had dropped entirely away, down his life, into a meaningless void.

The Abiding Star, fiercely radiant, would not be his return to the formless after all. Instead, he chose to use its mounting force to shape for himself a new form into which he could copy himself sufficiently. He wanted to seek out the ones who sought him. But he could not go in his present form. Not yet. Not until he was certain that the children of the margrave offered some hope of staving off the terrible future he had seen in the clouds.

Out of whim and Charm, the sorcerer shaped himself a most explicit body of light – small, keen, and agile – a bird. He made it green-feathered and just strong enough to carry his mind's eye. And then, he sat down on the cold flagstones of crystal that ledged the Calendar of Eyes, and, with a flurrying snap of wings and a shining cry, he set the bird free of his grasp – and he flew.

Jyoti paced a stone creek with the languid restlessness of a panther. Wistful bird calls glittered in the dun thorn shrubs on the shaded bank where Poch lay curled upon himself, covered with leaves, watching her. He wore a scowl of worry on his young, freckled face. Several times he had called to her to hide, but she had ignored him. At last, he had fallen silent and tucked himself small, glowering with fear, clutching his amulet-tunic tighter about him.

They had been camping on the Kazu sand rivers when the horror began. It had been a casual trip, an impulsive decision of Jyoti's to do something with her younger brother that he would enjoy. She had simply wanted to spend more time with the lad while he was still young enough to enjoy dune-sledding and campfire stories. Originally, two of his playmates were to accompany them, but at the last minute they were called off to usher a clan wedding at Primrose Stilts.

Who could begrudge young adolescents a chance to experience the majestic opulence of Primrose Stilts, the most elegant temple grounds in Arwar Odawl, where the Peerage traditionally held its coronations? So, Jyoti and Poch had gone alone to Kazu. They had not even bothered to request an escort. Why would they require guards on the open ranges of the sand rivers with Arwar Odawl visible on the horizon as it drifted south for the winter?

Jyoti and Poch played games on the sand rivers of Kazu. The cold morning air walked through their bones as they traipsed among the dunes, sledding down the slipfaces, scampering around hulks of cacti, laughing and frolicking at the lizards that scurried to escape them among the rocks.

In the distance, Arwar Odawl floated. It was the oldest of the floating cities, erected at an antique time when hover charms were still new and the city required steering rudders to guide itself through the air. The rudders dangled below the city in long metallic tentacles. And though they were no longer necessary now that the technology of Charm had advanced to the point of controlling weather, the city retained the pendulous vanes and cables that lent it the appearance of a metallic medusa.

In the afternoon, they had sat on a black granite ledge above the thorn and tall dry grass, enjoying a picnic of currant cakes and wind apples the kitchen had sent by flyer-box, when the attack on the floating city began. At first, Poch had thought the black swarm appearing above the horizon was a storm cloud. Jyoti had known at once it could not be, for it moved against the wind. Through their niello eye charms, they magnified Arwar Odawl on the jungle-tasseled horizon and gaped in terror at the ravenous flock of cacodemons.

Within minutes, before the margrave's children could alert their father on their aviso crystal, jets of green fire erupted from the city. *Green fire!* The margrave's children had known at once that such lethal flames appeared only when Charm was broken.

The cacodemons had smashed the hover charms!

Terror-stricken, they had watched Arwar Odawl tilt sickeningly, green plumes flaring from the tabernacle pyramids. Screaming in unison, they followed with wide stares as the city spiraled beyond the horizon and an enormous firecloud billowed above the jungle. The thunderous roar deafened them, and they fell to their backs before the hot pressure of the blast wave.

All day they had remained on that granite bluff, stunned before the black, churning tower of smoke that rose from the crash site. Their niello eye charms could not reach beyond the horizon, but the numb feel of their seekers informed them no one had survived.

Poch had sobbed while Jyoti had stared in shocked silence. Only their charm-tunics held hysteria at bay. At night, when their escorts would have come to take them back home, no one had arrived. The horizon where the city had fallen breathed flames, and by that scarlet glow could be seen the ascension of the dead.

There were so terribly many that half the night sky was blotted as the nocturnal tide lifted the corpses into the wind and then drifted them toward the Ocean where the ebb current of the Gulf would sweep them into the abyss with all other dead things.

A nauseating stench of char and volcanic miasma sifted across the sand rivers, and the brother and sister activated all their hexgems to filter out the stink. Against the stars, the ascension of the dead and the black swarm of cacodemons swirled.

The margrave's children fled before this grisly sight, and morning found them well south of the black rock escarpment where they had witnessed the destruction of their home. Jyoti felt that all her 7,048 days before this morning had been a happy dream, a quiet prelude to a terrible time. She paced the stone creek before her brother, pondering what to do next.

With impotent rage, she reviewed all that she had witnessed of yesterday's holocaust. *Cacodemons are not real!* she repeated to herself, wanting to understand what she had really seen. But niello eye charms did not lie, and she had to admit finally that fabled monsters had attacked and destroyed Arwar Odawl.

Sharp and strange, that truth hurt her. She had trained her whole life long to emulate her forebears, the ancient warriors of pre-Charm times. Her beloved grandfather, Lord Phaz, had inspired her to believe that the hardy and archaic virtues of the first people could only enhance the modern powers of the Charmed generations. But neither old-fashioned warrior spirit nor contemporary magic had prepared her for cacodemons, monsters that existed only in children's stories – until last night.

Jyoti amplified to maximum intensity the two power wands she wore at the collar of her amulet-tunic, at the base of her neck, resting atop her clavicles. Their strength soothed her helpless fury and lent a cold precision to her thinking. This horror was only a beginning. Her parents were dead – Lord Keon and Ladyship Erna – and Grandfather Phaz – and all of her clan, all of her friends, all of her people. Dead.

Mourning lurked behind the calm strength of Charm. Deeper than her shock, grief lay coiled around her heart, hoarding its toxins. In time, it would come for her. But for this grim day, she required mental alertness, and she would not diminish the strength of her power wands or hex-gems. She had to reason out a plan, and for that she had to know what had happened.

*From where did the cacodemons come? Are they a ridiculous disguise for some known enemy?*

The somber hum of bees droned from the sunny bank, where a tiny bird with green, silver-tipped feathers strutted among knobs of cactus. She stared at the bird but did not see it, for her mind ranged among horrific possibilities: Her eyes gleamed with malicious hurt as she considered old family rivals who might have discovered some new magic . . .

'They will see you out there,' Poch warned again. 'Come hide.'

Jyoti faced her brother with a soft expression. He was a gentle youth extravagantly spoiled by their parents and catered to so much he did not even know how to read the accumulation of signals gathered by his amulet-tunic. He had always relied on others to protect him – their parents, the guards, herself.

'You don't have to hide, Poch,' she told him once more. 'The eye charms see no threat to us at this time.'

'Maybe the eye charms are blind to the cacodemons,' he whined. 'How else could they get into the city?'

'We saw the cacodemons with our own niello eye charms, Poch. Stop cowering there and start thinking straight.'

Poch sat up but did not budge from his covert under the thorn bush. 'Try the aviso again.'

Jyoti found the tiny black crystal in the breast pocket of her tunic and rubbed it alert. A blue spark danced in its faceted interior but no sound came from Arwar Odawl, not even static. As she pointed the small communicator in another direction, a harsh screeching pierced the morning. She thumbed the volume plane of the aviso, and a frenzied voice bounded on to the creek bed.

' . . . approach impossible. They're everywhere. In the canopy. In the cloud cover. The jungle is filthy with them. No one has gotten through.'

*Everywhere!* Jyoti shuddered and peeked again at the niello eye charms on her shoulder pads. The thorn shrubs, the stony creek bed, and the broad pans of cracked clay that stretched to the sand rivers beyond appeared empty of threat. And above them, the blue depth of the sky held no clouds.

'They're cacodemons,' the voice reported. 'Don't tell me it's impossible. We have multiple confirmations. Cacodemons! And we can't stop them. Unlikely as it sounds, Charm doesn't seem to touch them. Wait. We've got another sighting. Nearby. Looks like one of them in the river grass. Watch it! It's seen us. Pull back! Hurry!'

A havoc of frantic breathing and thrashing vegetation ensued. Then, the unmistakable sound of firecharms shooting in rapid bursts. Static from the discharges smothered the shouting voices of the warriors.

Shredded with breakup, the voice returned, panting: 'We're hitting them . . . direct blasts from firelocks and calivers! Point blank! . . . nothing . . . It's nothing to them! . . . Hey! Watch it! Stand back! Stand back!'

Roaring flared through the aviso.

'One of the damned things snapped a firelock in its teeth! Broke the Charm-breech wide open. The blast blew two gunners to ashes. They're gone! But it's still coming! It walks through green fire!'

More rapid bursts from the firecharms disrupted speech. A scream gargled above the thudding automatic fire of a caliver, then silence.

'Give me that.' Poch held his hand out for the aviso.

Jyoti tossed it to him and continued pacing across the creek's cobbles, stupefied by what she had heard. *It walks through green fire!* Not even the soothing lave of Charm from her power wands could ease that horror.

What she yearned to do was remove her amulet-tunic. She wanted to bring forth her grief. She wanted to mourn. But she dared not. *Not yet. Maybe never.* Her alertness took in shadow patterns among the thorn bush, bees humming among empurpled blossoms, a vivid green bird watching her, and a front of cumulus swelling in the north offering cover for an approaching nightmare. At any moment, the cacodemons could appear. More than ever, she needed her amulets. Yet never before had they weighed so heavily.

'Listen!' Poch turned up the aviso's volume.

'. . . only death! For I am Hu'dre Vra, the Dark Lord. As an example to all, I have this day set my cacodemons upon Arwar Odawl, and that oldest and fairest of cities now burns in the jungles of Elvre. So shall it be for any who oppose me. Do not resist my might. Lay down your arms and bend your knees before me and you shall be spared. For those who dare stand against me, there is only death! For I am Hu'dre Vra, the Dark Lord. As an example to all, I have this day set my cacodemons upon Arwar Odawl, and that oldest and fairest of cities now burns . . .'

Poch silenced the aviso. 'It's a loop broadcasting on all the local public bands. The whole dominion must be hearing this.'

'Who is he?' Jyoti glared up at the empty sky and felt the heat and cold of rage and fright clashing within her. 'That is no name we know.'

'Dare we find out?' Poch asked, holding up the aviso. 'We can reach the local sender.'

'And call down those monsters on us?'

'He says if we bend our knees we'll be spared.'

Jyoti looked hard at him. 'This Dark Lord destroyed everything we cherish. Father and Mother are dead!'

Frowning with perplexity, Poch groaned, 'Must we die, too?'

Jyoti gnashed a cry, lurched forward, and seized her young brother violently. She hauled him out from under the thorn bush and with two deft tugs unstrapped his amulet-tunic and yanked it from him.

'Hey!' he protested with a shrill cry as she tossed the tunic with its clattering amulets behind her on to the stone bed of the creek. 'What are you doing?'

'Charm has blinded you.' She moved to block him from retrieving his tunic. 'You stand here now without your Charm and tell me you want to bend your knee to the killer who destroyed all we love.'

Poch trembled, as much from fear of his sister's fury as from the abrupt loss of Charm. 'Jyoti – give me back my Charm!'

'How does it feel?' she asked and unstrapped her own tunic and dropped it at her feet. A welter of emotion sluiced through her – a vortex of wild fear, anger and shock – and at its immutably still center, a green ache of implacable loss.

Poch clawed to get past her, but she stopped him, vigorously thwarting each of his frenzied attempts to dodge past her. She slapped aside his grasping arms and shoved him backward so hard he tripped and sat down hard.

'Why are you doing this to me?' he cried in anguished frustration. Without Charm to quiet the hysteria, the terror was unbearable. He felt like a mote in a vast storm. The destructive winds had blown away everything he knew – parents, home, teachers, friends, and his whole future, all blown away into the void. And all that was left was his small, quivering self and his mad sister.

Jyoti stared hard at the abject fear in her brother. It was the same dismay she felt. But he lacked the training. Father and Mother had reared him to rule with Charm, in the manner of all their noble ancestors – except for eccentric Grandfather Phaz, the throwback to aboriginal times. Poch had wanted nothing to do with that tough old man and his harsh disciplines. No one had. Jyoti herself showed her first interest only out of pity for the solitary and grizzled elder. Then, to her happy astonishment and the misgivings of her family, she discovered she actually enjoyed shedding Charm and focusing her mind on perceptual extremes while learning the athletic limits of her body. Not Poch. Not then – not at this time. The weepy fright on his young face hurt her, more keenly now that he was all who remained of her family. In his chemise that showed his rib-slats and bony shoulders, he appeared wholly helpless, a mere child. She picked up his tunic and handed it to him.

'I'm sorry,' she said and retrieved her own tunic. 'This Dark Lord – whoever he is – is our enemy. We will never bow to him. Never.'

Poch sat small and huddled in his tunic, not looking at her, sobbing quietly.

She turned away and held her own tunic out at arm's length. *This thing*— she thought, *this thing that makes us strong makes us weak*. A pang of lamentation hurt her to think of Grandfather Phaz dead among all the others, and she gazed at the garment with cold eyes.

The tunic itself was white suede, made of the softest antelope leather. Two power wands yoked the collar. The gold-thread that bound them also conducted their Charm and trimmed the edges and patterned the panels in spirals and fretwork. Atop this circuitry, tiny blue rock studs affixed amulets in clusters that focused their energy over the body's vital organs: Hex-gems in translucent ruby lozenges starburst the left breast, black mirrors patched the length of the spine and outlined the ribcage, iridescent emerald panes covered the kidneys, and platinum sigils guarded the alchemy of liver and abdomen.

She peered into the epaulets of black prism, seeking within the niello eye charms any sign of danger lurking nearby. For weapon, all she had was a small barb gun for fending off predators. It was nothing compared to the firecharms she had heard on the aviso vainly blasting the cacodemons.

*We are defenseless – on a journey with no destination.*

Grimly, she donned the charm-tunic and secured the gold hasps. At least when they came, she would not be struck blind.

'What are we going to do?' Poch asked in a voice tight with tears. 'Everyone is dead.'

Jyoti sat down next to her brother and put a gentle arm across his shoulders. 'Not everyone. We are alive. We have each other.'

'I'm useless to you,' he sniffled. 'You're better off without me.'

'Why do you say that?' Her arm tightened across his shivering shoulders. 'Are you so scared you would just give yourself to the enemy?'

Poch did not answer. He kept his watery stare in the dirt. Finally, he mumbled, 'Where will we go?'

*Where?* she wondered and removed her arm. Slowly, she rose and paced again the stone bed of the creek. The low electric buzz of the bees continued as though nothing had changed in the world. Where? No answer came, and the violent muscle of her heart twisted harder to realize there was nothing at all left of their lives but their own bodies and the charms they wore.

'No!' she practically shouted as her heart unclenched and offered a new hope. She faced her brother with bright and wicked purpose. 'There is one other. Of course! He wasn't in the city. He left almost a thousand days ago. You remember him. The old sorcerer . . .'

'Father's weapons master—' Poch whispered and lifted his

face. His traumatized features looked starved they were so scared – eyes staring from pits, mouth slack – yet, for this one moment, they took on a little of their former vitality.

'Caval,' Jyoti said. 'We must find Caval. He will help us.'

'Yes. He will!' The boy stood up, alert to this real possibility of salvation. 'Father always said Caval is the best weapons master on Irth. He will know how to fight the cacodemons.' He grasped his sister's arm. 'But where is he? Father retired him long ago.'

'We must find him.' Jyoti took a seeker from her tunic's inside pouch. Its starshape woven of gold filaments encased a homing bauble that held a lock of their father's hair.

'That won't help us,' Poch said grimly. 'He's dead.'

Jyoti shot him a dark look. 'Caval is a sorcerer. He worked for father a very long time – a lifetime. There may yet be a bond between them, and this could be our link to him. If we call, he might hear us.'

Poch looked skeptical. 'Might as well pray to the Abiding Star.'

'Look, Poch. If Caval is yet on Irth, he will surely be aware of what has happened to Arwar Odawl. He may come to help us.'

'Why would he?' Poch stared at her. 'He was not of our clan.'

'No,' she said and met his stare calmly. 'But he is of the Brood of Assassins, a mercenary whom father hired as a young man. Caval served no other master. I believe we can depend on his loyalty.'

Poch scowled. 'Loyalty to whom? The margrave he served is dead.'

Jyoti knelt beside the frowning boy. 'Poch – Father *is* dead. And Mother, as well. That means that I am our brood's margravess now.'

'There is no brood!' he shouted. 'They're all dead. All dead! Everyone is dead! Don't you see? You are no margravess. There is nothing left for you to rule.'

'There is the dominion,' she said softly and adjusted the power wands at his collar to soothe his anger. 'We have Elvre. We will build a new city.'

He pushed her hands away. 'Shut up. We are doomed. The cacodemons are going to kill us like they killed everyone else.'

'That's why we need Caval.' She held out the seeker. 'Put your hand over mine. Call with me. The sorcerer will hear us, and he will come.'

Poch stared at her sullenly, then placed his hand over hers so that the seeker was between their palms.

'Now reach out with me for Caval,' she instructed. 'We have the Charm. He will hear us.'

They closed their eyes, and their beseeching began. *Caval! We need you! Where are you?*

Their psychic cries glinted in the air like spun-sugar caught on the wind, and the time-loop abruptly closed for Caval.

The small bird with the green, silver-tipped feathers burst into flight, unnoticed by the two crouching figures on the dry creek bed. The bird flew directly into the white-hot glare of the Abiding Star and vanished.

Half a world away, Caval awoke in green and red twilight. A day had passed.

The glazed surface of the crystal flagstones burned with cold. He concentrated his diffused Charm on the quivering pelt of his body and warmed himself.

Tossed from his trance, he felt disoriented.

*The thin air*, he thought.

Yet, even as his Charm recharged his blood with oxygen, he groped to comprehend how he could be lying there under evening's red velvet. Moments before, he had been a gleaming bird beneath morning's radiant gaze.

Time was turned inside out. A rain of starlight drizzled through the dusk.

*The Calendar of Eyes*, he told himself, *rises above the clear boundaries of time.*

He sat up taller and groped to understand what he had witnessed in his charmed flight.

*Hu'dre Vra . . .*

The name sounded hollow – a cheap mask for the scavenger Wrat. *Hu'dre Vra*, he repeated, and again, *Hu'dre Vra!*

Across the lake of twilight, his chant shaped a vision of Hu'dre Vra's future: Smoldering ruins ranged the horizons of Irth. *The man is mad!* the sorcerer realized. Craters pocked the land where the floating cities had crashed, and cacodemons crisscrossed in the ashen skies above the godless wastes. *Mad!*

Caval stood, rigid with outrage. He brought his Charm to bear on the edge of night and the beginning of stars. There, he invoked his memory of the young survivors who had cried out for him.

*Jyoti!* he called into twilight's deepening scar. *Poch!*

Again, he saw their bodies splayed open beneath the fang-leering hulk of a cacodemon, their spilled entrails like dark glistening fruits.

*Deeper!* the sorcerer called.

Charm probed deeper into chance. And still their bodies lay torn upon the ground, ripped flesh glimmering red, exposing bones rasped clean as shafts of moonlight.

*Deeper!*

Charm reached through chance toward zero.

The sorcerer dizzied. He sagged to his knees, yet did not blink but kept his gaze firm. And he saw, staring back at him across countless fatal chances the green-blue irises of Jyoti and Poch.

Caval seized upon that dim and distant vision and poured his Charm into it.

The space around them swallowed light. Darkness enclosed them. And by that, he knew there was slim hope indeed.

*Yet hope!* he exulted. *What is seen in the Calendar of Eyes may yet be!*

He struggled upright, swerving his arms to maintain his balance, all the while holding fast to the two figures in the dark socket of furthest vision.

In the night that surrounded them, at the edge of time, possibilities shifted position: Cacodemons writhed in shades of black, teeth and claws glints of tarnished silver – and from the absences between them, outlined in their separations, like paper cut-outs, was his own shape, repeated many times.

He saw then that only his presence offered the slim chance of separating Jyoti and Poch from the cacodemons. *But to what avail?* he wondered and pressed his sight harder against the kaleidoscope of black shapes surrounding the young ones. Intently, he stared through the scarlet chords of nightfall at the black outline of his own body in the dark and demanded of his Charm, *Show me!*

The deep emerald door of day's end opened. Inside, he saw Jyoti and Poch in a pure light, the shine of the void. He was there, too, but only vaguely, his body erased to a dim blur in the emptiness. Was that him gone at last to the Beginning within the Abiding Star? Or was that his form blurred by death? He could not tell. Yet, it did not matter, because there before them were the floating cities – Dorzen – Bryse – Mirdath – Sharna – Keri – adrift once again in a new dawn's aquamarine sky and all the final horizons of Irth empty of cacodemons.

The vision closed. A mist of stars touched the darkness where he had stared through time and chance to a tentative future.

*The hope is so small*, he despaired.

He gazed flatly at the last smoky remnants of twilight under the gauzy constellations. *Small hope for Irth – and for me?*

His hard face did not flinch and the diamonds in his eyes did not waver. He could not abandon Irth even if that meant oblivion for himself. What small, unborn hope there was would have to be good enough. He dared not fail.

Without hesitation, he crossed the open court to the side farthest from the sanctuary and began the long descent from the Calendar of Eyes. All his life he had wanted to be a sage, to serve the spiritual, the truth beyond the actual, beyond form. That desire to serve what was higher forced him then and there to commit all his Charm and his very life itself to reshaping the iron of what was real.

He felt great gratitude for having at least glimpsed the immortal. Beating Wrat and his cacodemons out of the iron of reality would be hard work, the hardest task he had ever set for himself.

A mournful yearning for the Beginning, for the rapture of freedom, haunted his exiled heart. Yet, he did not glance back, for he was Irth's one small hope and that was bigger than all his longing.

Under violet dusk, he descended from the heights at the margin of time toward the treacherous world of life and death. His footsteps left blue holes in the snow. And as he went, his strong body narrowed smaller and withered. By the time he reached the gravel slopes, the years he had shed in climbing to the limits of time found him again, and under their burden he picked his way slowly over the rocky terrain.

His beard shriveled scabrous and white upon his sunken cheeks, and his hair thinned to a gauze pierced by stars. With stooped, bent shoulders and knobby legs quavering upon the mountain's bricks, the aged sorcerer felt his way downward through the darkness.

Jyoti and Poch strode through the jungles of Elvre on a road of moss-covered brick known as a spice trail, a trade route that connected interior plantations to the dominion's cities. Jyoti had cobbled together a crude seeker from components of their amulet frocks. They had no item from Caval to focus their seeker so Poch offered a tiny hex-ruby from a guardian ring that their father, the margrave, had given him.

'The ring never belonged to Caval,' Poch stated, 'but with Father dead, this is as close a link to his weapons master as we have.'

Jyoti did not care whether it actually worked or not. She just wanted to get away from Elvre, far away from the smoldering ruins of Arwar Odawl and the deaths of their brood. They followed the faint impulses from their makeshift seeker to the jungle trading capital of Moödrun.

The treetop city, built in the canopy of the jungle, was in a panic. The citizenry believed that the cacodemons would strike their busy sky bund next, and everyone was eager to escape – though no one knew to where.

In the frenzy, no one paid attention to the two lone survivors of Arwar Odawl. Jyoti and Poch blended into the swirling crowds on the bough streets and scaffold roads that rayed across the top storeys of the forest.

The governor's palace carved into the central bole of a massive pilaster tree stood starkly abandoned, its hanging garden balconies and fern terraces empty of the brokers and trade agents who usually managed Elvre's commerce from this hub of webbed avenues. The governor himself, Earl Jee, a faithful friend to Lord Keon, had gone into hiding, and there was no hope of the fugitives seeking help from him.

With the three quoins and two prisms that they had between them, Jyoti and Poch booked passage on a market dirigible heading north, which was the direction that their crude seeker pointed.

The slow journey up the coast revealed no signs of destruction or of the cacodemons. The fishing villages and farming thorpes over which they flew appeared idyllically serene. On board, however, gossip circulated about the horrors inflicted on the Peers of Dorzen. Whispers carried news of the Palace of Abominations under construction somewhere in the south, where it was said Hu'dre Vra interred his prisoners in pain cages charged with a black magic that never allowed its victims to die.

For most of the journey, the brother and sister avoided prying questions from the crew by keeping to their tiny cabin, an empty tuber bin between loamy stalls of mud beets. At each stop, they hoped their seeker would point the way to Caval, but not until the final stop in Zul, at the most extreme limit of Irth's dominions, in the industrial cliff-city of Saxar, did the seeker beckon them to disembark.

Saxar seemed only dimly aware of the Dark Lord that early

morning when they arrived. The factory chimneys still billowed smoke, and the vertical city bustled with everyday activities. The unique character of the city intrigued them with its numerous bridges, pulleys, and quaint ornate lifts. Imperial villas and frugal chalets, cottages, and huts all had tile roofs and overhanging eaves that curved upward to protect occupants and passers-by from falling objects.

Jyoti and Poch followed the strengthening impulses of their seeker down smoky Everyland Street deep into the Saxar refinery district, where the city's character changed darkly. They hurried through narrowing lanes and alleys among torn shadows of steam escaping from gutter gratings.

Behind a massive factory of black brick, in a warren of weeds and discarded steel drums, the seeker signaled their arrival. A mousy young woman in rags, with stringy hair and soot-streaked face, looked up startled from the heap of refuse where she was on her knees digging. She stared at them in open wonder.

'You two kids better get back to where you belong,' the waif warned. 'You'll get those amulets and fine clothes torn off your backs in an eyeblink you slum around here.'

Jyoti and Poch exchanged a bewildered look, and the boy backed away and pulled at his sister's sleeve.

'Hey, wait, before you two go – you think maybe you can put a newts-eye or two on me?' The trash-digger stood up and approached them. 'I ain't seen food in days.'

Jyoti nodded to Poch, and he handed his sister the seeker. She offered it to Tywi.

The waif took the alms eagerly. With surprised fingers, she examined the patched-together amulet, noting the high-quality black mirror panes and hex-ruby that comprised it. 'Dragonpiss! This is good stuff. But why's it patched together like this? What's it supposed to be?'

'It's a seeker,' Poch answered from behind his sister. 'It led us to you.'

'Me?' The vagabond laughed like a cough. 'Who you looking

for? And who *are* you, walking around here dressed better than factory bosses?'

Jyoti, who had been scrutinizing her niello eye charms, looked to her brother. 'She's wearing an Eye.'

Poch squinted at the smudged woman in her patched garments, then gazed into the epaulets of his amulet frock. There he glimpsed an aqua shadow, a vague aura about the tattered woman.

'The hex-ruby is from Father's guardian ring,' Jyoti figured, 'so apparently the seeker led us to the strongest guardian Charm it could find – this Eye of Protection.'

'What're you talking about?' the waif asked, fidgeting impatiently. 'Who are you?'

'My name is Jyoti. This is my brother, Poch. We're from Arwar Odawl.'

'The city that crashed?'

'Our father was Lord Keon, the margrave of Odawl, ruler of all Elvre.'

'Dragonpiss again! You're not bosses' kids at all. You two are Peers.' The woman gawked at them blatantly, understanding now their opulent garments. 'What are the likes of you doing down here?'

'We're looking for our father's weapons master, the sorcerer Caval,' Jyoti explained. 'But our seeker led us to you instead, because you're wearing an Eye of Protection.'

'Look—' She opened her arms to fully expose her patchwork trousers and tattered jerkin. 'My name is Tywi. I haven't eaten in days. I sleep in closed trash bins so the night tide won't take me out. I don't have no Eye of Protection on me, whatever that is.'

'It's a spell,' Jyoti told her, 'a protective spell. Only an advanced worker of sorcery with a great deal of Charm could cast such a spell and make it stick without you carrying charmware.'

'I don't have no charmware – except what you given me.' Tywi examined again the hex-ruby in its delicate setting of tiny black mirror panes. 'Thanks for this. It's going to save my skinny shanks. I hope you don't want it back.'

Jyoti shook her head. 'No, Tywi. It's yours. That seeker is no use to us any more.'

'Do you think Caval put the Eye on her?' Poch queried.

'Maybe.'

'Why?' Tywi asked. 'I never even heard of this Caval till now.'

'Then obviously we've made a mistake,' Jyoti admitted. 'If Caval were in Saxar, the seeker would have found him, I think.'

'What are we going to do now?' Poch asked, looking around nervously at the black brick walls and the alleys that climbed like shafts among the dank cliffside buildings.

'We have to leave the city,' Jyoti decided. 'On our journey here we heard the terrible stories about what the Dark Lord does to Peers. We have to find Caval before the cacodemons find us.'

'Where you going to look?' Tywi asked. For all her rough appearance, the waif did not have an unpleasant manner, and there was a glimmer of intelligence and curiosity in her face.

'The Calendar of Eyes, maybe,' Jyoti answered thoughtfully. 'It's a sanctuary for Mages in the Malpais Highlands. Caval always fancied himself a mage and spoke now and then of that sacred place. I think he may have retired there.'

'The Malpais Highlands—' Tywi frowned. 'That's way across the Qaf. Won't find no overflights from Saxar. Our Lady Altha ain't no friend of the Highland's witch queen, and you won't find no trade routes between our dominions either. You got to fly south to Mirdath and take a connection.'

'Too risky,' Jyoti said. 'The cacodemons are coming north. We'll get swept up with the others if we go back. We have to cross the Qaf.'

'Yeah, you and half of Saxar,' Tywi said. 'Word in the warrens is, Hazar's gathering his army north of the city right now to cross the Qaf. He's going to hide in the wilderness and strike back at the Dark Lord. Glad luck to him, I say. Glad luck because he's the only way out.'

'We can't travel with Hazar,' Poch spoke querulously.

'You're right,' his sister agreed. 'The cacodemons will be

looking for Peers. We'll have to rely on our amulets to help us cross on our own.'

Tywi grimaced, then shrugged. 'Unless you've got weapons, children, you'll be so much meat for the trolls.'

'We'll take that chance,' Jyoti asserted. 'Can you direct us to the best way from here out of Saxar and into the Qaf?'

Tywi shook her head. 'You're lucky you got this far without getting jumped.' She thought a moment, then added, 'You need protection if you're going to move through this city without weapons. And I see you don't have nothing but your fancy clothes.' She glanced down at the amulet in her fist then faced them again with a determined look in her eye. 'Let me take you to a thief I know who will get you anywhere in the city – if you're willing to pay him.'

'A thief?' Poch asked anxiously. 'Can a thief protect us?'

'Sure, this one can, if it comes to that.' Tywi nodded with grim assurance. 'He's beastfolk from the warrens. They don't come no tougher. But more importantly, he knows this city better than anyone. He'll get you through. Then all you have to worry about is the Qaf.'

'Take us to him, Tywi,' Jyoti asked and took her brother's arm as the waif turned and led them across the warren to a dark alley. They climbed notch-stairs to another level, an oil-stained esplanade overlooking the derrick and trestles of a lading yard.

A large man with bold beastmarks paced the cobbles, hands clasped behind his back. He wore a harness that strapped power wands to his ribs, and he looked dangerous.

'Dogbrick, look here. It's me, Tywi,' the waif called. 'I brought you some work.'

'Don't need work,' the creature retorted in a rumbling voice. 'I am replete.'

Tywi motioned for the Peers to wait on the slick steps, and she approached the muscular thief. 'What are you talking about? I've got me two Peers here. They're fugitives from Arwar Odawl.'

'We are all fugitives from that fallen city, Tywi,' Dogbrick groused. 'Anyway, I'm running a job right now that can make me enough Charm to buy a lifetime far away from this grimy city.'

'You don't look like you're running nothing.'

Dogbrick regarded the waif with defensive pride. 'Well, if you must know, curious mouse, it's just gone down. So I'm thinking through where to go from here. Foresight, my drear dear, is more precious than Charm. And if the rumors are right, Charm isn't going to be worth dung when the Dark Lord gets here.'

'The rumors *are* right, bold Dog.' Tywi nodded to where Jyoti and Poch watched from the alley steps. 'Those are Lord Keon's kids, so they claim. They're the only survivors of Arwar Odawl.'

Dogbrick glared at them. All he could think about was the trance wrap that his partner Ripcat would be delivering in a few hours at Mirage Climb. 'What do they want from me?'

'Safe passage to the Qaf.'

Dogbrick barked a laugh. 'Safe passage to hell, you mean.'

'They have the amulets to pay,' Tywi whispered conspiratorially. 'That's why I think they got to be telling the truth about who they are.'

'I don't need any more amulets. Especially if the cacodemons are coming.'

Tywi shrugged. 'You said you're going to Mirage Climb anyway, right? Come on, Dog. Where's that noble heart of yours? Take them with you. From the Climb, it ain't far to the city limits and the Qaf. Do it for me and give me the amulets. I never asked you for nothing much before. You owe me.'

'I am indebted to you,' Dogbrick admitted and nodded his large head resignedly. 'Of all the urchins who've spotted for me on my jobs, you've certainly been the best. I have never been spied on your watch. Not once. So I will do this favor for you, girl. Tell those fancy-pants kids to hurry along. I'm leaving now.'

Tywi waved the siblings closer. 'Dogbrick – Jyoti and Poch.'

Dogbrick looked them up and down carefully, assessing the worth of their amulet tunics. Then, he reached out and plucked several hex-gems from their tunics. 'Payment up front,' he announced and handed the gems to Tywi. 'Spend them now, while they're worth something.'

'They're already spent, Dog,' Tywi informed him. 'I'm going with Hazar's army today. These sparkles are buying a slot for me in the caravan with the troops. I'm gone.'

Tywi nodded her gratitude to the Peers, hastily thanked Dogbrick with a smile, and loped down a narrow lane.

'And don't try stealing anything from those soldiers,' Dogbrick yelled after her.

'I won't steal nothing, Dog,' she shouted back. 'I know how to make my own way.'

Dogbrick watched after her with a worried scowl, then turned his formidable bulk toward his new wards. His hard stare appraised them. 'So – you are Peers,' he said coldly and watched the play of emotions on their faces.

The boy stood before him paralyzed in fright, and the young woman observed him intently, shifting her weight subtly yet decisively as if she were actually about to spring at him.

*Timidity and temerity*, the thief observed and relaxed his hostile stance, feeling he now knew better whom he escorted.

He motioned with his head for them to follow. 'These are cruel times for you,' he spoke as he guided them up a steep ramp littered with broken crates and metal shavings in tangled coils.

'For us all,' Jyoti agreed and tugged at the sleeve of her reluctant brother, who stared with alarm at the large, beast-like man.

They emerged behind warehouses where a charmless gang milled about a blazing steel drum and a skinned cat roasted on a spit. The malefic stares of the gang as they took in the amulet tunics cut like a cold wind through the Peers. Poch slid closer to Dogbrick.

'Ah, don't fear them, lad,' the robust thief whispered. 'They are Irth's charmless. With the amulets you have on your back you should feel nothing but pity for them.'

Poch and Jyoti followed silently, warily peering into the dark alcoves among the factories and assembly shops and finding threat everywhere – wild dogs, squatters guarding with clubs and sticks their shanties in the sewer mist, and roving bands of charmless people kicking over trash drums and glaring predaciously as they passed, too intimidated by Dogbrick to approach or even call out.

Along the way, the thief regaled his wards with his philosophy. 'Talk is glory. It is what makes us human, is it not? Words. Words. And more words. The corpuscles that make up the storied blood of our souls! That is why I make a point of talking with myself at all times. At *all* times. It is an excellent way to know one's mind and express one's heart. How else to make those important and often snap distinctions in life between what is true and what merely useful. Otherwise, one easily becomes lost in oneself. Is that not also true among the Peers? How large a place the human heart is!'

They crossed a rusted span above a churning cascade of clanking mill wheels, and the loquacious thief turned to help Poch across. He saw then the distraction in their faces. They were attentive to a world they had never visited before, this curious architecture of winches, spans, and trestles conjoining the towering cliff faces.

'Drakesblood!' He cursed himself and smiled, showing fangs. 'I talk too much! Especially when I'm with strangers and can speak freely without fearing that I'm repeating myself. You see, words have been both the poison and the cure in my life.'

The zoic philosopher climbed a switchback stairway toward modern stone buildings awash in daylight and rearing above the fuming precincts like a parapet to a higher world forgotten by the scorched denizens below.

'They are dangerous powers, words,' Dogbrick rambled on. 'Words, symbolic and unreal as they are, demand a genuine friendship with the actual, you see. They want to become real. They want to be included in the circles of necessity that define our lives. They strive, even against our will, to share and shape the other dreams and visions that flower from the Irthen bed our flesh in fact is. To live with words – as must we all – requires us to negotiate constantly between these energies of the body and the arts of action. Do you understand?'

Jyoti and Poch nodded vigorously, though neither of them had been listening. The cityscape had opened around them as they climbed out of the refinery district on to a terrace of townhouses and merchants' shops. Below them industrial smoke seethed, and among rips in the vapors they beheld the sooty depths from which they had risen. Forge fires flashed in the fuming grottoes, crimson and sudden, like an infernal semblance of celestial lightning.

Dogbrick urged them away from the railed landing into the daystruck boulevard. At a street corner station, they caught an uptown trolley and rode the rest of the way to Mirage Climb and its tiers of jigsaw trees.

'Follow that gravel path through the park,' the thief directed them with a burly arm. He pointed at a flinty trace among the mauve and yellow trees. 'It starts here as a trickle, wanders a while through that grove, then widens immediately afterward into the wasteland. Glad fortune to you both in that blighted expanse. You have water, of course.'

Jyoti indicated their flagons. 'We have water and a water seeker. And our amulets are fully charged.' She said this in an encouraging tone, for Poch's sake. 'We even have some food left from our flight in. We'll be fine. Glad fortune to you, Dogbrick, for getting us this far.'

'You paid Tywi well enough,' he said with a smile that showed fangs again. 'Glad fortune. Glad fortune, all!'

They were relieved when Dogbrick finally took his leave, sauntering away into a grove of broken daylight.

'What a blowhard,' Poch muttered when the beastman had departed.

'But a useful blowhard,' Jyoti said. 'We surely would have been jumped down there without him. If we hadn't gone in during

126

those early hours when everyone was still waking, we probably would have been assaulted then, before we found that girl, Tywi. All I have on me is a utility knife.'

'What I can't figure out is, who could have put the Eye on Tywi if not Caval?'

Jyoti thrust her thumb back at Saxar, the carved cliffs glowing blackly in the daylight like a cauterized sore. 'This is a city of charmwrights, Poch. Masters of sorcery come and go from here all the time. It could be any of them.'

'Jyoti – look!'

Over the horizon, a dark thin line undulated. It could have been gulls – but at that great distance they were far too large and black.

'Look at them! It's the demons!' Poch shrilled, clasping his sister's arm. 'They've arrived!'

Jyoti took his hand and rushed with him up the gravel trail. The jigsaw trees parted, as the thief had predicted, and they mounted to a ridge at the scalloped edge of the Qaf. Tracts of cinder and slurry swept to the horizon.

The Peers balked at the massive sight of the badlands and regarded each other with trepidation.

'We have Charm,' Jyoti reassured him yet again. 'Our flagons are full, and we'll find more water as we go. If we stay—'

They both looked back at the cankerous city. The thin, distant line of demons was not visible from this vantage, but they both knew the threat that lurked among the smoky cliffs where they could not see. Hand in hand, they stepped into the dead land.

## Lord of the Nethermost

Lord Drev paused in his wanderings at a clear pool among the northern mountains of the Malpais Highlands. He had climbed high and all around him snow peaks soared against the fathomless blue. Like the convolutions of a giant brain, dark gorges and valleys mazed far below, where no light from the Abiding Star reached. A griffin circled through the vastness in silence, its white feathers bright as tufted starlight.

On the mountainsides around the wizarduke, giant trees crowded the slopes and ridges and softened all edges with a carpeting of yellow and bronze leaves. With each turn in the wind came rich humus smells laced with bracing scents of iced rocks and snow. Drev breathed deeply and, for an ironic moment, marveled that he would never have known such beauty had not the return of Wrat forced him out of the fortressed comfort of Dorzen.

Yet, with this loveliness went a terrible solitude and an anguish for his brood and his dominion who were vulnerable to the Dark Lord's cacodemons. He dreaded what was to become of Irth with a rampaging madman like Wrat invulnerable to Charm.

The conviction gnawed at him that this was all his fault, that this nightmare would not now be upon them if only he had been more ruthless and had executed Wrat outright. He determined to lead the so-called Dark Lord on a chase for as long as he could. He had no doubt that the petty scavenger would want his revenge and would scour Irth for him.

Drev planned to journey north to the desert kingdom of Zul on the far side of the terrible wasteland of the Qaf. He would search for Tywi, the woman whom Charm informed him could be his true love. If these were to be his last days, he would spend them questing for her and keeping one step ahead of Wrat and his minions. Along the way, he would remain attentive to finding ways to defeat this maniacal enemy of Irth.

Finding Tywi offered him the hope of becoming stronger, not in Charm but in his ability to take this darkness in.

*Yet, even if I find her again*, Drev wondered, *will she be pleased? Or will she find me unworthy – a renegade without dominion and only the Charm I carry to share with her? What will she think of me?*

He knelt at the pool of tannin-dark water and gazed at himself, pondering if she would find him acceptable, or even attractive without the mirage of Charm to enhance his features. In his night-blue cloak, his brown uniform hung with charmed ornaments of turquoise and silver, and his low red-stitched boots of hide and wool, he looked like a common trooper. Worse, he felt like a fool, an undignified fool hiding like this.

Kneeling among the rose quartz and cinnamon fern, he parted his crow-black hair falling to his long shoulders and peered into the pool at his dark copper skin and oblique eyes blue as ice.

He looked striking, though not necessarily handsome, and he took comfort in the truth that fate had united him to Tywi. As a child, when he first learned how to scry, she had been the first one he sensed, a woman of low station and far from him, at that time not yet born yet already bound closer to him than any other. The river of time beat the drumskins of blood in both their hearts.

*Why?* he had often questioned. *Why her?*

He might as well have asked, why magic, why joy, why innocence, sweetness, violence, and death? Fate unified impulse and instinct. So he had been trained to believe as a child by Irth's finest sorcerers. In learning to scry, he gazed into the dangerous abysses of chance, fate, and the implacable future. He had learned that to scry was not to know but to suspect.

No hint of Wrat's return had ever been scryed by anyone, as far as he knew. The power to glimpse future time existed sketchily among the bright worlds under the Abiding Star and not at all beyond the Gulf on the Dark Shore.

And now that the Conquest had begun and Wrat had thrown chaos upon Irth, he might not ever find Tywi again. The future was changed, and yet she was there, somewhere, at the causal end of the string of events that had first brought her last newts-eye to him. She was there. But he might not ever find his way to her again, even though they were bound by fate, and time's river beat the drum that was their hearts.

Drev knew that if he was to find his fateful lover he would have to do so soon. In his niello eye charms, he watched flights of cacodemons scouring the labyrinth of valleys, searching for him. Immune to Charm, the cacodemons also were blind to it; so, they did not sense him observing them. By that means, he had been able to avoid them – so far.

Arwar Odawl had fallen, just as Wrat had threatened. Looking down from the high ranges, the eye charms revealed the ghastly crash site in the Elvre jungle, and gazing at the seething crater mounded with char and rubble, he wept. In the smoldering black anathema, he identified nothing of the lyric turret tower domes famous across Irth or the fabled walled gardens from the Primrose Stilts where his parents had wed and that he had often visited in his diplomatic tours as regent. Nothing remained of the living city. No shapes appeared among the vapors and rueful debris. And his heart grew darker with half-mindless, wayward thoughts of vengeance.

*Somehow I will elude the stalking cacodemons and learn to*

*destroy them,* he swore to himself. *Somehow I will face Wrat again, and he will answer to me for Arwar Odawl. I will avenge this terrible thing. Somehow . . .*

With a hand upon the sword Taran in its black scabard, Drev stood and again scanned his surroundings. Cold torrents plunged from the snow mists of the upper world of ice peaks and depthless blue. Nearby, beneath the great boughs of massive trees, rock gardens tumbled from one ledge to the next, cluttered with fern, saplings, and florets in every hue of fire. Squirrels darted and bright finches alighted upon lichened boulders.

He detected no enemy with his niello charms or with his own eyes, and thus he dared to draw his weapon and allow it to catch light from the Abiding Star and gain more power. It adjusted to his grip, enclosing his hand and flashing hotly as he danced with it. With each swerve of his arm, it changed shape, beveling itself to cut most swiftly through the air.

Pointing the sword north at the far distant crest of the highest mountain, the Calendar of Eyes, Drev contemplated going there. A sanctuary lay hidden upon its upper face, and the sword Taran could surely lead him there. Perhaps the sages in that sacred place would have knowledge of how to fight the cacodemons, and he listened to what the sword had to say about this strategem.

The reply came swiftly, and, in the wordless manner of the greatest magic, it shaped itself with his own thoughts. Deeper into the mountains lay the broken world – the world shattered by Wrat. And he knew at once that sanctuary was not a hopeful recourse for him, the prey of cacodemons. *No,* he realized, *I must continue my quest – through the mountains and into the Qaf.* That way led him toward wholeness, toward a woman who could love him before he died.

Drev turned and aimed his sword through the wistful vistas of cascades and arboreal uplands toward a faint silica aura shining from under the horizon that he knew was the desert. The sword hummed agreeably in his hand.

The silvergold blade returned to its black scabard, and he

adjusted the red belt about his waist, pulled his dark traveler's cloak around him, and continued hiking down the narrow, mossy path of the mountainside. Charm gave him agility and disallowed missteps that would have sent him plummeting into the chasms below.

Both by day and by night, he marched. Charm gave him strength. The collar and hem of his cloak had been fitted with a dozen power wands. To avoid griffins and dragons, he relied upon his niello eye charms. Hex-gems granted him vision in the dark, and he made his way boldly out of the mountains and into the sere grasslands that fringed the dread Qaf.

There would be little food and less water in the wasteland, and Drev took the time to resupply his provision sack. From a stammering rivulet of ice-melt, he filled his flagons and among the orchid-spangled hills gathered as many breadberries and nuts as he could carry. By the time he stood before the cinderland of the Qaf, he shouldered as much hope as was possible against the brutality of the desert.

The parched grasslands fell behind him and ahead lay a cracked plain luminous as shattered glass. To keep out of sight of cacodemons that might overfly the broken land, he meandered among eskers, long wandering ridges of gravel, boulders and sand deposited by ancient, vanished glaciers.

The danger afoot in these ashen wastes was trolls. Bolt-eyed as sharks, with metal-burnished flesh, quilled green hair, and clawed feet and hands, the carnivorous, snouted creatures could not easily be slain. Lopped limbs continued to live and stalk and kill. Only charm fire could burn them entirely away. But Drev carried no firecharms.

His first night on the Qaf, the trolls found him. They came from their caves in the gypsum archipelagos under the volcanic rims that seeped scarlet vapors into the night sky. Drev heard their claws scuttling over the gravel flats before he saw their lucent eyes shining like metal discs or smelled their sulfurous stench or heard their enormous groans of hunger.

The sword Taran whistled as he spun the blade overhead, warning the trolls. But their hunger exceeded their fear, and they came on, out of the starwoven darkness like clots of cinderous smoke, leaping over each other, naked and tufted with glaucous quills, males and females interchangeable in their boneshrunk forms.

Drev retreated to the ridgetop of an esker, and as the trolls swarmed toward him, he shouldered boulders and kicked rocks to slow them. They stumbled onward, slaverous and groaning, scrambling over those who had fallen.

The sword Taran lopped three heads in its first swipe, and the headless bodies would have clawed after him but for the others who pulled them down to get at him themselves. Charmed steel bit into the surging wave of trolls, and black blood spewed, amputated claws spun away, and the groans widened to roars of pain and fury.

Dancing death, Lord Drev spun across the summit of the esker, and the wounded trolls fell away under the desperate scramblings of ravenous others. He pressed the fight, hacking downslope two paces, then whirling back to the crest and chopping at those who surged up the slipface behind him.

The trolls offered no respite. Mindless of their losses, they surged on all sides, and the wizarduke gave himself wholly to the fight, a killing machine powered by Charm. He would cut at them all night, no matter the cost in power. Better, he believed, to deplete all his Charm and die of exposure under the smiting hammer of the Abiding Star than fall prey to trolls, who would devour him alive.

Pain stabbed his ankle. In a flash, he glimpsed a severed claw clamped to his boot, the talons embedded in his flesh and twisting. His leg flew out from under, and he crashed to his back.

Instantly, the trolls thronged over him. With a cleaving blow, he smashed the claw that had toppled him and spun his blade in a whistling arc over him. Black blood sprayed, and maimed howls went up like crying laughter.

Drev rolled and pushed to his feet. But as he struggled upright, other lopped limbs closed in. The nearest flexed and leaped, slashing his cloak. He cut it away swiftly and hurled himself about in a hopping circle, blade flourishing, slicing at his crowding assailants while kicking at the amputated limbs creeping toward him.

The bodies of wounded trolls came hurtling, thrown by trolls eager to overwhelm him. He knocked them aside with two-handed swipes of his sword, and they bounded back at him, and he slammed them aside again and again. The blood that splattered him burned acid blisters in his flesh and bleared his sight. He had no time to reach under his cloak for the amulet of theriacal opals that could counter the scalding blood. The trolls frenzied in the bloodsmoke of their fallen, attacking ever more fervently, hurling cut limbs and rocks at him.

Drev crouched, and a stone struck his shoulder with deep-bruising pain. Bellowing, he charged. Once the realization swept over him that this was no horde he could fend, he gave himself to a wild attack. Six more trolls fell under his spinning sword, but their spilled entrails snaked around his feet with lively vehemence, roping him and pulling him down.

Whooping trolls closed in. Shielded by hewed carcasses, they pressed forward to smother his slaying sword. Their snarling snouts and bolt-black eyes enclosed him, and he grunted his death-chant to the Abiding Star, to the Beginning that oversees all ends.

Glaring white light erased vision. In his momentary blindness, Drev heard squealing – the high-pitched cry of terrified trolls. Then, sight seeped back, and he saw the monsters around him scrambling away, tumbling down the slipface.

Another bright glare erased starlight and etched the desert in daybright hues and flung shadows.

*Firecharms!* the wizarduke realized dimly, simultaneously relieved and alarmed.

He clutched at his amulet of theriacal opals, pressed the cool cluster of baubles to his eyes. Vision cleared immediately. The trolls had vanished, scurrying away into the darkness, leaving behind the throbbing, writhing, creeping shapes of disseevered limbs. And in their place stood a small squad of Falcon Guard, a dozen troopers in dun assault gear: raptor hoods, combat vests, and gun bandoliers.

One of the troopers raised the vizard of his raptor hood to reveal wide red whiskers fanning out from a harshly scarred and dented head of yellow eyes and a pugnosed face cruel as a bat's.

'Leboc!' Drev shouted with surprise. He cut away the entangling loops of trollish viscera from his legs and staggered upright to address the marshal of the Falcon Guard. 'How did you find me?'

'We never lost you, my duke.' The old warrior bowed, and the other troopers followed in tight military precision. 'When Arwar Odawl fell to Wrat's cacodemons, I called for volunteers to serve you. These are the twelve who came with me. We have been in your shadow since you left Ux.'

'But – how? I detected no one . . .'

Leboc cocked a gnarled, rusty eyebrow. 'My duke, you have fought too many battles with the Falcon Guard at your side to ask that. We see all and are not seen.'

The wizarduke nodded distractedly, scanning the starsmoke for movement. One glance at the niello eye charms under his cloak confirmed his fear. Teeming reptilian shadows gathered at the southern horizon.

'They are coming,' the wizarduke warned.

'We know,' Leboc acknowledged. 'The firecharms attract them. Which is why you refused to carry such a weapon with you in your exile.'

Drev nodded tersely and cast a searching stare about the bleak terrain, noting crevices in the esker where individuals could burrow. Farther on were the gypsum hills occupied by the trolls. And beyond that, volcanic rills glowered with infernal red shadows. 'We must hide at once, Leboc.'

'And yet, they will find us,' Leboc said with calm certainty. 'There is only one way.' He raised an arm and displayed a hand-signal. Two troopers swiftly separated themselves from the others, drew their firelocks from the sheaths slung across their backs, and ran toward the gypsum hills.

'Stop them, Leboc,' Drev protested. 'The cacodemons will snatch them before they reach the hills.'

Leboc gestured the wizarduke to wait, then signed to the remaining troopers, who dispersed and melted away into the night shadows of the esker's crevices. The marshal took Drev by the elbow and led him hurriedly along the lee of the esker to a covert between two boulders.

From there, they watched the two running troopers fire several rounds toward the gypsum hills. The flash of their firelocks punctured the night with vivid colors and cast their shadows in long arcs across the broken plates of the desert.

Drev knew then what was happening. The two had volunteered to sacrifice themselves, and his heart churned with the urgency to call them back. But it was already too late.

Angular silhouettes soared out of the night, cutting sharply against the star fumes. The two troopers stopped running and fired in rapid bursts at the descending predators.

In the dazzling radiance, the cacodemons reared wholly into view. They moved with serpentine agility and swiftness, their serrated tails lashing the air for balance as their talons slashed in a blur. The hot bluewhite strokes of murderous energy splashed off their powerful bodies in a rainbow spray of refracted Charm.

A cacodemon pounced upon one of the troopers, knocking his firelock aside. Hooking him with curved talons under the collarbones, it pulled him closer for the avid totem of faces in its belly to devour.

The second trooper shot the first in the back, ending his torment. Then, even as another cacodemon seized him from behind, he discharged his weapon directly at his comrade's fallen firelock. The impact shattered the Charm-breech, and an explosion of green fire engulfed them both.

The cacodemons danced in the conflagration as bales of ball lightning bounced and skittered across the cracked desert floor. The shock wave sent rocks sizzling down the slopes of the eskers and spiraled luminous fragments high into the heavens where they burned hotter than stars.

Darkness descended, and the cacodemons roared triumphantly and flew off.

The agitated wizardduke waited where he lay between the boulders until he saw the last of the creatures disappear from the range of his eye charms. Then he sobbed a curse: 'I swear by the Abiding Star, I will kill Wrat with my own hands!'

Enraged, he glared at Leboc who lay beside him with his hands fisted in the gravel, and the marshal's riven face did not flinch.

'Better you had let me die,' Drev declared, gnashing the words. 'Two brave souls burned in green fire! No ascension for them. Only ashes now. Only ashes.'

'They died for their duke.'

Drev pounded his fist against the stones. 'I am no duke. I am but a man now that I have abandoned Dorzen and fled Ux. You know that, Leboc. It is damnation to know me. You should not have followed me out here.'

Leboc's cruel face tightened even more cruelly, and he spoke in a steely voice, 'We all chose to follow you, my duke. You shall always be our duke. The two who died this night to protect you – they volunteered, remember. And you will not again besmirch their memory by denying that you are our duke. You must accept what I am saying.'

Drev heard the compression of reproach in his marshal's voice. He had heard that tone before, on the field of battle, in those times when the wizardduke had wearied of war. Leboc's cold glower had always before shamed him back into battle as, again, at this time it shamed him back into the position of command and reproached him for failing his hereditary role.

Drev held his marshal's resolute stare with wet eyes as deeper

comprehension opened in him. *The blood sacrifice has been paid.*
If he had died in this cinderland, remorse and duty would have
died with him. But the ones who died in his stead had devoured
him as wholly as the trolls would have.

Leboc sensed the depth that his harsh words had reached in
the wizarduke and knew that the tears in Drev's eyes were not for
the dead troopers but for his own fate, his own dead freedom. He
selected his words carefully, to seal the pact between them:
'There is no freedom from our freedom, my duke. Two troopers
freely chose to die. Ten more freely await your commands. All of
Irth is free to rage against the savagery of the cacodemons. And
what will you do with your freedom?'

Drev's stare went dry, and he swallowed. He had been selfish
to believe he could simply walk away from his legacy. The deaths
of two good men shattered the delusion that he could take what
was left of his life for himself. He belonged, as ever, to his people.

'When we parted, Leboc, I told you that I belonged to fate.'
Hearing his own voice, the wizarduke realized that he had fully
returned to the broken world, but he would never forget that, for
a brief moment, he had glimpsed wholeness. To remind himself,
he placed a hand over the crude shoulderguard under his cloak
where he had returned Tywi's newts-eye to its place and felt again
the chime of his distant love. 'Fate has made me a wizarduke. And
fate has put in my heart the hope of saving our people. But we
don't know how. And so, I will wander where my fate leads me.
Perhaps I will discover how to fight the cacodemons. If you and
the others choose to follow, I will be glad to lead.'

'And we will gladly follow,' Leboc assured him, 'so long as you
do not forget that you are our duke.'

'I will not forget,' he promised with a firm voice. 'Never again.'

'Very good, my duke.' Leboc pushed himself upright and
offered a square hand. When the wizarduke accepted it and stood
upright, the marshal clasped Drev's shoulder strongly. 'We live
and we die – as one people.'

Drev nodded and watched coolly as the marshal rallied the

troopers from their coverts. *Is not Leboc the ultimate warrior?* he marveled to himself. Drev remembered that he had first come to serve the Brood of Dorzen as a boy-trooper under the One-Eyed Duke, Drev's great-grandfather, who had united the Seven Dominions. The union, of course, was a sham. The Dominions intrigued against each other and conducted almost perpetual guerilla warfare, but for the most part the regency had maintained a semblance of order in which the economies of Irth flourished.

The order that the One-Eyed Duke had won for Irth, tenuous as it was, provided a semblance of stability for people that Wrat's cacodemons now mocked and threatened. The danger that faced them all was the loss of all order. *What hope could love offer if the world itself is chaos?* Drev realized resignedly as he took his place before the gathered Falcon Guard.

Leboc looked to him to speak to the squad, but Drev could find no words. Speech seemed to him then like so much bright gutterings against relentless darkness. Silence alone matched the dark limits.

Lord Drev led the Falcon Guard on toward the smoldering calderas. By dawn they found themselves surrounded by cindercones and a sulfurous haze. They marched on, the Abiding Star above them the color of dull metal. The squad were motes in the glare of the alkali desert.

None queried where the wizarduke led them. He had determined to cross the Qaf, and he followed his strategem of keeping close to eskers, dunes, and volcanic ridges, within easy reach of hiding if the cacodemons appeared again. They did not.

In his niello eye charms, Drev spotted trolls. They watched from dune ridges and kept well away from the armed wanderers. Heat devils tilted sullenly on the horizon.

A mirage appeared in the watery distance. The sight of it ate holes in their hearts, for it revealed tasseled treetops, buttressed roots, and, afloat on the afternoon reflections of this viscous swamp, a smoldering mountain of debris – twisted girders, hot spalls of rubble, misshapen towers and façades drooling with great globs of steaming slag.

'Arwar Odawl—' Leboc identified the ruins, and dismayed mutters passed through the squad. 'Fallen into the jungles of Elvre.'

The wizarduke checked his eye charms and saw no sign of the destroyed city. 'Why does it appear to us here?'

'Atmospheric refraction . . .' the marshal speculated and sipped from his flagon.

The mirage melted away as they approached. By nightfall, under hanging willows of stars and watermeadows of green dusk clouds, they crossed the scoured waste where the simulacrum had wavered. Footprints marred the dusty scoria.

'Two, traveling very light.' Leboc read the prints. 'A woman and a small man or a boy.'

'Out here?' Drev asked in disbelief. He searched his niello eye charms again and could not find them.

'They must be cloaked,' Leboc reasoned.

'Then, they're Peers,' Drev knew, for cloaking amulets were forbidden to all but the peerage.

'Peers or clever thieves that know how to rig a cloak with a scalp or a skull,' the marshal said. 'Shall I bring them in?'

'No. If they are Peers, they will answer only to me.'

Leboc's rusty eyebrows knitted. 'And if they are clever thieves?'

'Then they will answer to my sword.'

The wizarduke followed the prints across a pan strewn with shards like broken crockery. Leboc and the Falcon Guard watched after him until he vanished among fluted columns of sandstone. Then the marshal flashed a hand signal that sent three troopers after him.

Darkness erased the last smudges of twilight by the time Drev spotted the two figures. They moved along a horizon slanted against the blanched face of Nemora, two sojourners remote and of vague substance in the nocturnal shine.

Drev purposefully did not activate his own cloaking amulet and approached atop a rock ledge, easily visible in the nacre light. When the two spotted him, they dipped out of sight.

From the provision sack under his cloak, he removed his aviso and rubbed the dark crystal until a blue spark danced within.

'This is the wizarduke Drev of Dorzen,' he spoke softly into the aviso. 'If you can hear me, please reply.'

He heard only open-air static.

Reading the terrain's mangled shapes of lava rock, Drev predicted the path of the travelers and ran across a bed of alabaster sand to cut them off. He emerged through a notch in an eroded crater and found himself nearly colliding with the two shadow figures in the ivory-blue light of Nemora.

One of the shadows, the smaller one, fell back in a fluster. The other came straight at him. One glimpse of motion-feathered hair and a firm jaw was all he had before she was upon him. He reflexively spun to his side to narrow his profile and crouched to receive her attack. But she slinked as if falling, bounded, curled in mid-air with surprising agility, and a blow to the back of his head splattered hot colors across his sight before his brain thought to dodge.

Drev splashed into the sand, and she was above him, her knee expertly placed between his scapulae, and the cold tip of a blade at the base of his throbbing skull.

'Who are you?' she hissed.

He understood then that her whip-kick could have killed him if she had not restrained herself. She was no clever thief but in truth a lethally trained Peer.

'I am Drev of Dorzen,' he groaned.

'The *regent*?' she asked in a gust of awe. The blade tip pulled away, yet she did not remove the pressure lock on his back that bore down so strongly that he felt his spine could snap. 'How came you here?'

'I am fleeing cacodemons sent to destroy me,' he answered candidly, squeezing words from his pressed lungs. 'You would be wise to release your lock now. I am traveling with my Falcon Guard, and they will surely kill you if they find us like this.'

The pressure relented and, light as a shadow, the woman slipped into the darkness.

'Who are you?' he called after her, his voice charged with wonder. She had displayed a physical skill he had only read about in the annals of the old wars but had never witnessed before. *She attacked without Charm!* And yet with exquisite control. He strained to find her. But she was gone. He peered into the problematical shadows of starlight and boulders and spotted the smaller figure huddled in a concealing cleft. 'You, there. Come out.'

The shadow stood and stepped forward with raised arms. Planetshine from Nemora illuminated a young adolescent male with large, frightened eyes. He wore a sportster-style amulet tunic and the padded slacks and cross-strap boots popular among the affluent young. The gold circuit tunic with its expensive blue stone studs and intricate amulet overlay could only belong to a Peer. *Stolen? No.* The boy had the look of one accustomed to privilege: stylish, feather-cut hair, penciled eyes, delicate hands, and a stance at ease with these opulent garments.

'What is your name, lad?' Drev inquired, trying to steady the skittish boy with a tone of gentle command.

'Sir, I am Poch, Margrave Keon's son from the Brood of Odawl.'

'Lord Keon's son?' Drev echoed in amazement. 'At ease, lad. We are allies. Your father was my friend . . .'

Footfalls turned Drev about, and he saw a Falcon Guard running toward him, eager to assist with the captive. Out of a narrow enfilade among the reef rocks, a shadow violated its oath of stillness to the naked stone that cast it and lunged at the trooper.

The Falcon Guard dodged, but too late. He tumbled to the ground with the impact, and the two rolled as one. Sand splashed around them.

Drev clearly saw in the brash starlight the woman who had stunned him. Lithe as a panther, she clung to the trooper using the momentum of their fall to pull him on top and then over. She followed fluidly in a reverse flip and an abrupt twist turn in mid-air, pouncing upon his back even as he rebounded to somersault away.

From a ledge on the corroded crater wall, another Falcon Guard dropped and scrambled to help his comrade. But the attack was already over. The woman pulled sharply away, snatching the trooper's firelock from the holster slung across his back.

'Disarm!' she ordered.

Drev noticed she was not even breathing hard. She, too, wore a heavily-laden amulet tunic and fashionably padded slacks and cross-strap boots. *Dressed for a casual sport outing. she has bested an armored Falcon Guard!*

'Do as she commands,' Drev told the trooper.

But before he could act, a third Falcon Guard showed himself, moving out of the darkness behind Poch. He had his firelock trained on the boy.

'No!' She fired one dull red burst, and it hit the trooper behind Poch squarely in the chest.

The Falcon Guard collapsed backward with a loud grunt, dropping his weapon. He quickly snatched it again and jerked upright.

'Stand down!' Drev shouted. He turned a calm countenance toward the woman whose firelock was aimed at him. Again she had exhibited precise control, having fired a low-impact burst to protect Poch. The trooper she hit in his combat vest had had the wind knocked out of him, no worse. 'I admire your restraint, woman. Now tell me who you are.'

She lowered the firelock and stepped forward, a young, lean woman with athletic limbs and a wide, freckled face, hair tied in a knot and sun-dusted even in starlight. 'Lord Regent, forgive me for striking you. You startled us.'

'Not unwarranted. You are forgiven, young lady.'

She passed the firelock back to the trooper from whom she had taken it. 'I acted against your guard because I feared they would attack us. In the darkness, in this wild place, they might well have misconstrued who we are. Especially after we took you down. You said so yourself.'

Drev smiled. 'I did indeed. Please, be assured you are in no danger from me or my guard.' He gestured to Poch, who edged away anxiously from the Falcon Guard, dusting sand from the seat of his pants. 'I have met Lord Keon's son, Poch. You must be his sister. I see the resemblance.'

'Yes,' she acknowledged and went to her brother's side. 'I am Jyoti, Margravess of Odawl.'

'All Irth is grieved at the tragedy of your brood and outraged at the fall of Arwar Odawl.' He searched their faces and saw on deeper inspection the bitter melancholy and fright in the boy and in the young woman. 'All the Dominions stand united to defeat Wrat and his cacodemons.'

Poch lowered his head, and Jyoti smirked cynically. 'Forgive me, lord regent, for saying this, but the Dominions are united in truckling subserviently before Hu'dre Vra,' she said coldly. 'We fled Elvre on an airship bound for Saxar, and we heard ample news of the Dark Lord's victories. Your own city of Dorzen capitulated without a fight. Romut rules there now, Wrat's right hand recruited from the Bold Ones. They say he has made your brother-in-law Baronet Fakel his personal servant and taken Fakel's witch dancer wife Lady Von for his mistress. As for your dead sister Mevea's children—'

'Stop!' He put a hand to his brow to shield his eyes. 'I cannot bear to hear of my sister's children suffering.'

'They suffer no longer, my lord regent,' Jyoti said stiffly. 'Rumor says they are dead. Romut gave them to the cacodemons in public display to satisfy his hatred of you and to tighten his rule of terror on Dorzen. No one now dares oppose him. Arwar Odawl will not be avenged.'

Drev huffed angrily and had to turn away from her. She spoke truth, he knew, yet her derisive, angry tone incensed him, and he had to remind himself that she spoke out of even greater suffering than his. 'We will find a way to break Wrat.'

'Is that why you are wandering the Qaf, Lord Regent?' Jyoti pressed.

Drev slowly turned and faced her. 'Margravess, I flee the cacodemons because I cannot fight them. But I am determined to find a way to strike back.'

She lifted her chin in challenge. 'How?'

'I don't know.' Perplexity darkened his brow. 'But I do know that all beings under the Abiding Star are mortal. Wrat brought these monsters across the Gulf from the cold worlds. That is why Charm is useless against them. Yet, surely, among all the sorcerers, witch dancers, and sages of Irth, there must be some knowledge that will reveal the weakness of the cacodemons.'

Jyoti studied the wizarduke intently, then passed her gaze to the Falcon Guard, and finally to her brother. Then she looked back at Drev with a brighter gleam in her large eyes. 'That is our hope as well, my lord. That is why you find us here in the Qaf. We are questing for our father's weapons master, the sorcerer Caval. Our inquiries suggest he may yet be among the sages in the sanctuary of the Calendar of Eyes, not far from here. We hope that he can help us get the knowledge we need to fight the cacodemons.'

'I hope your hope is fulfilled,' the wizarduke said. 'I would offer you escort, but that would only mark you more boldly for our enemy.'

'We have come this far on our own,' Jyoti said. 'We have a trek of three days before we reach the Calendar of Eyes.'

Drev signaled for the nearest trooper to hand him his firelock. 'Take this with you.' He passed the holstered weapon to her. 'There are trolls in the gypsum hills south of here. The sight of the weapon alone should keep them at bay. Use it only if you must.'

'I know,' Jyoti finished for him. 'Firecharms attract caco-demons. They are scouring Irth for all the Peers. Wrat wants every one of us dead.'

'Do you need provisions?' Drev asked. Looking at these two, with their kin traits of broad bones, freckles, and pale skin shining in the white shadow of Nemora's full disk, he felt touched by prescience. Briefly, he saw them dead. A cacodemon squatted over them, the mess of their guts hanging from its jaws.

The image dissolved and disappeared in trickling lines of time: He glimpsed the causal streams of events that would guide sister and brother to their fate, the arduous journey on the river of time with its nameless distances of desert, jungle, and bogland that these two would endure – and everywhere they went, like echoes rebounding from the river canyon's walls, cacodemons thronged.

'On the airship to Saxar, we traded hex-gems for provisions,' she replied, then saw the indrawn vacancy of his stare. 'My lord – are you all right?'

'Yes,' he responded at once, and common sight snapped back into place. 'Now and then, I glance sidelong into time. I saw a little of your hard journey ahead. You must be careful. Of course, you don't need me to warn you that, even with all your fighting skills, you wander perilous paths.'

'So do we all.' She clasped her wrists with her hands and bowed formally, and her brother followed curtly. 'Farewell, my lord.'

Jyoti slung the firelock across her back and led her brother into the night shadows. They followed a rock beach along interlocking crater rims, keeping to the dark side of the tall and riven walls.

When they had walked long enough to be well out of sight of the wizarduke and his Falcon Guard, Poch spoke in a piteous tone, 'He scryed our doom, you know.'

She hushed him and kept her eyes on the pathless way ahead, toward the silver sill of the starry horizon.

'You're not listening, Jyo!' Poch spoke shrilly. 'He saw across time.'

'The time to come is uncertain,' said Jyoti. 'Even for those who can scry. And do you think he's any less doomed than we are? Want to go back and travel with him? He's going north. He'll be cacodemon scat in a few days.'

'He saw *our* doom,' the boy spoke sullenly. 'I know it.'

'That would be the obvious thing to see,' Jyoti said derisively. 'You don't have to be a wizard to see that we're doomed. But if we look deep enough, we'll see a way out of our doom.'

'He didn't see that.'

'Then he didn't look deep enough, did he?' she replied testily. 'Caval will. He will see a way that leads not to doom but to victory. We will destroy the cacodemons. We will slay Wrat. And we will rebuild Arwar Odawl.'

'How can you be so sure?'

'We've talked about this, Poch,' she said, trying to check the burr of impatience in her voice. 'More than a few times.'

'Don't be mad at me. It's dark, Jyo. It's better for me in the dark when I hear your voice.'

Greased shadows of starlight showed the way toward the windward face of dunes and, beyond, the rock escarpment of other extinct volcanic craters. Jyoti sighed and made an effort to soften her scolding tone. 'Then listen to me, little brother. I know it's hard for you. If we accept that we are doomed, tonight would be a good night to use this firelock on ourselves and let our souls and bodies rise into the Gulf wind and ascend with the nocturnal tide. Would you prefer that?'

'No!' he replied at once. 'Please, I don't want to die. I don't want to be doomed.'

'Then we shall live,' she affirmed with a smile. 'We shall find Caval. We have taken the shortest route to him. If we had approached from the south, we would have had to cross the Spiderlands and climb through the Malpais Highlands. Riding the black dirigible north to the Qaf has saved us many days of wandering.'

'But look at this place!' Poch cried. He squinted with disdain at the austere terrain of flints, dunes, and reefs of naked rock. 'Could the Spiderlands be worse?'

Jyoti cast a baleful look at him and refused to condone his question by a reply.

'The regent said there are trolls here.' Poch studied both epaulets of niello eye charms to be absolutely certain no trolls were currently in their vicinity. 'Have you ever actually seen a troll?'

'No.'

'I think we're going to.' He looked out on the great expanse of wild and stony terrain before them, silvery gray and blotched with impenetrable darkness. 'It's a long way to go without seeing them, if they're really here.'

'You fret too much, little brother. We have a firelock to protect us.'

'And how did we ever think we were going to cross these badlands without one?' he asked in an accusatory tone.

She shrugged off his complaint. 'I tried to buy one on the airship and at every trade-port along the way, but no one would sell to us.'

'Sure. They knew who we are. They don't want the Dark Lord charging them with helping their enemies. We were lucky to get passage.'

'We rode as unregistered cargo, that's why. But a firelock can be traced.'

'So, what *would* we have done out here without a firelock?' Poch challenged.

'What do you want me to tell you?' Jyoti asked with exasperation. 'That I've thought this all through? You know everything I know.'

Poch shuffled onward silently for a spell, then spoke dimly, 'Tell me again, Jyo.'

'We're going to find Caval.'

'And then?'

'We will return to Arwar Odawl.' She spoke in a flat tone,

mechanically. 'We're going with Caval into the archives. They are vaulted in the city's core. No harm has come to them. They were designed to be indestructible. Designed for a tragedy such as this.'

'And we'll find the magic there to destroy the cacodemons,' Poch said with dry sarcasm. 'That is, *if* there is a magic to be found that can work against them.'

'Our archives are the oldest on Irth,' she answered his doubt. 'Older than the most venerable sanctuaries or even the ancient temple at the Cloths of Heaven.'

'Yeah, yeah.' Poch kicked a stone violently and sent it skidding ahead, striking small sparks along the way. 'We're the oldest family on Irth. Older than Charm. And now we're old and dead.'

'Not dead so long as we yet live,' she insisted. 'That is why we cannot fail. To all Irth, we are emblems of tradition. That is why Wrat seeks to destroy us.'

'Don't call him Wrat.'

'That is his name.'

'Maybe it was,' Poch conceded glumly. 'But now he is Hu'dre Vra. And we don't know that he wants to kill us.'

Jyoti stopped walking and stared at her brother with disbelief once again. 'You ninny – he destroyed our family, our city – everything!'

'To force submission from the others,' Poch explained. 'He chose the smallest of the cities.'

'And the terror in Dorzen that we heard about on the airship?' she asked, brittlely. 'The cruelties of Romut? What of that?'

'The Dark Lord wants vengeance against the wizarduke for having broken the Bold Ones.' He leaned forward inquisitively. 'And were the Bold Ones evil? They were but scavengers striving for something greater. Lord Drev broke them to preserve his hold on power – to protect all the Peers.'

Jyoti stood arms akimbo, her features scrawled with disbelief. 'And so we should submit to the murderer of our parents, the slayer of our people, the destroyer of our city?'

'We will die if we don't. The wizarduke saw it. You know that. He scryed our doom.'

'Wrat will kill us if we submit.'

'I think not.' Poch crossed his arms and spoke matter-of-factly, 'We are the last of the oldest brood. I believe Hu'dre Vra will preserve us, for tradition. Conquerors want validation. We can offer him that by submission. He won't kill us. He will make a showcase of us. And we will live on to continue our brood into the next era of Irth's history. It will not be the first time that our clan has adapted to survive.'

'I can't believe you are saying this.' She dropped her arms to her sides and continued walking. Over her shoulder, she threw a question, 'Have you no love for Mother and Father? For all our brood?'

'They are dead.' Poch strode beside her, staring hard at her with conviction. 'We don't have to die just because they died. We can choose to live.'

Jyoti shook her head. 'Don't do this to me, little brother.'

'Do what?' He edged his voice with scorn. 'Disobey you? I don't want you to think for me any more. I'm over 5,000 days old. You can stop being my know-it-all sister now.'

Again, she stopped in her tracks and turned abruptly to face him. 'I am not just your sister any more, Poch. I am your margravess. I lead our brood now.'

'Our *brood*!' He spat the last word. 'We are no brood. Our brood are corpses. It's just you and me, sister. Just you and me.'

'Even so, I am margravess,' she persisted with authority. 'And you will obey me.'

'Or what?' He pushed close to her, his features tight. 'You can't make me obey you.'

Jyoti fumed, speechless. Then she pulled herself away from her brother's angry stare and continued hiking in long furious strides.

Poch hurried to keep up with her. 'When we get out of here,' he promised, 'I'm going my own way.'

'Why wait?' she shot back. 'Use the aviso. Call for your beloved Dark Lord. I'm sure his cacodemons would be delighted to pick you up.'

He trailed after her silently for a while and then admitted, 'I don't want to go alone.'

Jyoti hissed a rueful laugh. 'Why? Don't you want to be a conqueror's showcase specimen?'

'You have to come,' he pressed. 'You're the margravess.'

'Oh, is that it?' she sneered at him. 'I am the margravess. That is the truth. I am the margravess who is going to destroy Wrat. I will never submit to him. If you're going over to the enemy, little brother, you go alone.'

They walked on in silence through that night of starfire and the strange contours of rocks. And they walked on in silence well into the radiant day of glaring sands and thermal gravel beds, toward pale mountains that seemed to float upon a lake of shimmery nothingness. And when at last they did speak it was small and routine talk of water, Charm, and the lifeless distances between them and the conjectural snow ranges of the south.

From atop blue mesas far to the north, the wizarduke watched them until they became so small in his niello eye charms that they vanished as motes among the pocks of craters at the rim of the world. Drev looked up and stared across the lonely void. His prescience had been clear about the margravess and her brother. They would soon become cacodemon scat. With their deaths, the brood of Odawl would become extinct, tragic precursor to the fate of all the Peers if Wrat continued unchallenged.

*But what counterstroke to an invulnerable foe*, Drev pondered, *except evasion?*

The Falcon Guard asked no questions of their lord. They marched with him along the high mesas, silent and alert as if their privileged destiny were to patrol these nether limits to the end of their days. Leboc alone wondered aloud at their ultimate destination As they descended the narrow defiles that switchbacked among stratifications of purple and maroon rock, the marshal addressed his lord. 'Zul will be infested with cacodemons by the time we arrive there.'

'We are not bound for Zul.' The wizarduke swept his arm toward the anvils of surrounding mesas. 'This is my dominion now, Leboc. Here I am lord. Lord of the nethermost.'

That silenced Leboc, for in his commander's reply he heard madness. *And how could he not be deranged?* the marshal asked himself. *How can any of us pretend to sanity now that chaos runs rampant upon Irth?*

Drev felt into the silence surrounding him. Modulating his breathing to induce trance in rhythm with the cadence of the squad's march, he searched ahead through time. Scry shadows appeared upon the seabed of lava below. Phantoms of wandering refugees from Zul crisscrossed the pan of cracked volcanic glass. Among them would be charmwrights, witches, mentors, sages, and workers of sorcery. It was his task to cull them in his prescience and find those who had knowledge of cacodemons, who knew how to fight them.

The wizarduke could not accept that anything in the world was immortal. And though the world was a huge place and hid many secrets, all secrets could be disclosed by persistent inquiry. And there, in the Qaf, where those with Charm would flee to escape the invaders, he was convinced he would find the ones who knew how to unravel the strength of cacodemons. *But how to identify them?* he asked himself, gazing upon the stark promontories crowding the low range of gravel flats, albino dunes, and scorched cinder fields. Ghosts abounded, shades of exiles yet to trespass these badlands.

He ignored those with the brightest Charm. They were powerful, certainly wealthy, but they could not help him. Instead, he fixed upon apparitions with a dull but lustrously iridescent and compacted shine. The muted glow told him that those individuals had fewer power wands and less mental amplification from hex-gems like rat-stars and sharpeyes. And the iridescence was the hallmark of mirror-chips, trance-inducers popular among charmwrights and frequently used in sorcery.

While still high in the mesas, the wizarduke selected several promising candidates among the time shadows and carefully marked in his memory the pathless vectors these blue, dusky rose specters followed across the wasteland. He intended to meet each of these travelers, and he adjusted his direction through the directionless land accordingly.

The vaporous quality of the vision assured him that the first encounters were yet days away. The squad marched on in silence. The land demanded strict discipline, and the Falcon Guard were well matched to this arduous task. If Leboc or any of his squad entertained fears for their duke's sanity, none showed it.

There was scarce time. Trolls abounded in the graphite hills and often came charging down the slopes, only to scatter and flee the moment the troopers unholstered their firecharms. No shot was fired in panic, for all knew the terrible consequences of such rashness.

Yet, careful as they were to favor the hard footing of rock ledges and shale clines, they still left scattered, intermittent tracks. And on a wine-red morning, the wizarduke's niello eye charms warned of approaching cacodemons. Two of the monsters scuttled across the desert floor reading the squad's spoor, tracking them remorselessly across the rocky terrain. Others circled lazily overhead.

'We must separate,' Leboc realized. He raised the visor of his raptor hood, the better to sniff the air. An acrid taint of sulfur soughed from the west, from an infernal rill of volcanoes beyond dense hillocks of sand. 'You'll hide there, my lord, with half the guard. The others will come with me and lead the cacodemons that way.' He pointed east toward an outlandish skyline of standing rocks, needle-spires, and twisting stone arches.

Time shadows blurred at this juncture of fate and mortality, and the wizarduke could see no viable alternative. Like frightened animals, he and five of the Falcon Guard burrowed into the sandy hillocks. Leboc and the four other troopers swept away the tracks of the duke and his escort with their cloaks and clambered up the eastern inclines of pea gravel and rock shards into the eroded architecture of the wilderness maze. Protected from smothering by his power wands and a mask of theriacal opals, the wizardduke lay perfectly still as the cacodemons clattered past. Their avid breathing sizzled, and he could also hear the gnashing of their abdominal faces, hungry for prey. He watched them in his eye charms as they scratched at the flinty ground with their talons. The tiny black beads of eyes embedded in their lobed brows almost grazed the ground, reading the tracks of Leboc and his troopers. Then they turned their horned and scaly backs on where Drev and his guard lay interred, and scampered howling toward the monument rocks.

The howls yammered weirdly as the cacodemons bounded through the stony labyrinth. The eelish creatures ferreted into every shadowed alcove and toppled poised boulders in frustration. A trooper screamed and was hauled out of a kettle hole and into the sky, snagged in the claws of a leering cacodemon.

His firelock fired point blank at blue-white maximum intensity and did not faze the beast. Other cacodemons flocked closer, slashing at him, ripping him apart as they fought for gobbets of his flesh. And in moments, he was devoured.

Two other troopers were eventually found, dragged from under rock shelves and consumed alive by ravening fangs. The cacodemons circled overhead for several hours, searching for any others who might have eluded their voracity. Then, obeying alien instincts, they drifted away through the shimmering sky and vanished altogether into the heat of the empty day.

## What Lives After

❖—I—❖

Ripcat made his way silent and unseen through nightbound Saxar to the industrial district. If eyes were to peer out from the enormous walls of the assembly hangars with their many cavehole windows hung with concrete drippings and sumac, they would have glimpsed only a fluid shadow slinking quickly over the canal spans and along the tow-paths.

The thief knew well these back alleys behind the warehouses and silos. His curved green eyes gathered transient threads of tarnished starlight sifting down through mazy heights of trestles, winches, buttresses, duct pipes and cables, and shaped sight where others would have seen stubborn darkness. And he accomplished this night-vision without amulets.

On his half-naked person, clothed only in black cord trousers and ankle-slung boots, he wore no devices whatsoever. Devoid of Charm, he moved undetected by most watchers. Niello eye charms alone could spot him and then only if the person using them knew what to look for. Automatic devices relied upon disturbances in Charm fields caused by the intrusion of amulets. Even a single newts-eye could trigger the sensitive alarms employed in this mercantile district. But Ripcat moved everywhere unseen.

Without Charm, the thief had to endure the limits of weariness and its sole remedy, sleep. But on this night, he was well rested and moved with his usual lithe grace. His partner, Dogbrick, had informed him of a cache of unmarked trance wrap ripe for the taking, because the shriekers who guarded it were gang-rotated in a known pattern and timetable. All he had to do was move fast.

Along a stone ribbon-walk above the torpid black water of the canal, he padded, occasionally running deftly along iron railings to avoid pools of sulfurous light cast from polelamps. At the masonry arches of the viaduct leading to the factory that held his treasure, he paused to ponder the best way in and out.

He stood atop a gnarled trashbin on the far side of the canal from the building he intended to burglarize. From there, he could see the pocked brickwork of the imposing walls devoid of windows or shuttle chutes. Blue globed lanterns shone at the attic towers. The owners' painted names in giant block letters offered faint outlines where thousands of days of daylight had bleached all clarity.

Ripcat lowered his sights to the tarred street and a ditchside water main behind a rusty mesh fence. No other thief would think of such an approach, for the street, the ditch, the fenced foreyard with its stacked lumber and crates, and the grating through which the waterpipe entered the building itself were all scrutinized by charm alarms. He could see them hanging in plain view from the fence poles – crystal pendules aglow with dusty blue light.

Quickly, he climbed into the vaulted undercarriage of the viaduct and crossed beneath the bridge to the far side. Soft as soot, he dropped from the girders and landed on the pillowblock where the bridge joined the factory lading yard. The canal's black murk lapped susurrantly beneath him, spooling its dank odors and slow voice under the bridge lamps and into farther gloom as he scuttled along the embayment and then climbed up on to the tow-path.

He lurked for a while among a warren of ramshackle tool shops opposite the factory, to be certain that no one patroled the canal bank or the narrow street. Convinced that he alone occupied this reeking corner of the city, he boldly crossed the street, walked up and over the tall fence, ignoring atop the posts the crystal davits of charm alarms whose blue inner lights saw him not at all, and plopped soundlessly into the cinder lot of the foreyard.

The ditch that bedded the water main led him to the grating that greeted the pipe and blocked all other entry. Another charm alarm stood watch above the grating, and he paid it no heed as he removed a small folding ratchet wrench from his bootcuff and began working the grating bolts. Corrosion welded all but two of the bolts, yet the thief managed, with much pushing and pulling, to wedge open a gap just large enough for him to squeeze through.

Inside, darkness reigned. Acrid machine odors directed him across cracked concrete and under low-hung pipes to an iron stairwell. Up he spiraled, and the hatchway above opened upon a cavernous assembly den with worktables, blocks-and-tackle, drill presses, milling cutters, hoists, and weigh beams all stenciled in the sepia glow of night lanterns.

At the far end, scaffolding ladders ascended to a catwalk that receded into chambered distances of cable rigging and pulleys. Up there, at the most remote extreme, the thief knew he would find a cage stacked with bolts of trance wrap waiting to be boxed and shipped. But before he dared make his move, he had to wait until he spotted the pass-through of the guards on their rotation. Then he knew he would have just enough time to traverse the lengthy catwalk, retrieve as many bolts as he could carry, and flee. If he was slow or for some unforeseen reason the sentinels returned early on their rotation, he could expect to die, for these were no human guards but shriekers.

Several heartbeats later, the next rotation passed through. From his floor-level vantage, he watched the portals to adjacent assembly dens open and the gang of shriekers enter. Their crisp green uniforms and sturdy boots did not hide the fact that the guards were corpses animated by Charm and programmed to attack and kill all intruders. Families desperate for Charm sold their dead to the factories instead of releasing them into the nocturnal tide.

Ripcat suppressed a shiver at the sight of the shriekers' lipless grins and mauve teeth. Their varnished skulls peered through masks of tattered face-flesh, upturned eye sockets agleam with charmlight. Empowered by Charm, they were lethally swift, and powerful enough to tear a man's limbs from their sockets.

He lay perfectly still, the hatch above him cracked only a hair, until the shriekers completed their silent round and departed the den through the portals they had entered. Then, with liquid speed, he darted out of the stairwell and charged over the chill buckled linoleum the length of the den, hurdling workbenches and bounding between machine stations to the scaffold ladder.

It creaked from his weight as he flew up it, and the catwalk rattled under his sprinting legs with iron vibrations that echoed through the vacant chambers. He had to slow down or risk alerting the shriekers, and he cursed under his breath.

The cage he sought showed itself in the blue radiance of three large charm alarms set in the groined rafters. The trance wrap within the cage stood stacked in a pyramid of crisscrossed bolts. The agate fabric gleamed with citrine swirls and cinnabar depths like a prismatic gold liquid. Its Charm was sealed within so long as the crimson binding cord securing each bolt remained in place. The thief knew this, yet he thought he sensed chimerical images within the gaudy luster of the cloth – spectral revenants of his own dangerous dreams: a sable-haired young woman with languorous eyes among quicksilver glimpses of an autumn forest riddled with thin shafts of daylight and elvish shadows.

Ripcat dropped his startled gaze and concentrated on the work at hand. The three azure spotlights from the charm alarms shimmered brightly against the blue fur of his shoulders and scalp as he bent before the cage door to retrieve a lockpick from his bootcuff. A few nimble twists of the pick, and the door slid aside before the heap of luminous trance wrap.

Gathering seven bolts into his arms, he dashed from the cage and had to restrain himself from pounding along the squeaky catwalk. Yet, even so, his greater weight elicited metallic groans from his trespass. Less than halfway to the scaffold ladder, a portal below opened and in strode a shrieker, its scabrous head swiveling to search the heights and its blue-flame eyes flaring hotly at the sight of him.

A piercing cry, like torn sheet metal, screeched from the guard's burned mouth.

Ripcat burst into a mad run, hopelessly desperate to attain the ladder before others appeared. The shrieker who had found him ran for the ladder as well, gliding with a supernatural speed. He was half up it by the time the thief reached the end of the catwalk, and four other shriekers crowded below, screaming shrilly as they bunched together, readying to climb up after him.

With his teeth, the thief untied the crimson binding cord on the top bolt and, holding the loose end, dropped the trance wrap in an unraveling flutter. He whipped the fallen length of fabric so that the shining cloth snared the climbing shrieker and entangled the others.

A lucid dream snapped through Ripcat before he released his grip on the trance wrap: The sable-haired woman skipped laughing through windfallen yellow leaves, and sunlight winked around her in a thousand toppling gold coins. A scream cracked the chill blue afternoon and jolted him awake.

The shriekers lay below, collapsed upon themselves, entranced by the gold fabric draped over them, dreaming obscurely in their mummied brains of their past lives and the dire events that broke them. They twitched and moaned but made no move to stop Ripcat as he came down the ladder and hopped over them.

With the alarm sounded, the thief flaunted all pretense of secrecy and hurried toward the lading gate, feet slapping loudly on the warped linoleum. Portals banged open, and shriekers piled into the assembly den, caterwauling raucously. They closed in from all sides, blocking the paths to the exits.

Ripcat hopped on to a work table, kicked a bin of tacks at the crêpe-faced guard before him, jumped to the next table, and chewed off the crimson binding cord on another bolt. With a body-twisting heave he sent the bolt spinning toward the lading gate, paying out trance wrap over the heads of the shriekers. He followed, chewing off another binding cord as he vaulted over the work tables.

From the hook end of a large weigh beam, he pierced the wrap, adroitly threw the bolt over a ceiling pipe, and sent the beam spinning. Streamers of trance wrap flashed gold through the assembly den, and he scampered under and leaped over the whipping fabric, springing to the workbenches and daring to pounce atop the bodies of the fallen shriekers.

At the lading gate, he dropped two more bolts in his frantic effort to unfasten the locking bar before the remaining shriekers reached him with their gluey hands. The din of their angry cries lashed him. Afraid to glance over his shoulder, he concentrated on unclasping the bar. The gates banged open before his thrown weight, and he hurled himself into the night.

The shriekers came after him. Siren howls cutting into the darkbound city, they flung themselves off the lading dock and spurted in swift pursuit with grasping arms and streaking fire-cored eye sockets. No human runner could have escaped them.

But Ripcat was not wholly human. With fleet feline strength, he fled, running low and sleek, the two remaining bolts under one arm, his free arm churning. At the fence, he did not even break stride but scrambled straight up the mesh and dove from its top like a swimmer off a falls.

He landed with bent knees in the middle of the street and sprung with another prodigious leap into a lightless alley nestled among a cluster of oblique shacks and tool-and-die shops. Only after racing hard through a maze of cramped sandy lanes and finding himself in a deserted precinct of corrugated warehouses did he slow gradually to a panting halt.

Heart punching in his throat, he bent double and sucked air from between his knees. Limbic music from his contact with the unbound trance wrap back in the factory competed in his brain with the iron smell of engine drippings. He heard her voice, distinctly, nearby – his long lost love saying with a laugh, 'Look, a fairy ring in the goldenrod! Let's dance worship.'

He looked up at a cove of battered trash barrels squatting among withered pokeweeds and shook his head, trying to dislodge the dream.

A needlesharp yell shrilled from behind, and he curled about in time to see a shrieker's gray greasy face flying out of the dark. Its burnt-spider hands already clutched the sweaty air around him, its fingers like dripping candles, the bonetips showing, snatching for him.

He ducked, and the shrieker toppled over his back and spun immediately upright, clawing wildly and squealing in rage. Ripcat struck the zombie's head with the bolts of fabric and staggered the creature.

The thief flung himself backward into the trash cove, dropped the bolts, and picked up a metal barrel. He banged it sharply downward on his assailant's head, and the shrieker crumpled under the impact. Another hurled barrel rocked the living corpse to its side. Quickly, Ripcat seized the two bolts of trance wrap, leaped over the stunned shrieker, and ducked into the dense shadows of an alley.

This time he ran steadily, weaving among the many oldbrick lanes between the hangars, following the canal. He forced his aching muscles to climb mossgrown stairs of ill-joined cobbles to a trolley station on a terrace high above the industrial hell of the city. Then, with the bolts dropped between his feet and both hands clutching his heaving lungsore ribs, he peered down at the inkwash of midnight shadows and the jammed factory yards below.

No shriekers were visible, and he raised his weary face gratefully to the starblown darkness. Then he looked about to orient himself. This was Hiphigh Street, a small avenue of fishmonger stalls and vegetable stands, shut for the night. He picked up the two bolts and shuffled down the street several long blocks, past empty auction platforms and tiers of vacant market bins.

A clay gully path between a meat mart and a vegetable and fruit booth, both shuttered for the night, invited him. He hobbled into the dark, pressed his back against a vine-tangled wall, and sidled to the ground exhausted. Clutching the bolts of trance wrap to his chest to keep from floating away in the nocturnal tide, he nodded to sleep and dreamt of her again.

He saw her with the deep violet haze of autumn woods behind her and yellow blotches of goldenrod and fallen leaves around her. She stood in a fairy ring of mushrooms, the fungi like a talismanic circle of boneshards, and she was laughing with a childlike glee, her black hair brushing across her face in the afternoon's rimpling wind.

He woke with a salty taste of sorrow in his mouth. Morning's auburn light seeped into the alley, and he heard boisterous noises of the markets setting up for another day. From a stack of emptied fruit crates, he extracted a burlap liner and wrapped the bolts. A newts-eye bought him a honey peach and two blue bananas, and he ate breakfast as he slowly made his way along the street listening to the day's fervid gossip about the fall of Arwar Odawl and the terror of the Dark Lord. Business slowed almost to a standstill as the populace awaited dire events.

At the corner of Hiphigh and Dark Meander, he came to a station with an empty trolley. As soon as he boarded, it continued its route, and he sat in the back eating his fruit and watching the city trundle by. A gaggle of young students on their way to lyceum boarded, yammering about cacodemons, and hushed when they saw him. A charmwright and her two apprentices got on, glanced darkly at him, and continued muttering about Saxar's vulnerability, wedged as it was between the Qaf and the Gulf.

At Everyland Street, Ripcat disembarked and caught an uptown carriage so crowded he had to stand on the runner and hang from the side. He changed again at Cold Niobe and rode that trolley up Dreamborne Boulevard where Dogbrick and Whipcrow awaited him in a grove of jigsaw trees.

'That's it?' Whipcrow griped when Ripcat removed the two bolts of trance wrap. The factory manager pulled back the cowl of his cloak and released the sticky spikes of his black hair. 'Just two bolts? There must have been two dozen in that cage.'

'Shriekers were all over me,' Ripcat explained.

Whipcrow's dark, narrow face squinted with distrust. 'You're holding the rest. That would not be smart. We have a deal.'

Ripcat frowned angrily and gave the bolts to Dogbrick.

'Ah, Whipcrow—' Dogbrick shook his maned head. 'If you are smart at all you will apologize at once to my partner. At once.'

Whipcrow stared hard into the slanted animal eyes of Ripcat, recognized the taut promise of violence, and backed away a step. His thin blue lips sneered. 'You can't cheat me, anyway. I'll find out from the factory report what was stolen.'

Ripcat turned away in disgust and left Dogbrick to haggle with the informer. He walked through the grove to a grassy slope overlooking banks of flowering hedges. Across the tops of the blossom shrubs, he cast a slow gaze, over fields shelving a blue vein of stream that fell in frothy torrents among green boulders. That was the Millgates. A crowd thronged there from the sedgy fringe of the cascade up the tilted sward to a slate ridge, where the silver figure of 100 Wheels addressed them.

The thief raised his line of sight above the Millgates and its enclosure of opulent estates and fixed on a flock of black dirigibles afloat over the city skyline. He had often watched the trade vessels come in but had never seen so many at one time. They would be filled with refugees, he reasoned. The Dark Lord terrorized the south and people from every city would flee to remote Saxar to escape the cacodemons.

A growl from Dogbrick turned Ripcat, and he saw his partner and Whipcrow glaring at each other and tearing between them the burlap sack that contained the trance wrap. He slouched toward them.

'The diligent Crow insists on delivering our trance wrap to a charmwright to be cut into three equal segments,' Dogbrick explained. 'I say we go together.'

'Then let's go,' Whipcrow insisted and tugged at the sack, ripping it further.

'I thought we had met here so we could watch the festivities below,' Dogbrick said, annoyed. 'We will go later.'

'Not later,' Whipcrow scolded. 'Now. I want to reach this charmwright while he is still in his shop.'

Dogbrick snarled. 'Don't make me angry. I want to see the surgeons stir up the rabble. That's why we're here. We'll go later.'

'I'm going now.' Whipcrow spoke harshly. 'I will deliver your shares here tomorrow morning.'

'Anything can happen in a day.' Dogbrick took the bolts of fabric firmly back into his hands. 'We go together or not at all.'

'You don't trust me, Dogbrick?' Whipcrow's thin face axed forward irately. 'These two bolts would not be ours to share if I hadn't told you where to find them.'

'So what?' Dogbrick pulled the bolts against his massive chest, covering his amulet harness. 'Getting it took all the risk.'

'And what did *you* have to do with getting it?' Whipcrow's sharp features twisted derisively. 'You did nothing. This prize should be shared between me and the Cat alone.'

'How would you even know of the Cat if it weren't for me?' Dogbrick showed his fangs.

'Enough!' Ripcat seized from Dogbrick the trance wrap in its shredded burlap. 'I don't want any of it. Split it in two.' He shoved one bolt at an amazed Whipcrow and slapped the other one into his partner's hands. 'That's all there is,' he said to Whipcrow, fixing him with a green stare dark as coming nightfall. 'I didn't hide any of it.'

'I'll know if you did,' Whipcrow said harshly, sliding the bolt of trance wrap under his cloak and gliding away. 'I'll know. And I'll make you pay.'

The thin man hurried off and soon disappeared among the

crazy quilt shadows thrown by the jigsaw trees.

'You gave that parasite a small fortune,' Dogbrick groused. Then, his heavy features recomposed to a sly, tongue-wagging smile. '*Did* you put a few bolts aside?'

Ripcat flung a hot stare at him and turned his back. He ambled to the slope and sat atop a boulder overlooking the Millgates.

Dogbrick joined him and leaned against the rock. 'I will share my trance wrap with you. Even though I think giving half to clever Crow was foolish.'

Ripcat shook his pug head. 'I don't want it.'

The large man scowled with disbelief. 'You earned it, and more.'

Ripcat shushed him. 'Use your eye charms so we can listen to what 100 Wheels is saying down there.' He pointed with his chin to the Millgates, where a bright platinum figurine paced on a natural stage of shale before an attentive crowd.

Dogbrick obligingly unsnapped a black-amber power wand from a side panel of his harness and the niello eye charms from the shoulders. But before he set them down, he tried once more to understand his partner. 'Stop evading me, Cat, and tell me why you won't take your share of the trance wrap. Is it perhaps warped or stained?'

Ripcat regarded him coolly. 'It makes me dream.'

Dogbrick huffed, perplexed at this answer. 'Of course. We all know that. But you don't have to *use* it, you silly beast. Sell it. You could get many incredible amulets with one of these bolts.'

'I have all the amulets I need in my trove,' Ripcat responded indifferently. 'I've already a bag of hex-gems, sharpeyes, and rat-stars. And in my time I've stolen whole crates of power wands. More loot than I could ever have used. I don't want any more.'

'Then why did you dance with the shriekers?' Dogbrick persisted. 'My stars, Cat, they could have ripped you to pieces.'

'It was a last dance. I did it for you.'

'For me? What do you mean?'

'Don't you see? No festival last night. 100 Wheels is down

there recruiting factory laborers and thieves. And all everybody's talking about is the Dark Lord. Look—' He gestured to the sunny towers of the city and the long line of black dirigibles stacked in the clear sky around the sky bund. 'The refineries are shut down. When was the last time that happened?'

'They smell doom,' Dogbrick moaned. 'The Dark Lord comes. I keep thinking it's all a bad dream.'

'Would it were,' Ripcat mumbled. 'So, I wanted to score big this last time for you. I wanted to repay you for making a place for me in Saxar.'

Dogbrick waved aside his gratitude. 'You didn't really need me. You would have made your own way.'

'Perhaps.' Ripcat shook his head in grim remembrance. 'But when you found me in the Qaf, I remembered nothing. I still don't. At least you helped me make a life for myself. You showed me how I could steal what I needed from those who had more than they needed.'

'Ah,' Dogbrick acknowledged airily with an upraised finger thick with callus and hooked with a yellow nail. 'More importantly, I showed you the folly of giving your loot away to the impoverished, did I not? You thought you could help. Ha! You thought you could change their lives with your anonymous gifts. How many amulets, prisms, and quoins did you foolishly leave on the doorsteps of the indigent? You were most benighted, almost as a child, in those early days. You did not then realize that when a life has not succeeded, it is not because of lack but because there has been a misjudgment between what is righteous and what is merely so. No amount of amulets can correct such a misjudgment.'

'You have taught me a great deal,' Ripcat agreed tersely. 'With this trance wrap, I have tried to repay you. I wish there were more.'

'It's a handsome payment, indeed.' Dogbrick patted the bolt appreciatively. 'I am grateful. And yet I do not miss your wider meaning. You think there will be no further opportunity for thieving. Am I right? Worse, you believe that Charm itself will have less significance in the days to come. Yes?'

'Shh. Listen, 100 Wheels has started.' Ripcat peered down at the Millgates.

From the waist-pouch of his harness, Dogbrick removed two metal clasps, which he used to attach the niello eye charms to either end of the power wand. 'This cannot compare to an aviso, yet it will serve,' Dogbrick said agreeably, and adjusted the couplings until static sizzled from the wands.

He climbed on to the boulder beside Ripcat and pointed the assemblage at the gathering below. Crowd noise packed the air. Grumbling to himself, he aimed the binocular eye charms at the slate ridge where Crabhat had joined 100 Wheels. The two security officers paced before the gathering, arms waving.

' . . . from the streets and alleys,' 100 Wheels spoke, her stern voice so close that it made the small hairs rise on the thieves' necks. 'If we cannot use Charm, then we will use subterfuge. We will resist by shutting down the factories, the refineries, and the shops.'

The crowd roared their approval.

'The Dark Lord will get nothing from us!' Crabhat shouted, his squat, burly body hopping, his famous spiked helmet scattering rainbow glints. 'In time, he will have to capitulate. Only we can make Saxar work. He needs us! Don't ever forget that.'

The throngs cheered, and Dogbrick lowered his improvised ear-charm. 'That it has come to this,' he moaned, shaking his head sadly. 'The very surgeons loathed and feared by all, now cheered!'

Ripcat lay back on the boulder and studied the arguments of light in the clouds while Dogbrick wandered off to find a meatstick vendor at the park's streetside. Later, with a carafe of iced blue tea and a basket of twist bread and meatsticks to share, they listened to the pipers and chorale singers hired by the factories to calm the crowd.

Afternoon cast its diamonds on the stream above the Millgates by the time 100 Wheels and Crabhat stood atop the shale ledge again. Ripcat had wearied of their exhortations and stood to depart when, without warning, he saw the dark line to the south. Initially, he thought they were more black dirigibles fleeing to Saxar's remote haven. But the cold wail of sirens from the factory cliffs made him look closer.

'Churlsbane! It's cacodemons!' Dogbrick shouted, standing. He saw them in his niello eye charms, a black, particulate line dissolving into individual flyers as they neared. His first view of a cacodemon fluffed the bronze hair all over his body and loosened his ponderous jaw. In the eye charms, he observed with distinct horror their mallet heads with spider eyes under bulbous brows, the snaggled rows of hooked fangs ringing like flames in their black snouts, and the reptile faces embedded in their torsos, blistered with drool.

Dogbrick sat down heavily, his face frozen in shock. With much coaxing, Ripcat finally budged him, and they sought cover under the rootcoils of the jigsaw trees at the mossy edge of Mirage Climb. From there, they watched the formation of flying demons dissolve. Flocks dropped into the factory district. Others spiraled down on to the residential terraces. A dozen descended on the Millgates, attracted by the crowd.

Gaudy screams flitted from below as the cacodemons set to their slaughtering. With evil design, the monsters began at the outer flanks of the multitude, lopping heads from the shoulders of runners and flaying open the backs of those who cowered.

Firelocks flared blue from the shale ledge, where the security officers had determined to test the invulnerability of the invaders. A cacodemon arced toward them, splashing flames from continuous direct strikes. In one movement, its serried whip-tail sliced through Crabhat, and his head flew high into the air, blood sparkling with the rainbows from his helmet spikes.

100 Wheels used her fabled speed to flee. In a silver blur, she reached the gravel path above the ledge before a cacodemon swooped over her and plucked her off the ground. Above the

screaming crowd, the evil beast tore her to pieces, ripped apart her silver armor and dropped the bloody gobbets like chunks of an exploded star.

The trapped people below writhed under the furious assault of the cacodemons, but there was no escape. The alien creatures circled the crowd and hacked with furious abandon, chopping at everyone that moved and seizing up in their talons the dead and the living alike by their ribcages. The cacodemons rolled in the bloody mire and came up with entrails dangling from the hideous faces in their abdomens.

Terrified by what they witnessed and afraid to be seen, the thieves hidden in the rootcoils atop Mirage Climb did not move. Dogbrick pressed his face into the loam and moaned. Ripcat watched keenly. Searching for some weakness among the enemy, and finding none, he tapped his friend's shoulder and whispered, 'We must go.'

'Where?' Dogbrick asked, his big features woeful with fear.

'Away from Saxar.' Ripcat squirmed out from under the jigsaw trees.

'Into the Qaf?' Dogbrick scrambled after him. 'There are trolls out there.'

'Charm can kill trolls.' Ripcat moved quickly through the grove, and his large partner took heavy strides to keep up.

'But the Qaf kills everything.'

'Would you rather die here?' Ripcat looked sideways through the trees down to the Millgates where the cacodemons picked vigorously among the dead. 'Saxar belongs now to the Dark Lord.'

They kept off the main paths and traversed Mirage Climb; through shrubbery lanes and dusky tunnels of interlocking trees, they eventually made their surreptitious way up through rubble gullies and junk lots strewn with broken hulks of machinery, bottomless steel drums, cast-off waterheaters and stoves, all devoid of Charm and rusting in the weeds – and finally climbed a scarp wall streaked bright with oxides.

That led them to a hardpan waste of eroded craters and ghostly salt hills pockholed with viper slots and crusty caves. This was Sky Edge, the desolate eyrie limits of the cliff city, where the thieves kept their trove of stolen treasure.

Ripcat crossed the raw landscape to one chalky sinkwell among thousands, reached in and came out with an old red leather pouch. He fastened the stuffed pouch to a loop in the waistband of his black cord trousers and walked over the caked salts to help his partner.

Unlike Ripcat, who had given away most of what he had stolen, Dogbrick had hoarded all his loot for this very day, though he could never have foreseen as dire a time as this. In a daze, he cleared out bricks and cobbles from a rime-toothed cave and pulled into the light two brass-cornered trunks, both fitted with deadware locks. From beneath his brindled beard, he removed a rat-star gem, swiped it over the skullgrin of one lock, and opened the trunk. Inside, a neat array of hex-gems, theriacal opals, witch-glass, conjure-metal, power wands, prisms, quoins, and newts-eyes smashed daylight to rainbow chips and hot shards. He placed atop this lucre the bolt of trance wrap he had been hugging during their flight from Mirage Climb, mournfully closed the lid, and locked it with another pass of the rat-star.

With a sad shake of his head, he announced, 'A lifetime's labor, and all of it worthless in a world of cacodemons.'

'Not all worthless,' Ripcat retorted. 'Theriacal opals will still heal wounds and rat-stars sharpen minds.'

'Ah, friend, *again* you succumb to the useful and disregard the true,' Dogbrick groused. 'Don't you see? I could have retired years ago if all I wanted was a hoard of useful amulets. I've striven all my life for something else, something far more precious.'

'So I have heard,' Ripcat said with a rueful smile. 'You seek the truth.'

'Yes, truth!' The beastman banged a frustrated fist atop the trunk, and dust sprites danced mockingly around them in the circling breeze. 'No more hiding in shadows. No more deceiving and stealing. No more lies to defend us against security officers and other thieves. I want truth, which is, when all is said and done, nothing other than simplicity. I want truth for myself at last. I want the simple life of a man with his own home, in a city with civilized amenities available for those who can afford them. The simple life of truth. And this treasure could have bought me that. *Could have* – the two most reproachful words a person can speak.'

Ripcat met his partner's scowl with a cool slant green gaze. 'All this Charm will get us across the Qaf.'

'No, my friend.' Dogbrick pulled the rat-star gem through the skull mouth of the other deadware lock. 'Those hex-gems will make our life comfortable on the other side. But this other trunk here, *this* is our passport through the Qaf.'

He opened the second trunk and revealed two blunt-nosed rifles with chrome barrels scaled green-blue from heat as if wrapped in metallic snakeskin. The black metal housings and zebrawood shoulder stocks had been chiseled and sanded to remove military insignia. Gold-jacket charge cartridges packed the trunk, and they, too, had been filed to remove identification codes.

'Firelocks,' Ripcat said with cold surprise. 'Only the Peers can issue these. Where did you get them?'

'Where do we get anything?' Dogbrick responded with a wry smile.

'If we encounter regal troopers in the Qaf or beyond and they find us with these, we will face summary execution,' Ripcat stated flatly. 'Possession of firecharms by citizens is a capital offense.'

'Citizens?' Dogbrick weighted his voice sarcastically. 'For there to be citizens, my dear fellow, there must be a state. And the only state I see now is chaos. The Dark Lord reigns. Do you think her Ladyship Altha and her fawning gigolo Lord Hazar yet rule? I am sure that the cacodemons will serve them as they did Crabhat and 100 Wheels, eh?'

The big thief tossed one of the firelocks to Ripcat, who plucked it out of the air, hefted it, and turned it curiously in his hands.

'Do you know how to use that?' Dogbrick asked.

Ripcat shook his head.

'The trigger is useless,' his partner explained, 'unless there's a cartridge in the breech and the charge pin is set.' He flung a cartridge to his partner. 'The black end is out and the contacts go into the breech like this.' He fitted the cartridge to the gap in the black metal housing and slapped it into place. Then he gripped the slide behind the bore and pulled it back. 'This is the charge pin. Where you position this slide determines how powerful a charge the firelock will shoot. Once it's set, just aim and shoot.'

He sighted on a salt dome stained with cobalt leechings and fired a yellow bolt that flashed like a ray of daylight, almost invisible against the glare of the pan until it struck its target. Like exploding crockery, the salt dome shattered and sent chunks whirling in sparkling arcs across the blue afternoon. The râle of blasted rock echoed loudly among the alkali cones and brimstone gutterways of Sky Edge.

Ripcat peered apprehensively toward the cluttered cliffs of haze-blue Saxar. 'Let's go, Dogbrick. Before the cacodemons find their way up here.'

Dogbrick emptied his firecharm caisson and packed as many gold-jacket cartridges into the treasure trunk as would fit. Others he jammed into his amulet harness. Ripcat fitted several in the pouches of his cord trousers, and the rest they abandoned.

At the bottom of the caisson, Dogbrick had collected an assortment of military supplies: a combat vest, raptor hood and camouflage cloak, and utility belts outfitted with assault knives, coils of filament rope, flagons, compasses, and lenses. They each donned a ultility belt, and, with a few skillful cuts of a knife, Dogbrick fashioned from the raptor hood a cowl-hat for his partner. 'I have my mane, but you will need protection from the desert rays. Even the Charm of amulets has its limits in the Qaf.'

With a forsaken and ripped pallet recovered from a junk lot

below, they devised a travois and mounted the treasure trunk atop it. A length of burned-out cable cut from a gutted trolley served as a tow line, and Dogbrick affixed it to his harness and hauled his treasure after him, lilac dust roiling behind.

Firelock slung over his shoulder and cowl-hat shading his eyes, Ripcat led the way down goatpaths, through quaking heat, into the Qaf. *What a curious return*, Dogbrick thought to himself as he resignedly followed. Only five hundred days ago, he had found Ripcat wandering blind with heatstroke in this infernal landscape. Too often called a muttwit, the blond-maned thief had entered the Qaf to explore himself and determine if he was truly a man.

He laughed silently to himself at that memory, recalling how he had railed at the gypsum reefs and the sandstone arches, demanding that the heat djinns reveal his true nature to him. *How you die decides that!* the sybil in The Wise Fish had recently told him, and he knew that was the truth.

Ah, but back then he had not been clever enough to accept himself as he was. Man or mutt, his destiny depended entirely on how he behaved. A mere five hundred days ago, he had not yet realized this. He had wanted some existential evidence of his intrinsic self, of his core identity. He never found it. Instead, he had stumbled upon Ripcat.

As though reading his partner's thoughts, Ripcat said, 'Ease your mind, Brick. If you hadn't doubted yourself all those days ago, you wouldn't have been out here babbling to yourself – and I would have died then.'

'Are you thanking me, or regretting I interfered?' Dogbrick asked pointedly.

'I'm not the philosopher – you are, Dogbrick.' Ripcat spoke without taking his eyes from the blighted terrain. He watched the terrain for sand-adders, sinkholes, and troll spoor. 'I don't have the depth to regret life. You know that. You told me that. Remember? I prefer to live on the surface with my instincts.'

Dogbrick laughed aloud, and his guffaw drifted slowly out into the ashen plain of cindercones, vanishing with lonely diminutions among the carbonized rocks. 'Why, Cat, those were the most words you have ever spoken to me at one time in the five hundred days we've been together.' He barked a laugh again, and again the jocular sound curdled among the balesome hills into echoes of wistful distance. 'The circle of our union is complete. And returning to where we began inspires dread thoughts, does it not?'

Ripcat did not answer. He gauged the time to nightfall, the time when he would have to sleep again – and dream. His partner, he knew, had never slept in his life and knew of dreams only from trance inducers, such as blue beer and the wrap in the treasure trunk. Dogbrick would watch over Ripcat's body as he slept and the amulets in the red leather pouch would help, too. But they would need water, and he determined to find it before dark.

He extracted from his pouch a seeker whose gold-woven starshape encased a bauble that held pure water. Almost daily he had used this seeker to find water at Sky Edge or on the desert fringe of Everyland Park, coverts where he liked to sleep because few people visited those barren places. The seeker guided him to a monolith of nude sandstone stratified in pastel bands of buff and rose. Where the seeker's cool wind entered the slab, he struck with his assault knife, chipping away the soft rock until water seeped under his blade, oozing down the contours so perfectly transparent that only the spinning grains of sand where the flow milled in the cupped stone at his knees revealed the pool.

As they filled their flagons, Dogbrick suddenly stiffened and whispered, 'Wait. Someone approaches.' Peering into his niello eye charms, he saw a slim shadow adrift in the quaking heat haze of standing rocks that floated in mirage rootless as clouds. He had to squint to make out who it was: 'Bane! It's Whipcrow. He's tracking us with a seeker.'

Dogbrick climbed on to a ledge from where the factory manager could easily see him. The man, garbed as ever in ebon cloak and cowl, shouldered a formidable backpack and leaned heavily on a walking staff of amber glass tall as himself – a giant power wand.

'I cut a small lock of your hair,' Whipcrow greeted the large thief, 'when we met on the Devil's Wynd – to feed my seeker – in the event you dared cheat me and tried to escape.'

'Is that why you shadow us?' Dogbrick asked accusingly. 'You think we cheated you?'

'Oh no,' the slender man acknowledged at once. 'The agile Cat spoke the truth at Mirage Climb. I learned that the shriekers indeed very nearly seized him. He was most lucky to get away with two bolts of trance wrap – and his life.'

'Then why are you here?'

'The Qaf is formidable,' the informer admitted. 'Wouldn't it be better if we traveled together?'

'Nothing doing. The more there are, the easier the target for roving cacodemons,' Dogbrick said, and Ripcat stepped on to the ledge beside him. 'It is best for all that you go your own way, Whipcrow.'

'Perhaps.' His sharp chin pointed up at them. 'But hear me out: I see you carry firecharms. I should not want to be in your company if you come upon a regal squad. The penalty for bearing such weapons is death, you know. Perhaps then it is best I go my own way. In fact, I am aware that Lord Hazar has defied her Ladyship the Sorceress Altha, who wishes to capitulate to the Dark Lord. He leads a large company of troopers from Zul into the Qaf. I shall then seek to join up with them – and if we should perchance cross again here in the wilds, I will speak well for you. Though, as I say, the penalty for bearing firecharms is a swift death.'

'That is a threat, Whipcrow,' Dogbrick growled.

'Is it?' The informer cocked a wispy eyebrow. 'I do not intend to threaten, merely to warn. Of course, should you allow me to travel with you, I could help you to avoid encounters with regal troops.'

'We have our own niello eye charms,' Dogbrick said. 'We can see what's around us well enough.'

'Yes, but one who sees is also seen,' Whipcrow countered.

'Lord Hazar and his company also have niello eye charms, to be sure. But now, if you had an aviso, you could monitor their movements from a far greater distance than eye charms can see.'

'You have an aviso?' Dogbrick asked, impressed.

'Of course.' Whipcrow removed from a pocket of his cloak a smoky gray crystal, which he rubbed with his thumb until a blue tongue of flame wagged at its interior.

Static resolved to small, distant voices: '. . . oh seven hundred. Visibility unlimited. Keep to the shadowside. We want a low-profile crossing. At the basin far side, squads oh four hundred and oh six hundred deploy north, bearing two eight one. Squads oh seven hundred and oh nine hundred, fall back to leeside of the dune massifs . . .'

Whipcrow silenced the aviso. 'You may have unlimited use of this tool. All I ask is to travel in your company, under the protection of your firecharms. I can procure my own food and water, and I have ample Charm in this power wand for my needs as well as yours. I will keep fully charged all of your amulets. Do we have an agreement?'

Dogbrick looked to Ripcat. 'Whipcrow is the answer to your concern about bearing firelocks. I would feel easier myself with his aviso handy.'

Ripcat nodded. 'I have no objection. But you would travel faster without us, Whipcrow. At night, I sleep.'

'Sleep?' Whipcrow's swarthy face flinched. 'You've plenty of Charm. Why do you sleep?'

'To dream.'

Whipcrow squinted at the beastman. 'Are you mad? Dreaming is a luxury ill suited for the Qaf.'

'To remember, then.'

The informer turned his head suspiciously, thinking, *He must be mad. Who else would face shriekers for no gain?* And he wondered if seeking them out as protection against the perils of the Qaf had been such a wise idea after all. He asked, 'Remember what, Cat?'

Dogbrick spoke up first, 'He tells you, curious Crow, only because it seems we will be spending time together. He dreams to remember.'

'Who I was before.'

'Before?' Whipcrow looked inquiringly at Dogbrick, then back to Ripcat. 'You mean to say, you were not always thus?'

'I don't know.'

'I found him in the Qaf five hundred days ago,' Dogbrick revealed. 'He doesn't remember how he got here – or who he was before.'

Whipcrow clasped the jut of his chin ruminatively. 'If you want to remember, spry Cat, then why have you not sought out a worker of sorcery? Such a one could spell you back to what you were before this.'

'Better to dream.'

The dark face frowned in query.

'Don't you understand, Whipcrow?' Dogbrick squatted on the ledge to better face the factory manager. 'If my partner was but a *whole* beast that some mad magician transformed into Ripcat, then sorcery would revert him to an animal. The spell would be broken. And he would lose his humanity forever.'

'Ah – so it is better for you to dream, fearing and yearning simultaneously, to snatch rags of memory out of sleep and so to piece together your former life.' Whipcrow's jagged features relaxed with understanding. 'And what have you seen these past five hundred nights, dreamy Cat?'

'Not enough.'

Dogbrick stood impatiently. 'All right, men. We must get going, especially if we're traveling only by day.'

'But why must we stop at night?' Whipcrow asked. 'I have plenty of Charm, Ripcat. I can power sharpeye amulets to keep you wakeful and strong without sleep until we finish this damnable crossing. Once on the other side, you can continue your dreamquest.'

Dogbrick passed a hopeful look to his partner. 'It *is* dangerous sleeping out here, you must admit.'

Ripcat swung his gaze across the nitre plains to the jawbone horizon and, reading there accurately the devouring journey ahead, acceded with a reluctant nod.

'Good.' Whipcrow thumped his walking staff on the desert floor. 'I will bond a sharpeye brace for you at our next water stop. Now, let us be on our way.'

They hiked onward together in silence, Dogbrick dragging his travois of treasure behind him. Later that day, they crossed through a sandstone metropolis fashioned by the wind, replete with buttressed towers and majestic boulevards. At the far end, where the sandstone hardened to terracotta, a rill trickled under the shards, and they replenished their water. Whipcrow kept his promise and fashioned for Ripcat a neckbrace of sharpeye amulets linked with conjure-wire and clasps of hex-metal.

The thief wore the brace, and sleep did not burden him with fatigue after the calamitous fires of twilight dimmed to freezing darkness. The amulets all three wore protected them from the rigors of cold and their exertion during their steady march through the star-festered night. Throughout the next day, Ripcat experienced no weariness whatsoever during the crossing of black glass lava beds. Neither heat nor effort overcame the Charm of the amulets. Again in the frigid night, the power wand gave him indefatigable strength. Cold and exhaustion seemed like dimly recalled symptoms of some past illness he had endured and surpassed, and he concentrated flawlessly on finding the best footing across the chimeric nightscape under slurred starlight.

By the crackling counsel of the aviso, the three nomads avoided encounters with Lord Hazar's company. But there were other refugees of Saxar that they did meet, outfitted less ably for the Qaf. A party of factory workers lay sprawled across the broken scree of a bluff, their flesh shrunk to leather, and worn through to the bone in places, eroded to rags by the sandblasting wind. They had died of exposure and thirst, having fled in a panic from Saxar with inadequate provisions. One of the corpses still clutched the cheap, witch-glass seeker she had attempted to use to find water – but the tiny wallow they had clawed from the rock with their last strength stunk of sulfur acid.

Farther on, they came upon the grisly remains of a charmwrights' party, their bones and skulls scattered over the arid benchland, all snap-broken and sucked of their marrow by trolls. Their smashed and discarded amulets and shredded backpacks alone offered evidence of their identity, for all physical individuality had been devoured save their gnawed and dispersed skeletons.

The tracks of the trolls led toward slag cones and windy plateaus. The three travelers would not have chosen to go that way except that the static-chewed reports on the aviso warned them that all other directions conjoined with Lord Hazar's army. So, through the roasting day and another frosty night, they aimed toward the ragged horizon.

Toward midnight, the aviso blared with terrifying noises: 'Cacodemons! . . . Scatter! . . . Seek cover! . . . Squads disperse!' The heavy thud of calivers firing their massive charges of Charm broke up the broadcast with pulses of static. In the background, a din of rapid fire, shouts, and screams raged against the bellowing roar of cacodemons – and then, silence, abrupt and final.

Among dawn smoke, grimly climbing down the scrabbled trails of the granite tableland with the treasue trunk hauled between them, they spotted the hives of the trolls under chimney rocks and ashen hills. Lord Hazar's company had followed the shorter route around the plateaus and reached this gray place of lava dust and flint fields at midnight, and it was here that the cacodemons had found and slaughtered them.

Frozen in gruesome postures, hundred of bodies lay spraddled among the dusty outcroppings; all of them were gutted, many headless, most without limbs. The stink that fouled the air rose with the day's heat that blackened pools of ordure and blood congealed by the night's cold. Trolls by the score scurried about slathered in gore, cracking bones against rocks for the marrow.

Dozens rolled in the spilled viscera, gibbering maniacally, too stuffed to eat more yet too jubilant to depart the bounteous feast of the cacodemons' killing ground.

Whipcrow and Dogbrick turned away, horrified. But Ripcat did not avert his eyes. In a lava rock coulee, he spotted a living figure among the corpses. It was a woman soaked with reeking blood and powdered with ash. She had been hidden by the dismembered and disemboweled sprawl of the newly slain. But in moments, the creeping dawnlight would expose her to the trolls. He could tell that she sensed this and she searched wildly for another refuge, only to see in the brightening day no escape among the carnage.

To his companions' chilled amazement, Ripcat bounded down the trail, shouting to call attention to himself. Puzzled, the trolls looked up from their frenzied feeding and flared toward him. Without breaking his stride, he unshouldered his firelock and brandished it threateningly. Hooting and hissing, the trolls pulled back, the black bolts of their depthless eyes fixed hard upon him as he came pounding down the stony spill.

'Woman!' he called to the bloodslaked refugee crouched in the lava coulee. 'Come with me!'

For a moment, the woman hesitated at the summons of this beastman with the blue-furred shoulders, pug ears, and slant green eyes. She cowered until he pranced closer through the torn bodies, firelock trained on the trolls gnashing the needleteeth in their scorched snouts and bristling the green quills along their backs. Then, once more, he beckoned her with an outstretched hand – a human hand.

She climbed out of the gully and ran to him. The trolls surged forward. But again Ripcat stalled them with a flourish of his weapon, and they backed away chittering and clawing at the air.

Ripcat led the woman hurriedly up the stony slope to where Dogbrick and Whipcrow waited. When they looked back, the trolls, afraid of the firelock, had resumed their feasting and none bothered to follow.

'Tywi!' Dogbrick shouted at the sight of her, but she only gaped back mutely, too shocked to recognize him in this bleak setting.

'You know this pathetic creature?' Whipcrow asked, backing away from the blood-grimed woman.

'Yes,' Dogbrick replied pityingly, leading the stunned woman higher up the talus slide. 'She's one of the urchins I used to hire to stand watch while I worked. She's the best of the lot.'

They crossed among the granite outcroppings until they were well away from the place of slaughter. Dogbrick sat Tywi on his treasure trunk, gave her a flagon from which to drink and applied theriacal opals to her wounds. They were superficial scrapes and healed at once.

Whipcrow affixed a braid of opals to his walking staff and applied sufficient Charm to the woman to purge her of the ichor that covered her. It fell off in trickling brown streams and fluffed away in the wind, revealing a young, hollow-cheeked woman with brown hair cut bluntly short and watery blue eyes shrill with fright. Garbed in gray factory smock and worn-out cloth sandals, she surprised no one when she announced, 'I'm cold.' A stricken look fixed her haunted features, and only the residue of Charm from Whipcrow's power wand kept her free of shock. 'I bought protection from Hazar's troops – and they . . . they tried to protect us. They tried. But the cacodemons found us! You saw!'

To calm her, Dogbrick pressed into her hands a goldplate amulet studded with hex-gems and theriacal opals. She gazed at it perplexed, gripped immediately by its soothing force, and handled it with awed fingers as one who had never before touched Charm in such concentration. Her starved, crazed features relaxed.

'Tywi,' Dogbrick called to her gently. 'Do you remember me now?'

She clutched the amulet to her chest. 'Dogbrick! I thought I was dreaming! It's you, here—' She gazed at the shattered landscape.

'Come, Tywi,' Dogbrick summoned. 'We must depart this terrible place at once. It is your past now. You do not belong here, for you are what lives after. Come. Come away quickly. By this time tomorrow, we shall be out of the Qaf.'

Calmed almost to the point of trance, Tywi regarded her saviors with a dreamlike clarity, and her vision blurred with tears. 'Thanks,' she whispered and pressed the amulet harder against the hurt in her chest, squeezing Charm to the psychic wound inside her. She sought out Ripcat's oblique features. 'Thanks to you, too, friend – for coming for me.'

They moved on. All that day, as they descended the stony spillways to the cracked clay floor and traversed the desert among stony stubs of weatherworn boulders, Dogbrick laved her with philosophic chatter, hoping to fill the gaping emptiness gouged in the waif by the horrors she had endured. Whipcrow fitted together a vest of power wands from Dogbrick's trove and tailored it with conjure-wire to fit the skinny young woman.

Made strong by Charm and the care of her rescuers, Tywi hiked vigorously through the day's staggering heat and twilight's crimson wool into the crystal night. She heard all that Dogbrick said, yet listened to none of it. Whipcrow's amulets filled her with a vitality that defeated all the impoverished sorrows of her life, even the terror that had ripped her free of the others, a lone survivor.

She had never before experienced such an abundance of Charm, and she wanted to know more about Dogbrick's companions who bore such bold beastmarks and yet cared for a waif in the wilderness. But she dared not ask. She feared to disturb her salvation. She feared it would all be taken away from her, and, bereft of the healing strength of Charm, she would revert to her paupered self, again prey to terror.

So, she walked silently among the beastmen through the night that smoked her breath and yet set no chill in her flesh.

At dawn, the immensity of the terrain revealed snow mountains to the south, dim and blue. Ripcat parted from the others, announcing he would seek more water and would reconnoiter at a windowrock of red stone just visible on the far side of a cracked bed of smoking slag.

Instead, he disappeared among the steaming kiln rocks and used his greater speed and agility to dash ahead to the windowrock. There, he removed the neckbrace of sharpeye amulets and left it on the sill of the rock with the firelock, the cowl-hat, and the utility belt where the others would find them.

The silver rinds of Nemora and Hellsgate hung in the day sky as he moved on his solitary way toward the snow ranges. He had repaid the kindness of Dogbrick by risking his life for the trance wrap, and he had kept his word to his partner and Whipcrow and escorted them across the Qaf. He had taken nothing of theirs for himself. He moved free of all ties through the shimmering heat and across cracked rock plates toward blue mountains and a future that held his past in his dreams.

# The Cloths of Heaven

❖

In his niello eye charms, Dogbrick watched Ripcat wander away into the ruinous landscape, his narrow image inverting in the heat lens above the desert floor so that he seemed to walk on the sky, head brushing the dry rocks below. The large thief said nothing to the others until they reached the windowrock, where they recovered the firelock, amulet-brace, and garments that Ripcat had left for them to find.

'He's mad,' Whipcrow determined. 'He can't survive without Charm.'

'He is another order of man,' Dogbrick said and strapped the firelock to the treasure trunk.

'I do not think he is a man at all,' Whipcrow spoke with annoyance. 'What man would walk on into the wilderness without firecharms or amulets? He is a jungle cat imperfectly disguised as a man by some demented wizard.'

'He's a brave man,' Tywi said softly.

'For you he was,' Whipcrow admitted. 'But for us he is simply gone.'

'He left us so he could continue to dream,' Dogbrick understood. 'He knows he would only impede us on the path of our destinies by stopping each night to sleep.'

'Good.' Whipcrow slipped the neckbrace of sharpeyes into his pack. 'Now we are free of him. Ahead are the Malpais Highlands. Among its numerous dales and valleys we can hide from the cacodemons.'

They trudged on across the sooty and rusted terrain, and by noon scrub grass and nettle weeds began to appear among the windshaped boulders. The snow ranges that had floated like a mirage that morning anchored themselves to the horizon beyond visible tracts of forest. Nightfall, full of zealous colors and soaring cloud castles, found them on a grassy field under the dark talismans of tall trees. They stopped to recharge their amulets with Whipcrow's massive power wand, and they sat in the swaying grass under the pale stars looking back the way they had come.

'The Qaf,' Whipcrow spoke with thick pride from under the cowl of his dark cloak. 'We crossed the Qaf. We can survive anything now.'

'Even cacodemons?' Dogbrick questioned, arching a blond eyebrow.

'They have no Charm,' Whipcrow said. 'They cannot see us from afar. So all we must do is be where they are not.'

'And how is that to be done?' Dogbrick took from a pouch in his belt a packet of honey berries and served the two others.

'Clearly, we must stay away from the cities,' Whipcrow replied, munching desultorily on a handful of the berries. 'We must make a life for ourselves in remote places. At least here there will be food. We've lived on nothing but these damn berries and Charm for days. I hunger for some real food. Perhaps we will find a hamlet with an inn. Though, more likely, we will have to make do with what we can forage.'

Dogbrick groaned. 'My whole life, I've only known Saxar. I labored all my days to earn my way to some truth in that city. And now – now success means finding a tasty tuber! All my efforts in Saxar are worthless.'

'Not worthless, sturdy Dog.' Whipcrow gave a stick of nutmeal to each of his companions and gnawed on one himself. 'You have your treasure. Keep your power wands under the gaze of the Abiding Star often enough and they will stay well charged and run your amulets for a lifetime.'

'For years I was too poor to afford even one power wand more than I needed to charge my harness,' Dogbrick remembered unhappily. 'And so I had to keep working just to replenish my amulets. Now, when I finally have enough wands to keep my amulets running, when my days of thievery are at an end, I am exiled from Saxar – from all cities. What kind of life can there be for anyone out here?' He waved his stick of nutmeal at the radiant dust of nightfall settling among the somber trees and the cobblestones of the desert.

'You at least have Charm to sustain you,' Whipcrow spoke through a mouthful of nutmeal. 'But look at this poor child. You have nothing of Charm but what we've given you, isn't that right? And am I wrong to say that you've never had Charm in your whole life?'

'Never.' She concentrated on eating her nutmeal and honey berries and did not regard the two men but kept her face lowered behind a veil of lank brown hair.

'You worked in the factories for newts-eyes and with them bought simple fare and a prism to ward off sleep.' Whipcrow nodded with the certainty of his assessment.

'I've slept,' she admitted, not looking up. 'I'm not ashamed to say it.'

'Yes.' Whipcrow continued nodding, measuring her with his tight dark eyes. 'I wager there were many nights when you had to choose between bread and prism. Better to sleep sated than be awake with an empty stomach.'

'It was like that for me as a child,' Dogbrick interjected. 'I used to crawl under trash bins and lock myself in with bricks to stay grounded while I slept.'

'The nightcrawlers will get you there,' Tywi said.

'True enough.' Dogbrick showed wan, silvery tracks on the inside of his arms. 'I still bear the scars where they crawled into my veins trying to get inside me. Where did you sleep?'

'In the factories where I worked,' she answered. 'Until I got caught – and fired. Then, inside trash bins.'

'Ugh.' Dogbrick wagged his beard in disgust. 'I've too keen a nose for that. It stank bad enough under them.'

'Out here you will have to lash yourself into the tree canopy like the first people,' Whipcrow said. He folded back his cowl and revealed an ax-thin face swarthy as leather, lips and eyes lined in blue, and black locks coiled to spikes. 'Unless you are inclined to stay with us.'

Tywi looked up fretfully, her famished face tight to her skull. 'I don't know what to do. I don't know why I ran from Saxar. Where'd I think I was going? I never been anywhere else. I just wanted to get away from the cacodemons.'

'Now we are away,' Whipcrow said in a quiet voice and placed a thin hand on the gray worn fabric that covered her thigh. 'You are an attractive woman, Tywi. I would be inclined to provide all the Charm you need if you were my consort.'

'Thanks, for sure. But I ain't worth it. I'm just a street orphan.' She hung her head again, and her sallow hair hid her face. 'I'm glad for all you done for me – saving me from the trolls, healing my fright with your Charm, cleaning me up, and getting me across the Qaf, sharing your water, and now this— You're giving me so much. But – I ain't nobody. I have nothing for you.'

Dogbrick spoke to her in a wry tone while looking hard at Whipcrow: 'I believe the amorous Crow is interested in you for who you are.'

Tywi shook her head decisively. 'I can't be yours, Whipcrow. You're a man of Charm and I'm charmless.'

'Is that it really?' Whipcrow removed his hand from her. 'You are charmless. And I? I have Charm for you. But that's not it, is it? I am not just a man with Charm, am I? I am a man with beastmarks. That *is* it, isn't it?'

'Beastmarks don't mean nothing to me,' she repeated, softer. 'It's you I don't much like.'

'Bah!' Whipcrow stood and put a hand on his amber walking stick, jangling the amulets that hung from it on coils of conjure-wire. 'Then if I am not good enough for you, you can return to me my amulets.'

'Whipcrow,' Dogbrick protested, standing and scowling. 'She is in our care.'

'Yet she will not care for us.' Whipcrow leered. 'If she will but give what she has, I shall be generous with what I have.'

'That is crude, Whipcrow.' Dogbrick admonished the informer with a hot stare. 'You sound like a brute.'

'These are brutal times, Dogbrick. Brutal times.'

Tywi rose and removed the neckband of theriacal opals Whipcrow had given her to replace the brace he was recharging. She held it out to him, and he snatched it angrily.

'You shall have Charm, Tywi,' the thief promised. 'I will give you the amulets you need.'

Tywi shook her head. 'I can't take your amulets, Dogbrick. How am I going to repay you out here? What work is there to do?'

'You've worked long enough for me. Now we have to work together to survive.'

Tywi gazed inquisitively at the beastman with his flared mane, coppery in the day's last rays. 'Why you doing this for me, Dog?'

'Yes, noble Dog,' Whipcrow wondered, 'are you going to grace with Charm every orphaned refugee we meet?'

'All Irth is not in my care,' Dogbrick said. 'But this young woman is.'

'Why?' Whipcrow challenged. 'Because Ripcat was fool enough to pluck her from the trolls?'

Dogbrick squared his shoulders. 'The truth is, we have a history, sketchy as it may be. She is in my care. That is the simple truth. And I serve the truth.'

'The truth! Ha!' Whipcrow removed the amulets from his staff and shook them. 'The truth is we are alone in the wilds. This could well be our final day. Cacodemons could descend upon us at any moment. That is the truth! Why then should we not take our pleasure where we find it?'

'Whipcrow, you are not a good man.' Dogbrick turned away in disgust. He began unstrapping his trunk.

'This is not a good world, Dogbrick.' The informer again shook the amulets in his grasp. 'I will give you a brace of rat–star gems *and* a brace of theriacal opals for the woman.'

Dogbrick faced about slowly from his open trunk. 'I do not barter people.'

'Then consider it a very generous payment to simply walk away.' Whipcrow's blue lips curled upward as his small eyes thinned. 'I see no one else here who could stop me from taking her.'

'You are right, wicked Crow.' He looked to Tywi and saw the fright in her starved and helpless face. When he turned back to Whipcrow, his nostrils flared. 'I will stop you dead if you dare touch her. Go now.' He thrust an arm toward the dark lanes of the forest. 'I don't want to see you again. Go – before I forget I am a philosopher and cut you down like a troll.'

Whipcrow thrummed with rage and shook his fist. 'You cannot dismiss me, you mangy muttwit.' He swiped a firelock from where it lay on the ground and aimed it at the thief.

Dogbrick showed his fangs in a snarl of revulsion and leaped forward. He grabbed the muzzle of the weapon as it fired, and the blue pulse of Charm that seared past his head singed his mane and exploded in the branches, showering them with sawdust and leafmeal. Outrage roared from Dogbrick as he ripped the firelock from Whipcrow's grip and struck the informer in the brow with the shoulderstock.

Whipcrow dropped to his back, eyes rolled up, mouth agape.

Tywi rushed to Dogbrick and put a hand to where his scorched mane wisped thin smoke. 'You hurt?'

A blistering pain scalded the side of his head, and within him a mineshaft plunging into the netherworld stood exposed. His war cry echoed dimly down that inner darkness, harking his near extinction. 'I'm alive. Amulets can heal what pain there is.'

Tywi looked at Whipcrow sprawled in the heavy swales of grass, eyeballs agog. 'Is he dead?'

'No.' Dogbrick picked up the amber walking stick and the informer's pack. 'He's only unconscious. But I will have to kill him if we are still here when he wakes. He is a dangerous man to anger. He knows nothing of truth – and so he is capable of any atrocity in his mad pursuit of what is useful.'

She stepped back from the unconscious man. 'He tried to kill you.'

'Yes.' Dogbrick closed his trunk and began securing the straps. 'The firelock was set to vaporize my head.'

'And you're not going to kill him?'

He handed her the neckbrace of sharpeye amulets from Whipcrow's pack. 'I'm a thief, Tywi, not a murderer. And so I will take from him everything of value – and should that lead to his demise, I will feel no remorse.'

'He could come after you,' she said and accepted the amulets with both hands.

'If he wants to learn more of pain, he's welcome to my school.' Dogbrick tied the second firelock and the factory manager's pack to the travois. 'I teach the truth – and for one such as Whipcrow, the truth is always painful.'

From Whipcrow's cloak, the thief removed all the amulets and left him nothing. Day's last purple wire stretched taut across the desert horizon behind them as Dogbrick fitted himself to the harness and, with Whipcrow's walking stick in hand, pulled the travois into the forest.

A pendant of theriacal opals healed the thief's burned head, and by midnight he was whole again. They traipsed under the dense brocade of hanging moss from giant bearded trees, collecting along the way edible mushrooms and asparagus shoots. Vapors of starfire sifted through the languorous boughs and illuminated avenues of kelp-like grasses among the forest's dark architecture.

'You are as noble out here in the wilds as you were in Saxar,' Tywi said and stared up at him with large eyes in sunken sockets. 'I thought – I mean, in the warrens we all think – well, you know, that those with beastmarks are dangerous.'

'Oh, but we are,' Dogbrick readily affirmed, his heavily browed eyes scanning the dark.

'You ain't. I mean, in Saxar I thought you was dangerous. That's why I never messed up on the job with you. I was afraid to make a mistake. Afraid of you. We all were. Because you're so fierce. But you're no way like Whipcrow.'

'I am a philosopher.' He bent down to pluck another asparagus shoot and tossed it atop the trunk among the pile of others they had gathered.

'How?' She sought out his gaze. 'How'd you get to be a philospher?'

'Like all philosophers.' He glanced at the niello eye charm on his shoulder, searching for other presences in the forest. In this gloom, even with the eye charms, visibility lacked the precision he had enjoyed in the desert. 'I had a teacher. Her name was Wise Fish. She rescued me from the warrens. And she taught me the truth.'

'The truth. You talk that up a lot. What is the truth?'

Dogbrick scooped up more mushrooms. 'The truth is what is. It is not always useful. Not always kind. Not always beautiful. Not always anything. It changes and yet it is always the same.'

'How can that be?'

'What is, changes. Always. Change is the truth that never changes.'

'You mean, nothing stays the same.'

'Nothing.'

'Not even the Abiding Star?'

'Ah—' Dogbrick's large teeth shone in the dark with the breadth of his smile. 'You have the makings of a true philospher, Tywi. That is a perceptive question.' He used the walking stick to part a veil of hanging moss as they tramped on. 'Do you know what the Abiding Star is?'

'The Beginning. That's what the street witches say. It's in their book, *Origins*.'

'Yes—' He lifted his face toward the forest awning, where starvapors leaked, and he quoted, ' "Above Irth blazes the Abiding Star. Its radiance dazzles the primal darkness like a door standing open on heaven. That is the Beginning." Origins two, nineteen—' He looked down at her, his bushy brows lifted inquisitively, 'You've read *Origins*?'

'No.' She watched a nightbird glide soundlessly across their path into a higher nave of the forest. 'The witch-mothers who run the orphans' house on Cold Niobe read from it before every meal. I used to stay there sometimes. But you can't stay long lest you want to become a witch. Which I don't.'

Dogbrick heard a rustle, glanced at his eye charms and kept talking. 'That is a noble life, celebrating the seasons, crafting amulets for the poor and the sick. You know, every witch is an expert charmwright. If there were enough witches, there would be no poor on Irth.'

'But witches never marry,' Tywi said. 'They make ritual love to the sages. That's not for me, Dog. I – I feel there's just one for me.'

Dogbrick spotted a white hart in his eye charms and watched it bound away at their approach, explaining the rustling he had heard. *Calm down, brave heart*, he counseled himself. *Fear is its own enemy.* 'And who is this one who is meant only for you?' he asked.

'I don't know. I just feel there is. I always felt that.'

'Good.' Dogbrick beamed at her. 'Such feelings imply a future and at this uncertain time in our journey, young Tywi, that is a welcome feeling indeed.' He grunted to pull the travois over a rootledge and went on, 'Now, about the Abiding Star – ah, but wait.' He pointed with his staff to an alcove among the big trees where a brake of feathery canes shimmered in a shaft of starglow.

'Those are sugar stalks. They will make a tasty addition to our meal. Cut a few for us, will you?'

Dogbrick handed Tywi a knife from his utility belt, and she went over to the brake and began harvesting the stalks. As she knelt to cut closer to the sweet root, a large hand reached through the canes, grabbed her by the collar of her smock, and pulled her into the darkness.

The thief shouted, threw off the travois cables, and leaped toward the great trees, trampling the sugar stalks.

Tywi had utterly vanished.

'Dogbrick!' Her cry curled out of the dark distance and stabbed him with its fearful anguish.

'Tywi!' he called back.

No reply followed. In the niello eye charms, he had to search hard before he found her, already almost a league distant. She was a bundle thrown over the shoulder of an ogre. The huge anthropoid charged crashing through the undergrowth of a gully screened almost entirely from his eye charms with hanging moss and ivy.

Dogbrick gave chase, flinging himself into the darkness, ignoring the slashing thorn vines and nettle weeds. He oriented himself by his eye charms until he heard the ogre far ahead of him, devouring the leaf-strewn distances with mighty strides.

The thief activated all his power wands, risking heart rupture. His legs churned, and the sturdy walking stick beat aside intrusive vines and grassy obstacles. Her one cry to him had hooked him under the breastbone and pulled him after her with inexorable stamina. He leaped boulders, splashed unhindered across viper-haunted streams, and pulled to within sight of the fleeing ogre even as his heart boomed with mortal thunder in his aching ears.

The kidnapper was gigantic. Its enormous, naked thews gleamed in the starlight with the sweat of its exertion. Glimmering through the forest's lacy shadows, it glanced back at its pursuer with a small, pugnacious face inset in a mammoth head of black fleece.

Dogbrick unslung his firelock without breaking stride, but he dared not shoot for fear of striking Tywi inside the shoulder-thrown sack. Instead, he fired a rapid burst ahead of the big creature, hoping to slow it down. Green tracers illuminated the cathedral depths of the forest and exploded on the banks of the gorge, toppling two trees in a crisscross barricade.

The ogre spun about, crouched, its tiny face bent with fury under hunched shoulders of sliding muscle, and for one frightful instant, the thief thought that the howling goliath intended to charge. Dogbrick leveled his firelock, but the ogre dropped the sack, sprang upward, and tumbled over the fallen trees. A crashing sounded from the far side as it continued on its way.

Slapping off the power wands on his harness, Dogbrick collapsed beside the sack, heaving for breath, blood whining loudly through his heart's coils. His sharp fingers tore open the coarse cloth and his wildly dancing heart cramped coldly in him at the sight of packed leaves. A bellow of despair emptied his burning lungs and dropped him sobbing for breath over the ripped decoy.

By the time he got back to his travois, the ogre who had taken Tywi had ransacked his treasure trunk. Its colossal footprints had dented the ground around it, but it had not taken anything except the utility belts and the food. That ogres despised Charm he had heard all his life, though he had never met an ogre until this night. He had also been told that they were supreme tacticians, and they had certainly convinced him of that.

He took the two bolts of trance wrap from the upturned trunk and bent to retrieve his spilled amulets. Only then did he apprehend with an intuitive flash that the hex-gems and talismans had not been carelessly strewn. The ogre had arranged them to look scattered when in fact they served as a cover for the firecharm cartridges below. The cartridges had been joined in twos by their contact ends. Rat-star gems wedged between each of the coupled cartridges glinted with live current. If any of them were disturbed even slightly, they would spark and the whole pile would explode.

*Those ogres hate Charm so much they've learned exactly how to destroy it*, he thought, trying to calm his quaking body, astonished at the wicked intelligence of such brutish creatures.

A leaf whisper made him glance upward, and he saw a rock lob through the branches. The ogre had been watching from somewhere nearby, and when it saw him backing away, aware of the trap, it acted to finish him.

Dogbrick flung himself backward, lifting the trance wrap to protect his face. But it was already too late. The ogres had outwitted him again he realized as the thrown rock clattered amidst his treasure.

The blast lifted him off his feet and flung him into absolute darkness.

Green fire exploded upward through the trees and stained the night. The captives in the chattel-carts on the far side of the forest saw it swirl into the sky and spread in sticky emerald unfoldings, an eerie nebula crawling over Irth. Thunder twisted in the wind, and they knew the ogres had done more evil and taken more prisoners. They shared woeful knowing looks in their caged carts but dared say nothing, for the basilisks that towed the carts had been trained by the ogres to hate the human voice. If anyone spoke, the horned and slinky red creatures slid their scaly black tails into the chattel-carts and whipped everyone bloody.

As dawn's orchids unfolded in the sky, the captives heard the ogres returning and sat up from where they slept on the straw-matted cage bottom. Gnawl, the dark-fleeced ogre who had raced Dogbrick into the night, arrived first, carrying sacks of foraged foods – mint grass, honey berries, asparagus spears, eden nuts in clustered vines, and sugar stalks – and passed this fodder by thick handfuls into the caged carts.

Gryn, rufous tufts of coarse hair furred in blotches on his capacious bald scalp, came in with a waif under his arm, a shred of her filthy smock stuffed in her mouth. He tossed her into the nearest chattle-cart and went directly to the basilisks to reward them for guarding the captives. Out of the other cart, he hoisted the eldest, a silver-haired woman in a tattered and soiled witch's gown. She made no protest or struggle but kept her gaze upon the Abiding Star rising sparkling through the treecrowns.

The ogre threw her to the ground between the beasts, and the basilisks set upon her with avid ferocity, their turtlebeaked jaws vanishing into her flesh to the dark caves of their eyes. She gave out one agonized cry and went silent as the twisting jaws tore her apart.

The new prisoner stared with bulging eyes until a female captive in the leather vest of a charmwright turned her head. 'Don't look.' She removed the cloth from the waif's mouth and untied her wrists. 'What is your name?'

'Tywi,' the terrified young woman said.

'Listen to me now,' the charmwright said. 'When the basilisks feed is the only time we can speak. Otherwise they beat us terribly. We are all prisoners of the ogres. They roam this forest snatching travelers. They feed only the old and the sick to the basilisks. We think we must be bound for some labor camp, probably the coast, to scavenge the tidal flats at night for our new masters.'

Tywi stared hard at the brown-eyed woman with the smudged face and gray-streaked hair tied up by a cord of vine. She stared hard not to hear the crunching bonemeal in the chewing jaws.

'Were you traveling with anyone?' the charmwright asked.

'Yes.' Tywi nodded vigorously. 'Dogbrick. My friend.'

'Did the ogres kill him?'

'I don't know. There was an explosion . . .'

'Green fire,' the charmwright whispered. 'Charm blowout. We saw it. Dogbrick must have had firecharms.'

'Yeah. And amulets. Lots of them.'

'That's it. The ogres destroy amulets wherever they find them. Maybe your friend Dogbrick escaped. He may alert others to our plight. We need something to keep our hope alive.'

The feeding sounds diminished, and the charmwright peeked

over her shoulder. Tywi glimpsed between the two scarlet reptiles a froth of blood and brainpulp, and nausea whirled up in her.

'Hush now,' the charmwright warned. 'They are nearly done, and they will tolerate not a word from any of us. We will talk again later.'

Between the immense pylons of the trees, Gryn and Gnawl conferred, their voices low and rumbly as a distant storm. Then they whistled and strode into the woods. The basilisks followed, pulling the two chattel-carts behind. Tywi clasped the wooden bars and stared into the morning sky above the treetops where a slur of green fire still hung in the air.

Whipcrow saw it, too. Rousing from Dogbrick's blow, he clutched his aching head in both hands. The far-off explosion of the Charm cartridges could have been the throb of his own pain. But the bloom of green fire deep in the forest lifted his attention beyond himself.

He staggered upright and wheeled drunkenly through the grass, looking for his walking staff and his pack. When he realized that they were gone, taken by the thief and the waif, he cawed angrily and the thick black hackles of his hair stood up.

'Muttwit!' he screamed. 'I will find you! And break you!'

Whipcrow's rage chilled quickly to angry muttering before the brutal truth of his predicament. Without Charm, he had no protection from the forest's beasts, no enhancement of his body's strength or his mind's aptitude, and no way to ward off sleep. When exhaustion eventually claimed him, he would be vulnerable to predators and, at night, the tide that wafted the Charmless into the void. The residual Charm in his garments had alone prevented him from drifting off into the Gulf this past night – and that residue was now gone.

Striding purposefully along the matted track left by Dogbrick's travois, he racked his brain for all that he knew of Charm, trying to figure a way to survive without it. Charm, every schoolchild knew, radiated from the Abiding Star. Plants absorbed it directly, and animals held it within their living bodies.

Only people needed amulets to endow themselves with Charm. He thought of all the reasonings for this from the sages and the witches – all their palaver about evolution and the migration of consciousness away from the Beginning and out into the void to populate the cold worlds – and, with an irate hiss, he dismissed it all as superstitious nonsense.

Humans suffered from an unfortunate mutation. That was what he had learned as a charmwright before becoming a factory manager. The first people, the aborigines of Irth, had lived for ages without Charm. He would survive as they had. At night he would stay awake. Consciousness itself seemed to be an aspect of Charm and was sufficient to keep one grounded. By day, when the tides abated, he would sleep. Though that, he bitterly acceded, would be difficult. Predatory creatures abounded everywhere. And by day, he would be most visible.

Dogbrick's revenge seemed truly terrible the more he pondered it. Only Whipcrow's fury kept him from paralyzing despair. *Muttwit, I will break you!* he repeated to himself as he hurried after the thief.

Shortly past noon, he reached the site of the explosion. A crater had excavated the ground deeper than the burned ends of root-cables, penetrating to a granite depth where gasps of green mist still lingered. The trees on all sides leaned away as if repelled by the acrid stench of scorched soil.

No trace of any of the amulets remained, yet Whipcrow knew what had happened here. *Charm blowout.* He thought, *The muttwit did this on purpose, to spite me. He shattered the Charm-breech on the second firelock and destroyed all the amulets so I could never get them back!*

Believing that the thief and the waif were traveling lighter, he searched the surrounding woods for signs of their passing. Then, in a scrim of leaf litter and lichen, he found prodigious footprints, each impression clearly displaying nimble prehensile toes.

'Ogres!' he gasped. He crouched and stared all around him with startled eyes. Leaflight glinted like teeth and shadows lumbered nearby. He pulled his cloak tighter about himself and did not rise until he saw that he was alone, misreading the winking daylight and passing cloud shadows.

The footprints were easy to spot in the loam, and he turned to flee in the opposite direction. Two paces later, he turned again. Without Charm, the forest would devour him. Dangerous as ogres were, Whipcrow recognized that his best chance of survival was to follow them. They lived, like the first people, without Charm and would know the safest routes through these woods. And though they were fabled for their cruelty to people, that might work to his advantage if they eventually led him out of the forest to some human settlement in their quest for people to enslave.

He pursued the tracks across small creeks, alert for vipers. Twice he spotted shaggy green bears, but they ignored him as he crept past with footfalls muted by moss and duff. By late afternoon, he found where the ogre tracks joined with the rutted impressions of cartwheels and the long, quartz-like droppings of basilisks.

Exhaustion dogged him, a weird wooziness after a lifetime of Charm, and he decided to sleep until dark. He swung up into a tree and lashed the hem of his cloak to a bough to hold him in place and nestled against the groin of the trunk. A dream of big-headed ogres with their blacktoothed grins startled him awake.

He thought only moments had lapsed, yet folds of sunset creased the western sky. And there, below him, a figure moved. He blinked twice to focus his eyes in the murky gloaming and saw Dogbrick leaning on the amber walking staff and reading the rut tracks in the forest floor.

The thief had been blown into a treetop by the exploding Charm. His harness of power wands and the amulets fitted to it had protected him from the force of the blast, though the impact had rendered him unconscious. After he woke, he found his firelock, the walking staff, and the bolts of trance wrap lodged with him in the attic of the forest.

Seeing his foe, Whipcrow grasped at once what had happened. *The ogres have kidnapped Tywi – and the muttwit is off to rescue her!*

Whipcrow waited until the thief had vanished among the trees before hopping down from his perch. He had to be wary. Dogbrick had eye charms. But the factory manager knew how to elude their searching gaze by keeping his distance. The thief would follow the tracks, and Whipcrow would be not far behind, hidden by the trees' beards of moss and the creeks' shawls of ivy.

After twilight, clouds masked the stars, and the forest seeped in blind darkness. Bioluminescent tendrils dangling from the black canopy and ledges of glaucous fungus on tree boles illuminated vague pathways through the night. Though this slowed down Whipcrow and left him more anxious than ever about the creaturely howls and shamblings he heard around him, he felt fortunate that the rains did not come and wash out the ogres' tracks.

Lightning quaked soundlessly and stenciled the forest corridors in fitful glimpses. Whipcrow crawled slowly onward, fighting weariness and the doomful sleep that night proffered.

Dawn rose with brimstone radiance, underlighting stormclouds trundling eastward, wind-tossed leaves scuttling after them. He pulled a blanket of slick ivy over himself and plummeted immediately into a dark sleep. Again, the blacktoothed grin of ogres thrashed him awake.

Streams of afternoon radiance angled through the treetops and rendered the world in a fiery green incandescence. Briefly, he spied elves in their silk robes and sparkling auras jog across the loomwork of vines and grass, merry of aspect and swift.

Remembering his vengeful mission, he shoved himself upright and stumbled with weakness. He had to eat. He had never known hunger pains before and had mistaken them for a fatigue sleep could mend. Reeling out of the creek bed, he wobbled among the trees until he located pendant vines of eden nuts. He tore down several loops, dragged them to the creek bed, and shucked the nuts with a rock.

After sating himself, he continued his pursuit. Along the way, he tore up canes of sugar stalk and gnawed the sweet roots, drawing into himself the vitality he needed to go on. Daylight faded hours before nightfall, and a gray mist swirled up from the creekbeds and shrouded the root ledges and rotted logs. Cold penetrated him, and he shivered so hard his teeth ached in their roots.

At dusk, with the sky the color of stone above a chill green pool in the west, he shuffled through mauve leafdrifts and low whorls of fog to the forest's edge. A salt wind tinged the air and burned branch tips and grass to curled ash. He found himself atop a bluff that fell away in heather slopes and gray weathered bramble to a duneland below and, beyond that, the slate horizon of the sea.

A crude wooden barge sat aground on a sandbar, listing hard to one side, the tide retreating behind it in a froth of pawing waves. Even at this distance and through the misty scud of twilight, he could clearly see the big, hide-covered bodies of ogres building a driftwood fire on the beach. Two chattle-carts sat on a sandy saddle between dunes. A dozen people slogged single file through the sand and tide pools to the barge, where an ogre directed them up a ramp and into the hold.

Farther down the beach, two basilisks thrashed, feeding voraciously on something, their black tails snapping like whips. He could see the greasy stumps on their scaly red backs where the ogres had docked their wings. So intent was he on viewing these maimed creatures with their spiked elbows, serpent necks, and spiral-horned heads that he almost overlooked the small shape of a man in the dunes behind them, kneeling in the sand, burying something.

Whipcrow squinted and saw that it was Dogbrick. The thief worked energetically, scooping sand with his hands and pushing it away from the hole with his feet.

Confident that Dogbrick was preoccupied with his task and would not heed his eye charms, Whipcrow made no attempt to hide himself but moved boldly along the margin of the forest until he was directly above the dune where his foe was digging. There, he crawled under the pulpy decay of tree husks, humus, and mushrooms and watched Dogbrick bury the walking staff and the two bolts of trance wrap.

When the thief was done, he covered the site with a tangle of seaweed and a twist of driftwood and ran off bent double to stay out of sight of the feeding basilisks. Whipcrow stayed himself from going down after his staff and the trance wrap, because from his new vantage he could see what the basilisks were devouring. They struggled noisily over the remaining orts of a human being – a skull crushed to brainpulp and boneshards.

While they finished their meal, he observed the thief.

Dogbrick strode over the belly of a dune directly into the ogres' line of sight. He had already decided not to attack them with his firelock and risk losing his battle and Tywi to their superior martial cunning. Instead, he chose to confront them and appeal to their avarice.

Much as the ogres despised Charm, they well knew the value of amulets, which could be sold to traders for what the ogres coveted and could not make for themselves – exotic dew-wine, that most rare and intoxicatingly fragrant vintage from the grassland arbors of Sharna-Bambara. That was what made their willingness to explode all the amulets in the thief's treasure trunk so frightfully devious: Ogres indeed proved themselves supreme tacticians to the philosopher-thief by willingly suspending their greed to destroy a potential enemy.

Dogbrick's entrails shook with fear when the ogres bellowed at the sight of him. *Why would they trade Tywi for what they intended to destroy in the first place?* he fretted. *They must! I am a philosopher, not a warrior. I cannot hope to slay them all.*

He held his firelock in both hands over his head, intending to show that he approached without aggression – yet ready to use the weapon if they attacked.

Gnawl stepped away from the others hunkered about the bonfire in the evening gloom. The ogre immediately recognized the dogman who had pursued it through the forest several days earlier.

'Dogbrick!' Tywi's voice called from the barge, and he saw her pressed against a window-grating in the prow. 'Dogbrick!'

He took his hand from the firelock's muzzle and waved to her. From down the beach, the basilisks roared at the sound of a human voice and came bounding out of the dunes. Gnawl shouted a guttural command, and several ogres leaped up to quell the beasts.

'Woman!' Gnawl pointed its giant arm toward Tywi and showed its black teeth in a lush grin. 'Yours!' Its tiny face in its great-skulled head wrinkled with abrupt lines of merriment. Then it looked at the firelock and sneered. 'Kill me – die!' Its little eyes motioned toward where its comrades had unsheathed bows long as young trees and had pointed quartz-tipped arrows at him.

'I have not come to kill you,' Dogbrick said. 'I am here to barter. Ogres are honorable. You trade without treachery for what you want. Yes?'

'Barter!' Gnawl roared. 'What?'

'That woman, Tywi, for trance wrap. Enough trance wrap to buy twenty barrels of dew-wine. Twenty barrels!'

'Blown up!' The ogre made a vicious face, its small eyes vanishing in creases of malice. 'You blown up!'

'No, I'm not blown up.' Dogbrick slapped his harness. 'My amulets protected me. And the trance wrap. I got it out before the charges went off. I have it hidden. Two bolts of it. Enough for twenty barrels of dew-wine. And you can have it all for Tywi. Give her to me, let us go, and you can have the trance wrap.'

Gryn came up behind Gnawl and muttered something ominously, glaring at the firelock the thief held before him.

'Look, you two,' Dogbrick ventured, 'I hear that ogres are tactical masters. The best on Irth. Surely, then, you see how it makes sense to trade one prisoner from a score of others for a bounty of dew-wine. This deal is so good, I will stake my life on

206

it. Here. Hold my weapon till the deal is done. The honor of ogres is well known. So I don't need this weapon to threaten you now that you understand what I have to offer.'

The thief held out the firelock, and Gnawl snatched it away in a flash. 'Get woman,' he growled. 'Get wrap.'

Gryn lumbered toward the barge and yelled to the ogre at the bow, who disappeared below deck.

'Get wrap!' Gnawl commanded.

'Tywi—' Dogbrick objected.

'She comes!' The ogre bowed its vein-gnarled head. 'Get wrap!'

Dogbrick led the way into the dark dunes, keeping a tide-stacked mound of driftbramble, bleached logs, and seawrack between him and the snorting basilisks. From behind, Gryn came running with Tywi slung over his naked shoulder.

Spume and cloudshreds muted the starglow, and Dogbrick wandered disoriented in the darkness among the tussocky dunes, twice passing the site where he had buried the trance wrap. He did not at first recognize the location, because a gaping hole stood in its place. When at last he stopped before it and Gryn lowered Tywi to stand beside him, he stared wordlessly, uncomprehending.

'I didn't really think you was coming for me,' Tywi breathed excitedly beside him, clutching his arm.

Her voice came to him from far away, across a vastness of despondency he had never before conceived.

'Get wrap!' Gnawl shouted.

Dogbrick faced Tywi, thick brows sadly arched. 'I'm sorry, Tywi. I had the trance wrap here. But now – it's gone.'

A powerful hand seized Dogbrick by his mane, pulling him away from Tywi. He flailed helplessly as Gryn tore the amulet harness from his body. Gnawl snapped the stock off the firelock, then broke the muzzle and heaved the breech angrily toward the sea. With Dogbrick gripped firmly by his mane and Tywi held by both her hands, Gryn dragged them after him through the sand, mumbling grouchily.

Into the muted glow of the stars stepped a slender human shadow holding a tall walking staff. With a brisk flourish, the staff lit up amber-bright and revealed Whipcrow, cowl unfolded, black hackled hair fanned wide around his hatchet face.

'I have the trance wrap you want,' he announced to the ogres. 'It was mine originally, before this thief stole it from my factory. You may have it and all the dew-wine it will purchase in exchange for safe passage to the next human settlement. Are we agreed?'

'Whipcrow, you liar!' Dogbrick shouted, and Gryn shook him to a blur that left him dizzy in a dazzle of neural stars.

'Agreed!' Gnawl pronounced, and Gryn nodded with satisfaction and a tight, smug smile in his minuscule face as he lugged his captives onward.

That night, Dogbrick and Tywi sat in the dark and stink of the barge's hold among the other desolate prisoners. Many bobbed against the low ceiling, weightless with sleep. Others pressed against the hull, peering through the tiny chinks and seams at the inaccessible stars, grateful for the salt breeze that leaked through.

'It is safe to sleep here,' Dogbrick said in a desultory whisper and closed his eyes.

'I'm glad you came for me,' Tywi said, nestling against his fur.

'I failed you. I failed us both.'

'Whipcrow betrayed you – again. You should have killed him when he tried to kill you.'

'I am not a killer or a soldier . . .'

'Yeah, right. You're a philosopher, I know.'

'And so I must endure the fate of philosophers,' he groused softly. 'I only regret that you must suffer with me. Fate put you in my care, and I have failed you.'

'Not failed me,' she muttered. 'Joined me.'

A faint smile peeked through his beard. 'You are a philosopher, too, I see. Good. Together we will share the truth. Together we will discover what it means to have largeness of heart. For if I have learned anything it is that the smaller the circle of imprisonment becomes, the larger grow the dreams of escape.'

Tywi grew lighter against him, rising into sleep, and he put an arm about her and held her close to him.

Morning flood tide rocked the barge, and both Dogbrick and Tywi woke to find themselves pressed against the low ceiling. They dropped to the deck with hard thumps that jolted them fully awake. The hold resounded with the loud thuds of numerous bodies falling back into consciousness as thin rosy rays of dawn threaded through the cracks in the upper hull.

Seasickness overwhelmed many of the captives crammed into the tight and sweltering hold, and a rancid stench rose from the retching bodies. Both Dogbrick and Tywi succumbed. Day and night, they curled around their soft bones, weak with nausea, sleeping in fits. The greasy slop lowered into the hold in rusty pails only sickened them more with its sour stink.

Whipcrow paced the open deck above, limber as a mariner, his black cape flapping like wings in the stiff maritime wind. A grin like a blue slash opened the wedge of his dark face every time he thought of Dogbrick suffering below. And this was just a prelude to the torments yet to come.

The ogres, true to their word, had granted the factory manager safe passage on their barge. They would have released him the following dusk when they came to shore farther south on the pebble beach within sight of Old Shard, the colossal granite port on the headlands of Mirdath, but he refused to go. Above the port's famous helical towers, in the orange shades of day's end, floated cacodemons.

Gryn and Gnawl, well pleased with the ample bolts of trance wrap delivered to them by Whipcrow, confided in him the purpose of their mission. They were bound for a desolate swamp in the Reef Isles of Nhat where the refugees they had collected would populate work camps established to serve the Dark Lord. Obeisant to nostalgia, Hu'dre Vra had spared Nhat from the devastation he was visiting upon all other dominions. The realm where he had once slaved as a scavenger scouring the tidal flats for valuable flotsam would now serve as a vast labor camp for the

Dark Lord's many enemies. And the ogres had been commanded by him to run this vengeful site with all the brutality for which they were renowned.

Whipcrow pondered this and decided to take his chances with the ogres who favored him rather than wander aimlessly among cacodemons. And so, he remained on board the entire voyage, amusing the ogres with the games of cruelty he devised for culling the weakest prisoners to feed daily to the basilisks. Captives danced on trap doors above the hold of the basilisks and the first to drop exhausted fell through and was devoured. In a variant game, a pulley line was rigged above each trap door so that the door had to be pulled shut by a body's weight, and the first prisoner whose grip gave out fell to the ravening jaws.

The factory manager came up with new ideas every day. But what secured his position among the ogres was the remarkable feat he accomplished in the coastal city of Drymarch on the littoral plains of Sharna–Bambara. Flanked by Gryn and Gnawl, Whipcrow entered the low-lying metropolis of pastel dykes, grass verges, sand roads, bright yellow cottages, white pickets and flower-strewn yards bordered with pink conches and periwinkles, and met with the mayor.

The portly, ruddy-faced woman feared the arrival of the cacodemons. She listened avidly to Whipcrow's news of the ogres' alliance with the Dark Lord and, eager for some hope of reprieve from destruction for her beautiful municipality, arranged for a hundred kegs of dew-wine to be laded on to the barge. The ogres carried Whipcrow back to the ship like a hero, raised high above their heads.

As the barge sailed south the following morning, they spotted a chevron of cacodemons arrowing toward Drymarch. Shortly afterward, columns of black clouds rose from the city, and the ogres put ashore to gather the evacuees fleeing through the salt marshes. Among the new captives marched on board that evening was the florid mayor, her eyes vapid, her pudgy flesh pale with shock.

For the rest of the voyage, Whipcrow no longer had to pace the boards or brace himself with the deck cleats in rough weather; instead, he enjoyed the comforts of a quarterdeck cabin with a hammock and a wide desk shelved with tomes from sacked libraries and set before a bay of mullioned, prism-glass windows. The ogres gifted him with the amulet harness that they had taken from Dogbrick, and they went out of their way at subsequent ports to secure for him fine foods and drink – fried squash flowers, abalone soup, octopus salad, and blue beer. They also returned to him the two bolts of trance wrap, since they no longer needed them to trade for dew-wine.

When, at last, the misty Reef Isles of Nhat hove into view, Whipcrow was well rested and nourished. With staff in hand and wearing the amulet harness tailored to fit his gaunt body, he stood at the prow with Gryn and Gnawl as the barge sailed past the Cloths of Heaven, the most archaic ruins on Irth.

Sphinx-columns stood mired in miasmal bog, winding serpentcoil stairways curled to nowhere, and roisterous vines and incessant creepers strangled domed porticos and tiled atria. Visible above the seething mists, moss-splotched porphyry towers and gilded spires flared to weeds and stormbent trees at their jagged, broken crowns under the speeding clouds.

The barge docked at a crude wharf of lashed logs that squatted among giant medusa trees in the foggy depths of an impenetrable marsh. To one side, across a span of onyx water fetid with oily black rainbows, the broken coral columns and cancerous walls of the ancient ruins brooded. In the other direction, beyond a riotous wall of swamp growth woven from the sordid tanglings of strange parasitic silks, ropes, and tendrils, beyond sepulchral depths of fallen trees and monstrous black root boles full of glisteny seepings, dripping rot among shifting vapors, an evil place loomed.

A lunatic teetering of scaffolds reared above the dark galleries of the somber swamp, full of trestles, ramps, and catwalks skewed at weirdly obtuse angles, and swarming upon this immense skeletal construct a thousand cacodemons crawled and hovered, smudging the sky with their numbers. They were constructing something. They were fitting sheets of alabaster together to fashion a huge pyramid. In the foreground, along the cobbled road that led to the wharves where barges delivered the construction materials and stone sheets, corpses hung from leafless trees. Carrion birds had plucked their faces to skulls, yet all could still recognize upon their dead bodies the amulet tunics and silken raiment of Peers.

The ogres herded the prisoners away from this horror toward a gloomy nave in the marsh that enclosed the labor camp, a rude prison shut in by tall palings of ghostly-white wortwood topped with thorny coils of nettlebraid. Whipcrow did not linger on the wharf to gloat at Dogbrick. He went immediately along the wharf road of mushy planks toward the bizarre construction site of the cacodemons.

His heart beat madly inside him, and he had to draw Charm heavily from his amber walking staff and amulet harness to find the strength to go forward. Yet, he knew that his destiny awaited him in this place that the ogres called the Palace of Abominations.

As he rounded the bend in the plank road that took him through the wild walls of drooling compost and stranglelocked vegetation, he came into full view of the terrible place. Cacodemons crowded the crazy heights of the tilted structure so tightly that light came through in dusty, luminous shafts at crisscross angles. On the lower tiers, scores of people hung in thorn-cages, the blood from their wounds floating around them in red wisps. Their moans and cries echoed remotely from the cathedral heights of the eerily silent cacodemons.

At the ground level, separated from the construction by tall thorn hedges, opulence sprawled. Crystal globes suspended at intervals radiated a kind of Charm, stirring fronds of breeze and soft perfume. None blocked Whipcrow's way, and he entered trepidatiously.

Walls of green and blue glass opened through alabaster portals upon an august garden of topiary hedges, pollarded blossom trees, and espaliered arbors. At the center of this serene chamber, surrounded by thrusts of marvelous rocks of chrysoprase, chalcedony, and agate shaped in cataclysm and polished by time and wind, stood a gray stick upon which hung a wrinkled empty skin of brown leather flayed from a human body. The flounces of limbs and pleats of fingers could easily be seen, as could the grisly face furred with green fungus, its eyeholes gazing vacantly, its nostrils mere slits, its gaping mouth void of teeth or palate yet tongued with blue flame.

That fire-flicker hissed, 'S-step clos-ser, Whipcrow.'

Despite the sedation of his Charm, the factory manager jumped. 'Who are you?'

'I am the warlock Ralli-Faj.'

'I have come to petition the Dark Lord,' Whipcrow blurted before this frightful being. 'I have in my possession two bolts of trance wrap as a gift of tribute to the great Hu'dre Vra.'

A mocking laugh sizzled from the mummy rag. 'S-s-silly man! The Dark Lord possess-es-s all Irth!'

'Of course! Of course!' Whipcrow hung his head. 'I have come to honor him and offer my services.'

'I know why you have come.' The blue flame wagged in its peel of skin. 'I know who you are. I have been waiting for you, Whipcrow. You are here to s-s-serve me.'

Whipcrow lifted his flinty face, frowning with perplexity. 'But the Dark Lord . . .'

'S-silence!' The blue flame torched from the gaping mouth with acetylene intensity.

Whipcrow staggered backward, his black hackles flaring outward in a crest of fright.

Ralli-Faj hung like a dead thing and yet spoke: 'The Dark Lord is-s touring his-s world. He has-s left me here to torment his enemies-s most worthy of pain. And I have s-sent for you to help me. Oh, I have been calling urgently, Whipcrow – urgently. For there is-s much work to be done.'

# Dark the Seed

—✦—

Jyoti and Poch hiked through pools of daylight in a grove where branches waved, buoyant with blossoms. She carried across her back the firelock the wizarduke had given her, and he dangled a gurgling flagon from each shoulder. Both wore the hoods of their tunics pulled up, to protect themselves from the direct rays of noon.

Though the margravess had given her younger brother permission to depart from her and submit to the Dark Lord, he stayed at her side. He was afraid to stand alone. Except for his sister, everyone that he knew had fallen into the source of night. He did not want to lose his sister, too. He did not have the heart to walk a solitary path.

Since leaving the Qaf, food and water had been easy to find, and their amulet tunics protected them from the elements. Of the highest quality, the power wands on the collars of their tunics drew Charm directly from the Abiding Star and would charge their amulets for many days before needing to be replaced. They possessed the means to continue Jyoti's quest for the sorcerer Caval – so long as they avoided detection by the malevolent cacodemons.

Their eyes traced paths through the sky, searching for the monsters and reaching ahead toward the auburn plateaus where they were bound – the Steppes of Keri. From there, they would cross into the Malpais Highlands, whose ranges of staccato mountains hung blue and vaporous on the farthest horizons.

'What if he's not there?' Poch asked and peered once more into the tunic's epaulets of niello eye charms.

'The sages will know where he went.'

In his eye charms, Poch saw no threat, only harpy snakes wheeling under the Abiding Star, daylight glinting on their wings and tailfeathers. 'But what if he was never there?'

'The Calendar of Eyes is where he went,' Jyoti answered patiently. 'It's the only place on Irth where a body can return to the light, to the Beginning. He went there.'

He lifted his hooded face toward the hot zenith, shadowed his eyes with his hand, and tried to gauge the distance to the Steppes of Keri. Sometime in the night, they would begin that tedious climb. 'Is it far to the Calendar of Eyes?'

'It's very far. It's at the edge of time. From the summit, you can see across the ages. But you have to hold a lot of Charm in your body just to get there. There's no air and it's terribly cold.'

'Well, how will we get there?'

'We're not climbing to the summit.' Jyoti squinted through the bright pollen that swirled with the breeze in the radiant shafts of daylight. 'We're only going as far as the high slopes, to the sanctuary. Our amulets can carry us that far. And if he's not there, they might have something of his that we can use with our seeker.'

'But what if he's already climbed the Calendar of Eyes? What if he's gone back to the Beginning.'

'Then we will have to find another worker of sorcery to help us.'

'There is no other worker who knows the archives of Arwar Odawl.'

They emerged from the blossoming grove into a grassy swale of chittering birds and flickering butterflies. 'We know the archives.'

'I don't,' Poch responded. 'And you've never been down there, either.'

'It's a blood memory. A strong enough Charm worker can summon that memory in us.'

'And what if we do?' he pressed. 'What if we go down there and then find that there is no magic that can stop the cacodemons?'

'Little brother,' she smiled at him wearily, 'you ask questions only time and deeds can answer.'

'I'm frightened, Jyo.' He peeked into his eye charms again. Ruby asps writhed away in the tall grass, and he watched their swift currents rush off like streaks of red energy. 'Even with all these amulets, I'm frightened. I can't stop thinking about Mother and Father dead. And all our brood. Dead. I feel we should be dead, too. I feel our brood is waiting for us to finish our dying.'

'That is your fear talking,' Jyoti admonished. 'Now let your courage speak.'

'My courage says, we should be brave enough to accept the defeat of our brood. We should be brave enough to go to the Dark Lord and submit before his might. If he slays us, then our dying is done.'

Jyoti gazed into the shadow of his cowl. 'I will never submit to evil.'

'Why is he more evil than any other conqueror in history?' Poch returned his sister's stare with a worried mien. 'Our ancestors submitted to other conquerors. That is how our brood survived to be the most ancient of lines. Grandfather Phax grew up in a household that had submitted to the One-Eyed Duke of Ux. Was his father and mother less for yielding?'

Jyoti shrugged. 'That is why Grandfather used Charm to summon the blood memories from before Charm. It was impossible to fight his enemies with Charm. They were too powerful. He fell back on the old ways and learned how to fight without Charm, with his body alone.'

'So let us yield as his father yielded!'

'No!' Jyoti spoke sharply. 'It is different. Terribly different.'

'How?'

'The One-Eyed Duke of Ux fought to unite the Seven Dominions,' she explained with a taint of impatience. 'He destroyed only those who resisted. This so-called Dark Lord destroyed Arwar Odawl without provocation. He never gave us a chance to yield or resist. He used the death of our brood to terrorize the others into submission. That is evil.'

'I do not have the heart to fight evil.'

'Who does?' She helped herself to one of the flagons hanging from her brother's shoulders. 'Only evil has the heart to fight evil. It is enough that good be strong enough not to submit. In time, evil consumes itself.'

'I don't understand.'

She sipped the chilled Charm-sweet water. 'Why do you think Grandfather Phax taught himself the ancient fighting ways? He had no hope of fighting Charm with his bare hands. It was not a useful martial skill in modern times. What hope could such skills offer against firecharms? And yet he devoted his life to mastering open hand fighting. Why?'

'Father said that Grandfather was an eccentric who hid away from the world inside himself.' He accepted the flagon Jyoti offered, and drank.

'Father was Grandfather's son. He was disappointed that his father was not like other men. Grandfather did not hide in himself. He resided there. In his heart. The place of angels and demons, he called it. He mastered open-hand fighting not to defeat others – but to conquer himself.'

'Is that why you learned from him – to conquer yourself?'

'Not at first. I just thought Grandfather was strange, and I wanted to know why he spent so much time tumbling and rolling about like a court zany. Then, he had me try it, and it was fun. That's all it was for a long time. Fun. A sport. I liked it, and I got good at it.'

'You spent a lot of time at it, Jyo.' His voice softened with rueful memories. 'Mother and Father worried about you. Mother thought Grandfather had cast a spell on you. But Father said Grandfather was charmless. He worried that you were wasting your time on a ridiculous sport and he was afraid that people would think you were as crazy as Grandfather was. He wanted you to prepare to take his place, to be margravess, not a court zany.'

'I mastered my other studies.' Jyoti sounded hurt.

'But you sure spent a lot of time letting Grandfather push you around.'

'I miss him most of all.'

'I miss Mother and Father.'

The margravess set her gaze toward the iron-blue horizon beyond the maroon shelves of Keri. 'We will avenge them all.'

They continued across the grassy plains that day and advanced into the late afternoon's long shafts of hot light with their heads down, faceless beneath their hoods. A pack of muscular wolves followed them into the night, their yellow eyes shimmering like heat in the twilight. The thin aura of Charm around the two wanderers kept the big lobos at a distance, and by nightfall the pack loped away, long noses to the ground, tails waving like banners.

Hours later, as Jyoti and Poch climbed scrabble paths among twisted dwarf-trees, Hellsgate rose gibbous and pocked, followed soon by Nemora, a great naked face. By their planetlight, sister and brother could plainly see the wolvish tracks widen and stretch in the dust, transforming across the steep landscape into human prints.

A tribe of ragged nomads squatted at the end of the tracks, blocking the trace that led up the escarpment to the rimland of Keri. Men and women wore hacked hair cut to uneven lengths with stone knives. Mud plastered their nakedness with grass and twigs, and they stared with hungry yellow eyes and strangely grinning mouths.

'Food for your fortune,' the tribal leader spoke with surprising lucidity in Irthorc, the world's common dialect. He was a brawny aborigine with a bleached beard of sun-cured fur twisted into a tangle of braids. 'We shall read your fortune and you shall share your provisions with us.'

Before either of the wanderers could reply, the tribe's prophetess leaped down from the ledge and jangled a chain of bones before them, chanting, 'Whirlwinds of fire! Tilting this way! Traveling that way! Whirlwinds of fire crossing Irth's open hand! We are all whirlwinds of fire on the great open hand of mystery. Spinning this way. Moving that way. Crossing the distances that are the stories of our lives.'

She stopped abruptly and offered the bone chain to the travelers. That close, they could smell her parched scent of dried mucilage and rancid wool. Her abnormally stretched mouth hung wide, each tooth fang-pointed and the jaw itself heavy as a vise and stubbled with whiskers that appeared scorched off.

'Hold one end each,' she instructed, her breath dense as baked blood, 'and pull.'

The tribe watched avidly, crouching forward with leering mouths, the starlight and planetglow casting a glossy sheen on their grizzled crowns.

Poch did as he was instructed, and Jyoti met the keen stare of the prophetess and saw in the yellow flatness of the stare a raw and unflinching directness. She took the other end. They pulled, and the dried ligament binding the chain snapped, spewing the bones among the night-shadowed gravel and stones with a cheerless clatter.

'Time afar shows itself,' the prophetess cried. 'And it became so. It became so!' She knelt, and her blackhaired hand crawled spiderwise over the spilled bones. 'You are hunted and you hunt. What hunts you will find you three times. And each time you will stand on the shadow of death. And if you die, your story dies with you. And there is no more. No more. Dark the seed that dies in the ground. Yet if you survive, you will survive this way – by the strength of your bones and the speed of your muscles. Alone by these strengths will you break through to the light and survive if you survive at all. Three times death's shadow falls on you. And all three times, Charm is charmless. On your journey, Irth is flat – and you stand on its edge. Dig deep your roots, for if you fall, you will fall forever.'

The prophetess looked up and nodded her head solemnly. 'Time afar shows itself. And it became so!'

The tribal leader strode forward. 'Your fortune has been told,' he said gruffly. 'Now share with us your provisions.'

'We have little,' Jyoti said and opened the flaps on her belt pouches. 'But what we have, we will give you. Our Charm will sustain us until we find more on the steppes above.' She nodded to her brother, and he opened his belt pouches as well.

They removed handfuls of honey nuts, several sugar stalk roots, and red figs. All this they placed ceremoniously in a pile among the augur pattern of bones.

'You may have our water, too,' Jyoti offered. 'It is Charm-chilled and cleansed. It is refreshing and sweet.'

'Nuts and fruit!' the leader shouted in dismay. 'We cannot survive on such meager fare. We require meat. We drink blood.' The tribe howled agreement and rose as one.

Jyoti unslung her firelock. 'Then we will hunt for you. There are antelope on these slopes.'

'Tonight we have a taste for other meat.' He smiled a mesh of fangs.

With blurred speed, the prophetess snatched the firelock from Jyoti's hand and tossed it behind her. The leader fetched it out of the air, and the tribe jumped down from their perches and closed in with jubilant cries.

Poch screamed and fell back.

Jyoti spun about as if to flee but twisted full around and delivered a slamming circular blow to the prophetess as she lunged forward to pursue. Even as the woman went down, her attacker leaped over her, tumbled, and uncoiled feet first into the leader's chest.

He collapsed backward under the full-body impact, the air kicked out of his lungs with a surprised grunt, and for one instant

Jyoti stood atop him while his arms were still in the air. With a violent twist, she yanked the firelock from his weakened grasp, kicked him hard under the jaw, and charged back the way she had come.

Poch crouched in terror before the pouncing wolf-tribe. The first to reach him grabbed his upraised arms and lifted him upright, the better to gut him.

Jyoti fired point blank at the wereman holding her brother. The blue flash scattered the night for an instant, and the tribe reeled away in a fright. The man she shot dropped Poch and flew over him with the force of the searing bolt, skidding down the pebbly slope and crashing into a dwarf tree. There he lay, spongy with blood, unmoving.

The firelock's muzzle glowing, Jyoti waved her weapon at the tribe with one hand while grasping her stunned brother's arm with the other. She led him up the trace, toward the snarling wolf tribe. They clawed, spat, and hunched, preparing to pounce as one, and Jyoti fired several bursts over their heads.

The luminous bolts sizzled, ionizing the air along their fiery trajectories, and the tribe shrieked and dispersed.

Jyoti and Poch ran up the trace, through the defile in the escarpment, and on to a wide weedy slope of hunched dwarf trees. They kept running until they attained a ledge of blank shale. From there, they dared glance back and saw the tribe huddled about the one Jyoti had shot, tearing him to pieces, ripping the flesh from his bones with their teeth and feeding with noisy ferocity.

They continued their climb with renewed vigor. Poch, at last, was glad for his sister's acrobatic training, which he recognized that night as something far more lethal than sport. He wanted to tell her, but the rigor of their ascent and the sullen wind calling from the steppes urged him to silence.

Dawn found them on a highland heath cluttered with bald granite boulders and piles of rock deposited by vanished glaciers. The lowlands they had crossed lay in darkness below them even as ruddy morning light blazed from the snow peaks and harpy snakes wheeled in the blue depths.

'Jyo!' Poch cried out, his head turning to peer first into one niello eye charm on his shoulder and then the other, confirming his fright. 'They're coming!'

Jyoti, who had been breathing deeply of the cold air and admiring the alpenglow on the snow ranges, checked her eye charms and saw two cacodemons soaring up from the dark void along the path she and Poch had climbed. 'They're tracking us. They must have seen our charmfire last night.'

Poch whimpered and began running for the forested hills beyond the heath.

'Not that way,' Jyoti called to him. 'They'll catch us in the open before we make it. Over here. Follow me.'

She pointed to a tall cairn of mounded boulders where she hoped they could hide in the crevices. They dashed through the purple gorse and reached the rock pile as the cacodemons glided up from the night's depths into the morning shine. They crawled into the wedged spaces between boulders and squirmed about to see if they had been detected.

The cacodemons read the tracks they had left on the heath, one stalking them on the ground, the other hovering above, scanning the red dawn for signs of them. They were close enough to reveal the iridescent gloss of their scales and the scarlet gleam of gums gripping their dagger-fangs.

As they closed in, Poch moaned with fright, 'Shoot me, Jyo! Kill me fast. Don't let them get me.'

'Shut up!' Jyoti pushed Poch deeper into the crawlspace. But there was not room for both of them in this crevice. 'Stay here and don't move.'

'Jyo!' Poch wept. 'Where are you going?'

Jyoti pulled herself out of the crawlspace and swung around to where the cacodemons would spy her first. Quickly, she read the shadowside of the heaped stones, searching for a cleft large enough to accommodate her. She did not dare spare even an instant to glance at the monsters, yet she was aware they had spotted her. She heard the triumphant squawk of the soaring cacodemon beginning its dive, and the crackling of the heather alerted her to the charge of the other.

Into a chute barely as wide as her shoulders, she shoved herself. Claws clacked against the stone as she squeezed into the niche and fired upward with her weapon. The powerful bolt smashed harmlessly into the saurian visage pressed against the opening, and the tight space filled with the styptic stink of seared rock and ozone.

Dust and pebbles churned around her with the aggressive attack of the cacodemon, who pried at the jammed boulders. From the roaring and frenzied scuttling above, she knew that both cacodemons worked to get at her. They had not yet found Poch, and she was glad for that. Perhaps when they took her they would be satisfied and not realize he was hidden nearby.

Cloudy shafts of daylight blinked around her as the cacodemon's powerful limbs widened the chute. In moments it would be large enough for it to scoop her out. She contorted and pulled her knife from its sheath in her boot, preparing herself to die fighting.

*Grandfather!* she called upon the spirit of her teacher, trying to smother her fear in bravado. *Death has found me with my knife in my hand! I will die as I know you died, my last breath a war cry!*

A fierce roar shook the flesh on her bones, and had she not determined to die slashing her enemy, the raving jaws bellowing above would have blasted all vigor from her muscles and para-lyzed her with terror. Instead, she screamed back at the malefic swamp-brown face, and she forced herself to see every detail of the thing – lobed brow, black-rimmed slits for nostrils, and lidless black glass eyes, tiny, rayed with malice, the left one surrounded by a maroon stain like an acid burn. She kept staring even as talons hooked her amulet tunic and hoisted her out of the cranny.

She whacked the cacodemon with her firelock, striking it hard on the cleft of its snout, and when it reflexively flung its head to the side, she drove her blade into the monster's left eye, and the maroon stain glistened with spilled vitreous fluid.

With a shriek of agony, the cacodemon released Jyoti and toppled over, tumbling among spinning rocks into the heather, where it writhed in pain.

Jyoti landed among the rocks with a bruising thud, her hand and knife glutinous with the ichor of the beast's pierced eye. She leaped up at once to find the second cacodemon. It had run to its companion, and both hunkered below her. Obeying a lethal instinct, she climbed to the crest of the rock pile, lay on her stomach and fired a burst at the boulders below. They avalanched with an explosive rumble, and the cacodemons disappeared in the dust fumes.

Clambering down the rock pile, she called, 'Poch! Come out! Hurry!'

Poch poked his head out of his covert and saw Jyoti skid past him. The sky seemed to shake with the crazed roars of the cacodemons. He jumped from the fissure and landed running on the heath, flailing his arms to catch up with his sister.

They sprinted for the wooded hills, throwing terrified looks over their shoulders. Behind, they saw the cacodemons struggling to free themselves from the rockslide. The stabbed one shoved loose first and staggered about clutching its gashed eye, screaming.

The heath climbed sharply toward the trees, and Jyoti and Poch clawed at the bramble and weeds, arms and legs churning to power themselves up the tussocky slope. They flung themselves into the forest and rushed splashing down a rill that carved a narrow, somber avenue through the dark woods.

Until the Charm of their amulets could sustain them no longer, they ran. Exhaustion dropped them in a glade of blue flowers, blossoms so brilliant they looked like pieces of the sky fallen to Irth. Gasping for breath, cheeks pressed to the ground, they saw broken bottles, a twisted cartwheel orange with rust, wood slats with chipped paint and splintered ends, a metal drum gashed and dented and lichenous with corrosion.

'Junk,' Poch wheezed.

'Jettisoned from Andezé Crag,' Jyoti reasoned. 'They dump rubbish on the Keri Steppes. Read about it in a Dominions report.' She sat up, scrutinized her niello eye charms, and, seeing no cacodemons in the forest, drew a deeper breath and exhaled with relief. 'We're just days away from the Malpais Highlands.'

Poch rolled to his back, attention fixed on his eye charms. 'How?' he asked and sucked harder at the mulchy air. 'How did you get us out?'

Jyoti raised her knife, which she still clutched. 'I cut one of them. In the eye.'

'You did that?' Poch sat up on his elbows and saw the gluey blade. 'Did you kill it?'

'I don't know.' She wiped the blade in the loam. 'I don't think so. But I hurt it. And that means – we can fight them.'

'Not with Charm,' Poch marveled, 'but with blades!'

'Maybe.' Jyoti sheathed her knife and supported herself with her firelock as she stood. 'We don't know how they heal. How quickly. Maybe we can't kill them. But we *can* inflict pain.'

'Will they come after us?' Poch asked, again studying his eye charms.

'I'm sure of it.' The power wands had already erased her fatigue, and she looked about for food. 'We must keep moving.'

The forest ascended gradually among hills that opened to high meadows in a cold blue twilight. Rain flurried throughout the night, and they marched over the mushy ground with their hoods up. Gray dawn led them higher into the steppeland, to vast plains of wind-broomed grasses taller than they were. Green bears, griffons, and herds of white antelope occupied this hissing land, and they had to pay close heed to their eye charms to avoid dangerous encounters.

They bore west, toward the snow mountains, and two days and two nights later emerged from the plain on to a sloping champaign. Redthorn and stands of bristle pine covered the campestral downs, and they stocked up on berries and pinyon as they proceeded toward the tundra heights. Several times on the upland trails they spotted cacodemons circling the purple zenith, and they crawled into the shrubs and lay still until the sky was again clear.

The cacodemons flocked on the eyrie cliffs surrounding the capital of the Malpais Highlands, Andezé Crag. Hanging like lizards from the goat-steps of a rocky pass, Jyoti and Poch observed from afar that obsidian city with its numerous needle spires and cliff-hive towers like black coral shapes. Dirigibles floated serenely to and from the sky bunds, and traffic appeared brisk on the ramproads and switchbacks. By this, the wanderers knew that the mountain capital and its Peer, the witch queen Thylia, had capitulated to the Dark Lord.

Aware of that, Jyoti and Poch avoided the pasture hamlets and kept to the wild traces above the gorges. They traversed flower fields of fire colors, bees humming around them, and crossed into a cloud forest of shaggy trees and mountain mists. Night there offered only foggy darkness, and they made their way over the mossy shelves by the blue shine of their amulets. That attracted moths of every shade of ghostliness, and when they exited the dripping forest into orange dawnlight, fumes of tiny pale winged insects came with them.

The moths dispersed with the heat of day, and the Abiding Star rose upon silver breezes of cirrus and a rocky terrain of tundra stubble and barren granite shoulders above abyssal ravines. A vast wall of glassy mountains soared before them, and behind and below ranged swatches of cloud forest, precipitous ledges of tattered mists, and farm terraces connected by wooden bridges dangling with flower vines.

A day of stony walking led to a cold, clear night and views of Hellsgate and Nemora hung in frost-halos. They attained the snowline by morning, and followed glacial streams upward over ice-glazed boulders. Swift, soft clouds flew overhead through a sky of darkest blue. Far, far below, green meadows shone in daylight like spilled jewels.

A long, scarlet twilight guided them over snowy, treacherous tumulus, slippery footing that twisted at their ankles and knees and that led them into another crystal night. They navigated by starfire, crossing ice bridges and the crusty surfaces of glaciers, meandering among canyon rims high above roaring torrents and broad cascades falling like a giant's silver tresses under the luminous star vapors.

The Calendar of Eyes, the tallest mountain in the range, marked their journey's progress, looming larger as they negotiated the maze of steep mountainsides, loose scrabble, and icy cliff faces. After midnight, they came within sight of the sanctuary, a rock-walled settlement of stupa domes and minarets beside a ribbon waterfall.

They reached the sanctuary early in the morning and found devastation. The cacodemons had attacked days earlier, and all that remained of the sages were gnawed bones and rags strewn across the rock fields where they had fled.

The outer vallation of the sanctuary had been toppled to rubble in several places, and snowdrifts migrated across the cobblestone courtyards. More torn carcasses lay scattered there, the bones webbed with flesh leathered by the wind and the cold. Tall, stately windows smashed, the great hall howled and sighed like a cave of winds.

They departed without talking. There was nothing to say. They knew not if the sorcerer Caval was among the anonymous dead or if he had fled or if he had ascended to the timeless heights on the Calendar of Eyes. But they could not remain in this inhospitable place. They only hoped that their power wands would hold enough charge for them to get down from the cold heights.

Knowing that the Dark Lord held the Malpais Highlands, they traveled south, out of the snow mountains and eventually to the riverine plains in the Falls of Mirdath. They conserved Charm by using only one power wand at a time. On a bosky stream they found a kayak lodged against a tree that had fallen into the water and riffled the current with river kelp caught in its submerged branches.

They righted and bailed the kayak and rode it downstream, avoiding the main river and its settlements and keeping to small tributaries that wound in emerald-dark tunnels under mossy branches hung with air plants, orchids, and bromeliads. After a few days on these chattering streams, portaging small foaming falls and brisk rapids, they shot out of the steep country into the shoals. The tributaries trickled over sandbars and vanished into pebble flats on the grassy banks of a prismatic wall of gigantic trees – the Rainbow Forests of Bryse.

Out of the sandy ground with its duff gritty as glass shards, thick boles grew with crystalline bark of glossy scales. The shiny trunks divided high overhead into boughs of varied colors, so that each tree displayed sprays of spectral leaves in many different hues. The corridors of the forest filtered light into sparkling rays of all wavelengths. The color-shattered light of the dense woods awed and disoriented them.

Wandering the shimmering boulevards of the forest, they misread the bright mottled shadows around them and in their niello eye charms, and they snagged themselves in the web of a dragon-spider. Big as a man, the red-and-black splotched arachnid pranced toward them silently, its eight legs a mad blur as it hurried to pierce its prey with its scissoring pincers.

Poch screamed as his struggles bound him tighter, and Jyoti screamed with him when her firelock tangled in the gummy web. She managed to twist her arm behind her back and reach the charge pin and the trigger. Her first shot cut the guy lines of the web and splattered sparks of wild spectra from a shattered bough.

The spider fell upon Poch, and his screams weirded to a yodeling pain.

Jyoti pulled the firelock free, and her second blast smashed the spider to brown pulp and twitching leg-parts. She hurried to her brother and staunched with one hand the bubbling wound at the base of his neck while her other hand groped for the theriacal opals in the inside pocket of her tunic. At their touch, the bleeding stopped, and the wound began healing. It was deep and it would be a few hours before he could move.

Poch grimaced with frantic fear, amplifying the terror of the spider-attack: 'They must have seen it! They must have seen it!'

Jyoti activated all the power wands to calm him down. 'We're deep in a forest, Poch. They won't have seen it.'

But she did not believe that, nor did he. The two bolts of charmlight had flashed brilliantly through the millions of prisms that were the forest leaves. The vigilant cacodemons could not have missed it.

As soon as Poch felt strong enough, she dragged him to a covert among the huge buttressed rootcoils under the glittering hiss of the eerie and beautiful trees. They waited in silence. The theriacal opals completed their healing, and Poch was left with no scar but the ghastly memory.

Footfalls thudded in the tight, shining alleys of the forest.

Poch curled tighter under the root arch. 'They're coming!'

'No. It's just one. Listen.' Jyoti distinctly heard the heavy gait of a large beast. In her niello eye charms, almost camouflaged by the stained glass shadows of the forest, she found it. Lumbering beneath the interlocked boughs, the scaly creature advanced slowly, its tiny inkdrop eyes reading their tracks in the silica leaf litter.

She saw then, by the maroon stain around its right socket, it was the second of the cacodemons that had attacked them on the Steppes of Keri, the one she did not stab. It was alone. *Is the other one dead?* she wondered and hoped, *Maybe I can slay this one, too.*

Then a bizarre singsong crying began. It sounded like the imperfect utterances of a malformed being – mutilated phrases and half-sense: *Blind nothing – no thing is what is – blind, blind, blind nothing – no thing is what is – blind nothing . . .*

Several voices spoke, yet she saw only one monster in the crooked shadows. Then she saw them: The gorgon faces pressed into the creases of the cacodemon's torso had begun to move their bent mouths, chanting odd words—

The image in the niello eye charm faded. She looked at her other epaulet, but that eye charm, too, had blurred.

'I can't see anything!' Poch called in a desperate whisper. 'My eye charms are empty!'

A sudden fatigue weighted the brother and sister, a sorrow in their muscles, a lethargy in their bones that was not synchronized with the wild fear in their scramming hearts. Jyoti reached to adjust the power wands in her collar, but they had gone dead. All the amulets in her tunic had lost their Charm.

Reflexively, she checked the firelock. It remained fully charged, and by that she knew that the cacodemon's blinding song had only drained the Charm circuited to their bodies. It was a mesmermur song that had opened them to the demon's influence. But that thing could not hypnotize her firelock. Her grip relaxed, and she set the charge at full and slung the weapon over her shoulder.

'Jyo!' Poch rasped. 'What's happening?'

'Hush.' She drew her knife. 'The cacodemon is casting a spell.'

Lying flat and peering around the tree's pediment, she watched the cacodemon slouch into view. The crazed faces in its belly had stopped yammering, and their eyes glinted like stars.

Then the great lobed head spoke, its voice twisting like smoke, 'Jyoti – Poch – you are close. I smell you now. A red smell. Your blood spinning. Soon spilling.'

Jyoti pulled her head back. 'Stay here,' she told her brother. 'I'm going to lead it away. When it comes after me, you run the other way. Try to keep to the rootledges. Leave no tracks.'

Before Poch could protest, Jyoti rolled away and ran bent low around the colossal tree.

'I stole your Charm,' the voice of smoke said. 'I – Ys-o. Now you cannot run. You can only die.'

Jyoti burst into the open, and a roar brattled the tree branches as Ys-o saw her and charged. She ducked under shrubs, and the cacodemon ripped them away with one slash of its claws. She was gone, scuttling and rolling through the underbrush. The cacodemon pursued, kicking through the bushes and bellowing angrily.

Without Charm, Jyoti tired almost at once, and fear alone powered her over rootcables and under thorn arbors. Cutting hard among the trees, she forced the cacodemon to slow down and gained precious distance in her flight. But too soon, her breath burned in her lungs and her legs wobbled. When she knew she could flee no farther, she threw herself against a colossal tree and fired rapid bursts into the forest awning.

The cacodemon lunged to smash her against the tree-wall, and a heavy bough struck it behind the head. As it went down, Jyoti shoved forward and drove her knife into the beast's face, ripping toward the nostril. A roar of maddening pain flung her backward, and she ducked and rolled into the underbrush.

Again, she turned and fired bursts, this time at the trunk of the mammoth tree where the cacodemon thrashed itself upright. The shearing blasts shattered the glassy bark and sprayed hot flechettes at the enraged beast. It covered its eyes and writhed with grotesque, misshapen cries, and the faces in its torso shrieked in a horror of agony.

Bawling cacophonously, the cacodemon fled, crashing blindly through the underbrush. It collided with a tree and staggered about. Jyoti aimed at the trunk, and bursts of blue charmlight exploded its rosin bark to fiery projectiles that shredded the nearby bushes and gashed the monster, tearing away gouts of its scales and spilling black blood.

It sprang into the air and crashed to the ground under the weight of its wounds. Screaming, it wrenched upright and shambled away.

Jyoti wanted to hunt it down now that she knew how to hurt it, but she was too tired. Having severely maimed Ys-o, she hoped Charm would return to her power wands, and she stood in a shaft of daylight, wanting the amulets to recharge. But they did not. Wearily, she shuffled in the opposite direction from the cacodemon and found her brother hiding inside a hollowed log.

The cacodemon had fled north, and so they continued south, much slower and far more carefully without the strength of their amulets. Adrenalin powered them through most of that day, but at nightfall, exhaustion asserted itself. They lashed themselves with vines to sturdy roots and took turns sleeping, yet even when they slept, they clutched a knife.

In the night, predators drifted through the aluminum light of the forest. Molten eyes watched from the shadows, the lumens of hunger dimming when the sentinel threw a stone or waved the fire-lock. The radiations of howls and cries permeated the dark hours and drenched sleep with dreams filthy with danger and fright.

By day, the wanderers moved gingerly, watchful for dragon-spiders and camouflaged adders. They collected water only from springs that gurgled out of rock, tart with a lithic aftertaste but free from animal contaminants. Their sure but aimless destination was to find a way through the Rainbow Forests, away from the colorful and lethal deceptions, to one of the large cities of Bryse – Lake Apocalypse, Mount Szo, or Soft Anvil – there to tell the Peers about the vulnerability of the cacodemons.

But the trek was arduous and tediously slow. Fortunately, the woods abounded in edible fruits and nut-ladened shrubs. They ate well. From the windy summits of trees, under the flying clouds, they searched for settlements and saw only vast, chromatic tracts of forest.

One slick night, with rain drooling through the canopy and nearby streams rocking loudly in their beds, a sibyl sought shelter in the root cove where they had lashed themselves. Poch was asleep, his unconscious body buoyant in its moorings, and Jyoti's gasp did not waken him.

The sibyl, no larger than a small child, stood dripping under the eave of the root buttress, her crimson and green wings bedraggled, her marble nakedness jeweled with raindrops that sparkled with the faint, breathing glow that suffused her perfectly white flesh. Her clawed, three-fingered hand brushed inky streaks of hair from her vivid, inhuman face. Her curved eyes, glazed as quartz, studied the sister and brother.

'I am cold,' she said in a silken voice from far away, her tongue of fire a blue radiance in her round mouth.

Jyoti set the charge pin on her firelock to its lowest setting and pointed the muzzle at the visitor. Its thermal breath luffed over the sibyl, and she gratefully raised her winged arms and revealed her sleek nakedness gleaming with iridescent streaks of rain.

When she was dry, she folded her wings about her and curled against the rootwall. The blue spark in the bore-hole of her mouth flickered, 'Ask me what you would know.'

'Where is the nearest settlement, sibyl?' Jyoti inquired at once, eager to find her way out of the perilous woods.

'Soft Anvil is east,' she answered in her soft voice. 'Twelve or more days as you would walk. But danger awaits you there.'

'Why? Are there cacodemons in Soft Anvil?'

'Not yet.' The sibyl fluttered her crossed wings and leaned closer, confiding, 'But your destiny is not there either.'

'What is my destiny?'

'Do you not remember?' The sibyl sat back with surprise. 'The weretribe told you.'

'I don't remember.'

The sibyl closed her eyes, lifted her crescent face, and sang in a wispy voice drifting into vastness: 'You are hunted and you hunt. What hunts you will find you three times. And each time you will stand on the shadow of death. And if you die, your story dies with you. And there is no more. No more. Dark the seed that dies in the ground. Yet if you survive, you will survive this way – by the strength of your bones and the speed of your muscles. Alone by these strengths will you break through to the light and survive if you survive at all. Three times death's shadow falls on you. And all three times, Charm is charmless. Remember, on your journey, Irth is flat – and you stand on its edge. Dig deep your roots, for if you fall, you will fall forever.'

*Three times!* Jyoti thrilled with understanding. 'The caco-demons have found us twice already.'

'And twice you have survived by strength and speed.' She lowered her head under the weight of a pause and opened her luminous eyes. 'What hunts you will find you again.'

'When?'

'When you sleep.'

'Soon?'

'Your soon is not mine.'

'Where will it find us?'

'In the south,' the sibyl promised in her remote voice. 'In the grasslands of Sharna-Bambara. If you avoid it, you will never find what you hunt.'

'Caval!' Jyoti remembered their original quest as if from a former lifetime. 'Where will we find the sorcerer Caval?'

'At the Cloths of Heaven. He has gone there to gain strength for the tasks ahead.'

Jyoti was sure that what the sibyl said was true. Her scalp knew it.

'Rest now,' the sibyl said and closed her mineral eyes. From the socket of her mouth, starlight seeped and with it came a music of vacancy, so empty it could hold everything, like a mirror with its perpetual questioning of all it confronts, constant and passionless. These mesmermurs lulled Jyoti to sleep. When she woke and sank back to the ground in her vine-tangle, morning's prismal colors stood outside the root cove, and the sibyl was gone.

Poch was unhappy to hear of the sibyl. 'What if she lied?' he asked as they hiked south through the iridal forest. 'The Cloths of Heaven – those are ruins. Why would Caval be there?'

'What better place to hide from the Dark Lord?'

'But it's in Nhat – the Dark Lord's dominion.' Poch's upper lip shivered. 'We can't go there. What about our plan to find a nearby city and tell them how to kill cacodemons?'

'The sibyl said we would never find Caval if we do that.'

'What if she lied?'

'Sibyls can't lie.'

'Maybe you misunderstood her.'

'No.' Jyoti spoke as she scanned the variegated depths of tree lanes and tiered shrubs. 'She was very clear. We have to go south. To Sharna-Bambara. We have to stand down the cacodemons one more time. It will come on your watch.'

Poch moaned. 'The prophecy said if we failed, we'd fall off the Irth forever. Are they going to throw us into the Gulf?'

Jyoti slapped an open hand against her brother's chest and stopped him in midstep. At his scuffed boot tip, a scarlet scorpion-asp coiled, nearly invisible in the red shadows, only its fangs and stinger glinting like diamond points.

'If you don't pay heed,' Jyoti warned, 'you'll throw yourself into the Gulf.'

They proceeded in watchful silence. A breeze, charismatic with fruit pollen, led them to a grove of blue banana. They ate and moved on. Late in the day, they crossed through a wide depression warted with limestone, remnants of an ancient lake. Sinkholes matted over with ivy plunged remorselessly at random intervals and offered ample fatal opportunities. When they climbed out the far end at twilight, they slewed staggerfooted with fatigue, their eyes dizzied and aching from reading pathways in the shattered rainbows.

That night they moored themselves to the red stilts of a fig tree and fell asleep together. Poch woke at midnight to find tiny, barbed landcrabs crusting his hands and face, eating salty wafers of skin. He screamed and flung them off him and screamed again to see his sister equally matted with the thorny parasites. The crabs vanished into the litter of the forest floor, and Poch readily agreed to take the first watch.

The Rainbow Forests of Bryse held them in their labyrinth of prisms for a dozen more frightful days and restless nights, reducing their tunics to tatters. Even their boots wore thin and had to be patched with bark and twine. On the brilliant afternoon that they stepped through the trees on to a bluff of mushroom rings above the soughing grasslands of Sharna-Bambara, they looked like wraiths.

Vision dazed from their long wandering among the heatless flames of the forest, the plains below appeared pale, faded, and apparitional as a mirage. The horizon's thick mane of grass tossed in the wind and carried to them minty scents of sedge and rain. Wearily and with fearful apprehensions, they descended toward the colorless land and its slippery cloud shadows.

Their approach released arrowheads of birds. Small animals darted through the reeds.

'How far is Nhat?' Poch wanted to know.

'Days and days, brother,' Jyoti answered, standing on tiptoe to peer above the tall hay. Veils of rain smudged the distant sky and threads of lightning tangled and vanished without thunder. 'Sharna-Bambara is larger than Bryse.'

'What if Caval is not at the Cloths of Heaven when we get there?'

'He's a sorcerer.' She regarded Poch, and the sight of his long, unkempt hair and tanned flesh drawn taut about startled eyes staring from sunken sockets hurt her heart. 'Perhaps *he* will find *us*.'

The boy asked nothing more. Before the Cloths of Heaven, before the hope of Caval, lay the third encounter with the cacodemons, the one that the sibyl prophesied would come to him. He tried to forget about that and put his mind on the trek before them. Waves and ripples on the grass ocean scattered across the world, tossing glints of pollen and airy clouds of butterflies.

Lacking vines to moor themselves at night, the nomads took to cutting burrows in the soft loam with their knives. They weighted their torsos with soil and what rocks they could find and left their faces and arms free. But that was not as satisfactory as the ties they had utilized in the forest, and more than once the sleeper budged free of the soil and had to be woken by the sentinel before the nocturnal tides lofted them into the Gulf.

They tried sleeping by day and hiking the flat terrain at night under the starglow. But they could not see as far and twice in one night trespassed the lairs of animals they would easily have seen by day. One was a hive-cluster of viper-wasps, dirt towers tall as a man and fragile with knobby protuberances of egg-cases. Colliding among the fragile mounds and smashing numerous bulbs in the dark enraged the hives, and viper-wasps bloomed in inky clouds against the stars.

Fortunately, the cool night slowed the swarms, and the trespassers fled without being stung. In their haste to get away, however, they barged into a camp of sleeping hippogriffs. Crazed wings exploded into flight, claws ripped the air with searing screams, and stout thighbones kicked hooves and pounded the ground like cannon.

To keep from getting crushed in the stampede, Jyoti fired bursts of red flares that drove the screeching beasts away from them. The shrieks and thunder of the herd evoked panther roars and yowls of startled dog packs. All that night, sister and brother sat back to back, scanning the starfields for silhouettes of cacodemons.

Under the morning groundmist, Poch slept. Jyoti took her turn at noon. And that was when Ys-o and Ss-o arrived, crawling snakewise through the tall grass, glittering with silver dew.

Poch heard a hiss, turned and saw eel-grins and spider-eyes peering at him from the cane shadows. He wanted to shout his sister awake, but the cacodemons had begun to sing a dreamy noise that scraped the will from his nerves and left him jaw-slung and voiceless, staring with wild eyes at the lizard masks: *Blind nothing – no thing is what is – blind, blind, blind nothing – no thing is what is – blind nothing . . .*

The black depths in the cacodemons' tiny eyes looked back into him, and he did not move. The monsters did not move either. The boy held the firelock, and it pointed at the ground before them. Each blast would spray rock and quartz nodules at them with mangling force.

'Put down the firelock, Poch,' Ys-o whispered.

'We have come to take you to the Dark Lord,' Ss-o added quietly.

Poch shook his head. Words opened and closed like butterfly wings: 'You – tried – to kill – us . . .'

'No—' Ys-o hushed him.

*Blind, blind, blind nothing – no thing is what is – blind nothing . . .*

'The Dark Lord sent us for the margraves' children,' Ss-o explained with soothing softness. 'But your sister attacked us. She hurt us.'

The cacodemons slowly edged closer, and daylight touched their wounds: Ss-o tilted its long head to reveal the gashed socket emptied of its eye, crusty with pain; Ys-o, too, looked deformed, its snout cleaved to an ugly scar and its frilled throat and muscular shoulders mottled with black scabs.

'We forgive you the pain,' Ys-o assured.

'We are but servants of the Dark Lord,' Ss-o spoke gently. 'Come away with us.'

They rose to their full heights, and the sight of the warped faces pressed into their bellies startled Poch. He gasped, and his finger tightened on the trigger.

*Blind nothing – no thing is what is—*

He lowered the weapon and gazed up in awe at the flexing talons and widening fangs.

Jyoti, roused by her brother's gasp, lay still, peeking through her lashes, measuring distances. The queer mouthings of the abdominal faces lulled her pounding heart and kept panic in check, leaving room in her mind for calculation. In this crucial moment, she was grateful that she made a habit of sleeping with her knife in her hand.

One more step, and the cacodemons would be close enough to strike. Jyoti did not wait. She flung her knife at Ys-o, and the blade pierced its belly, cleaving the brow of a singing face. Following through her movement, she hurled herself over her brother, pulled the firelock from his hands, and rolled off firing.

The first shots cut high, splashing harmlessly against the cacodemons' legs. Ys-o, ragefully shouting with pain yanked the

239

knife free, swung about and lashed with its serrated tail. It sliced grassheads to chaff and scythed a whistling inch from Poch's head. The boy dove under the writhing tail and scrambled away.

Ss-o leaped after him, but Jyoti's second burst struck the ground under the lunging cacodemon. The explosion of dirt and stones heaved the creature into the air and dropped it to its back.

Firing rapidly, Jyoti gouged the ground, flinging incandescent rocks and fuming soil at the howling beasts. She advanced, intent on destroying the killers, and they fled before her, spouting black blood and maimed cries. She exhausted one cartridge, tossed it aside, grabbed another from her belt, and slammed it into the breech, pausing only briefly in her fusillade.

The cacodemons bounded skyward and circled back. When they dove, Jyoti fired at their shadows on the ground. The blasts geysered deadly jets, and the cacodemons pulled back abruptly and gazed down from an impotent distance.

Jyoti ducked into the grass and in moments vanished from sight. The cacodemons glided overhead for a while and then departed, weakened by their wounds. Their furious cries climbed down the sky for a long time.

Poch sat sparking with cold sweat, his terror unmitigated by Charm. Jyoti tried to soothe him, but he shoved her away.

'They came to escort us to the Dark Lord!' he shouted bitterly.

'You believe that?' Jyoti knelt before him, scowling with incredulity.

'They could have jumped me.' He spit the words.

'They were afraid of the firelock. If you had put it down, they'd have gutted you on the spot.' She waved the weapon at him, its muzzle still warping the air around it with its heat. 'This is all that saved us.'

The boy said nothing. He stared hard into the switching grass shadows. When Jyoti spun away angrily and stalked off to search for her knife, his face wrinkled, and he wept.

## A Maiden in the Fastness of Ogres

＊—＊

Ralli-Faj hung from his stick among fragrant silks of perfume in a garden beneath the Palace of Abominations. Around him, walls of green and blue glass enclosed flowering trees, vine arbors, hedges shaved to animal shapes, and a cirque of boulders hewn of raw gemstones. This was his piece of heaven.

The Dark Lord had blessed him with this serene paradise and made him master of the hell beyond. So long as he managed well the terrors of Hu'dre Vra's prison, all the pleasures of this soft world were his to exploit. The tenderly spiced air lofted the warlock to unprecedented heights of rapture.

Most of each day he spent deep in euphoric trance, a seraph of light singing in the sky's abyss among the seven-horned stars. Dumb with joy, all inner narrative silenced in him, he drifted free and triumphant, a mystery of flame and pleasure. This was a fulfillment far grander than anything he had won for himself with Charm.

As a warlock, he had learned to float in a small space of bliss, and he had enjoyed it so thoroughly that he had allowed his very flesh to wither away to a husk. But that thrill had been a paltry and wan glimmer of the radiance that the Dark Lord gave to him.

By Hu'dre Vra's magic, he lofted upon the very wings of stars, high above the blue wall of day.

At nightfall, the happy dream ended, and he returned to Irth, which in his lightstruck eyes seemed a thing of shadows. All form was a flimsy aggregation of atoms hung in a void of immeasurable blackness, all life so much diamond ash molded in frail and ludicrous shapes. To bear it, he breathed deeply of the garden's soporific perfumes until the glare of his dazzling trance dimmed and he could see clearly once more in the dense and dim world of matter.

Then he made his rounds. Thousands of days ago, Ralli-Faj had lost his physical powers of locomotion and learned how to project his consciousness out of the hung skin of his body and into his surroundings. It was not possible for him to go far. Charm carried him like a mote in the wind, skittering about in a general direction. That had been sufficient for his purposes in the catacomb citadel from where he ruled his dominion.

But since arriving at the Palace of Abominations, he had received from the Dark Lord the magical power to walk among the shadows of the world, a shade himself. At his whim, he could remain invisible or reveal himself to those around him. And he could journey as far as a man could walk to midnight and then walk back by dawn. He had never actually done this, because among the Reef Isles of Nhat there was nowhere to go. Thus, he constrained himself to a nightly tour of the Palace of Abominations, the work camp, and the tidal flats where, sometimes, he wandered out among the scavengers to watch the ebb flow retreat in a shiny black wall toward the Gulf.

This night, he began his rounds as usual within the palace. After the fragrant and supple scents of the garden had grounded him in his physical senses once again, he stepped out of the limp skin of his body. Invisible and chilled, he walked through the trim garden casting not even a shadow under the blue glow of the suspended crystal spheres.

An alabaster portal in the glassy wall led to a helical ladder that ascended toward scaffolds, derricks, and trestles – an immense framework jutting at skewed angles into a sky bright with the day's frayed ribbons. Hordes of cacodemons roosted on those skeletal ramparts, a shifting black cope that vaulted toward a zenith where the first stars ignited.

The demons were in the midst of constructing the white stone façade of the palace. It would be a vast pyramid when it was completed. The warlock had gruesome plans for the labyrinth of chambers, shafts, and pits that the four triangular walls would enclose.

At the apex, the Dark Lord's adytum would overview a plunging maze of torture cells where the Peers of Irth, embalmed alive in black magic, would suffer eternally in their pain crypts. Their anguish would power a winding engine that the warlock envisioned pulling a chain of torture boxes endlessly around a circle – a circle that Hu'dreVra's magic would suspend vertically on the face of his pyramid, under the apex, at the portal to his adytum. And on that pain chain would ride the most infamous of Wrat's despised foes – Lord Drev the arrogant wizarduke and his haughty brood reduced to so much living suffering, so much cargo on pain's relentless journey to nowhere.

Ralli-Faj delighted to behold this dark fantasy coming to reality at his whim. He strolled among the torture tiers, rampways where soon permanent stone vaults would be installed to house the damned. For now, the living bodies of the Dark Lord's enemies hung encased within oval cages of amber.

Baronet Fakel was in one cage, and his two sons, the wizarduke's nephews, shared the cage beside him. They looked like foetal creatures embalmed in bloody yolks. Naked, curled upon themselves, and glistening with wet crimson feathers, ripped tissues, tattered frills of flesh, they floated in an oily smoke of ruby seepings. They were alive – and they suffered.

The warlock marveled at the Dark Lord's power. His enemies twitched with jolts of pain and their eyes swiveled with anguish in their bruised sockets and yet their bodies appeared already necrotic, days dead. *How does he sustain them?* he asked himself and shrugged. *How does he do anything?*

Continuing on past other tortured bodies, all Peers and former allies of Lord Drev, Ralli-Faj considered the host of cacodemons perched above him. Large and ferocious and animated with savage intelligence, they nonetheless appeared to the warlock like apparitions, fiercely vivid ghosts. They ate nothing. They drank nothing. They had simply fallen out of the night with the Dark Lord and stood vigilantly in attendance upon him.

Theirs was like no magic Ralli-Faj had ever witnessed in deed or history. It defied all the laws of Charm. He would not have believed such abominations could be possible if he himself had not witnessed their tangible reality. Many times, to sate his curiosity, he had gone up to them and touched their scaly hide, outlined with his ghostly fingertips the grisly faces embedded in their torsos, and felt the ivory razors of their upturned tusks.

He paid them little heed on this tour. They obeyed an evil power he did not fathom, and, at last assured of their dangerous reality, he was content to leave them to their avid watchfulness. His assignment from Hu'dre Vra was to attend to the torment of his enemies, not to wonder at the Dark Lord's power.

Before each cage, he paused and reached out with his sensitivity to ascertain that the prisoner lived and suffered. He had strict orders to make certain that none of the captives died. Indeed, most of the Dark Lord's victims had the power to end their lives. They were masters of sorcery, for they were Peers. And though their Charm was helpless to free them, it was sufficient to snuff the lifespark within themselves. All that prevented them from taking their own lives and ending their torture was the warlock's surveillance.

When a caged Peer dwindled too close to death, the warlock had to bring over one of the crystal spheres. They relayed the Dark Lord's magic. Usually, Ralli-Faj kept those spheres in the garden, the better to enhance his daily rapture trances. And when more than three were dispersed at a time to break the Charm of the Peers, his bliss diminished. But that had only happened a few times, in the first days when the will of the Peers was yet strong.

Recently, there was not enough Charm in the captives for them to defy the cruelty that bound them to their torture. Yet Ralli-Faj insisted on watching them closely. He did not want to invite upon himself the wrath of Hu'dre Vra and find himself in one of these eggs of torment hatching a new species of suffering.

And so, he was grateful for the help of Whipcrow, the ally that the warlock had summoned by his own Charm. With him to watch over the labor camp, Ralli-Faj was free to pay greater heed to the captured Peers – and to enjoy his raptures.

Hu'dre Vra had appointed the ogres to run the labor camp and to take their share of treasure, but he wanted Ralli-Faj to oversee them and ensure that the workers served the Dark Lord and not the overseers. Also, only city dwellers and those of the fortunate classes were to labor. Those who had been scavengers or who had lived at the lowest levels of Irth society as aborigines and nomads were to receive the treasures gleaned from the tidal flats.

The warlock left these tasks to Whipcrow, though Ralli-Faj made a point of including the labor camp and the flats on his rounds, wanting there to be no chance of the Dark Lord finding disfavor with him.

Sometimes he made himself patrol the camp in his physical form so that all could see him and recognize his authority. To accomplish this feat with his boneless husk of a body, he had the cacodemons strap him tightly with crude, heavy thongs to a crossbar fixed between two stilts. The hard ironwood of the stilts carried amulets – power wands inside the hollowed tops and talismans mounted at the top ends and connected to the crossbar and his tied-off skin by conjure-wire and amulets of small bones and gourds. By their Charm, the stilts walked like scissors, the very sharp points marking his gait on the stone pavement of the palace: *Tok. Tok. Tok.*

On the dirt paths of the labor camp and on the sandy beach, his Charm hovered him a wormwidth off the ground so that he could advance across any surface, even water. But this frightened everyone – the prisoners *and* the ogres – and interfered with productivity.

And so this night, when he was confident that the Peers in their cages languished in mortal agony, he did not require his skin to be secured to the stilts. In his disembodied form, he proceeded down rampways flanked by cacodemons to the swamp path. It curled among fallen behemoths of trees with dislodged rootcrowns tall as hills and broken trunks luminous with fungal gills and nodules. Marsh mist pooled among the forest's mangrove stilts and drifted in whorls across the trail.

The labor camp had emptied at nightfall. Two ogres remained behind to watch after the handful of laborers assigned to clean the latrines and the galley. Smeared with excrement, the ditch workers gleamed like salamanders. The ogres paced before the sturdy log warehouse where they stored their treasure, their muscle-packed bodies moving with surprising litheness while the small faces in their large heads attentively watched the prisoners.

Ralli-Faj entered by the front gate of lashed bamboo, open to allow the laborers to cart out the ordure and dump it in the marsh. Satisfied that all was well in the camp, he exited through the back gate, where the rutted path led to the wagons that the workers pulled along the shore while retrieving the tide's treasures.

Over a thousand scavengers shuffled toward the sea under hanging vines and ragged draperies of moss. The ogres shepherded them with long gnarly staves and gruff shouts, and bioluminescent moths flitted about them, drawn by the torches set in the sconces on the wagons.

Whipcrow, dark as a piece of the night with his black flamboyant hair spikes and swarthy wedge of a face, stood in one of the wagons enticing the yoked workers to pull faster with promises of favored positions on the flats. Since his arrival, the labor camp had become more productive. Unlike the ogres, he did not bully the scavengers but employed techniques he had learned as a factory manager to motivate the crews. He offered incentives of food and rest for those who worked effectively, and he carefully organized and rotated the crews to avoid rivalries and disputes.

Ralli-Faj appreciated Whipcrow's expertise, yet he invariably revealed himself to the manager on his rounds, wanting him to know that he was being watched. The warlock climbed on to the trundling wagon and unveiled his mask-like face with its empty eyeholes and its round mouth bright with blue fire.

'Who are the new prisoners?' he asked in a voice more resonant and less sibilant than the sounds that hissed from his physical husk. He turned his vacant eyes toward the large man with the furry blond beastmarks yoked beside a small, mousy woman. 'It is not like you to mismatch such a pair.'

Whipcrow bowed in a fluster of fright and reverence. The abrupt appearance of the warlock always shocked him. The man was a ghost, a living dead thing. 'Master, I have my reasons,' he said in a hushed voice, meant to be heard only by the wraith before him. 'These are two I know from my time in Saxar and my journey out of the Qaf.'

'Two that you loathe, clearly.'

Whipcrow peered from under his pencil blue brows at the warlock. There was no hiding anything from this being, and so he spoke freely: 'They betrayed me. Of the thousand and seventy-four laborers who serve you, I ask for the authority to torment only these two.'

'The laborers do not serve *me*, Whipcrow,' the floating mask spoke angrily. 'They belong wholly to our lord, Hu'dre Vra. Your request to torment them is denied.'

Whipcrow bowed deeper to hide his frustrated scowl.

'Torment is out of the question,' the warlock insisted. 'But harassment is not. So long as these two remain as productive as the others, you may trouble them for your vengeance as much as you please.'

'Thank you, Master Faj!' Whipcrow responded with gratitude

— but when he looked up, the warlock had vanished. The manager did not doubt that Ralli-Faj was yet nearby, and he continued to nod with grinning satisfaction. 'Thank you. I shall inflict pain upon these two with the utmost finesse.'

Dogbrick's keen ears had heard this exchange over the noise of the wagon wheels, and he looked to Tywi with concern. But she had heard nothing. Not that it mattered. Since arriving at the labor camp, she had behaved as though death alone could offer her freedom. He bent harder under the yoke, trying to lift from her small shoulders as much of the burden as he could.

Whipcrow clapped, pointed, and several other laborers gathered at the sides of the wagon and helped to push. The parade of work crews marched through cypress archways where nightbirds clicked and fretted. In the dark tunnel, the salty tang of the sea thickened and the sound of the surf crashed. Then the swamp's murky avenue opened among dunes bristly with salt cane and seagrapes.

The ogres herded the work crews toward their various jobs, raking the tide litter, scouring the sand, dredging the shallows, and, most dangerous of all, trawling the deeper water where the combers collapsed and foamed. Whipcrow pointed toward the distant phosphorescent glow of collapsing waves and ordered, 'Get your nets.'

'Send me,' Dogbrick said, staring up at where the manager stood in the empty wagon grinning at them. 'Leave Tywi to rake the sand. She does not merit your ire.'

Whipcrow slanted his sharp face toward where the ogres stamped through the sand shouting in their thick voices at the work crews.

Tywi picked up her coiled net from the equipment cart, and Dogbrick glowered at the manager. 'Recall what your master said, Whipcrow. If harm comes to her, he will not be pleased.'

'Go!' Against the star-flung sky, Whipcrow's silhouette shook like a black flame.

Dogbrick held his harsh gaze a moment, then turned and took

248

the heavy net from Tywi. They waded past the crews raking the shoals and stood briefly in the chill water watching the big waves looming up, contemplating the shore, and collapsing into smoking heaps of froth and spume.

The outbound current nagged at them, and when the foam flew past and dragged back, Tywi clutched at Dogbrick's arm.

'Stay behind me,' he advised and cast the weighted net on to the seething water.

Tywi anchored one end of the seine while Dogbrick sloshed deeper and pulled in the weights, bringing up seaweed and leathery eggs. They threw the eggs back, moved several paces along, and cast the net again. This time they snagged a large ribcage webbed with kelp, a chimera's skeleton. Dogbrick waved for a recovery crew, and they shoved a floating barrow through the churning water to where Tywi and Dogbrick rocked among the waves, untangling the net from the slatted bones.

The next several throws brought in the rest of the skeleton – the chimera's blunt skull with its fabled crimson teeth, the thick thighbones, and the vertebral coils of the serpent tail and its barbed tip. The recovery crew laughed with delight at their luck and offered a ride to shore on the barrow. A large find like this guaranteed a food break and an easier assignment, but Whipcrow waved them back into the waves.

'He wants to kill us,' Tywi despaired. 'He ain't going to be happy till we're drowned.'

'Don't cry,' Dogbrick said and maneuvered himself before her to take the brunt of the waves' impact. 'That's what he wants. Deny him that and he will weary soon enough of this harsh game. Come, Tywi. The night is beautiful. We will make play of this work.'

But the battering of the waves and the entangling undertow offered no joy. They netted mostly seaweed and driftwood and only a few kraken teeth. And though Dogbrick strove bravely to protect the small woman from the pummeling breakers, by midnight her legs gave out and the riptide swept her away. He dove after her and pulled her sputtering from violent water.

On shore, she lay shivering in the sand. The ogre who stalked down from the dunes and stood over her spoke only one word, 'Basilisk.'

Tywi cried and struggled to her feet. Dogbrick stood protectively before her. 'No!' he said gruffly to the compact face of the ogre. 'She can rake the tideline or work the shoals.'

Whipcrow arrived, a blue sneer on his lipless face. 'My offer from the forest remains. Will you give yourself to me, Tywi? Or to the basilisk?'

Dogbrick hoisted Whipcrow off his feet by his throat. 'Touch her and I will break all your bones!'

A thick hand seized Dogbrick by his mane, jerked him into the air, and shook him until he released Whipcrow. The manager fell choking into the sand and rasped through his bruised larynx, 'Punish him!'

The ogre holding Dogbrick by his locks carried him away at arm's length. The thief swung his legs, trying to twist free, but that only tightened the pain in his scalp. He winced a hurt stare and then forced himself to look back at Tywi valiantly, 'Do not fear.'

*Do not fear!* He could think of nothing else to say, and he felt smaller for that. There should be much more to say of courage in so desperate a moment. But the pain in his scalp left no room for bold thoughts, and without his rat-star gems, his mind felt like a bird without sufficient feathers.

The ogre lugged him through the dunes to the swamp verges. There, it threw him down among squalid tentacles of creeping fungi and nightwort. Before he could push to his feet, the ogre snatched both ankles in one powerful hand and hoisted him upside down. It pounded his head against the mud-caked lip of a viper-wasp hive until the swarm seethed forth. Then it rammed his head into the hive and dashed away.

Dogbrick tore his head free and thrashed among the strangler vines and lichenous compost under a vibrant red cloud of viper-wasps. Howling, he bounced to his feet and ran toward the dunes slapping at himself. Among the mats of seagrape, he collapsed, his muscles cramping with toxins.

Tywi shoved Whipcrow aside. Terrified of his threat, she had let him lead her from the water's edge toward the dunes. But when she saw Dogbrick prostrate in the weeds under a venomous swarm, she ran to him, throwing handfuls of sand to drive off the stinging bugs.

Whipcrow backed away from the enraged viper-wasps and watched with grim amusement as Tywi tugged at the thief and swatted at the stinging attackers. With her help, Dogbrick managed to wobble to his feet and hobble to the sea. They stumbled into a tide pool and wallowed there.

When the swarm thinned away, the ogres picked them up and threw them both into a wagon laden with that night's treasures. Among gummy bones and buckled sheets of corroded metal, they lay in feverish pain. Their flesh puffed and throbbed. Nausea curdled their blood. At one point, Dogbrick stopped breathing. His diaphragm had become fiery metal and welded shut, and he had to labor strenuously to drag air into his lungs.

Tywi listened to him struggling to live and wanted to die. But there was not enough venom in her body to kill her. From each of the many welts where she had been stung a flame cooked her flesh, and the necrotic smoke curled through her veins and sickened her.

Dawn trembled overhead, and the wagon rolled back into the swamp tunnel on its way to the camp. The ogres sang their ponderous songs, and the scavengers shuffled listlessly, already half-asleep on their bones.

The reed huts caught the morning's rays through their woven seams and shone from within like ovens. While the others collapsed in the stained darkness and plunged into sleep, Tywi and Dogbrick lay awake on the hay-matted floor of the hut, gnawed by rats of pain they could not see but heard chittering as the blood boiled in their ears.

Dogbrick moaned, barely audible, 'It is big inside a human heart. I am no dog but a man. And it is big inside me. Yes, it is big.'

Tywi sat up on one elbow to hear more closely what her protector mumbled.

'He quotes The Gibbet Scrolls,' a haggard voice said in the mottled darkness. A woman in a charmwright's leather vest drifted out of the spongy dark and knelt beside her. This was the same person who had helped her after Gryn had tossed her into the chattel-cart with the other prisoners. Her gray-brindled hair tied back with cords of vine and large, liquid brown eyes lent her an aspect of wisdom. 'Beastfolk often recite that quote. They yearn to be human and so believe that if their hearts are strong enough to endure all suffering they will become human. It is sad.'

The charmwright bent closer and examined the thief's swollen features, the eyelids bruised a glossy black. 'This is Dogbrick, the one whose amulets caused the charm blowout in the forest – the one you hoped would save you.' The older woman shook her head sadly. 'Hope is sour desire. That, too, is from The Gibbet Scrolls.' She put a hand over his heart. 'He is strong and will survive.'

'Who are you?' Tywi inquired, appraising the woman more closely, noting the gaunt cheeks that looked long and hollow like tracks rain had deepened.

'Who I am does not matter,' the old woman confided. 'Not any more. The Dark Lord has changed everything.'

'What do I call you?'

'Owl Oil,' she replied with a faint smile. 'Now lie back and rest.'

'I can't rest,' Tywi protested yet relented to the elder's gentle hands that pushed her down on to the straw ticking.

'You are in pain, I know.' Owl Oil's hand curled in the air as if plucking an invisible fruit. When she opened her palm, she held a theriacal opal, shining inside with lilac milk. 'This will restore you and Dogbrick.'

Tywi gazed with surprise at the charmwright. 'You kept this hidden from the ogres?'

'From everyone.' The old woman touched the opal to each of Tywi's welts, and the inflamed flesh cooled at once to smooth, unblemished skin.

'You got others?' Tywi asked, thinking of Dogbrick.

'No.' Owl Oil placed the opal between the thief's swollen eyes. 'There is sufficient Charm in this gem to begin healing your protector.'

'Why?' Tywi asked, staring with wonder at Dogbrick as his puffy features and limbs began to deflate to healthier contours. 'Why use your gem for us?'

'Dogbrick is the strongest of us,' Owl Oil said with a sagely nod, 'and you are his ward. If there is any hope at all of freeing us from this prison, it lies with him. And I have a taste for that most sour of desires.'

The theriacal opal dulled to common stone, spent of its Charm, and Owl Oil slipped it into a pocket of her leather apron with such deft speed it appeared to vanish from her fingertips.

'He is not wholly healed,' she said, regarding the weals that still afflicted his tawny pelt. She stroked his brow, and he relaxed into sleep. 'But it is for the best that he not appear recovered too quickly. We do not want to rouse suspicions.'

'The ogres are clever,' Tywi agreed. 'And Whipcrow is Dogbrick's enemy, for sure.'

'Far more dangerous than Whipcrow or the ogres is the warlock who oversees the Reef Isles,' Owl Oil warned. 'Ralli-Faj patrols the camp regularly.'

'I seen him on his stilts,' Tywi acknowledged with a shudder.

'More often he comes as a shade. He thinks he is invisible. But those with the right Charm can see him well enough.'

'Do you have – "the right Charm"?' Tywi asked, looking into the weatherworn face for some indication of power and finding none.

'Charm is not only held in hex-gems, witch-glass, and conjure wire,' the elder whispered. 'A body can hold it, too – if the mind within that body knows how.'

253

'You're a sorceress!'

'I did not say that.' The elder turned her hands palms up. 'What I am is as unimportant as who I am. This is the time of the Dark Lord, and the values and identities of the past no longer pertain.'

'Yeah, but you ain't like us.' Tywi gestured with her eyes at the other prisoners in the hut, sprawled on the ground, some curled upon themselves, others sitting with their backs against the walls, hollowed out with exhaustion. 'What do you see?'

'Someone watching you,' Owl Oil said. 'There.' She pointed toward a corner littered with shadows and straws of sunlight.

At first, Tywi saw nothing. Then, the elder placed a soft hand on her shoulder, and she discerned a glinting energy in the shadows, fleeting and recurrent as needles of rain.

'What's that?' the young woman gasped with surprise.

'Not what, Tywi.' Owl Oil removed her hand, and the grainy apparition dimmed but did not vanish. 'Who.'

'Who, then?'

'We have talked enough for one day,' the charmwright answered and crept away. She lay down among the other sleepers, turned her back toward Tywi's following gaze, and did not stir.

When Tywi looked again for the energy, it had dimmed but was still visible, and it wavered like wheat caressing the wind. She sat up taller and squinted and saw that, as the power waned, it narrowed to the shape of a man. The harder she stared, the more it faded until it wholly vanished.

She lay back in wonder. The oppression that had made living seem unbearable had become lighter, and she drifted toward sleep with a hopefulness she had not experienced since Saxar.

The clangor of the ogres' wake-up bell roused her from a dreamless sleep, and she sat up into a scarlet haze of twilight seeping in through the woven reeds. Many of the others in the hut had already woken, and when she searched for Owl Oil she could not find her.

Dogbrick sat on the tamped ground rubbing his eyes with his

palms. The residue of eerie dreams left him feeling desolate and forlorn, and he was glad for the ache of his stung flesh because the pain sharpened his wakefulness. He was happy, also, to see Tywi appearing clear-eyed and revived.

On their way to the camp field where the ogres distributed the day's rations and divided the labor force into crews, she told him about Owl Oil and asked him, 'What did she make me see?'

'The warlock she warned about?' Dogbrick guessed.

They spotted her among the hundreds of workers gathered about the forage carts, on her way out of the camp to gather food from the swamp for the next night's rations. She did not return Tywi's wave and marched into the crimson dusk without acknowledging her.

'That old thing has Charm?' Dogbrick asked, unable to believe that anyone with power would appear so aged. 'The ogres will be feeding her to the basilisks before too long.'

'Hush!' Tywi scolded. 'She spent her last hex-gem yesterday to heal us.'

'Better she'd have used it to get us out of here,' he moaned, seeing Whipcrow watching them from atop a wagon.

With a curt gesture, the manager assigned them once again to the scavenger detail, and they glumly fell into line and accepted from an ogre their meager rations of tubers and berries. They said nothing more until they were shuffling with the others toward the beach. Then Tywi questioned, 'How'd you get your beastmarks?'

'No wizard put them on me, if that's what you mean.' He straightened proudly. 'My parents were beastfolk, what little I remember of them. Like most of my kind we had little Charm, and after the housefire that killed them, I had none but what I could steal for myself. But I tell you, if I had all the Charm of a wizard, I would not imitate the wealthy. Those with Charm remove their beastmarks and pretend to be wholly human. I will always be just what I am.'

'So, Owl Oil was wrong to say you wanted to be human?'

'Am I man or am I beast?' Dogbrick lifted his bearded head ruminatively. 'With those such as I, that is ever the question. But a sibyl has already answered that for me. How I die decides that! And I tell you I will die a man, because in me the beast serves the man.'

'That's why you was quoting The Gibbet Scrolls in your pain?' Tywi asked.

'Of course.' He thumped his chest and winced from the pain of his hurt flesh. 'It *is* big inside a human heart. There is room there for every nobility and every iniquity. To be a beast, instincts are enough. But to be human, one must be a philosopher.'

At the beach, under the fuming constellations, Whipcrow separated them. He sent Dogbrick out to net the waves with another burly man, and he assigned Tywi to rake the sand.

'I have been kinder to you this night,' the manager whispered from behind her, making her jump. 'I can be kinder yet if you favor me. Dogbrick, too, can be spared the difficulties that await him.'

Tywi glared at him but said nothing.

Whipcrow wanted to seize her on the spot, but he dared not act on his impulses, not with the warlock's invisible presence skulking about. Instead, he came to her again throughout the night, taunting and threatening her. Yet not once did she speak to him, and he began to contemplate more deceitful ways to get what he wanted.

At dawn, he assigned her to a hut apart from Dogbrick and contemplated how to get her alone with him in his garden chamber at the Palace of Abominations. There, among the blossom trees within the green and blue glass walls, he plotted. By day, he knew, the warlock drifted entranced. He could bring Tywi to this place without any fear of discovery. And though there were many women among the captives that he could take, he wanted Tywi, for she had significance to Dogbrick and he sought vengeance on the thief who had defied him.

By noon, he had resolved to simply carry her off. *Who can stop me?* he reasoned and marched with bold strides to the labor camp. But outside the hut where Tywi slept, he stopped abruptly, seized with icy fright. In the stark daylight moved a slim, pearly shadow of human proportions, disembodied and wobbly as watershine.

*Ralli-Faj!* Whipcrow feared and quickly retreated from the camp, running headlong down the mossy path, cloak flapping birdlike as he disappeared in the shadows of the forest's fallen behemoths. He did not look back, not even when an ogre awoke in its sleep-basket at the crest of a tree and called after him.

In the Palace, returned to his residence among flower trees and blossomy hedges, he clutched the large power wand that was his walking staff and soothed his tripping heart with Charm. No woman, no vengeful act, was worth the risk of inflaming the warlock's wrath, he decided, glad that the shimmering shadow had not pursued him. From then on, he determined, he would confine his brazen harassment of Tywi to the night. And with that resolve, he passed through an arbor of black roses to a garden alcove where a crystal sphere hovered. He stood there, laving himself in its fragrant breeze, readying himself for a soothing trance.

Had he dared to confront the shining shadow he saw in the camp, he would have known at once it was not Ralli-Faj. Several paces closer and he could have discerned a face within the vague manshape – the fierce and decisive features of the wizarduke Lord Drev.

The wind glossed like silk around the wizarduke's body of light and bore the contours of his form bleared but recognizable. The somber shade of his face did not waver when Whipcrow approached nor gloat when he fled. Tempered by the loss of his dominion and endless days wandering the badlands of the Qaf, Lord Drev had filled with the silence of the stones that drank the blood of his lost troopers. He felt no fear or delight at his own fate, only a proud and tense expectancy at finding his way to the one woman on Irth bound to him by a blind destiny.

*Blind no more*, he exulted, entering the hut where she slept. At grave jeopardy to his life, he had left his physical form in a deep trance at the other end of the world, in a volcanic cave among the lava fields of the Qaf. Trolls could descend upon his body at any time, and Leboc and his remaining troopers would have to use their firecharms. And then, the cacodemons would come again.

It was a terrible risk, yet the wizarduke was unsure what he hoped to achieve by following the charmlines that connected the newts-eye in his shoulderguard to this hut. During his many nomadic days in the wasteland, he had slowly developed the connection, gradually intensifying the dim fatefulness he sensed in the newts-eye until it thickened to a tangible filament he could follow with his Charm.

The thread of fate led him through a slanted doorway of dried moss into a darkness riddled with splinters of daylight. Twenty slumbering bodies crowded the interior. Yesterday, he had come this close but had been unable to focus his attention sufficiently to see anything clearly. A night of charmwork, adjusting the focus of his power, returned him to this sordid camp with keener sight, and now he stared about at the primitive hovel with thick unhappiness.

He had hoped to find the woman that fate had selected for him in better circumstances, and now he only wished that she had her health, for in this starkly crude hut there was no chance of Charm or any of its virtues. The sleepers looked haggard, and shrunk to their bones, their clothing shredded remnants. The men, nearly faceless in their wild beards and tangled hair, and the women dirt-smudged and mottled with scabs and scratches, seemed weary denizens of a prehuman epoch.

The filament of Charm guided him among the bedraggled bodies to a young woman, no less filthy than the others, with lank hair the color of withered brown reeds. Her slight body and the bleak hollows of her eyes and cheeks evidenced her humble origins, and the wizarduke pondered how it must have been for her, to have come from Irth's sadder regions, charmless all her life.

The Eye of Protection he had placed on her was gone. It had worn away at some point in her travels to this dingy place, and the wizarduke was certain she would not now be alive without the Charm that the Eye must have imparted to her.

He studied her with fascination, imprinting again on his memory the dimpled chin, the curved fullness of the upper lip barely covering a rabbity overbite, the diminutive nose with its wide nostril wings, the dark eyebrows, bold lashes, and a rounded forehead like a child's.

No desire stirred in him for this waif, yet an immediate warmth suffused his chest, an affection born of soulful recognition. He wanted to reach out and touch her, stir her to wakefulness so that he could tell her of himself and find out what sentience occupied this soul almost too poor to be human.

Lord Drev sensed the pressure of a watchful presence, and he looked up from his examination of his bride to see staring at him an older woman with gray-streaked hair pulled back from a tawed face. Through a crooked smile, she whispered, 'You do not have the strength to wake her.'

The wizarduke drifted across the hut to where the old woman sat with her back to the woven reeds. A slash of daylight made her brown eyes seem orange. 'Who are you?' he asked her, testing to determine if she could hear him as well.

'Who I am is not important,' she answered, and her smile deepened at his sustained expression of surprise.

'You can see and hear me,' he said, looking her over and noting her torn and scuffed charmwright's apron. 'That makes you important to me.'

She passed a finger through his glossy shadow and felt an astral chill. 'You are Lord Drev of Ux, the wizarduke of Hoverness. That is what matters. Two days now I have seen you in this camp, lurking about young Tywi. Why?'

'Tywi.' Lord Drev looked back at the sleeping woman. 'You know her?'

'Yes.'

'Where are we?' He questioned the charmwright with an anxious tone. 'Why is she made to sleep in filth and with no Charm?'

'You don't know?'

'I am a fugitive from Wrat the Scavenger and his cacodemons.' His flittering silhouette darkened at the very thought of his enemy and nearly vanished. 'I lack the Charm to see my way clearly in this form.'

'Yes, you are but a body of light.' The crone squinted her eyes. 'And a slim one at that. From where do you come?'

'I am hidden far from here.'

'You need not fear me, my lord.' She opened her arms and exposed her evident distress. 'You can speak freely, for I am not your enemy nor allied with them. I am myself a prisoner in this place.'

'This is a prison?'

'Of course.' She cocked her head, taken aback by his ignorance. 'You are in Wrat's labor camp in the Reef Isles of Nhat.'

'That far?'

'You do not know how far you have journeyed?'

'I am trance traveling, stranger.' He turned an inquisitive stare on their dismal surroundings. 'I have no notion yet where my Charm has taken me.'

'Ah, then you must have hitched a charmline to the Abiding Star and followed that here. But why?'

The wizarduke turned his attention sharply back to the old woman. 'I see you know something of charmworks. You are no common charmwright graced with sight.' He examined her for signs of Charm and recognized none. Yet he knew. 'You have advanced knowledge of wizardry.'

'You have not answered my question, my lord.'

Drev frowned, and his shadowy features blurred like smokedrift. 'How can I trust you? I don't even know your name.'

'You may call me Owl Oil.'

'You are a sorceress?'

'I am, as you see, a prisoner. What little Charm I have is held in my body.' She wrung her hands. 'It is not sufficient to free me from this grief.'

'Holding Charm in your body?' He edged closer as if to see deeper into her. 'That is advanced wizardry indeed. You must be a Peer. Reveal yourself to me.'

'No.' Her eyes jittered in their sockets. 'Already you have put me in grave peril. I have revealed too much.'

'I am no danger to you. We are allied against Wrat.'

'Yes. But there are Peers allied *with* Wrat.' Her voice softened almost to silence: 'Among them is the warlock of the Spiderlands. He guards this camp.'

'Ralli-Faj!' A jolt of alarm spun him toward Tywi. If the warlock found out about her, she would experience such horrors of Charm that death would seem a gallant gesture.

'By day he drifts in rapture trance,' Owl Oil said. 'We are probably unseen by him. But occasionally he breaks his routine and tours the camp while we sleep. If he comes through, he will see you as I am seeing you now.'

Drev retreated at once. His shadowshape folded into itself and vanished in a flutter of hot motes, star twinklings that left behind emptiness so pure that Owl Oil felt compelled to put her hand in it. She felt nothing, for nothing was there.

Lord Drev awoke at the bottom of the lava chute where he was hidden. In the blue desert sky above, winged snakes floated like notes of an escaped song. Leboc and his Falcon Guard waited for him, hidden among the boulders around the pit, watching their eye charms for the approach of trolls or cacodemons.

For many minutes, the wizarduke did not move but held intact by his stillness the success of his quest: He had once again found his mate, found the one chosen for him by the nameless powers beyond time and Charm. He lifted her image before his mind's eye and studied her again, his orphaned woman.

He wanted to speak with her. Her image was not enough. He

had to look into her eyes and see her seeing him. Until she spoke to him and he met her soul, he felt that he would not really know himself.

He decided that he must make the more dangerous journey to her by night and risk the treacherous eddies of the nocturnal tide that would pull tenaciously at his astral form. If his charmlines tangled and he lost his focus, the tide would sweep him into the Gulf, and he would fade to nothing among the stars. His body would stop breathing and no amount of Charm could keep him from shriveling to dried leather.

More dangerous than the tide was the threat of Ralli-Faj. Empowered by the black magic of the cacodemons, the warlock was a master of bodiless transit. If they met, the wizarduke would suffer to escape with his life if at all. And Tywi – she would know living death.

*Even so*— He felt compelled to go to her. Fate had bound them, and he possessed no other direction in his life. He had been stripped of his dominion, his family, and all hope save her.

'Leboc!' The wizarduke stood upright, and the dust that had settled on him during his trance scattered in a mauve puff, shed by the amulets that also dispelled all weariness from his body. Spry as a spider, he clambered up the chute and emerged into the quaking heat of the Qaf.

Leboc and the Falcon Guard awaited him, their raptor hoods in place, protecting them from the brutal heat.

'I am going south,' Lord Drev spoke, 'to the Reef Isles of Nhat.'

'My lord!' The black filter mask could not mute the surprise in the marshal's voice. 'That is at the other end of Irth.'

'Leave me to make this journey alone,' the wizarduke said. 'You have traveled far enough with me.'

Leboc's hood shook adamantly. 'Too many of our own have died for us to abandon you now.' He turned to the others to see if any disagreed. They stood unmoving, silent with determination. The marshal turned back to his lord and said confidently, 'We will go where you lead us. Just tell us why we are going to the Reef Isles. Wrat has made his residence there. Are we striking at him?'

'If we can.' Drev pulled his hood into place but left his face mask dangling so that the troopers could read his features. 'I have not yet discovered how to fight our enemy. Yet my fate leads me to Nhat. My hope has ever been that by following my fate I would learn to overcome Wrat and his cacodemons. I can offer no assurances, other than that I will remain true to the powers that have always guided me.'

'You are the Duke of Dorzen,' Leboc spoke firmly for the others. 'We are your Falcon Guard, sworn to serve and protect you with our lives. Lead us where you will.'

They marched south through the nacre waste, wending among ashen dunes and corrugated expanses of gray slag. At nightfall, the wizarduke called a halt on a gravel slide under twisted towers of naked rock and announced he would spend the dark hours in trance. He situated himself on a slate shelf under a rocky promontory, and his guard took up positions around him, hidden among the enfolded stone, watching the burning migrations of the stars for shadows of evil.

Drev closed his eyes and began the patterned breathing that would induce trance. Alone inside himself, he gathered the airy powers of his Charm, the meditative feathers that would lift him above the sinking depths of sleep, and he flapped free of his body.

Electrical clouds billowed in the darkness, the magnetic auras of the tall rocks, fields of force unfurling like green and yellow banners against the fixity of the stars. The Falcon Guard in the dark appeared to his tranced eyes like pieces of dusk broken off from the end of the day and dropped randomly among the stony crevices. They pulsed with thermal hues of red and orange, vibrant manshapes crouched in the black crevices of the night.

He felt for the charmlines that radiated from the newts-eye in his shoulderguard. What had once been no more than a subtle sense of destiny and then, after much attention and Charm, a thin filament had become a thick cable in his ethereal grip. It had fed on the power he had generated during his two previous journeys and was sturdy enough to lead him with unerring swiftness to Tywi. But without the Abiding Star in the sky to renew its Charm, it began to thin immediately, its force bleeding away into the stellar abyss, drawn off by the nocturnal tide that carried charmless bodies and the heat of the day into the Gulf. He would not have much time with Tywi before he would have to return to his physical form, for if the charmline wore out entirely, his body of light would be swept away from Irth.

Drev put both of his spectral hands on the charmline and pulled himself toward it. A cold wind gusted through him, vision smeared to a fiery blur, and he abruptly found himself among hanging vines and veils of tattered moss. The charmline in his grip tautened down a tunnel of overarching swamp trees toward the ghostly glow of ocean waves and star whorls.

Slowly, he followed the clew, watchful for the breathing red shadows of other entities. Owl Oil, though she wore no amulets, had seen him yesterday without his imparting any Charm to her at all, and perhaps there were others in Nhat who had this power, sentinels posted by Wrat. Perhaps Owl Oil was one of them. If so, then he had already betrayed Tywi, and that was his strongest motive in returning to her this night. He had to know that she had not come to harm because of him.

At the end of the arcade of swamp trees, he found dunes maned in salt grass on their leesides, their slipfaces concave and luminescent in the starshine. From there, he watched the scavengers working the strand and spotted Tywi at once. She raked the high-water margin, gathering shells into one basket and oddments into another. Separate heaps consisted of kelp and driftbramble.

Several ogres lurked on the dunetops nearby, though the wizarduke had no concern of them. Wholly charmless, they could not detect him. But Tywi did have the shadowy escort of a slender man in an ankle-length mantle, and he clutched a sizable power wand as tall as he was. Drev recognized him from his spiked hair as the man who had fled from him outside Tywi's hut two days before.

That Tywi seemed unharmed was all that the wizardduke required from this bodiless journey, and he considered returning at once to the Qaf. The charmline that bound him to his physical form had already thinned from a cable to a rope, and he could feel the tidal tug and the chill distances of night. But a daring possibility stayed him.

He stepped boldly out from behind the dunes and strode in plain view toward the sea. The man with the hefty power wand started with obvious alarm and moved immediately away from Tywi and down the beach, busying himself with shouting orders to others.

Quickly, Drev approached Tywi. She did not see him and continued her desultory raking. Seeing her awake, she seemed to him less childlike, almost old, with thin but sturdy arms used to labor and a sober face that had known little of joy and rarely smiled. Her blunt-cut hair waved with the motions of her exertion, and the sinuous length of her body, bending under the night, carried the whole weight of human darkness.

He reached out and touched her with his luminous hand, and she straightened at the soothing touch of Charm and dropped the rake. The energy he gave to her through his touch thinned his charmline to a cord even as it infused her with strength as cheerful as clean snow.

She gasped and turned to look at the man with the giant power wand. When she saw that he was not directing magic at her, she turned full around. The ogres on the dunetops sat eating tubers roasted in their driftwood fires and chatting. None paid any heed to her.

'I am here,' Drev whispered and, when she jumped, added, 'Don't be afraid, Tywi. I am – your friend.'

He touched her with enough Charm to see him, and her pale eyes grew wide. The influx of Charm defeated her fear, and she gazed up in amazement at the tall man with the broad, dark face and startling blue eyes. 'Who are you?' She took in his full height, the naked length of him shifting with feathery illumination, lit from within and fluttering like a paper lantern on a gusty night.

'I am Drev. A wizard from Ux, where once I was a duke. Wrat – the Dark Lord – he is my enemy, and I am in hiding from him and his cacodemons. I have come to you in my body of light because—' He hesitated, not sure what to say. 'Because my magic tells me that – you and I – we belong together.'

Tywi stepped back and looked around again, searching for the source of this illusion. *It's Whipcrow's trick*, she was certain. But he seemed oblivious of her and had moved far down the beach to monitor the dredging of the shoals. The ogres remained preoccupied with their roasted tubers.

'How you know my name?' she asked and backed away another step.

'I visited you yesterday while you slept,' Drev told her. He withdrew the energy he had initially used to calm her, fearing to overcharge her with Charm and risk a depressing letdown when he departed. 'The charmwright Owl Oil told me your name. Do you know her?'

Tywi did not reply. She stared at him suspiciously and, furtive as an animal, swept her gaze along the shore. The nearest other rakers had noticed she had stopped working and were themselves casting nervous glances at the ogres.

'Pick up your rake,' Drev said. 'I don't want to get you in trouble.'

She retrieved her rake without removing her stare from him.

'I am a wizard, just as I've told you,' he explained. 'As a child, when I first learned to scry, I felt you. I didn't know it was you. I didn't see you. You weren't even born yet. I simply felt your presence in my future. I knew then you were my polar double – a woman as I am a man, with little Charm as I am a Peer, orphaned as I am head of my lineage, alone even as I was embraced by the brood of Dorzen.'

Her gaze lowered from the sable locks that spilled across his large shoulders along the sleek swerve of his torso to his phallus and cod in their dark radiance of nether hair. 'If you're a duke, why you naked?'

'I am in exile,' he answered forthrightly. 'I have no charm-clothes, only my work uniform, which does not carry Charm and so cannot garb my body of light.' He hung his head slightly. 'I am sorry. I am naked, because I have lost everything but a handful of amulets. My dominion, my brood, my treasures – all are taken from me by Wrat.'

Tywi recognized the pain in his wrung features. 'What you want from me, Lord Drev?'

'Do not call me lord,' he begged with bent brow. 'I am not your lord but your fateful double – your mate, if you would have me.'

'Your mate!' Her raised voice lifted the heads of rakers farther down the strand. She spoke softer but with no less intensity, 'You don't even know me!'

'Oh, I know you.' He smiled at her mettle. 'Not your history. Not really. But your being. And in your depths, you know me. We are both human, and a river of instinct carries us together through this life.'

'I'm a prisoner.' She slapped the sand with her rake. 'And you're a ghost. This is crazy.'

'No. I am real.' The charmline in his hand had diminished to a thread, and he could not linger any longer to explain himself. 'I will return. I have to go now.' He opened his right palm and showed a wire red as gold whose one end trailed into the sky like the line of a kite lost among the cluttered stars. The other end pointed at her and dwindled to the finest thread at the point where it touched her heart. 'Tell no one you've seen me. Our enemies are cruel.'

He stepped back, and the fine filament touching her snapped and vanished. The apparition of Drev disappeared, and his departure left her feeling as exhausted as the seaweed strewn under her rake.

From a dunecrest a gruff cry hurtled toward her, and she

looked up sharply to see an ogre motioning for her to work.

She resumed raking, her head windy with thoughts. Dared she believe what the handsome wraith had told her? How could it be that fate would choose her, a factory waif, an orphan, for a duke? *No.* She could not trust the giddy hopefulness that this encounter inspired in her. *It's a trick. Whipcrow's trick. Or worse.*

She remembered Owl Oil's warning: *Far more dangerous than Whipcrow or the ogres is the warlock who oversees the Reef Isles. Ralli-Faj patrols the camp regularly.* Perhaps this was his trick.

Yet wonder persisted amidst her bewilderment. Two days ago, when she met Owl Oil, the charmwright had enabled her to see a shadowshape, a specter within the hut. *Was that Drev?* She wanted to ask Owl Oil and remembered the wizard's admonition that she must speak to no one of their meeting.

*And Dogbrick?* How could she not tell her protector?

Another husky shout descended on her from the ogres on the dunes, and she bent more strenuously to her task. Currents of air swept off the sea's dark shoulders and circled around her. A faint smile touched her worried face. The futility of the future had been broken and out spilled hope – and danger.

# PART TWO:

## THE ABIDING STAR

❖

19 Above Irth blazes the Abiding Star. Its radiance
   dazzles the primal darkness like a door standing
   open on heaven. That is the Beginning.
20 Below and beyond Irth yaws the Gulf – the eternal
   night, the predacious blackness that devours the
   luminous Beginning and grinds its glorious fire
   into dim stars and frozen planets. Those cold
   worlds hung in the silence, adrift in the vacuum
   where the light fails, they range the Dark Shore.
   – *Origins* 2:19–20

**Everything watches.**
— The Gibbet Scrolls

## Thief of Shadows

❧

At night, Ripcat tied himself into the top branches of the tallest tree he could find and slept. In his dreams, he visited a peculiar world without Charm. Though the sky there was blue and clouds moved in herds on the migratory paths of the wind as on Irth, he saw no floating cities, no dragons, griffins or basilisks in the air.

The cities of his dreams rose directly out of the ground in steel and glass towers and houses sprawled around them for many miles in grids of streets and avenues. He sensed that he lived in one of those cities, on one of those tree-lined streets, in a pink house with white trim and a sloping lawn of hedges and shrubs. A discreet sign with calligraphic lettering on the wrought-iron lamp post beside the flagstone walkway welcomed boarders.

The people there seemed to know him, but he could remember no names. He saw them only briefly on his way in or out of the house. And always, as he climbed the left-hand stairway, his footfalls silent on the burgundy carpet, and approached the landing where a dark doorway of solid mahogany stood at the end of a corridor lit with small wall lamps and lined with wallpaper flora and dark wainscot, the dream shifted. He sensed that this heavy door with its glass knob and brass hardware opened upon his room, yet the dream never admitted him there.

In this strange world, he did not know what to call things, like the blue vehicle with four rubber wheels and iron breath that he rode in when he left the house. The vehicles crowded the streets, and he spent many dreams simply sitting in this machine turning the thin wheel before him to steer among the others. He paid little heed to these surreal episodes.

The dreams he remembered most vividly had the same sable-tressed woman in them. He met her usually in the city among clamorous streets jammed with smoking vehicles. He wanted to learn her name, and sometimes he actually spoke it but always forgot it upon waking.

She was not extraordinarily beautiful, yet whenever he saw her, an unspeakable loveliness claimed him. The sight of her dark, languorous eyes aglint, her black hair against the spicy tint of her slender neck, and her soft smile made his chest ache with want. She was the angel who ushered him to the bright places in the blackness of his memory, where dreams minted joy out of the heart's secret keep.

The happy news of this other world, however, had a dark limit. He drove with her out of the city of glass towers, out beyond the wide acres of packed houses, past tilted and vacant lots toward a blue seam of mountains under a sky ladened with cloudbanks and scribbled lines of flying waterfowl. They rode through the deepening shade of forests and pulled over beside a grassland in a gauze of goldenrod, and there shared the contents of a picnic basket.

Against the vaporous violet of autumn woods, they walked and laughed, and she ran ahead to trespass a fairy ring of mushrooms, fallen leaves of gold swirling about her in the chill wind like a phantasm.

'Let me dance worship with you,' she called to him from the fairy ring.

A sudden sharp scream cracked in the distance as if lightning spat. Time and space exploded. The forest plunged into night, and his lovely woman lay on her back naked in the moon-dappled grass, her pale flesh covered with mysterious sigils – and gashing wounds. Blood streaked her face.

Horror slashed through him when first this nightmare poisoned his sleep. Then, at intermittent and unexpected intervals, with each subsequent recurrence of the terror, a harder pain congealed in him, all the dull ores of grief. And he woke from those dreams as from a world lost.

On one such dawn, waking stained with sorrow, Ripcat found himself where he had lashed his body to a treetop to keep from drifting off on the night tide, but he was not alone. Others thrashed below on the forest floor. Seven men in raptor hoods and combat vests crashed through the briar bushes pursued by a voracious basilisk.

Ripcat had seen the spike-winged creatures circling among the red galleries of twilight and had taken the precaution before sleeping to hide from their hungry gaze by cloaking himself under a twig-and-leaf awning. The troopers below had obviously been spotted while crossing a nearby glade of wildflowers, where, from his height, he could read the trampled grass of their passage.

The crimson and black beast slithered among the trees with a rasping cry. The men had probably hoped to elude the winged predator in the cramped spaces of the forest, but they had underestimated its nimble attack. One of the fleeing men spun about suddenly and drew a sword of silvergold. And though the weapon obviously shone with Charm, Ripcat doubted it would offer much hope against the swift strike of a basilisk's claws.

The swordsman held the blade to shield his eyes from the basilisk's mesmeric gaze and shifted his stance to deliver the sole stroke upon which his salvation depended. With agile anticipation, the beast reared back from its assault and tensed to lunge.

A blue bolt of charmfire seared over the swordsman's head and struck the pouncing creature's breastbone, splitting its torso to windflung sparks and gouts of charred flesh. The basilisk emitted a parched scream and fell writhing to its back, its ribcage a brisket of azure flames.

'Leboc!' the swordsman shouted. 'I could have taken it through the heart.'

The hooded man who had fired lowered his weapon. 'It looked too chancy, my lord.'

'And what chance do you think we have now against the cacodemons?'

At the sound of that fearful word, Ripcat lifted his gaze immediately to the sky and its confetti of dawn clouds.

'You up there in the tree, come down!' the swordsman commanded. 'Don't think you can hide. We saw you with our eye charms a league off.'

The burned stink of the fire-gutted basilisk wafted through the boughs, and Ripcat swung down with limber ease. He landed soundlessly at the side of the trunk out of sword's reach and regarded the masked and hooded men with a cool green gaze.

'Who are you?' the swordsman inquired sternly.

'A thief.'

'From where do you hail, thief?' asked the trooper who had shot the basilisk – the hooded one called Leboc.

'Saxar.'

'Saxar?' Leboc's voice curled with incredulity. 'You crossed the Qaf? Without Charm?'

'Your charmfire has alerted cacodemons,' he reminded them. 'We should hide.'

'It may already be too late,' the swordsman spoke, looking into the dark prism of an epaulet. 'Three cacodemons are circling overhead.' He unsnapped one side of his mask and let it dangle by its ebony cords, exposing a wide, swarthy countenance of sharp planes and bony hollows, a severe mien whose deep sockets held a gentle gaze of ethereal blue. 'If we are to die together, you should know with whom you share your fate. I am Drev, and these others are Marshal Leboc and the five who remain of our Falcon Guard.'

'You are Lord Drev,' Ripcat said with surprise, recognizing the harsh features and kindly eyes from numerous gazette pictures at the news kiosks. 'You are regent of the Seven Dominions.'

'That means nothing any more. What is your name, thief?'

'Ripcat.'

'Then we will face death together, Ripcat.' He sheathed his sword and turned to his men. 'Quickly, then. Seek cover.' When he looked back, the thief was already gone.

Ripcat had leaped straight upward into the tree and ran among the interlocking boughs. He kept pace with Lord Drev as the wizarduke ran through the shadows below. That sword the regent carried, Ripcat realized, was the weapon that scavengers had made famous in their vicious bid for power hundreds of days before his memories began.

*Am I a victim of that rebellion?* he questioned himself. *Or am I one of the rebels perhaps? This man is a wizard. Is he the one who made me a beast? And now, has his Charm drawn me to him once more, this time to fulfill a blood debt?*

Waking from the dismal and murderous depths of his recurring nightmare to find himself thrust into the lethal presence of cacodemons, Ripcat felt prepared to believe in the mysterious consequences of chance. He leaped from tree to tree with adroit swiftness, bounding among the thick boughs soundlessly and with barely more flutter of leaves than the wind stirred.

So silent was his shadowing of the wizarduke that the cacodemons did not see him as they dove claw first toward the treetops. They smashed through the canopy only paces ahead of him, their screaming descent splintering boughs in a tumult of slashed branches and leaves. He hugged a trunk under an explosive spray of flying twigs and bark and swung sideways and nearly lost his grip before the splash of wind.

Through the rent hole in the forest awning, he peered down at the grisly sight of two troopers squashed under the cacodemons' claws to bloody paste. Lord Drev stood backed against an enormous tree, sword drawn, his open mask revealing a glaring expression of rage.

That defiance inspired Ripcat. This was the moment of death. The dead woman in his dreams was his soul, presaging this very instant where his own blood would spill. He had seen it all before, disguised as a sable-haired woman he loved, which was his very life. Thus, he had woken from one nightmare into another and knew it would end here in ultimate and dreamless dark.

With a shriek he unsheathed his boot knife and dove. The cacodemon confronting the wizardduke lifted its long head at the peeling cry, and the thief dropped on to its horrendous face. With maniacal speed, he drove the blade into an upturned eye till the hilt struck bone. The momentum of the wounded monster flinging its head withdrew the blade and tossed him upward only to have him twist about adroitly in mid-air and drive the blade hard into the second eye. Again hurled off by the creature's throes of agony, he spun about, hooked his knife behind the beast's jaw and let gravity seize him and rip a long gash to the monster's shoulder before he pulled his weapon and dropped feet first to the ground.

A convulsive lash of serrated tail forced him to duck and then leap over its backward swipe. The cut cacodemon collapsed in an upheaval of leafdust, shivered violently with scalding screams, and lay still and silent.

Lord Drev yelled triumphantly at Ripcat's victory, though his voice could not be heard above the bellowing of the other two attacking cacodemons. He leaped atop the dead monster and brandished his sword at the roaring beasts. Leboc and the three troopers had drawn their assault knives and affixed them to the muzzles of their firelocks. They attacked with battle cries, surrounding the two enraged creatures.

Ripcat, both arms slathered in blood, dodged among the snaking tails and leaped upon a cacodemon's back. It bucked to heave him off, but he pierced its hide with his knife and hung on with his legs flailing. Lord Drev exploited its frenzied distraction, ran boldly forward and plunged his sword into the mouth of an abdominal face.

Claws slashed for him, but he kicked away, pulling his sword with him. When the creature toppled, he advanced quickly and skewered the monster through its eye.

Leboc and the troopers fended the lone cacodemon with their fixed knives, and it jumped into the air and flew toward the torn opening in the canopy. With a slap of his hand, Leboc unlocked his assault knife, aimed, and fired.

The burst of charmfire carried the knife with it, and the blade drove deep into the back of the cacodemon's skull, pithing its brain. The beast caromed among the trees, its small faces shrieking, before it dove to the ground and convulsed to stillness.

'Haiii!' Leboc cried jubilantly in the sudden quiet, and the three Falcon Guards shouted with him.

Lord Drev stood panting for breath over the dead troopers. He rubbed the stunned flesh of his face with his leather-strapped hand, and when he found the breath to speak, he mourned: 'So many have been lost. Lost to our fear. Lost to our habit of relying upon firecharms. We forgot how to fight with our blades!'

'We must alert everyone!' Leboc said exuberantly and bowed to strip the corpses of their amulets. 'We must broadcast this news on the aviso.'

'No.' The wizarduke shook his head. 'The cacodemons will swarm. They have spared most of our cities so far because Irth has capitulated. But if we fight, there will be a terrible war. Many more will die.'

'But this news must be known,' Leboc spoke from where he knelt over the crushed bodies. 'The cacodemons can be destroyed by our own hands!'

'We know that now,' Lord Drev agreed, and he looked at his men and the thief with a steady, measuring gaze, wondering if they were up to the resolution shaping itself in him. 'We know the vulnerability of Wrat's army. Now we can take the fight directly to him.'

'Cut off the head!' Leboc stood and his voice conveyed through his mask the excitement he had caught from his lord. 'As a small force we can move quickly and unseen directly into Wrat's camp and destroy him!'

'Along the way, we will gather enough fighters from the dominions to penetrate his defenses,' the wizarduke said and faced the thief, staring fixedly into his curved and virid eyes. 'Fighters like yourself. Beastfolk with the physical power to wield the ancient weapons. Will you help us, stranger?' He extended his sword arm, his hand grimed with demon blood. 'If not for you, we should all be dead in these woods this morning. Will you fight with us?'

Ripcat stared at the proffered hand crossed with hex-leather and stained with ichor. 'Before I can take your hand,' he said, 'I must know a thing.'

Lord Drev drew back his hood, lifted his chin, and crossed his hands on the hilt of the sword embedded in the ground before him. 'Ask.'

The thief shifted his weight uneasily. 'Did you summon me here with your Charm?'

'No,' Lord Drev said at once. 'We saw you during the night with our eye charms. But we did not summon you. Fate alone brought us together at this dire time.'

'Then—' Ripcat spoke hesitantly, wanting to know the truth yet almost afraid to ask. 'You are not the wizard who – who put these beastmarks on me?'

The wizarduke's dark eyebrows raised. 'You are not beastfolk?'

'I don't know.' The blue fur of Ripcat's brow furrowed. 'I – I have human dreams. Of a human place without beastfolk or even Charm. But I don't remember how I came to be as you find me.'

'I have put no beastmarks on anyone. My enemies I have slain or cast into the Gulf.' Lord Drev rocked his head repiningly. 'Better I had slain them all. Wrat would not now be among us.' From beneath his cloak, the wizarduke produced a roll of flexible gold mesh studded with theriacal opals. 'With this amulet, I can undo whatever sorcery has been worked upon you.'

The sight of the hex-woven gold nubbled with iridescent gems shrove a unique fright in him: 'And if I am an animal some other wizard or sorcerer has made a man?'

'You will become again the animal,' the wizarduke confirmed. 'I will not be able to return you to Ripcat.'

'Put aside your amulet, my lord.' Ripcat offered his hand. 'I will serve you best as what I am than as what I might be.'

'Well said, Ripcat!' Lord Drev seized his wrist, and his austere features broke into a broad smile. 'You are a lethal fighter. With you at our side, we will bring death to Wrat and his cacodemons.'

Leboc undid his mask and dropped his raptor hood, showing a brutal face seamed with scars and fringed with stiff, rusty whiskers. He clapped the thief on the back and grinned with gruesome glee. 'You are a demonslayer, Ripcat! And we are proud to have you among us.'

Drev read the surprise in the animal traits of Ripcat's visage at the sight of Leboc's stitched-together face and laughed. 'Our marshal is a man who wears his scars as emblems.'

'Why erase with Charm what I suffered?' Leboc explained. 'Let the world read my pain – and my enemies beware.'

The Falcon Guard removed their hoods and offered the new recruit amulets and weapons.

Ripcat accepted an assault knife. The blade he had used was a fishmonger's gutting tool with a chipped edge and wooden handle that he had stolen in Saxar for protection against alley dogs. He was glad to replace it with green curved steel of Charm-honed razor length and black finger-molded grip.

Over the bodies of the two dead troopers, Lord Drev offered a mournful petition to the Abiding Star. The corpses were abandoned to the wild beasts and their remnants to the eventual tide of night, and the wizarduke led his fighters south through the hill forest.

Along the way, they cleansed themselves with hex-gems. Ripcat, freckled in fetid blood, did not object. Since departing the Qaf, he had been bathing in streams, risking the bite of water-adders, and was glad to feel again the cool electrical shimmer of Charm as the hex-gems sloughed the day's grime.

At nightfall, Leboc gave Ripcat a power wand to fend off exhaustion, and the thief fitted it to the loops along the waist at the back of his black cord trousers. He had grown weary of dreaming. From his sleep, he had hoped to extract memory and knowledge of his past. But instead, all he had attained was enigma and sorrow.

If the dead woman, whom he loved in his dreams, was not his soul, as he had expected when he met Lord Drev at the juncture of life and death, then was she truly a remembrance? How could he love someone as dearly as he did this dusky woman and still not know her name? For that matter, how could he recall a whole other world, replete with unique cities and machines and a house where he lived, and yet not know his own name?

He posed these questions to the wizarduke as they hiked through the night forest. The dark-skinned man watched him with ghostly eyes in the darkness and said somberly, 'The first lesson of sorcery is that every gesture of beauty bears an exact equivalent of pain.'

Ripcat puzzled over this. 'You sound like a friend of mine, a philosopher.'

'I mean only to say that whoever this woman is, dream or flesh, your profound love for her exacted a mortal cost.' Drev spoke softly for only Ripcat's ears. 'You see, only one's inmost destiny is truly worthy of such love – for that destiny has already been paid for in full by the truth of our births, which is ever nothing less than a guarantee of our deaths. Do you understand? Everything else is sentiment. Only one's fate can offer true love.'

'Could this woman be my fate?'

'You say she is slain. And slain on a world very unlike Irth. Your fate you carry with you, Ripcat. If she were alive and in one of these dominions, she could well be your fate. I know. I myself am bound by such a destiny to a woman in this world.' He told the thief about Tywi, and the beastman stopped walking.

'Tywi?' Ripcat's eyes enlarged in the dark, and he raised his open hand to his shoulder. 'She's this tall and has brown hair, like burnt brass, and buckled front teeth, and a dimple in her chin . . .?'

'You know her?' Lord Drev rocked back, astonished.

'She is a factory waif from Saxar.'

'Yes!'

'My partner Dogbrick, the philosopher, worked with her in Saxar. We found her again in the Qaf – a lone survivor.'

While Leboc and the troopers fanned out through the shadowy doors of the forest, searching for threats, Ripcat related how Tywi miraculously survived the massacre of Lord Hazar's army by cacodemons and trolls and how she, Dogbrick and Ripcat crossed the cauterized terrain of the Qaf with the corrupt factory manager Whipcrow.

'That explains much,' Drev acknowledged, realizing now how vital his Eye of Protection had been in preserving her life. 'In trance, I have seen this Whipcrow with Tywi. He works for the ogres now, and she is a scavenger in a labor camp somewhere in Nhat.'

'And Dogbrick?'

'I have not seen him. But the camp is large. It is not far from where Wrat has built his Palace of Abominations. That is where we are going.'

Ripcat tossed a wild look at the forest canopy and the powdery shafts of starlight. He felt derelict of his will, under consignment to some wider, more pervasive power. 'Your Charm did not bring us together?'

The wizarduke shook his head. He, too, pondered how circumstance and design had so deftly intersected to serve them. 'Luck.' The word felt odd on his tongue, and he gazed into midspace as if he could see this peculiar concept turning before him, revealing its unpredictable contours and in them a wholeness of precise and formal symmetry.

'It comes in two flavors,' Ripcat said with a vexed expression. 'We've tasted much of the bitter.'

'I know,' Drev said, staring into emptiness, still trying to comprehend this unforeseen propitiousness. 'I tasted that bitterness with the evil luck that returned Wrat from the Dark Shore. Perhaps, then, this is the counteragency to that misfortune.'

'Then we should seize this chance while we have it,' Ripcat said and stepped forward so that he was in the duke's line of sight. 'Is there any faster way for us to get to the Reef Isles?'

'If we take a light cruiser or a dirigible from any of the cities,' Drev predicted, 'the cacodemons will pull us out of the air.'

'Only if they know we're aboard,' the thief suggested. 'If we fly as stowaways . . .'

'We must trust too many others,' the duke said. 'That is too risky. There is a better way, a way known by very few. In a cavern among the Falls of Midrath is a charmway – a passage that connects remote areas of Irth. The charmway in Midrath links with the Spiderlands. There I know of another charmway that will take us into the Reef Isles.'

'The Spiderlands—' The thief blew a silent whistle of fright. 'I have heard that the spiders there thrive on Charm.'

Lord Drev sighed resignedly. 'Until the cacodemons arrived, the spiders of that dominion were the only creatures invulnerable to charmfire. We will have to defend ourselves with common fire and our blades – and, of course, luck.'

They wandered on into the night, wending south through the narrow lanes of the forest. Foraging as they walked, they made good progress through the rolling country. At dawn, they saw through the narrow windows of the forest the ice peaks of the Malpais Highlands etching the north sky like blue lace. The wind striding down from there chilled them with its frosty scents of arctic scrub and tundra resins.

Leboc, hood thrown back, mask dangling against his combat

vest, sidled up to the thief. He held out his hands, and Ripcat saw that they gleamed with the palest fire. He glanced down at his own body and beheld a caul of luminiferous air of no color but a distinct brightness.

'It's a charmwind,' Leboc said. 'Thylia, the witch queen of the highlands, has sent it to find us. And it has.'

'News of the dead cacodemons surely reached Wrat,' Lord Drev guessed and angrily threw off the cocoon of wind about him. It hung in the air briefly, limp as a jellyfish, then slipped away through the trees. 'Now we know for certain that Thylia serves him.'

'Who would have doubted it?' Leboc's lump of a nose wrinkled with disdain. 'She was never a friend of your regency or our brood.'

'What does this mean?' Ripcat asked and tried to shake off the sticky, flimmering wind. But it wobbled about him like a gelatinous sheath and would not loosen.

'We are in the witch queen's dominion,' the wizarduke said. He slashed his hands downward before Ripcat in an abrupt clawing strike that ripped away the viscous ether and left it dangling from his clenched fists like a crinkled sheet of transparency. 'She has the power to send these charmwinds roaming across the Malpais Highlands, looking for intruders. They are invisible to our eye charms, and now that they have found us they have released into the winds our location.'

'In a short while, Thylia will know precisely where we are in her dominion.' Leboc tore off the gummy ectoplasm in shreds, and it curled to the ground and fluttered away. 'When the cacodemons come this time, they will come in droves. We must hurry.' He snatched away the last patches of charmwind and helped the troopers who were clawing at the elusive substance.

They fled among the enormous trees, away from the mountain peaks stenciled with mist and ice. They ran fast and limber over the tangled rootweave, hurtling mossy benches and knobs of subsumed logs and stumps. Their tiny figures dwindled smaller among the gigantic timber vaults and vanished into the gloomy owl distances of the forest.

Yet, far to the north in the mountain fastness of Andezé Crag, the witch queen Thylia, standing naked before a crystal obelisk, watched their flight with eyes of black diamond. 'My charmwind has found them, lord.'

Wrat sat up among the colorful silk cushions where he had been pleasuring himself with the witch queen for the past several days. 'Drev?' he asked sullenly. 'You have left my bed to tell me of Drev?'

'Yes, the wizarduke,' Thylia confirmed. She turned away from the arboreal imagery in the obelisk and looked at the small man lying among the heaped silks. Knobby-shouldered, whittle-ribbed, sinew-shanked and pale as a slug's underbelly, he repulsed her physically. His pointy face with its slanted brow, narrow eyes, sharp nose, long nostrils, wasted cheeks, and caved chin seemed the most reprobate extreme of human visage. It required all her Charm to bear his presence, especially when his bony hands groped over her and he crawled atop and pressed against her with his leathery slitherings and his odor of oily sweat.

His was a reptilian lust, a constant and slow coupling, his slim murky eyes staring intently, finding sweetness in her woe. Days on end he possessed her, laboring with a creaturely shamelessness that sickened her soul and would have broken her health if not for her Charm. Joy flared in her that morning when her obelisk ignited with news from the charmwind that she had dispatched to locate the wizarduke.

'He will not tarry in my dominion, my lord.' Thylia seized the gray veils of her witch habit from the onyx chair where Wrat had thrown them and draped herself. 'You must now hurry forth to exact your revenge upon him while he is yet in our grasp!'

Wrat propped himself among the cushions the better to watch with prurient vigilance as the object of his desire sheathed her nakedness with the multiple and intricate folds of the witch's vestment. He had taken deep and abiding pleasure in tethering his carnal heat to a woman dedicated by convention to the sages – and a queen, at that. He wondered if he would ever tire of this passionate bliss.

'Let the cacodemons savage him,' he replied wearily. 'His death is a small thing now that I have taken everything from him. I am happy enough that he has been reduced to scurrying like a mouse through the woods, never knowing when the owl will strike.'

'You can make him suffer.' Her black eyes glittered. 'You can make him feel true suffering, suffering that yearns for oblivion.'

Wrat dismissed that notion with a distracted sigh. Now that she was dressed and was tying up her platinum tresses in a hair net and stepping into her fawn shoes, he wanted her naked again. He lay back and lifted his engorgement with one hand. 'The greater revenge is not Drev's suffering but my pleasure. Come, straddle me.'

Thylia crossed her arms and did not move. 'How can you be so indifferent to the man who cast you into the Gulf?'

'Had he not, would I be here now with you for my plaything?' He leered and wagged his phallus at her. 'I should thank him for what he did. But he is too dangerous.'

'Indeed, my lord.' The queen scowled with concern. 'You grossly underestimate Lord Drev. He is a formidable wizard, probably the Irth's greatest living master in the Lazor lineage of pragmatic wizardry. I do not doubt he could craft an amulet from a pebble and straw.'

'Enough!' Wrat sat upright, dark, narrow eyes tightening. 'His amulets do not frighten me. I am the Dark Lord! Charm is merely the light of the Abiding Star – and every light casts a shadow. I gather that darkness – and I smother Charm!'

Thylia dropped her arms to her sides and bowed her head contritely. 'I do not mean to impugn your greatness, my lord. But my love for you insists that I warn you not to ignore the wizarduke. He should be slain at once.'

'My cacodemons will destroy him,' he said and lay back again, exposing his renewed desire. 'Now come – sit on me.'

Reluctantly, Thylia edged closer. 'He has already killed three of your cacodemons.'

'I will send twenty – a hundred.'

'But now he knows how to kill them.' She knelt among the heaped cushions. 'Yesterday he gave you your first defeat. And today, will he escape? Tomorrow, how many more demons will you lose? And what will you do when he finally comes for you, if you do not first go for him?'

'Your fearfulness bores me, Thylia.' He rolled to his side and fixed her with a hard gleam in an underbrowed stare. 'If you had not already given me such exquisite pleasure and so freely, I would want to hurt you.'

She placed a querying hand softly on his knee. 'Are you not afraid of losing all that you have won?'

'Afraid?' He brushed aside her hand and rose to his knees. 'Me?' His sharp face flinched. 'Witch, I have been flung into the Gulf. I have stood upon the Dark Shore. Do you have any notion what that is like? No. You have lived a long life of Charm. Well, there is no Charm among the cold worlds.' He glared at her ignorance. 'The Dark Shore is the cloaca of the universe. Everything the Abiding Star eliminates seeps through the void to that ruder place – every illness, every deformity. And I lived there. I thrived! Steeped in sickness and weariness, surrounded by the ill-shapen and the deranged, I thrived! In those alien reaches, where people are so blunted by suffering they spend a third of their lives unconscious, asleep, unborn, I thrived! To a darker world I went, and I returned stronger. I am not afraid of anything on Irth!'

Thylia did not retreat before his rant but kept her noble features composed, without a hint of the loathing she felt for this graceless churl whom accident and ferocity had granted power. 'Very good, my lord. I spoke out of love. And now I will keep my silence.'

'Love!' His stringy brown hair swung over his eyes as his head snapped back. 'Twice you used that word freely with me, witch. Do you truly believe this is love I am inflicting on you? I have seen the disgust in your eyes. You do not love me. You endure me like a sickness, because if you did not, you would suffer far worse.'

Thylia's placid visage offered no sign of the distress constricting her stomach, withholding the vile aversion and maledictions rising in her. 'My lord, I respect you for what you are – a survivor, the only one ever to return from the Dark Shore. When I say I love you, what do I intend but respect, awe, and submission? Love is a question. You are my answer.'

'Do not quote The Gibbet Scrolls to me!' He shoved her away so violently she toppled to her back on the petrified wood floor. 'I may once have been a lowly scavenger with only the Scrolls for comfort, but now I am the master of Irth.'

She rose to her feet and confronted him without rancor or fear, though both competed in her. 'I never doubted that, my lord.'

'Of course not.' He sat among the bright cushions, arms locked across his chest, and his upper lip curled back from his wet brown teeth. 'Show me your love, then, witch-queen. Go and bring to me the head of Lord Drev. I will post it above our conjugal bed so that when I mount you next I can gaze into his lifeless eyes and savor that boldest of unions – passion conjoined with death.'

'My lord!' Thylia's jaw rocked loose, and she stepped back a pace. 'My Charm is no match for the wizarduke.'

'Take as many cacodemons as you want. But go!' An angry tic in his sunken cheek writhed like a lizard under his flesh. 'Bring me his head. And hurry. I will have to amuse myself with your court ladies until you return, and they cannot compare to a true queen.'

Thylia fled the bedchamber, relieved to be away from the lecher and yet wrung with anxiety about the deadly task he had set her.

*Can I slay the wizarduke?* she questioned herself, wondering if she had the lethal cunning to match her foe's Charm.

The ancient corridors of hewn stone carved with somber statues of her ancestors offered little solace. Her forebears had been enemies of the Brood of Dorzen since Lord Drev's great-grandfather, the One-Eyed Duke, slayed their leaders and forced the Malpais Highlands to submit to the regency.

She passed numerous niches and alcoves outfitted with censers, incense trays, veils and trance-slings for the witch ceremonies that had been the central function of Andezé Crag since it was chiseled out of this mountainside almost a million days ago. Many of the chambers were occupied with worshippers communing with the primal goddess of life whom all witches served.

As queen, her bedchamber occupied the highest tier of the spiral tower that corkscrewed into the grottoes of the metropolis below. There, the Dark Lord's cacodemons awaited her. Several hundred had accompanied him when he descended upon her city, and he had posted them among the many vaulted plazas and market squares that conjoined the maze of subterranean streets.

Hu'dre Vra had authorized her to conscript as many of the squamous monsters as she wanted, and she decided she would take them all with her, every one. She was certain that he could summon more if he needed, and for the time being her people, dwellers of perpetual night who naturally feared the beasts skulking about in the dark, would enjoy a respite.

Along the helical ramp that she descended, a wide vista of the highlands offered itself through the broad casements that penetrated the outer wall in colonnades of winged sphinxes. Charm kept the icy winds outside, but in pre-talismanic times the frosty blasts scoured these stones, and the sphinxes bore spalls and eroded features from those archaic days.

Handmaidens, witches in traditional gray veils, awaited her at the expansive balcony of tessellated tiles and gorgon pillars where she usually conducted her upper court. At her approach, they scurried to remove the chamois canopies from the Charm lenses where she cleansed and refreshed herself after her ceremonial duties or, of late, her lewd sessions with the Dark Lord. But, this day, she waved them aside.

'Send in the Dark Lord's sirdar,' she commanded, 'and leave us alone.'

The handmaidens departed in a whispering of veils, and Thylia paced quickly to her red-veined ebony throne. A tap of her beryl thumb-ring opened the Charm drawer in the pedestal, and sparkling trays of amulets fanned before her.

She selected a tiara of hex-rubies potent enough to ward off all unwilled physical contact, and she fitted it above the snood that secured her long hair. Fylfot bracelets of conjure-silver clasped her wrists, designed to call down and direct thunderbolts. About her throat, she placed an obeah cord from which dangled an emerald eye charm. Then, from under the Charm drawer, she extracted a cincture of power wands and tightened that about her waist with dragonclaw clasps of hex-metal.

Outfitted for battle, she closed the drawer with the toe of her buff shoe and faced the serpent-coiled portal where a red-splotched black cacodemon awaited her.

'Summon all the others,' she ordered. 'We are to fly at once to the southern ranges to find and destroy the wizarduke Lord Drev.'

'All?' the sirdar asked in its eroded voice.

'Every one of them – by command of Hu'dre Vra.'

'We number over five hundred,' it rasped.

'Then over five hundred shall escort me,' she replied firmly. 'They shall exit at once by the nearest flues and shall flock across the eastern terraces to rise here.' She pointed out of the balcony at the prospect of snow crags adrift in the mist like crystal sails against the blue zenith. 'Obey me now.'

The sirdar backed off and silently disappeared down the curved rampway, its limbless and tentacled hulk floating just above its shadow.

Thylia sat on her throne and contemplated her situation. She did not require Charmed insight or her training as a witch to realize that Wrat was psychopathic. Madness festered in him from the cruel days of his sufferings as a scavenger.

In the chambers of his quiet, when he lay calm with postcoital stillness, she had seen the abominations sloshing like brown sewage down the skewed corridors of his brain. Fevered with rage, he wanted them all dead, all the people of Irth who had lived better than he. From the Peers to the factory workers, they were all to be killed, all dead, dead by the millions, floating pulpy and rotted, bloated purple with death. In his mind, hosts of bobbing corpses lolled slowly in the seaward seethe that flushed their fecal murk into the tide's grimy drift.

*All dead*, she realized with horror. *He means to kill us all!*

She shuddered that his rancid brain possessed an enormity of power none on Irth could defy. She had to obey him. And though her ancestors were surely well pleased that her hand was forced to kill Lord Drev, the descendant of their mortal foe, she shrank from the task. Yet she had to destroy the wizarduke or be flushed away, herself a carcass, made slime before she ruptured the secret of Wrat's magic and discovered how to slay him and deliver his putrid body to the curing mud.

A sibilant summons steamed from outside, and a sooty darkness fell across the balcony. Beyond the carven marble balustrade with its gargoyled supports genuine demons rose. The swarm darkened the radiant sky, and she stepped to the balcony rail and hoisted herself atop it beneath a thunderhead shadow of amassed monstrosities.

She raised her arms in summons, and an invisible demonic force gripped her with chill brightness and lifted her into the air. Complexions of night shifted on all sides as she rose among the packed lizard flanks, flanged jaws, tar-bead eyes, past black hides leached to ashen gray underbellies impressed with wicked stares and tusked mouths, lifted to a privileged position at the crest of the swarm.

Charm muted her disquiet and thinned the garish stink of demon fetor. Emerald eye charm in hand, she chanted Lord

Drev's name, and his image appeared fugitive and small in the vast caverns of the forest. And with him ran four Falcon Guards in raptor hoods and combat vests and a beastman with a pelt of blue nap, small cub ears, long green eyes, and a panther's slouched stride. They splashed along the fern banks of a surly stream, charging fast through the arboreal shadows where daylight swarmed in hot pieces.

Thylia waved the emerald eye charm before her until she felt the precise direction. She pointed the way, propelled through the tilted and dazzling heights by a cold stream of black magic, and the cacodemons in their hundreds followed, rivering among the cloud chasms, south, toward the green nubbled slopes of the forest.

Flight above the rageful mists of the mountains took far longer than the witch queen had imagined, and when the emerald in her grasp indicated that the wizarduke was at last below her, the Abiding Star shivered as a red oblate disk in the treetops.

The forest fringe crumbled above a slate ledge. Rock-strewn grassland tumbled in steep bluffs and tottering boulders toward a misty horizon full of quicksilver gleams and twilight flares of red shafts and orange twinklings – the turbulent headwaters to the sprawling Falls of Mirdath.

The wizarduke and his five men leaped and cantered downhill, spinning around the monoliths in their way, their long shadows bolting beside them. They had seen the skyful of cacodemons in their niello eye charms before the armada loomed like a stormfront above the horizon, and they barreled over the stony terrain with arm-flailing abandon.

The Falls hovered at an impossible distance, and Lord Drev had abandoned that goal while still among the trees. Instead, he sought a particular chute among the sinkholes on the slope. The sharpeye amulet in his grasp felt the thin dry thread of Spiderland scent from the charmway hidden somewhere among the Falls. The distinct odor leaked out from one of the sinkholes ahead. By that cinereous wisp he knew that the one chute that the amulet sought connected to an underground labyrinth leading eventually to the charmway. Yet already he could see that the monstrous flock would descend upon them before they found the right sinkhole.

'Fix knives!' Leboc bawled when the roars of the approaching legion fell upon them like chunks of thunder.

'No!' the wizarduke countermanded. 'Too many to fight.' He stopped running, and the others staggered to a stop around him. 'We have to use the boulders.'

'Avalanche?' Leboc queried, his raptor hood shaking with disfavor. 'We'll crush ourselves.'

'Not avalanche.' Drev unshouldered his firelock, aimed at a thrust of rock, and hit its edge with a white-hot stroke of charmlight. Sudden arcs of lava sprayed upward with projectile velocity. 'Breakaways.'

Leboc scanned the front of the advancing horde and the placement of boulders around them, and he swiftly deployed the three troopers and found a firing position for himself.

Drev took Ripcat's hand and pressed into his palm the crystal rhomboid of the sharpeye amulet. 'Feel out the sinkhole where this amulet leads,' he said. 'When you find it, press the amulet to your brow and call for me. I will hear you. Go!'

Ripcat bounded away, at first feeling nothing, simply eager to comply. Then, he sensed it – a faint tremolo of vibration within the amulet that varied as he pointed the crystal. It led him through the scarlet glow and stretched shadows of twilight among tall slabs of rock and grassy bluffs. In the distances below him, mists from the extensive torrents and cascades of the Falls of Mirdath rose with the wind, frayed, and caught the setting light in red sparks and hot chaff blown high into the atmosphere.

The thief heard Leboc shout, 'Hold fire! Hold!' And he glanced over his shoulder to see the five hooded men kneeling in the sparse grass, firecharms poised. Above them, a black wave of cacodemons descended. A veiled woman, a witch, dove forward with them, her gray robes furling like smoke and her amulets shining sharply like broken carats of twilight.

The deafening roar of the demon army smothered the sound of Leboc's commands, and he raised his left arm high, withholding fire until the dread shadow of the multitude fell upon them. With claws and fangs thrust open to strike, the murderous throng swooped to the attack, and Leboc dropped his arm and opened fire.

Blinding bursts of charmfire blazed in a wide enfilade, struck the blunt edges of rubblestones and boulders and scattered fiery trajectories of burning rock across the purple gloaming. The front ranks of cacodemons exploded under the searing impact. Limbs, looping coils of viscera, and skull shards flew into the night. Wrecked bodies collided with the onslaught behind them, and more cacodemons tumbled into the lethal fire of shattered rock.

The witch queen rose higher, bullets of stone ricocheting off the invisible mantle of Charmed protection from her ruby tiara. Leboc sighted her and released several direct bursts in her direction. Most sliced brightly under the evening's hieroglyphic stars, but one struck her with a flash that erased the constellations. Her protective tiara fell apart, and she spiraled Irthward.

Two cacodemons seized her, one by each arm, and lowered her to the corpse-strewn ground. All around her, the throngs continued their assault, shielding themselves with carcasses and dashing left and right, trying to outflank the shooters. But Leboc had positioned the gunmen to chip away at the rocks from every side, and dozens more cacodemons fell before the blazing projectiles.

Thylia's trembling fingers came away from her forehead sticky with blood. Another direct hit would kill her. Yet with screaming carnage everywhere, she knew she was already dead in the Dark Lord's narrow eyes. She clambered among the mounded bodies, climbing into the line of fire, and cacodemons closed ranks to shield her.

While they shrieked and died before the withering blasts of stone, she raised her arms toward the sky and a night swept with stars. Intoning her most direful spell, the blood of her brow burning her eyes, she activated the silver fylfot bracelets and felt a great surge of energy gust upward from the ground through her and toward the breathing stars.

Her gray robes billowed in the frosty updraft and brightened to silver, and something magnetic flexed in her chest and twisted her heart painfully. She doubled over as if struck, and in the same instant lightnings flared from out of the clear heavens. A tree of electric fire reared above her, its branches tangling at the meridian in a darkness bleached by radiance and its writhing roots sizzling just overhead, lifting her long tresses in staticky disarray.

With agonizing effort, she straightened. Bloodstreaked face warped with pain, she stared through the loud glare, searching for her enemies. The brilliant tracers of their charmlight chewing away at the surrounding boulders located them for her, and she pointed vehemently toward one of them. A whipstroke of lightning lashed from the radiant tree and electrocuted a trooper, shriveling him to a burnt husk riddled with crawling worms of blue fire.

The witch queen clenched against the convulsive force racking her body and remained upright, seeking another target. The bodies of cacodemons hurled past, struck dead by flying rocks, and she pointed her aching arm in that direction. Another branch of the burning tree swung downward and clouted a second trooper. His firelock burst, and green flames consumed him so that only sparkling ashes remained, skirling upward on the thermal current of his pyre.

Ripcat, running in fits and starts, stopping to look back at every loud retort, felt the rhomboid crystal hum vibrantly in his grasp. He stopped short and looked down in the wavery shadows of flaring lightning and starsmoke to see a tufty-rimmed sinkhole socketed with utter darkness.

He pressed the amulet between his eyes and called against the cacophony of exploding rocks, bellowing cacodemons, and hissing lightning, 'I found it!'

The wizarduke heard him, felt out his direction, and signed frantically to Leboc and the remaining trooper to fall back. They sprinted into the fulgurant darkness, and the cacodemons pursued.

'Stop!' the witch-queen cried and contracted violently about the twisting anguish that linked the core of her body to the sky's blue-white flames.

But the cacodemons rushed on, inflamed with blood-rage.

With a hurt scream, she wrenched herself upright and peered down the stony incline for the wizarduke. She could not distinguish him among the three hooded figures running over the littered terrain. Quickly, before agony crumbled her again, she pointed, and a lightning blast jumped down from the sky and struck among the charging cacodemons.

Several heads detonated, splattering brain matter and skull fragments across the field.

Angrily and half-blind with her suffering, the witch pointed again and again and again, stabbing wildly. Three rapid bolts slammed into the slope. Rocks tumbled, and the cacodemons fell back. The wizarduke and his escorts ran unobstructed, and Thylia fought dizziness and molten pain long enough to steady her arm and point directly at them.

The next bolt incinerated the last of the Falcon Guard, and he crashed to the ground in a stinking charred mass. The reverberation of the strike jarred the marrow in the bones of the wizarduke and his marshal. Their eyeballs spun in their sockets and their knees buckled. They hit the ground and rolled, bruising themselves among the flinty stones.

As they lunged to their feet, Leboc cursed. He would not die running scared. He stopped and turned, and, with a furious cry, he tore off his mask, the better to aim. Shooting as fast as he could pull the trigger, he released a luminous volley toward the base of the tree of massive lightning.

The charmfire splashed harmlessly among the phalanx of cacodemons fronting the witch-queen and climbed dangerously higher. A scalding near-miss helped Thylia to find the strength to overcome her pain and raise her arm yet again. She gnashed her teeth and pointed down the line of incoming fire.

Ripcat had disappeared, hidden from the destructive thunderbolts, yet the wizarduke sensed him nearby and ran toward him. So intent was he on following his psychic impressions that he did not realize Leboc was not directly behind him until he heard the distinctive coughing of a firelock.

He whirled about in time to shout, 'Leboc! Stop—' Then the air burned white and the booming blow of destruction kicked him off his feet.

When vision winced back into his eyes, he saw the tarry remains of Leboc steaming in a circle of charred soil. He cried aloud with rage, unslung his firelock, and aimed. He got off two rounds before hands grabbed him from behind and hurled him down into darkness.

He struggled free and saw in the dark by the strength of his amulets that he knelt on a pebbly ledge surrounded by dirt walls embedded with rocky nodules. The thief crouched beside him, and he realized that he had been dragged into the sinkhole that they had sought.

Above, a coil of lightning struck where he had been standing, and a shaft of voltaic glare penetrated the sinkhole's depths, briefly revealing a honeycomb of tunnels and shafts.

'We are the last,' Drev said in a weary voice. 'They are all dead.'

'They died to save you,' Ripcat replied, his eyes iridescent in the dark. He placed the rhomboid crystal in the wizarduke's limp hand. 'Let them not have died in vain. Get us away from here before the demons come.'

Drev nodded and lowered himself through the chute to the floor of the sinkhole. 'We killed many,' he muttered, waving the amulet to feel direction through the maze. 'Five against five hundred!'

'That many?'

'Maybe more.' Drev selected a tunnel tall enough to enter standing. 'It grew dark before I could finish counting.'

Ripcat examined the walls with his fingertips and felt the smooth contours where water had once coursed. 'Where are we going?'

'Same as before.'

'The charmway? To the Reef Isles?'

'To the Spiderlands and then Nhat, yes.'

'But there are only two of us,' Ripcat protested in the merciless dark that not even his eyes could penetrate. 'Wrat has an army of cacodemons.'

The wizarduke answered with determination, 'We will recruit others along the way.'

'Perhaps you should go among the dominions and tell the Peers how to fight the cacodemons,' Ripcat suggested, thinking it more prudent to journey alone through the land of the enemy. 'I will travel ahead to Nhat to find Dogbrick, my friend.'

'You forget,' the wizarduke answered. 'I have someone more than a friend awaiting me in Nhat's labor camps.'

'Tywi.'

'Yes. She is my fate.'

'Does she know you are her fate?'

'Of course,' Lord Drev replied at once, and then added quietly, 'In her heart – if I can find my way there.'

# Three Blind Gods

·•·I·•·

Hu'dre Vra knew pain. Among the cushions of silk in the crown suite of the helical tower of Andezé Crag, he twisted with sudden hurt. The three naked witches cavorting around him with chromatic ribbons of trance gauze rolled away in a fright and leaped to their feet at the inhuman sounds that kindled in him. Clutching at each other, they watched with jarred expressions as the small, weasly man's skeleton began to glow with a blue-white intensity from within the lampskin of his flesh.

Pulses of radiance and shadow strobed along the knobs of his spine, and his shining skull throbbed behind a transparent face wrinkled with anguish. Spewing weird howls, he twisted upright. Like a blossom opening, the luminous claws of his ribs parted, tearing his flesh into ragged mummy cloths, and the ruby-black heart within him pushed outward, bloodwebbed and palpitating.

A snarling face pressed through the sticky maroon wall of the shuddering heart and thrust its malevolent gullet and harsh staring eyes into the room, releasing a ghoulish cry. It shook its ruffles of cankerous, fungoid flesh with pain, and the witches cried in horror and fled the chamber.

The evil puppet in its drapes of frayed heart muscle and torn arteries stood hatched within the living body of Wrat chewing screams. The dying cacodemons tormented it. Two or three dead parts of its ravenous hive and the pain remained inside the husk of its host. But the hive was dying by the dozen. The suffering ripped the fiend from its hiding, and it writhed in the open air, varnished in blood, its epicanthic eyes swiveling madly and its toothy, diabolic grin gnashing incomprehensible maledictions at this crazy world to which it had been carried.

The killing stopped. The pain ceased and left behind a murk of ache. The demon parasite spoke softer cruelties, its pikejaw rocking sideways while its split tongue flicked between green slimed incisors.

Wrat gaped down at himself and the hellish imp swaying sullenly between the jagged spindles of his split ribs. He moaned the chant he had learned on the Dark Shore from the black magicians of the cold world where fate had delivered him. The tatters of veins and crimson tissues began knitting together, stitching themselves out of the slither of bloodsmoke spilled from his body and the silver-blue light that seeped from the air.

That light was the power of this world, the radiance of the Abiding Star that the people of Irth called Charm. To the parasitical gremlin within him, it was pure magic. On the Dark Shore, such magic had to be distilled laboriously out of the void into which it had dissipated in its light-years journey from the Abiding Star, and the smallest quantities took enormous effort and time to garner. But here on Irth, just as he had promised this demon from the cold world, magic filled the air.

The Dark Shore chants worked instantly. The ripped-free heart pulled inward, drawing the gruesome and sulky demon back into its glisteny cocoon. Silver shining ribs closed over, and with the lost luster of his bones the pale flesh of his hairless chest went opaque and sealed over like cooling wax.

He sat down on the bed, blinked with amazement that he yet lived, and turned his head to look out the wide curved window at the twilight's shining spires of ice peaks and burning glaciers. His cacodemons were invulnerable to Charm. That had been the beauty of his return from the Dark Shore. But that beauty had become marred by a truth he had not anticipated: The brute physics of matter could slay his army, slash their flesh, break their bones, and spill the life from creatures that in this world of bright magic needed no food or water or even air to live.

From within, he heard the underwater droning of the evil thing that dwelled inside him. It felt betrayed. There was to be no pain. None of its hive was to die. They had come to feast and pillage in the shining fields of heaven. Now forty or more lay dead. The pain had been so unbearable that the diabolic imp had nearly broken free from its host and run raving into the ocean of light.

*Madness!* Wrat thought. Without him, the gremlin and its entire hive of cacodemons would dissolve in the seething radiation of the Abiding Star. The black magic that united them to him was spun from the spilled blood of Irthlings that they had imbibed. Rett. The Dog Dim. Grapes. Little Luc. Skull Face. Chetto. And Piper. All the Bold Ones who had survived the fall into the Gulf with him, all his former comrades, had been ritually slain and fed to the gremlin and its hive. Their blood enabled black magic in him, the power to bind the demons of the Dark Shore to his own Irthly frame and thus protect them from the destructive effects of this hot realm on their cold bodies. He was their talisman. They could not live on Irth without him.

Swaying upright, he stumbled to the window, where he leaned heavily on the sill. He gazed down into a giant snow bowl half scooped in purple shadows from the soft shrouds of the surrounding mountains with their orange tips of alpenglow.

*Thylia will pay!* he promised the droning gremlin enshrouded in his flesh. *She betrayed me. And she will pay.*

The realization of his vulnerability struck fear in the weasly man. A few more cacodemons slain and he would be lying among the cushions split like a shucked fish. In his giddy rush of power, he had underestimated his enemies.

*Not again*, he swore and wobbled away from the window. He

lay on the petrified wood floor, feverish and grateful for the cool glassy surface. As soon as Irth turned away from the Abiding Star, his need would summon more cacodemons from out of the Gulf. They would rise to him from the Dark Shore like the cold effluvia they were. And they would fall toward him out of the night sky, drawn to the evil in his heart and the magic strength of his own flesh that grounded them in this reality.

The hive had drunk of Irth blood. They were bound to him by blood, and they would come in the night with crazy faces leering in their bellies.

Lying helpless and naked in a scarlet pane of dusklight, he twitched to think of himself dead and his enemies thriving. A voice spoke through the wall of his chest, unintelligible rage. The gremlin's tantrum would become his own as soon as he had strength to bear it.

Seven shadows advanced from where night pooled in the chamber's distant corners. Seven ragged, unshaven men clad in jute.

*The Bold Ones.*

'The Dead Ones,' a turtlefaced man among the group croaked angrily.

*Chetto.* Wrat had fed him alive, like the others, to the hive – but the cacomaggots had been sated by the six before him and devoured him most slowly. He had bobbed in the caldera of grubs for days, a screaming skeleton of ulcerous sinews.

'The Sacrificed Ones,' a bald and hooknosed specter accused, the clusters of purple polyps on his face shaking with indignation.

*Grapes.* Wrat laughed darkly. 'Did you really think you would share all this with me?'

'You lied to us,' a squat man with the beastmarks of a canine groused.

He laughed even louder at this ghost, the Dog Dim. 'I lied! Did I lie when I promised that you would be free of scavenging? Did I lie when I swore we would assault heaven?'

A black man with his beard cleaved by a scar from his ear

across his mouth to his chin shook his head. 'Wrat, you are a homicidal maniac. We could have lived well on the Dark Shore. You betrayed us, one and all, so that you could come back here and have your revenge. Blood is what you crave. You killed us for our blood.'

'I did, Rett.' Wrat's insipid face flushed with insane mirth. 'I killed you one and all for your blood. And now here you are, back on Irth just like I promised. Back on Irth. As *ghosts*. And the Dog Dim says I lied!' He laughed so hard his vision bleared.

When he could see again, a man without a nose and no upper lip but bare brown teeth and purple gums glared at him. 'We *are* ghosts and the demons come again to pull us out of the air! You tell us why, Wrat. You tell us why we had to die so that you could have demons at your side instead of men.'

'Men!' Wrat tried to sit up but succeeded only in thudding his head against the floor, so drained was he of strength. 'You had your chance as men, Skull Face. I led you out of Nhat as men. And as men you climbed the stairs of heaven to the domain of the Peers. But you failed. You had your big chance – and you failed!'

'We failed together,' a short, towheaded youth with sad eyes said. 'We should have stayed together on the Dark Shore. We were the Bold Ones, Wrat. We could have ruled that world.'

'Rule the Dark Shore? Rule the gutter of the universe? How long would we have ruled, Little Luc? How long before some illness wasted us? Or old age shriveled us on our bones? Bah! When we found those pathetic gremlin kings who thought we were their legendary magicians returned from hell, you saw a chance to use their magic to rule a small world. I saw the way back to Irth, to freedom from sickness and decrepit old age. *I* saw the way back! *I!*'

The six wraiths that had spoken retreated into the darkening night shadows, depleted of their thin energy. Only one remained, a tall, pallid man with lustrous red hair and regal bearing.

'Go ahead, Piper,' Wrat spoke bitterly. 'Spit your venom like the others.'

Piper said nothing, only stared forth from somnolent depths.

'Come on,' Wrat cajoled. 'You were always one for sweet words. You knew how to make us feel good about ourselves even when we had nothing but bad to show for ourselves. Let's hear your sweet tongue speak sour.'

Piper said not a word but stepped back silent into the enclosing shadows, from where he stared with a solemn look of mute pity pressed upon his noble features.

'You're as much a fool as the others,' Wrat cried out and choked on his ire. He coughed fitfully, then spat blood. 'Don't look at me like that. I'm not the pathetic one. You are. You're the ghost. I'm alive. I'm the Dark Lord! Hu'dre Vra! The whole of Irth kneels before me!'

The phantom lifted a reed pipe to his mouth and blew a sad and flimsy tune. It was the music of their earliest days together as scavengers on the tidal flats of Nhat. That tune, sometimes jauntier, had accompanied them on their quest for glory and, sometimes with a noble lilt, had comforted them in their despair.

'Blow your weepy little song, you fool!' Wrat shouted and found in his anger the strength to sit up. 'You can't touch me with that! I laugh at all of you! You're all fools! You ate your defeat at the hands of Drev and his Peers. You ate it and would have lived out your puny lives on the Dark Shore, kings of the sewer! But I won't eat defeat! I'm going to make Drev eat it! And all of Irth will join him!'

In the darkness of night, the music veered away.

'You're all fools,' Wrat chortled again and wobbled to his feet. His chest ached where the gremlin had pushed through, and he pressed a fist to his sternum. 'Don't you ever do that again,' he warned the thing inside him. 'We have a world to destroy. If we have to swallow some pain to do it, so be it. And if we have to die, you little bloodsucker, it won't be because of pain or panic. You hear me? Death has to come to us. We're not running into its claws.'

He stood at the window and looked upon snowfields radiant

blue under the star fumes. Cacodemons fell toward him through the void. He could feel them. Their approach hammered iron dents in his blood cells, banging strength back into his body.

Soon he could see them, a black spiral against the sidereal incandescence. They funneled down toward him. Pieces of darkness settling out from the spaces between the stars' webs, they came at his silent summons.

He climbed onto the sill and raised his arms. His skinny nakedness swelled, and he felt the evil puppet in the cave of his heart jerk taller, yanked upright on taut strings of blood. Shadow leaked from his pores. It glistened darkly over his skin like fur, and his pallid flesh disappeared beneath a pelt of darkness.

Cacodemons descended from the sky's luminous spirals and hung in the dark air before him, big and silent as totems, watching him with their glassbead eyes and monstrous thoracic faces. No will in heaven or Irth could match the hideous wrath compacted in their hulking and sinuous shapes.

He drew on their power, and the penumbra enclosing him widened, expanding into glossy curved plates of barbed armor. A cowl of black glazed mirror covered his rat-profile, and he enlarged to the size of a cacodemon. He stepped through the Charm pane and off the window sill.

Across the span of night, Hu'dre Vra flew with his gang of monsters. A delirium of cruelties occupied his mind the entire flight – tortures he designed and perfected for the punishment of the witch queen who had betrayed him. But when, after midnight, they reached the ragged fringe of the mountain forest and alighted on the rocky slopes where demonic carcasses lay dismembered and reeking, weakness stymied his rage.

The slain demons did not rise in the nocturnal tide but remained in the obscene postures of their dying, rapidly decomposing. A haze of decay pooled over each corpse, and viscous shapes turned and mutated in the air. Foetal gnomes and hellish marionettes hung cobwebbed in sticky fumes above the mangled bodies. These were the squalid souls of the newly dead, greenly luminescent, astonished to find themselves alive and disembodied in the Charmed night.

The sickly presence of these ghosts drooling smoke depressed the imp caged in Wrat's heart and sapped his vitality. His knees wobbled, and the jointed seams of his armor buckled.

With a defiant cry, Hu'dre Vra raised both arms to the sky. Lightning crawled across the treetops, and a brisk stormfront scattered birds and leaves out of the forest. A wind drove by, dispersing the effluvial floss like dust, and the figurines of chimerical soul-images flew off in wisps of mist.

But the Dark Lord was still unhappy. He fisted both hands above his helmeted head as if trying to drag the starchains down from their celestial moorings. A gale howled over the forest, and the trees bowed their heads in unison. Pebbles scampered downhill, and the husks of the dead cacodemons stirred, rolled, and fumbled nearly upright. Severed limbs winged away, dissolving to ash and smoke as they flew.

Hu'dre Vra shouted furiously, and the tempest shrieked downward with a vertical force that smashed the corpses to powdery pieces. Reduced to a debris of humus and pulpy decay, the slain cacodemons went swirling away with the wind.

Stillness settled over the cleared killing ground. The Dark Lord reviewed the boulders gnawed by charmfire, their edges melted, fused sharply and stained with flamestreaks. He put a hand to the glassy scorch marks and shook his head. This was a danger he had not foreseen.

The hundreds of survivors from this horrendous battle waited farther up the grassy rise in the forest. He signaled, and they came forward bearing Thylia among them. She was unconscious, and he realized then that she had suffered to fight his enemies. What ire toward her remained in him evaporated at the sight of her blood-streaked face, and he felt pride for her ferocious effort.

The cacodemons laid her on the weedy ground before him and stood back.

'Rise, Thylia,' he directed, placing a hand atop her head, over the gash in her brow. The Charm of her amulets obeyed the pressure of his touch, and the head wound sealed at once and smeared away. Her lids fluttered open upon the black crystal of her eyes.

'I have failed you,' she said with obvious trepidation and did not move.

'On your feet,' he beckoned. 'Drev may have escaped for now, but you have won for me new understanding of my vulnerability.'

She rose slowly, surprised to find herself whole. The scalding effort of summoning lightning had knocked her unconscious beyond the healing reach of her Charm. She peered meekly at the Dark Lord. 'You are not angry?'

'I am enraged,' Hu'dre Vra snarled. 'But not at you. Irth will feel pain for what Drev has done here this night.' He turned in a majestic circle to confront his minions. 'Irth will feel pain!'

In a vortex, they rose into the night and flew south, away from Andezé Crag. Thylia hung close to her Dark Lord within the processional sky, relieved to escape Wrat's fury and anxious about their destination. She dared not ask and disturb the madman's delicate peace with her.

She stretched into her flight, in the warm and soothing current of the Dark Lord's magic. Under the blind stars in the indifferent dark, she and the hundreds of cacodemons aloft on the night wind were as locked in their trajectories as the orbits of the spheres beyond. She glanced about at the others. Limbs and tentacles tucked back, flanged viperjaws thrust forward, they drifted sleekly against the splattered stars.

Dawn spread a green mantle over the eastern rim of the world when the glassy spires of Dorzen rose before them. The floating city emerged from mountainous amber clouds high above the jade cliffs and exploding surf of Ux. Gulls wheeled among the crystal-domed belvederes and swooped under the buttresses and arcs of hanging sidewalks.

Flying closer, the source of the gulls' frenzy came clear: Corpses hung by their twisted necks from the city's renowned suspended sidewalks. Dead bodies also depended from the giant serpentine sky-arch. No commerce moved upon the city streets.

Hu'dre Vra signed for his cacodemons to assume posts upon the tower summits, and he and Thylia went directly to the opulent crystal palace and entered through the mammoth arcade of sardonyx columns. In anticipation of their arrival, the gold pylons stood open upon the vaulted, marmoreal court where once the wizarduke reigned.

Lady Von, in the gray and mauve veils of a witch dancer, waited there beside a tall, blond man with a handsome eagle's frown and wearing a jumpsuit of spungold. They stood before the hall's champagne marble altar under the tiered court galleries packed with cacodemons. At the approach of Hu'dre Vra, they bowed abjectly and offered sonorous greetings, but the Dark Lord ignored them.

He had come to stand in Lord Drev's central court from where he could activate the gem-star that the Ladyship of Sorcery, Luci Ux, the wizarduke's grandmother, had installed above Irth. By its charmlight, he could speak to the palace cities in all the other dominions.

The blond man separated from the diminutive Lady Von and advanced toward Hu'dre Vra, head bowed. 'My lord, I must address you.'

'What is it, Romut?' the Dark Lord asked, surveying the groined vaults above him and finding to his satisfaction that the gem-star projectors had not been vandalized.

'Lord—' The hazel eyes under their ledged, blond brows stared suspiciously around the barbed plates of Hu'dre Vra's armor at Thylia. 'You brought *her* here? The witch queen? Is that wise, my lord?'

Hu'dre Vra finally paid full notice to the muscular figure at his side. 'Romut, what are you doing in that absurd disguise?' Romut splayed his hands across his capacious chest. 'It's a skin of light, lord.'

'I know what it is, fool.' The Dark Lord stood arms akimbo

with disapproval. 'Why are you wearing it?'

'It is my wont, my lord.' Romut smiled abashedly, his blond face imploringly lifted toward his master. 'I am so ugly, I cannot bear to look at myself.'

'I prefer to see you as you are. I have no fond memories of your last disguise.'

Romut lifted both arms and nodded vigorously. 'Of course. Of course. Yet that skin of light saved my life, so that I could be here now to serve you. Otherwise – well, my lord, you yourself told me that had I been with the others – well, you know . . .'

The Dark Lord's angry voice in the enormous hall lifted toward echoes, 'I would have murdered you, too.'

'Yes, exactly.' Romut smiled timorously and glanced at the two witches, who watched with cool remoteness through their diaphanous veils. 'My lord, please.' He slumped his shoulders humbly and peered up meekly at the black armorial mask. 'May I speak to you in private a moment?'

'I have much work to do.'

'This is important.'

'It had best be.' They strode across the hall to an alcove of pillars entwined with marble ivy. 'What is it?'

Romut's noble brow creased with anxiety. 'My lord, I have seen them again – just this last night.'

'Who have you seen?' the Dark Lord asked impatiently. 'What are you talking about?'

'The Bold Ones,' Romut blurted and gnashed his teeth with fear. 'I saw them. I mean to say, I saw their ghosts.'

'Did you?'

'Oh, yes.' He nodded with such vigor his curly blond locks fell over his eyes and he had to brush their fleece aside. 'Seven of them – the ones you murdered. I saw them. They spoke with me!'

'Did they?'

Romut stepped back a pace. 'My lord, you mock me.'

'I mock your fear. You should know better, Romut, than to be afraid of ghosts.'

'They say terrible things, my lord.'

'Yes?' The Dark Lord's voice rumbled like muted stirrings in the tectonic depths of Irth. 'Did they rail at you that I murdered them, one and all, in a slow and horrible way so that I could climb the ladder of energy up through the Gulf and return to here?'

Romut shook his head and tossed his golden hair back. 'Worse, my lord.'

'Really? What did they tell you?'

'They say – they dare to say – well, they say that you are mad, that you are insane.'

'Do you doubt it?'

'That you are mad?' Romut's upper lip twitched, and he blinked several times. 'I – I should think not. You are the Dark Lord!'

'I *am* mad, Romut.'

Romut's hazel eyes grew large. 'You – are?'

'How could I not be?' The fathomless mask pressed closer. 'I have fallen into the Gulf. I have walked upon the Dark Shore. I carry inside my heart the very evil of that place. And by that evil I will bring death to all of Irth.'

'All of Irth?' Romut backed away another pace, wringing his hands. 'My lord, surely once the Peers are dispatched . . .'

'The Peers!' Hu'dre Vra straightened, fists upturned before him. 'They are my personal revenge. The rest belongs to the evil inside me. But first the Peers.' He turned toward the great hall. 'Come. Drev has dared strike at my cacodemons. I must punish Irth for that.'

'Wait, my lord.' Romut jumped forward. 'The witch queen. Is it wise to have her here?'

'She gives me pleasure, Romut.' A soft laugh silked through the needletoothed baleen of the ebony mask. 'You know, they are trained in special ways to please the sages. Ah, but you must by now have experienced those special ways from Lady Von. Does she not please you?'

'Oh, very much.' He affirmed that by clasping a fist over his heart. 'Her witch ways have given me delights I never expected. But that's just it, my lord. She is a witch. Witches work some kind of magic older than Charm. Some kind of power from their Goddess. It is dangerous to bring her together with the witch queen. They say of their Goddess, "When two witches travel together, She walks as the third." '

'The sisterhood does not concern me.' He stepped out of the alcove. 'They are interested only in helping the charmless, bringing comfort to the poor, and worshipping with the sages the old gods.'

'The Three Blind Gods,' Romut spoke in a fearful hush and hurried to his side. 'Her three consorts – Death, Chance and Justice. She guides them on their blind way. And Her witches attend. My lord, please, do not underestimate their power.'

'Their power presented no obstacle to us when we rose up as the Bold Ones,' the Dark Lord spoke while walking.

'Don't you remember, lord?' Romut turned so that he walked backward and could look up at the bloodglow in the adder sockets. 'I made peace with them for you. I promised them that the Bold Ones would never violate their coven houses or the sanctuaries of the sages. And, as you say, they strive to help the helpless and indigent – and as the Bold Ones, we championed the lowest, as do the witches.'

The Dark Lord stopped in midstride and stood in a wide stance. 'But now, Romut old friend, I champion only myself, is that it?'

Romut waved both hands in firm denial. 'You are the Dark Lord, lord. You are a new and greater order.'

'Ah, yes. My new order has been threatened. I have some work yet to do to maintain *my* law and *my* order. Come, Romut.'

'But the witches . . .' Romut pleaded, scurrying beside the giant.

'They are no threat to me,' Hu'dre Vra intoned confidently. 'I am the Dark Lord – master of all Irth.'

*He is indeed mad!* Romut thought and followed worriedly.

From the center of the court's spiral mosaic, Hu'dre Vra gestured at the coped ceiling, and a wet shaft of gemlight illuminated him. Romut walked swiftly to the altar and placed himself between Lady Von and the witch queen. Together, they watched as tableaux of courts from across Irth wavered into view like mirages encircling the wide hall. Apart from the hung skin of the warlock Ralli-Faj in his chamber of delicate trees and aqueous glass walls, no other Peers showed themselves.

Passers-by stood gawking, arrested by the sudden holographic appearance of Hu'dre Vra. He turned regally so that all might view his grim countenance. 'Hear me, denizens of Irth,' he intoned gravely. 'Continue to obey me and no further harm shall come to your cities. But defy me and death will descend upon you as swiftly and surely as it did on Arwar Odawl.'

He gazed into the startled faces, searching for fear, and found it abundantly. Most of the once-noble courts had been converted to markets, and where Peers had formerly trod exclusively, commoners milled about among their stalls and makeshift theater platforms.

'Those who dare strike at the cacodemons I have set over you will know painful death,' the Dark Lord continued. 'I will tolerate no acts of violence against your masters. In the dominion of Mirdath, the renegade Drev has dared attack my legions. For that affront, I will savage Mirdath and the communities of the Falls. Behold this terrible retribution and know the horror that awaits all and any who stand against me.'

At the sweep of his hand, the gemlight disappeared. To the stacked galleries he raised his voice, 'Go and destroy Mirdath. Every village, hamlet and thorpe is to be torn apart. Not a stick left leaning on a rock. And pull down the pillars of Mirdath's capital, the City in the Falls. Slay every Peer and all others who oppose you. Go – and bring death to Mirdath!'

With a loudly echoing uproar, the galleries emptied, and the cacodemons charged out of the crystal palace. Through the oblate panes of the skyroof, they were visible against the peach and apricot clouds of morning, a black thunderhead roiling toward the blue zenith.

'Romut,' the Dark Lord summoned, and the tall man stepped away from the altar and presented himself with his chiseled features raised. 'The bodies you have hanged from the walkramps and the sky-arch. Who are they?'

'Peers, my lord,' Romut answered with a sharp gleam in his long-lashed eyes. 'I have gathered several hundred in warehouses I have converted to prisons. I'm executing them at random, by games of chance whose rules continually change. I think you will find their despair amusing.'

'Show me what you have wrought, cruel Romut.' Hu'dre Vra's voice glittered with restrained laughter. Without facing the witch queen, he dismissed her with a brusque wave and a mocking tone. 'Await me here, Thylia. I would not offend your kinder sensibilities with the horrors my vengeful appetite require.' He hurled a laugh across the court so hard that its echoes tripped over each other.

The Dark Lord walked off jubilantly with Romut and his escort of cacodemons, and Thylia and Lady Von found themselves alone in the vast central hall staring bleakly at each other.

'My queen—' Lady Von began.

The witch queen silenced her with an uplifted hand. 'Say nothing unkind. I am the Dark Lord's consort, and all that you speak to me is spoken to him. Remember, sister, we are privileged among the Peers and so must honor Hu'dre Vra in all that we say and do.'

Lady Von understood at once. 'Then, my queen – we shall dance.'

'Yes.' Thylia released the stays of her robes so that her witch veils unraveled about her. 'Two witches in a hall this magnificent may complete a most wonderful dance.'

Lady Von lifted a power wand from the altar, gestured with it, and released dulcet strains of religious music, a slow duple rhythm to which she initiated the stately turning steps of the archaic Pavane for the Goddess. Such an old and traditional dance, so well known to every witch, allowed for the dancers to freely insert signs and code movements, conveying messages. In this way, Lady Von related to her queen the barbarities that the gnomish Romut had inflicted on her and all of Ux.

She danced a ghostborne account of massacres that left whole villages skewered on spikes – the villages where the Bold Ones had once been escorted in shackles on their way to the night cliffs and the plunge into the Gulf after their defeat at the hands of Lord Drev. She danced the terrors of the Peers. She danced flames and screams and the razor-claws of the cacodemons and the pitifully slow and anguished deaths of Peers stripped of their amulets. She danced their pain and the lewd laughter of Romut. And, finally, she danced before the salt gates of grief, recounting the atrocities committed on her body by that half-human creature.

In reply, Thylia's dance steps wove a cloth of compassion out of the shadowy air and the streamers of her flowing veils. Then she danced the truculent lust of the Dark Lord that had ripped her body and ripped her again each time Charm healed her. And, at last, she revealed the battle on the stone hills above Mirdath and how the wizarduke and his few men stood off five hundred cacodemons and slew forty.

'Can it be so?' Lady Von asked aloud, abruptly stopping her dance.

The witch queen danced on, silently describing the vulnerability of the cacodemons to physical assault.

'Charm!' Lady Von marveled. 'For so many generations it has been our strength. We were not prepared to accept it as our weakness.'

Thylia signed her again to silence, and the two danced to a more triumphant tempo, exploring the hopeful implications of the witch queen's discovery. They danced war. They danced the forms of killing. Sword flourishes, lance thrusts, arrow volleys hurried their steps. Until, sullenly, they slowed before the terror to be visited upon Mirdath.

Lady Von spun a question, wondering if Thylia could somehow persuade the Dark Lord to withdraw his lethal order to destroy the City in the Falls while this martial news was circulated.

The witch queen's sad dance stopped. She shook her head.

Lady Von gracefully reflected her understanding, unpacking quick, whipped steps that showed Hu'dre Vra's fear of his cacodemons' vulnerability. Then she too stopped. Mirdath was doomed.

Out of the long colonnades, maniacal laughter scampered. Wrat and Romut returned from viewing the torment of Dorzen's Peers. Flanked by cacodemons, they entered the central hall and amused themselves using the gem-star to view the flight of the assault demons toward Mirdath. At his command, the visuals were channeled to the courts of every major city so that all of Irth could behold the wrath of Hu'dre Vra.

Romut ordered a feast, and banquet tables replete with silver trays of the most sumptuous delicacies and flagons of dew-wine floated from the alcoves. The cacodemons retreated into the tenebrous archways. Charmworkers, with hot-colored ruffles and satiny costumes, entered in a flurry of trance vapors. At their appearance, mesmermur music lilted among chords of subtle perfumes.

Hu'dre Vra dropped his armor in a vortex of thistledown and appeared out of the swirling feathers as Wrat, garbed in chrome mail and a purple tunic. 'Take off that ridiculous skin,' he commanded Romut.

The gnomish man complied at once, peeling away the illusion with one swipe of a power wand. Revealed in his squat, long-skulled form, his scowling face swung about expecting insults and, receiving none, grinned with one side of his mouth, thick lips curling away from tarry teeth.

Wrat invited him to the table, and the two sat together chortling and guffawing. The morose witches sat opposite them, eating little and muting themselves with soporific drafts of charmsmoke. Neither man paid them any heed.

All that day, the Dark Lord and his comrade fêted, watching in the gemlight the horde of cacodemons flying to Mirdath. When the monsters attained their destination early in the afternoon, Wrat cheered their swooping attack upon the farming thorpes, and Romut whistled gleefully.

Villages burned, and shadowshapes of cacodemons flitted in the smoky depths. The shifting wind rent the vapors, revealing a mayhem of murder – crowds toppling over themselves in panic as demons ripped off limbs and heads and gutted people running, paying out guts as they bolted toward oblivion – and then the wind turned and stitched together the vapors, reducing the melee to a silhouette of clasped shadows.

Late in the afternoon, the rabid army arrived at the Falls of Mirdath. The horizons of explosive cascades and rushing torrents caught the light of the Abiding Star in a golden holocaust of mist, spume, and churning clouds of spray.

Wrat adjusted the gem-star's perspective to reveal the City in the Falls. Daylight smoked through the sheets of falling water in citrine draperies and illuminated a delicate coraline city of chalk towers, shell domes, and rime-melted shapes. Delicate mists wisped among fluted columns, mica-glinting cornices and plinths, and winding friezes hewn from the pale bones of Irth.

The cacodemons splashed through the toppling walls of water and attacked the support pillars of the cavernous metropolis. The stalactite walls buckled and leaked briny smoke. Piers snapped, buttress posts burst, and spongoid clusters of dwellings slid away in avalanches of dust and rubble. Whole cliff-faces groaned and collapsed, toppling into the skyline of spires and towers and razing all to heaps of slag beneath boiling thunderheads of stonedust and mortar.

Wrat leaped on to the tabletop, hysterical with evil joy. He and Romut peered with proud glory at the ancient gothic city reduced to a foggy cavern of unrecognizable rubble.

'No one now will dare attack my demons again!' Wrat exulted and leaped from the table.

'Nor will any dare offer succor to the fugitive Drev,' Romut offered.

'Yes, his doom is most sweet of all – because he knows now that I dominate all Irth. Everything that once was his is mine and more.' Wrat paced a mad, happy circle through the great hall. 'I have the whole world in my grasp. The whole world!'

'And Drev himself hides from you like a little animal.' Romut wagged his big warty head with delight.

'Yet he hides,' Wrat groaned. 'He eludes me. I cannot abide that.'

'Then let us make a game of him,' Romut suggested. 'We play death with all the other Peers. Why not play with him?'

Wrat stared sideways at the gnomish man and tugged his lower lip. 'What are you saying?'

'Let us hunt him for sport!' Romut crowed. 'Look around you, my lord! We are surrounded by all that once belonged to Drev's own person.'

A happy light flushed the Dark Lord's rat-face. 'Of course! A seeker!'

'It can be done,' Romut asserted. 'We can make seekers for the cacodemons.'

'And for ourselves,' Wrat agreed enthusiastically. 'We shall use them to find him wherever he burrows. We shall find him – and then we shall have some real sport.' He grimaced with mirth. 'See that it is done, Romut.'

'At once, my lord.' Romut clapped and beckoned the charmworkers.

Wrat placed his knuckles on the tabletop and leaned his weight on his straight arms, staring at the two witches. 'You have said nothing all day, either of you.'

'We share your joy, my lord,' Thylia spoke with effusive sincerity, 'without wanting to intrude on a pleasure that is rightly your own.'

'I'm sure.' The flesh between Wrat's murky brown eyes wrinkled devilishly. 'Prepare yourself, my queen. We are going hunting!'

He whirled away from the banquet table, and his ebony armor snapped loudly back into place, leaving only his pointy face exposed.

Lady Von flinched and placed a tremulous hand on Thylia's arm.

'You must do what we danced,' Thylia told her and squeezed her hand.

'If I must die myself,' Lady Von promised, her lemur eyes wide with fright, 'I will see that all Irth knows of what we danced.'

'And what would that be?' Hu'dre Vra boomed from across the great hall.

'The Pavane of the Goddess, my lord,' Thylia answered quickly.

'The Goddess?' The Dark Lord spoke from under the black shawl of an archway. 'What nonsense are you speaking? Or is it treachery?'

'Neither, my lord.' Thylia rose and walked around the table to join him. 'I have convinced Lady Von to see that all witches on Irth recall the ancient worship of the Mother of Life, She who bears all. For surely, as we have witnessed this day, there is much suffering to be borne before the Dark Lord.'

'And what has the Goddess to do with that?'

'She teaches us acceptance, my lord.' Thylia strode to his side, speaking with amicable assurance. 'Just as you would have the people of Irth accept you, She requires that we accept all that Irth offers, good and bad. That is the significance of the famous quote from The Gibbet Scrolls: "The Goddess provides. Life sucks." '

'Pithy.' He turned his back on her. 'Romut.'

The warty man had pulled the skin of light about himself again and stood tall and striking among the harlequin-garbed charmworkers. He left the festive group immediately and came to Wrat with chin on chest. 'My lord, the seekers are being prepared at this very moment.'

'Come along,' Wrat said, stepping out of his armor. 'I want to have a heart-to-heart with you.'

Thylia stepped away, but Wrat waved her to his side.

'Come, Thylia.' He smiled coldly. 'You are most dear to me. I should like you to witness this.'

They walked across the expansive hall to a marmoreal enclave crocketed and inset with alternating gargoyle dwarfs and cherubim. Thylia stood beside a winged pilaster carved in the form of an angel's lithe body and watched as Wrat led Romut toward a tall tapered window that admitted a frosty light through its tinted panes.

'The death of so many of my cacodemons has weakened me somewhat,' Wrat admitted and turned Romut so that they faced each other.

'Take your rest here in Dorzen, my lord,' Romut offered with a generous smile.

'Oh, I will take whatever I want,' Wrat assured him with a lopsided smile.

Romut's lips fluttered nervously. 'Are you displeased with me, lord?'

'Pleasure – displeasure—' Wrat's long nostrils widened. 'To a madman, what is the difference?'

Romut shuddered and made no attempt to hide his fright. 'My lord – I – I never once said I believed that – I never said that. It was the ghosts.'

'Yes, the ghosts.' Wrat jutted his lower lip, and his close-set eyes jittered, playing over Romut's handsome features. 'They are right, of course. But I've told you that. And you know it's true.'

'You suffered on the Dark Shore,' Romut acknowledged.

'Oh, indeed.' His sketchy eyebrows lifted. 'And you were not there.'

'But I am here for you now, my lord,' Romut said in a voice splintered with fear.

'And I need you now.' Wrat's avid stare hardened, and pearls of sweat glittered at his temples.

'You are in pain,' Romut observed.

Wrat said nothing. His eyes stared up from under his frowning brows and tightened with dread import. In each of the tiny baubles of sweat sparkling at the bridge of his nose, a minuscule and polished skull grinned.

'You're going to kill me again!' Romut wailed.

'No, Romut,' Wrat spoke softly, though the pulses in his neck and at the sides of his head throbbed. 'I'm not going to take your life.' With quavery fingers, he unclasped his chrome mail vest and pulled aside the purple tunic to expose his pale, bony torso.

Romut whimpered to see the flesh palpitating vigorously between the rib-slats of Wrat's chest.

Wrat groaned through gnashed teeth, 'I'm going to take your soul!' His breastbone buckled, and the skin unstitched, spitting blood.

Romut screamed and tried to turn to run. But Wrat seized his shoulders in an iron grip, and the captive's handsome face twisted ugly with terror.

With a wet, tearing sound, Wrat's chest split open, rending cobwebs of veins. Ribs parted like the skeletal fingers of an unclasping claw, and from out of the bloody viscid interior a hellish doll thrust its shellacked head, pugnacious jaws flashing fangs in an outraged scowl.

Romut bawled hysterically. Tiny hooked hands ripped away the goldspun fibers of his jumpsuit, and the furious puppet's face stabbed its sharp mandibles into his naked flesh.

Thylia staggered. *A gremlin!* Such monsters existed on other worlds far into the Gulf, and she had heard of them and their mindless voracity – but the sight appalled her. Under Romut's wild cries of pain and horror, she could hear the bone-crunching sounds of its jaws. She willed herself to flee and found her legs numb, wobbly, slipping from under her. She sagged to the ground, hand to her mouth as if to yank forth the scream that had lodged soundlessly there.

Locked in Wrat's steely grasp, Romut writhed, his howls drowning in blood, gargling strangled sounds. His head lolled, yet his eyes remained alert and staring.

The imp's dented skull vanished in Romut's thorax, shaking the man's body, rummaging for the pith of him. The skin of light flickered, and the gnomish body appeared and disappeared several times before the illusion sloughed away and left Romut's dwarfed figure shivering convulsively in Wrat's grasp.

The pain stopped, though the chewing sounds continued smacking and crunching. Romut's terrified eyes relaxed, and their black mirrors reflected Wrat's face that carried suddenly a woeful, stricken look.

Something remarkable was happening. Romut found himself not dying but living stronger. The imp that had burrowed its cephalic abhorrence into his body was not killing him. It had fused somehow with the lifeforce in him. Greater strength annealed with his being, and he found himself dazzling with energy.

Wrat, however, appeared weaker, his jaw slack, eyes rolling white. The might of the Dark One was entering him. All the bereaved dimensions of pain and fright collapsed, and Romut filled with visceral power.

Colors brightened, and the enclave appeared incandescent, hued with more vivid actuality. Sounds deepened, and he heard Thylia's panting fright and the crinkly collapse of the tissues in Wrat's body as the energy drained from him and his flesh shriveled.

As Romut realized that Wrat was growing weaker as he himself grew stronger, the process accelerated. Wrat's skinny body shrunk to its bones and slouched against him, desiccated as a mummy. Romut swelled bigger, and the hole torn into his body glowed, an erotic charge of wellbeing suffusing him from there. The squirmings of the gremlin impaled inside him buzzed with a magnetic fervor, electrifying his spine and sending cool tremors through his brain.

The windy pulses of energy amplified reality for Romut. He gazed about him with regnant clarity. This marble enclave disclosed all its secrets: He felt subtle drafts from the hidden door in the wall beside the pilaster, saw every flaw in the floor's stone seams down to the iridescent rays from the crystal fractures in the atomic matrix.

This socket of marble inconspicuously hewn into a shadow-littered corner of the immense central hall was the exact center of the cosmos. From there, Romut felt as though invisible lines of force connected him to every atom in the chamber and, by extension, to each and every single atom in the wide expanses beyond, all the way to the farthest measurable extreme of the universe.

He glanced at the witch queen on her knees, who looked back at him stunned to silence, and he felt her insides rotten with fright. In the shadows, he could see the dead beyond their dying. Ghosts stood within the arched portal watching dolorously – the seven wraiths of the Bold Ones fed to the cacomaggots on the Dark Shore. Their grave expressions offered no hope of pity or forgiveness.

He dizzied with exultation. The authority of the Dark Lord dwelled within him. Wrat was dead, his body shriveled to a dried husk. And now Romut was the new master of the cacodemons! He would terrorize Irth in ways Wrat had never imagined. That was why the gremlin had selected him. He was the greater soul, worthy of the cacodemons' obeisance by dint of his more wicked imagination.

Derisively, he sneered at Wrat's withered corpse and wondered that such a pathetic creature had ever inspired fear. He shoved the dead thing away – and something broke inside Romut.

The disgusting imp had not released its hold on Wrat's carcass and instead its warped head, jellied with blood and lymph, pulled free of Romut. It came out with a ghostly cord in its toothy jaws – the astral umbilical that circulated Charm from the Abiding Star – Romut's soul.

In an instant, the horrified man-gnome comprehended what had happened. Hu'dreVra had allowed him to partake of his glory, to taste his power, so that the taking away of that grace would inflict the most scathing injury of all on his psyche.

With a scissoring bite, the gremlin severed Romut's umbilical of Charm. The ectoplasmic tube spurted a vaporous milky substance, the very effluvia that bound Romut to his body. As the phosphorescent smoke leaked away, its fumes dissolving to nothingness in the air, Romut's consciousness separated from his body.

Looking down, he saw himself below, his big head hanging back, his crossed eyes sightless. The doll with its membranous rags and lace of blood vessels swayed as it sucked upon the cut end of his lifeline. The withdrawn effluvia entered Wrat, and his wasted body began to inflate.

While the enclave tilted and rotated slowly below him, Romut drifted further away. Distinctly, he saw the gremlin withdraw into Wrat's chest cavity and the flesh close over it, sealing him whole. Restored to his full vigor, he stood.

From a greater distance and less clearly, Romut discerned his own form moving, hands on his chest feeling for a wound and finding none. He squinted to see how his own form reacted without him there to guide it. But already he had drifted too far to distinguish more than the motion of small figures at the bottom of a shaft of moteless light.

Horrified, he gaped about and saw only darkness. Below him, far, far beyond him, the world of light dwindled. Soon it was no more than a remote star. On all sides, utter darkness ranged.

Romut shouted with outraged terror. 'Lord! Lord! You have killed me again! Bring me back! Bring me back!'

But the Dark Lord could not hear him, for he had released Romut from Irth and sent the flimsy waveform of his mind adrift in the Gulf. All that remained of him in the marmoreal enclave of the crystal palace's central hall was his body and its animal needs.

Wrat walked to the portal, and Romut followed him slowly, wearing a mindless stare in the permanent scowl of his heavy face. The Dark Lord offered a hand to the witch queen where she slumped on her knees, looking dazed.

At his gesture, she aimed a cold stare at him. 'You're not human. You're not a man.'

He smiled. 'I am the Dark Lord.'

'You're the puppet for a gremlin.'

His smile stiffened. 'Don't irritate me, Thylia. If you irritate me, we shall see who is the puppet.'

His close-set eyes narrowed menacingly, and she shifted her stare to Romut who waited passively behind Wrat. 'What have you done to him?'

'He hated his body, so I cut him free from it.' Wrat patted Romut's enlarged gnomish head affectionately. 'I set his mind free. It plunges now through the Gulf – on its way to the Dark Shore.' He offered his hand again. 'Come. I have a thing you must see.'

She stood without touching him. 'I have seen enough, gremlin.'

His whole face flexed as if setting tighter to his skull. 'Call me that again, witch, and you will join Romut.'

Thylia followed him out of the enclave and up a spiral stairwell to a gallery. In the window bay, they stood gazing out on the luxurious city of Dorzen. A Charm display arrayed like a tabernacle niche framed in onyx ferns and winged newts beside the window allowed Wrat to adjust the view. He passed his hands over the controls, and the city vista clouded away.

When the sheet glass cleared, they peered at the interior of a warehouse where scores of Peers lay about on straw ticks or sat with their backs against the corrugated walls, staring listlessly at the oil-stained woodboards and the splintered rafters. Many clutched amulets. Thylia noticed that a pearly aura of Charm pervaded the gathering and realized that they relied entirely on their amulets to keep them alive. Though each of them appeared impeccably dressed in elegant conjure satins and tailored trance silks, haggard features betrayed their suffering.

'They need food and water,' Thylia said in a tone dulled with hopelessness.

The flesh between his eyes pulsed. 'They shall have smoke and fire!'

Flames leaped like bright toads from under the planks, and the prisoners bounded upright, waving their amulets. But Charm could not stay this conflagration. In moments, the frenzied throng stood engulfed in the blaze. Clothes and hair ignited, silent screams broke from blistered faces, and the burning, thrashing bodies vanished in the twisting smoke.

Thylia slashed at Wrat with her nails, scoring his cheek and neck and cutting for his carotid. Instantly, she regretted her violent impulse. The wounds healed at once, like water, and he turned upon her a frigid grin. 'Look!' he ordered.

The smoke thinned, and she saw the charred and melted carcasses stirring. The dead rose. Ashes peeled and flaked off as the newly immolated stood and gawked about with unnerved expressions. The sloughed cinders wisped away, and soon the Peers touched themselves and each other, shocked to find no damage.

The flesh throbbed between Wrat's tight eyes, and again flames jumped like luminous frogs. Again, the captives panicked, faces contorted with pain and fear, and the fire ate hungrily among them.

'How many times shall I kill them?' Wrat asked as the churning smoke obscured their view.

Thylia said nothing. She no longer looked at the window but had sunk her vision into the inhuman entity beside her. She employed her Charm as she had many times before with this ugly man, wanting to see into him, into the nature that thrived there. Always before, he had remained opaque to her Charm. But now, the gremlin let her see.

Mute and infinite distance opened in him, through him to the Gulf beyond, where all boundaries broke. He was darkness itself.

He was the emptiness that swallowed whole all the light, warmth, and Charm of the Abiding Star. His void was an ocean vaster than planets, wide as the very drift of time.

The witch queen turned away, feeling cold and abandoned, the vacuum of space blowing through her. In the window, the smoke had cleared. The Peers rose in their shrouds of ash. Their blistered faces healed, and they gaped in terror when the toadish flames leaped again among them.

She saw yet did not see the world around her any more. Helplessness gathered its shadows in the placeless place of whatever dreamed in her, and she did not object when Wrat took her elbow and guided her out of the gallery and down the spiral stairway to where Romut waited.

Together, they strolled back into the central hall. Lady Von sat alone at the banquet table and rose at Wrat's return. The gloom in the witch queen's face and the vapid expression and animal slouch of Romut alarmed her, yet she restrained her emotions before Wrat's leering and searching stare.

'The charmwrights have prepared the seekers you requested, my lord,' she informed Wrat with lowered eyes.

'Excellent,' he chortled. 'Then my queen and I shall be away at once to hunt down the renegade Drev. And you, my dear—' He took her chin in his icy hand and lifted her face to meet his languid gaze. 'You shall rule Ux in my absence. I trust you to maintain the stringent standards I require. Do you understand?'

She nodded almost imperceptibly and stole a nervous glance at the passive, slack-faced Romut.

'Do not look to your consort for much guidance,' Wrat counseled. 'He is a changed man, you see. Animal appetites are all that concern him now. You will fulfill those, of course. I expect no less than your complete diligence, Lady Von. Otherwise – well, you will have to be replaced.'

Wrat turned away abruptly, took the witch queen's arm, and strode off with her toward where the charmworkers waited in the dark alcoves.

Lady Von stepped around the table and stood before Romut. She gazed into his eyes for the thing lost. Out of those obsidian mirrors, her own hapless expression reflected. With her Charm, she reached deeper, feeling fearfully for the robust lust of the gnomish man. Instead, she felt darkness, so black that she sensed the animal tread of his heartbeat and the simple hungers of his body parting around her like a school of blind fish.

Deep in Romut's core, she found the hole where his soul had been. A falling dream began there, and she dared not move too close. No wounds of wanting, no moods, no soul, only void remained.

She stepped back and felt her own soul come away stained with darkness.

## Ladder of the Wind

❖━❖

The Cloths of Heaven was haunted. Wizards and ogres alike avoided these ruins, for they were the most archaic on Irth and infested with wraiths elusive of Charm and greedy for bloodheat. When the sorcerer Caval entered the ghost city in the swamp, he expected to find none among the living, and he was not disappointed.

Old and bent from many thousand days of arduous service as weapons master to the Brood of Odawl and tired from his long journey out of the north, Caval moved slowly. His garb of bright tinsel and blue gauze windings fluttered around him in a charmwind that filtered the miasmal air for his aged lungs.

Briefly, he stood on a broken old slab of masonry blotched with mussel shells and gazed up at the sphinx-columns that guarded the entry to the ruins.

Behind him, the bog quaked and bubbled as the log that had carried him over the foggy waterways of the Reef Isles to this gloomy place sank. No trace would remain of his transit from the Calendar of Eyes to the Cloths of Heaven.

With a haggard visage that seemed hacked from cold sallow wax, he regarded the porphyry towers draped in moss and the serpentcoil stairways spiraling into cerulean emptiness.

Hollow voices called remotely from the ruins.

Caval nodded his approval and advanced wearily among the chunks of upturned and silted pavement and into the shadow of the sphinxes. Eventually, he made his way toward domed porticos shabby with vines and creepers. The eroded voices came from within.

The sorcerer hobbled along toppled walls so thick with lichen they appeared melted and, with bony hands, parted the curtains of overhanging tendrils. Charmsight enabled him to see in the dark, and there, among fallen entablatures and fractured pillars, he beheld the green ether of the ancient dead.

Swirling in a feculent stench, weightless as smoke, smoldering shapes rose. Arms like tentacles reached for him. Grievous voices swollen with emptiness droned a hypnotic chant. Caval felt it tightening in his already stiff muscles, paralyzing him so that the leprous shapes could gather around his bloodheat and feed.

In the afterlife, which was death's slander of life, all spirits were one ravenous hunger. There was no sentience here among these earlier lives, no wisdom to evoke and to converse upon anything but need. For hundreds of thousands of days, these specters of nameless magicians had staved off oblivion and the night ride into the Gulf by cleaving to the warm aura of life. Their magic preserved them – so long as they fed it.

Without humans to feed upon, the phantoms had resorted to clawing at slime and pursuing the slither of bog creatures. Burning bitter green and corrosive stains in the air, these shadows of the emaciated damned had nothing human to offer the sorcerer, and he shouted once, firmly and without wrath.

The force of his Charmed cry cleared not only the portico but the husk of spires beyond. Wraiths seeped out of the gaping holes in the stone towers and bled glaucous as rainsmoke into the swamp forest.

Like a wraith himself, Caval shuffled through the dirt and fungal beds of colonnaded passageways to a portal slewed with broken spandrels and collapsed tiles. He waved his hands above his head in small circles and two globes of cool yellow fire bobbed into the air. He sent them spinning ahead through the portal, and they illuminated the giant empty shell of a broken tower – a cavern of cluttered putrefaction: Petrified beams jutted from under piled black cobblestones, and a felled forest of busted pillars crouched beneath sagging vaults upheld by dense ganglia of roots.

Entering the wrecked chamber, he gradually worked his way through the crazed shapes of crumbled stone, making his slow way to a deeper recess lit from within. In this remote corner of the temple complex, random shafts of daylight stabbed through rents in the rubble roofing. They illuminated small, florid gardens of air plants and floating fire-blossoms and baked a sweet, medlar fragrance.

He joined the two globes of lux-fire and dropped them to the ground under the bright vermilion flowers. Spinning into a fulgent windspout, they cauterized a circle among the sooty debris and vanished with a sparkling flash of ruby dust.

The sorcerer sat himself at the circle's cool center and lifted his riven face into a blue dayshaft. Fragrant breezes stirred his long beard, and a thin smile touched his harsh and cracked lips.

This was the first rung on the ladder of the wind. From here, his soul could climb into the sky, to the Abiding Star and beyond, to the Beginning. He could not take his body with him, as he would have on the Calendar of Eyes. That would have to stay behind and rot here among the swamp dead. But his soul – that could fly higher than time, back to the source of all time.

Such was his wish. Yet, it was only a wish. The sorcerer knew that in a few days, the margravess of Odawl would discover his hiding place. He had been watching her with his long sight since he climbed down from the Calendar of Eyes, during his long trek to these ruins.

That was why he had endured the strenuous travails of secret journeying across Irth to come to this decayed temple. Time and destiny would deliver her to this site. And duty delivered him.

Trained as a weapons master in the Brood of Assassins, Caval could not turn his back on the doom of Arwar Odawl, the tiny kingdom he had served his entire adult life. If there had been no survivors among the ruling Peers, he would have been free to ascend to the Abiding Star. But there were survivors, the very children of his former master, and to them he owed the fealty of his training and lineage.

That had been the purpose he had chanted continually to himself since departing the Calendar of Eyes. Yet now that he had found a proper place to sit and reach deeper into himself he sensed wider powers that had conspired to lead him here. Blind powers. Chance. Death. And, of course, the third of the blind gods, the child, in fact, of the first two – Justice.

Chance had led him to the threshold of heaven at the instant the Conquest began. It had seemed as if his departure from Irth invited disaster. Death compelled him to return – death in the guise of the people in their thousands who had perished with the arrival of the cacodemons.

But how did this terror require him? What was the Justice that compelled him to come down from the mountain and sit in these moldered ruins, this place of sinking, where all succumbed to the darkness within Irth?

He told himself that he had come back for Jyoti and Poch, for their father's ghost, indeed for all the ghosts of the murdered Brood of Odawl. Yet that rang hollow. He was just one man. He knew better than to invest any faith in the conviction that he could save anyone, let alone a world.

He searched deeper into the blindness of his past, looking for what Justice had evoked in him. And so, for the next several days, the aged sorcerer sat in his cokebed circle among air plants and fallen walls, gathering Charm from the Abiding Star and focusing deeper into himself.

Around him floated blossoms from the dangling tendrils of

flora thriving on higher, sunnier storeys. Butterflies darted. Animal cries splashed in the droning forest beyond the decayed parapets, and Caval rooted himself in himself. From legendary depths, as deep as Irth itself, he summoned down the power of heaven, the Charm of the Abiding Star.

In the grassland village of Floating Stone, Jyoti and Poch came out of the wilds for the first time since riding a trade dirigible up the coast to Saxar. They had avoided people, aware of the bounty on their heads. But this agricultural Eden enticed them with its famous markets.

A mountain floated above a landscape of villages, farms, vineyards and orchards. Waterfalls ran off in silver threads on all sides, irrigating the lush terrain. Rainbows and vast, tiered hanging gardens trailed from the mountainside.

Floating Stone had been designated a sacred mountain at the beginning of talismanic times. It was then that the father of all wizards, the famed Goat Tree, succeeded in levitating this massif with the first hover charms. He led it away from its brethren in the purple ranges to the north and escorted it about a hundred and fifty leagues across the plains to this formerly desolate flatland. Over the thousands of days that it remained in place, it transformed the veldt below into a cultivated garden. But the mountain itself was never cultivated and remained pristine, a wilderness symbol of Irth herself.

Surprisingly no cacodemons had yet visited this wide, fertile community. For a day entire, the brother and sister sat on a rise of plum trees, eating fruit and observing the agrarian countryside in the blue shadow of the mountain. By nightfall, they felt assured that the land was not haunted by cacodemons, and they strolled cautiously down the hillside and followed a coach road into a market village.

Jyoti draped her amulet tunic over her arm and used it to cover the firelock. They wanted food other than the wild fare that had sustained them on their wanderings, and they approached the first vendors that they encountered.

In an open-air market beside a coach yard, travelers milled among stalls strung with gourd lanterns. Bins of fresh fruit and vegetables alternated among tables offering baked goods in golden heaps.

Poch helped himself to a loaf of nutbread and began eating voraciously. From her amulet tunic, Jyoti unfastened a hex-ruby and her heart talisman's conjure-wire and offered it as payment. The portly vendor looked startled.

'Can't make change for anything bigger than a quoin,' he frowned at Poch.

'It's probably not worth more than a newts-eye,' Jyoti began to explain. 'It's completely drained.'

'Hmm.' The vendor appraised the ruby with a squinted eye. 'It can be recharged. This is worth many prisms, even drained. Here, let me put a flush on it, and you can roam the market, help yourself.'

Jyoti returned the vendor's smile and turned her attention to the tables of assorted breads that were selling briskly to the travelers. But before she could sample the leek roll that had caught her eye, the vendor shouted from behind.

'Hoy! This won't take a flush!' He held the ruby in one hand and in the other a power wand fitted with a charging cap. When he fitted them together, the hex-gem should have absorbed the Charm in the power wand and flushed briefly with Charmlight, but it remained dark.

Jyoti understood that the cacodemons' black magic had not only drained the Charm but had also somehow altered the hex-pattern in the gem itself. But to the vendor the ruby was simply a clever counterfeit gem.

'Hoy, Roon!' the vendor called to a beastmarked man stacking crates of produce behind the busy stalls. He wagged the ruby. 'It's fake!' He pointed to Jyoti.

Roon put down the crates and advanced through the hurrying travelers, panther eyes sharp with malice. 'We've had enough thievery from you renegade Peers. You think we're simpletons and will take glass for food?'

'It's not glass,' Jyoti protested and pulled Poch behind her. 'It's a genuine hex-ruby.'

'What hex?' the vendor called. 'It won't hold a charge.'

'It must have been damaged,' she offered.

'Then it's no better than glass,' Roon concluded grimly.

Jyoti raised her firelock and glowered back at the agitated merchant. 'You want to see if *this* is holding a charge?'

Roon blanched and stopped short. Screams and shouts flapped from the crowd, and people fled the market and the adjacent coach yard.

Jyoti seized a cloth sack bulging with groceries that a panicked shopper had dropped and motioned for Poch to do likewise. He grabbed two sacks and hurried ahead of his sister out of the market.

'It *is* a real hex-gem,' she told the frightened vendor. 'Caco-demons broke it. Maybe the charmwrights can learn something about them from that. So, you see, we are not stealing. We're bartering.'

With that announcement, she bounded away across the vacant coach yard and on to the night road.

'Your firelock wasn't even set,' Poch griped when she caught up with him. 'What if Roon had kept coming?'

'Then I would have walked on his face,' Jyoti replied coolly. 'Let's get off this road.'

They jumped down from the highway's shoulder into the grassy verges and hurried along with their unexpected bounty under the frosty stars.

On Nynyx, one of the large western Reef Isles of Nhat, Jyoti and Poch hiked along the edge of a forest following the black and brown footsteps of autumn. Both wore the hoods of their tattered tunics pulled up against the crisp breeze, and Jyoti carried her firelock slung from her hip.

Evening descended over the moss-covered steps of the hills. The forest corridors filled with red shadows and scarlet depths, and indigo premonitions of night climbed the pastures and fields, up from the dark sea. On the coast, a ferry village twinkled, its lantern lights spilling slick reflections across the cove. The wanderers headed there.

Bells flurried, and a shepherd led his herd of red ponies along a dirt path down a nearby hill and across a stone bridge. In a copse of jigsaw trees, a hunter in green motley gutted an antelope. Bloodsmoke stained his hands, and the gray shade of the animal flitted past the hikers, rushing in a sigh back to the forest.

Before its panicked flight, crows scattered against the golden clouds of day's end, and Poch jumped at their sudden cawing. This was their first return to the civilized world in many days, since they had fled Floating Stone, and they were both anxious. To reach the Cloths of Heaven, they needed passage over water. All other routes were lethal without Charm.

'Maybe we should see if we can barter the firelock,' Poch suggested.

'That's against dominion law,' Jyoti reminded him dully. 'And besides, how will we protect ourselves in the swamps around the Cloths of Heaven without it?'

Near the mill, boys played with fire, jumping among flames that leaped from leafdrifts like pale friends. The children stopped to watch the cowled travelers pass.

Berries and most of the season's nuts had disappeared, and Poch wanted to stop at the mill to rest and barter work for food. But Jyoti decided against that. She was determined to get to Caval as swiftly as possible.

Night mended starlight above the hillsides, and they came down the steep trails and passed the tide pools. Fishermen dragged an enormous sable fish from a starlit pond, its cruel face full of whiskers and fangs. Above the voices of the reeds, men quarreled about something they had dredged from the ebb tide. Their red skiffs rocked in the shallows with the weight of it.

Jyoti and Poch avoided the hamlet, following a littoral path through wild onion and dockweeds. On their way, they passed scavengers in fishskin tunics, who dragged nets and hooks across the sandy trod on their way to the glossy flats. The workers glared at the bedraggled strangers but said nothing in transit to their nightly labors.

At the docks, the fleet was in, and the sailors had already retreated to taverns, fish houses, and cottages on stilts above the dunes.

The night ferry had loosed its moorings as Jyoti and Poch came pounding over the boards of the pier. They skipped across a plankwalk that a wharf-hand extended for them and jumped aboard, huffing for breath.

The ebb current carried them swiftly past the nightbound cliffs and toward the scattered silhouettes of other reef islands before the mate came down from the pilot house to collect fares.

A wiry, spry man in hemp sandals and oil-stained jerkin and slacks, he moved quickly among the passengers, short, quiet people with beastmarks of sleek otter fur and sloe eyes: dockworkers and fisherfolk returning to their homes on the outer isles.

When the mate came to Jyoti and Poch, he paused and nervously eyed the firelock. He jerked his thumb toward the pilot house, where the captain watched from the tall window.

The mate escorted them past the overtly curious stares of the travelers and up a corkscrew ladder to the bridge. The captain, a stout, turbaned woman in newts-eye bodice and rat-star gem earrings, raised one bold red eyebrow when they informed her they were bound for the Cloths of Heaven.

She asked no questions. She knew from their firelock and their tunics that they were Peers and all Peers were renegades.

'No ships approach the Cloths of Heaven,' she told them sternly. 'Only the Dark Lord's vessels have safe passage in those waters.'

'Take us as close as you dare,' Jyoti said and handed her a gold mesh brace set with theriacal opals. 'It's a healer's mesh, but it's charmless and can't be recharged. A cacodemon mesmermur song broke its hex pattern. Even so, it's of Peerage quality, and the materials, the elemental gold and silver, are valuable enough as scrap to fetch several prisms of actual Charm.'

The captain stared into Jyoti's earnest expression and accepted the fare without comment. The Peers returned to the deck. They sat by themselves on the cargo hatch until the ferry put in at its first port and deck benches cleared. Three more stops and they were the last passengers on board. The mate brought them two flagons of seaweed soup and skewers of braised fish courtesy of the captain, and they ate voraciously.

Dawn erased the last stars when the ferry turned and banked toward a brooding shore of spider-root trees, looping lianas, and spiral ferns. The incoming tide allowed the ferry to shoulder close to the willow shoals. The mate let down a plankwalk to a mossy shelf of black coral crawling with tattoo snails.

After the two passengers disembarked, the ferry backed away, boiling muddy water. Jyoti raised a hand, and the pilot jangled her bell. Swells of leafwaste and kelp undulated in the slapping waves on the verdant bank as the ferry moved out, the mate leaning on the rail watching pink shore birds soar upward like pieces of dawn taking their places in the sky.

Huddled in their tunics and scalded with insect bites, Jyoti and Poch slept fitfully till midday. In the afternoon, they trudged through the swamp, meandering along fallen trees and root mats, still bearing east, toward the destination given them by the sibyl many days before.

At night, they lashed themselves to trees with vines and took turns sleeping among the cancerous cries of predators. Blue plantains and abundant sugar grass provided nourishment, and they collected dew for drinking water. On the third day of their swamp crossing, they both fevered.

The world began to look warped and shimmery, and their bones leaked so much damp heat that they felt soft. For two days and nights, they lay shivering on a flat bough and watched the oily tide slide in and out among the canes. They clutched the remaining brace of theriacal opals for comfort, though the gems had no power to heal them, and they listened to the hot blood singing arctic tunes in their heads.

On the third day, Jyoti understood that they would die if they stayed. She cut walking sticks for them sturdy enough to bear their weight, and they hobbled on. Fiery shadows accompanied them. They could not tell if they were fevered illusions of their cooking brains or swamp ghosts. When they stopped to rest, the blown flames danced transparently closer and ate their strength. Jyoti forced Poch to march onward with her, crouching, shuffling, dragging themselves through the poisoned shadows, ever eastward.

Their dreams troubled them with forlorn childhood memories, the slow voice of their mother calling after them, their father's silhouette looking in at the doorway of bed chambers gone to ruin with all of Arwar Odawl. Lumbering through the jungle, enormous sadness accompanied them. The rue of the dead crawled with the fog that rose each evening from the mire. Phantoms with familiar profiles came and went in the mist, their lost family welcoming them back as they slouched onward through the swamp maze toward the edge of everything.

At one point, Jyoti's skin became the color of glass. She turned to show Poch, but he was gone. Wheeling through the underbrush, searching for him, she got lost.

Leprous with running sores, spider blisters, and fungal infections, she wandered into the night and fell asleep still searching. She woke in the canopy of the swamp forest and nearly broke her neck climbing down.

Later that day, in a bracken cove of hanging moss, she collapsed. The demented cry of a carrion monkey dwindled away as she toppled toward a lethal sleep.

Poch heard the same monkey's feeding cry and thought it

howled for him. He looked for his sister to see that she was still on her feet, and she waved him forward. He slumped after her through the bright squares of jungle light, rays sharp as glass. The gasping wind and the shaking trees scared him more than the icy numbness of his limbs.

He looked for Jyoti, and she beckoned him onward. But he was too weak to walk any more. She knelt, and he followed after her. Together they crept on to a shelf of pitted rock laced with lichen and lay down to rest again or die at last.

Poch clutched his sister's shoulder, and his mummied mouth hissed a cry. The shoulder was rock. He was alone. He lay on his belly and wept until the fever glistened to darkness in him.

'Wake up, Poch,' Jyoti's voice called.

The shivering boy opened his eyes and saw his sister kneeling above him, her parched head bending close to whisper encouragement. 'Get up – look!'

Jyoti helped him to his knees and pointed at the rock shelf on which they had sprawled. The lichenous surface was carved with the worn visage of a serpent woman – a giant smashed idol.

Suddenly excited by what this stone face implied, Poch forced himself upright, stood swaying, and glimpsed through the burning chinks of the treetops skeletal towers and immense broken bodies of winged sphinxes. He hauled his sister upright with all his ashen strength, and she saw the ruins and sagged back to her knees.

Again, Poch helped Jyoti to her feet, and they tottered through a decayed hole in the root dike that enclosed the Cloths of Heaven. They staggered with locked arms under the shadow of the immense sphinxes and passed through tangles of creepers to enter the lightless interior. Faint trickles of light led them deeper into a confusion of decayed collapse.

Poch protested and moaned, wanting to say *We don't even know Caval is here*. But he had no strength. And they had traveled too far.

In the darkness, they separated again, and when he reached for her, she was not there. Her voice whispered from an unexpected direction, and he groped that way and found her once more.

She clutched his arm more firmly, pulling him after her through the dense and black shambles. The ground trembled, cracking and sizzling under their weight. They whimpered in unison and inched forward.

With a creaky groan, the floor tilted. Poch clutched at Jyoti, and they both slid sideways among clattering bricks before jolting to a stop. They glared at each other in the dark, the whites of their eyes shining.

A deafening boom plummeted them into darkness.

Their screams, shrill as bat cries, ended abruptly, kicked out of them by a thudding impact among rocks. Debris crashed atop them.

In the hissing silence that ensued, Jyoti lay still.

Poch shoved away a cinderous beam rotted with fungus. The decayed stone broke in his hands like brittle paper.

He felt for his sister in the dark, his urgent hands crushing more stone until he found her inert body close beside him. He pressed his face close to hers, feeling for her breath while feeling with his fingertips for a pulse at her throat.

Terror astonished him in a stygian cellar thronging with bog rats and with his sister's corpse in his arms. Flawless fright electrified him. He shook with paralysis and could not let her go.

A soft blue light fell over them, and Poch saw his sister's face suddenly very clearly, slack as a sleeper's. He twisted around and winced up at a tall, long-jawed man with orange hair trimmed stiff as bristles, close to the skull so that his blunt head with its severe features looked square.

Jyoti snored.

Poch stared at her in the quiet blue light. Her nostrils flared, and he felt the knock of her pulse.

'Let her rest,' the man said reverberantly, azure radiance leaking from his pores. 'The healing has not yet set. Wait.'

'Are you——?'

'Yes, Poch.' The square, strong face squinted an avuncular smile. 'Don't you remember me?'

'You are the sorcerer Caval,' the boy said vaguely. 'I think. I saw you so rarely – and always from afar.'

Caval's orange eyebrows lifted compassionately. 'That's how it is with Assassins. We are known only by our intimates. Your father was my intimate.'

The sorcerer lifted Jyoti into his powerful arms and carried her into the dark. Poch scrambled to follow, drawing strength from the blue, healing charmlight that wafted off Caval.

But he was not swift enough. In moments, the sorcerer had disappeared, swallowed whole by the darkness. With him went his Charm, and the boy wobbled to stay on his feet.

Poch forced himself to move blindly forward. Presently, a dim glow appeared, more firmly outlining the mess of upended floor slabs and tilted columns. He wanted to cry out for help, but his parched throat only made croaking noises through his chattering teeth.

Dragging his body like a dead thing, he slowly made his way across the jumbled expanse of tarnished darkness toward the breathing light buried in the smashed architecture.

Hands outheld, he felt his way over jammed blocks and under bent girders corroded to rusty lace. Around a mound of cobbles, he saw Caval again.

The sorcerer sat crosslegged in a perfect circle of ash, air plants and fire-flowers hanging around him among shafts of daylight jittery with butterflies.

Poch gasped. In his windings of tinsel and azure gauze and with his long wisps of gray beard and shriveled body, Caval looked wizened as an insect. A blue radiance shone around him. It blazed brighter than the daylight in the shining fern glade where he sat at the clogged core of the shattered tower.

Peering over blocks flocced with fungus, Poch wanted to ask *Is that him?* but his throat would not work. *And where is Jyoti? Where is my sister?*

342

Staring long and hard, the boy finally realized that the wizened squatter sitting still as an idol was indeed Caval, much aged.

Poch choked back his fearful questions and advanced gingerly over the crumbly detritus, chary of a misstep that would send him plunging into hopeless depths.

Caval did not budge at his arrival. But the aura around him brightened.

Poch stepped from the gloomy shadows into the daystruck brightness of airy blossoms and floating butterflies and squinted, his mouth moving but no sound coming out. The long and perilous trek was over, and he stood shivering in the fragrant haze of prehistoric plants, wincing in the luminous presence of this withered and shining man.

*Jyoti – where?* His voice rasped incoherently.

Nut-husk eyelids opened on rheumy irises, and the sorcerer stared in real time at the brother of the margravess for whom his duty had stolen him from heaven. The boy stood before him, ulcerous with sores, his face shrunk to his skull, burning eyes sunken deep in their round holes. Even so, he recognized the father, Lord Keon, in the lad's tall brow.

He nodded and beckoned Poch closer.

They looked at each other briefly, joy and expectancy immixed in their harrowed faces, and then the boy came forward gratefully. As he stepped into the ashen circle, the blue aura of the sorcerer's Charm enclosed him and wounds sloughed away like snakeskin, falling behind in an emaciated shadow. At the dark perimeter, the shadow of wounds waited for his return.

Pain dimmed to ache, and Poch's mind sharpened instantly as if he had startled awake from a long and tedious nightmare.

The old man nodded and smiled.

'Master Caval!' Poch cried in relief. 'Master Caval! You are so old!'

'I *am* old,' the sorcerer admitted with a flimsy voice. 'The climb up the Calendar of Eyes used most of my strength.'

Poch put his hands on his chest, astonished to feel strength returning to his starved muscles. 'My clothes!' He gawped at his pristine tunic and pants and his buffed, shining boots, shocked to see that Charm had mended lifeless matter.

He touched his amulets. They were fully charged and hummed with Charm under his fingertips.

Caval sighed and unlocked his crossed legs. The blue aura disappeared. Its power drew back into his core, and he did not rely on it to pull himself heavily upright.

'Yes, I am old,' Caval drearily acknowledged again. 'Over 45,000 days old – and most of those days spent defending your father, Lord Keon.'

The old sorcerer bowed. Poch feared he might tumble over and moved forward to catch him. When the old man straightened, the boy found himself close enough to see the circuitry of burst capillaries in the sorcerer's long nose and in the gray sclera of his eyes.

'My sister,' Poch asked pleadingly. 'Where have you taken her?'
The sorcerer lifted the wisps of two arms. 'I do not have her.'
'I saw you carry her off.'
A smile webbed its wrinkles across his sunken face. 'That was my body of light. I sent it to guide you here. Your sister was an illusion.'

'Then, where is she now?' Poch peered about in the fulgent sunlight at the flame blossoms and spiral ferns. 'Is she dead?'
'Perhaps.'
'Don't you know?' Poch asked, alarmed.
'I don't know everything, young master.' The tired old man hung his head dolefully. 'It was enough to get at least one of you here safely. That it is you who is here now and not your sister was decided long ago by the blind gods. Will you question their decision?'

'Then you know why I am here?' the boy asked, his thrilled eyes searching the rugged terrain of the sorcerer's decrepit features for emotional cues and finding none, only fatigue and the ravages of time.

'We are here for the same purpose,' Caval asserted. 'Irth is in jeopardy.'

'Can you help us?' Poch blurted. 'Can you find my sister? She is your margravess now. You must find her. She cannot survive long out there in that fetid swamp. Don't you see? She has lost all her Charm!'

The torpid elder sighed. 'We will need far more than Charm to defeat our enemies.' He placed a pallid hand on the boy's brow.

His touch absorbed all exhaustion, and a mute vibration of peace and health passed between Poch's ears, consolidating the Charm he had already absorbed from the sorcerer's aura.

Caval motioned for the traveler to step forward, and Poch timorously slid closer and flinched timidly when the sorcerer reached to touch him again.

'Fear not, mousekin.' Caval smiled and showed perfect teeth behind his wispy beard. 'My touch gives but does not take. Come and rest in my Charm.'

Caval laid both hands on the boy's head, and Poch felt his feet grow light. He realized that, for the first time in many days, he was not tired. His body did not ache. Fear did not hunker in his chest.

He returned the sorcerer's smile and pressed his face into the old man's concave chest. His beard smelled of alpine resins, and the spikes of stars glinted behind Poch's closed eyes.

'You have traveled the length of the world to find me, child of my dead lord,' Caval spoke soothingly and stroked the boy's fair hair. 'And now I am your servant.'

Poch separated from the sorcerer and gazed hopefully up into his venerable face. 'Can you slay the Dark Lord?'

Caval shook his head. 'You have been too long without Charm. The touch of it makes you think I have powers greater than those of a sorcerer.'

Poch scowled and stepped aside. Immediately, he felt the light of his body dim. The shadow of wounds edged closer.

He turned and smiled gratefully at Caval, glad to no longer

carry the burden of exhaustion. 'I was afraid we might never find you.'

'Destiny was undecided,' Caval agreed. 'Death stalked you on your trek.'

'And still does, Caval. Cacodemons pursue us. They promise us the protection of the Dark Lord.'

'You are right to fear being seen,' the sorcerer concurred. 'Yet I sense no foes nearby.'

Poch's gaze hardened. 'Jyoti learned that the cacodemons are vulnerable to physical force. But there are too many of them, you see. We need a spell that can reach into the Gulf and draw down the power to defeat Wrat himself.'

'That is why the blind gods have brought us together, young master.' Caval motioned him to sit. 'It is time to use their blindness to see. Sit. I need your young strength. I am too old for so deep a trance. If you will keep still long enough, I can lean upon your youth to go deep and see.'

Poch squatted before the sorcerer, his hopeful face shimmering in a ray of daylight. 'See what, Caval?'

'Echoes of lost time, young master.' Caval composed himself, sitting still and tall as a heron in his beard, blue eyelids fluttering closed. 'Trance. The spill of dying, young master. The spill of dying, without the catch of death.'


In the deep blue shadows of the Falls of Mirdath, Lord Drev and Ripcat faced each other. The roar of the cascades shook the air and muted shouts to whispers.

'The way to the Spiderlands is through that cave!' Drev yelled and pointed to a vertical crevice in the rock wall behind them.

'What about the spiders?' Ripcat called.

'No Charm will protect us!'

The thief shook his head and turned his attention to the walls of falling water at the end of the rock corridor. He was about to suggest that they follow the torrent down to the riverlands and surreptitiously make their way south to the Reef Isles where

Dogbrick and Drev's fateful consort, Tywi, awaited them.

He and the wizarduke had come this far underground from the Malpais Highlands, following wisps of Charm to this gateway. No cacodemons had pursued. No witch queen had blocked their passage.

*Why risk the Spiderlands?* he asked himself, recalling with a needling chill the horror stories of those arachnid-infested badlands.

But before he could express his reservations to Drev, the sheets of tumbling water ripped and a dozen cacodemons slashed into the long cavern. Behind them came the black armored figure of Hu'dre Vra, a huge voice booming from the baleen of his spiked mask.

'I have found you, Drev!' The Dark Lord came forward with a gold seeker held high in one hand and his other hooked to a cutting tool. 'And now you will find death – again and again and again!'

Drev pushed Ripcat behind him and discharged an orange burst from his firelock. It dislodged slabs of stone from the cavern ceiling, and the cacodemons pulled back in a panic.

Hu'dre Vra smashed through the fallen rock like so much dead wood. His black magic offered no vulnerability to physical assault, and the sharp edges of his armor scratched sparks from the collapsed wall as he shoved closer.

Ripcat leaped first into the charmway, and Drev hurled himself after. The thunder of the Falls vanished. A sizzling silence enclosed them, and in an instant they tumbled on to their hands and knees in a cinereous wasteland. Clouds of ash obscured sight, and they coughed and choked as they scrambled to their feet, expecting pursuit.

The cinderdust settled, and the two men pressed their backs together, defensively confronting the strange terrain that surrounded them. Everywhere were jagged thorn trees and high brooming thistle grass hung with silver feathers.

As their eyes adjusted to the brash, unfiltered daylight, they recognized that these feathers were actually tattered cobwebs. Animals small and large had left their husks dangling in the austere vegetation: Shrunken birds, withered mice and a desiccated troll hung from the thorn trees, wrapped in shreds of cocoon silk.

The luminous day revealed an endless landscape of scalloped sands and sharp trees. Drev and Ripcat wanted to flee from the cleaved rock where they had emerged, but they were afraid to dash blindly into a trapdoor web. Slowly, they turned and edged among the cottony trees and their ornaments of perished animals, seeking a path.

None offered itself, and the next moment a noise of surf echoed from the charmway.

'They're coming through!' Drev realized. 'We have to hide at once.'

The wizarduke had no time even to scan his eye charms and bolted into the bramble instead.

Ripcat hurried behind him, and together they crashed through a brake of thistle grass into a hive of spider mites. Immediately, their flesh burned, sprayed with venom. Tiny red mites dusted them like pollen. As Drev had warned, Charm did not faze them, and the two men hunkered low in the tossing grass and rubbed sand and ash over themselves.

From their covert, they watched the cape of rock that hooded the charmway. The surf noise ceased, and the witch queen Thylia stepped into the blunt day, tall, regal, a charmwind fluttering gray veils that covered all but her black diamond eyes.

Behind her arrived the cacodemons with their lizard-leather skins aglint with water that smoked at once to haze in the hot dry air.

'They see our footprints in the sand,' Ripcat whispered, liberally rubbing ash over his furred body. 'Let's get away from here.'

'Wait.' Drev removed a power wand from his cloak of amulets and rubbed both hands along its amber shaft. Then, he stuck the wand in the sand, and when he raised his hands, they shone with golden light. Quickly and deftly, he ran his hands over Ripcat, then threw the golden light away to his side.

The Charmlight flattened the tall grass with the amorphous yet distinct shadowshape of Ripcat.

'Run!' the wizardduke commanded the shining shadow and pointed deeper into the grass. The double of Ripcat sprinted away, the grass bending before it and flattening under its tread.

Drev repeated the procedure with himself and sent his shadowdouble running in a divergent direction Then he motioned for Ripcat to sit still.

The thief found that command difficult, because the abrasive ash and sand did little to soothe the acid bites of the tiny spiders that infested them both. But the sight of the shambling cacodemons held him motionless with fright.

With her emerald eye charm, Thylia spotted Drev and Ripcat fleeing in separate directions. She sent half the cacodemons after the thief and pursued Drev with the others.

As they charged past the brake where the genuine fugitives lay, hot in the pain of biting spider mites, the eye charm blinked. But the witch queen assumed that was Drev attempting to shield himself, and she directed the cacodemons to fly ahead with her and swoop down upon him.

Drev waited several heartbeats before standing and swiping desperately at himself with handfuls of ash in an attempt to quell the burning. 'There is a charmway that connects to the Mere of Goblins – but it is a day's hike distant. We must hurry.'

From his seeker, Drev took direction, and as they moved out of the brake of thistle grass and into the forest of thorn trees, he used Charm to erase their footprints behind them. The canopy of cobwebs and spider nests obscured their progress from above, and they made good headway before the spiders began stalking them.

With a hissing noise like frying fat, the arachnids swarmed over the brittle branches, dried grasses, and caked ash of the forest.

Black leapers, big as a man's splayed hand, jumped from their tree nests and inflicted gouging bites before they could be swatted with the butt of the firelock or knife handle and stomped underboot.

The swarms of creeper spiders that flowed out from under the shrouded roots of the forest like green magma had to be avoided. There were too many to crush or to leap over.

The fugitives soon angled far off course, trying to elude the emptying hives of creepers. Streaked with blood, faces and hands swollen purple with bites, Drev and Jyoti knew they were going to die in the Spiderlands if night found them still in these lethal woods. The wizarduke decided on a bold strategy, too bold to share with his companion.

At the first opportunity, Drev fitted his assault knife to the muzzle of his firelock and exited the thorn forest into a swale of burrweed. Ripcat paused among the blowing threads of webs at the margin of the forest and called out in a voice clogged with pain, 'The cacodemons will see you!'

Drev waved him on and continued running through the sharp weeds. Spurred on by the frying sound of approaching creepers, Ripcat loped after him. He saw where the wizarduke was headed: Across the clearing and back into the thorn forest but at an angle that would bring them close to their destination – if they avoided being seen by overflying cacodemons.

A searing scream from above dashed that hope, and they scampered as fast as they could through the snaring weeds until a shadow fell over them. Drev jabbed upward with his knife-tipped firelock, and the descending cacodemon banked and alighted among the weeds. An ice-blue blast from the weapon buried it in upthrown sod.

Others appeared on the horizon even as the first threw off the dirt that had knocked it over and rose to give chase. Again, Drev turned about in his race for the treeline and fired at the ground. The cacodemon stumbled, and the fugitives scurried on. When the monster leaped into the air and came down on them claws first, they faced it with raised knives.

A talon strike flayed Ripcat's left arm even as Drev's knife scored the beast's torso, jabbing a shrieking maw embedded in its belly. It backed away, and the two men hastened onward.

Drev fired ahead of them. Dazzling blue bolts of charmfire slammed into the thorn trees, shattering them like glass.

Ripcat had no notion what the wizarduke intended until he saw the tendrils of smoke from the fires of the burning trees. Even then, he was not sure why Drev would create more peril. He was leading them toward a stand of trees heavily draped with spider cloths. A pack of wild dogs depended from those branches, their furry pelts shrunken to their skeletons.

Drev kept firing as they entered the forest. The Charmfire could not harm the spiders – but the forest fire could. It emptied hives and nests, and the woods sang with their vehement songs and with the screams and booms of the conflagration eating past the dried bark to the wet cores of the trees.

Only two cacodemons entered the forest before the pack understood the wizarduke's strategy. Falling webs spilled enraged arachnids that attacked the chasing cacodemons, and in moments the monsters had stopped pursuing and jumped upward into the air to escape. One burst free of the smoke and entangling webs. The other became snared in a scorpion spider's nest and struggled vainly to free itself from the dense skeins.

Drev and Ripcat shot ahead through the churning smoke. Spiders rained around them and crawled over their bodies, inflicting stinging wounds. By the time they ran clear of the blazing woods, the spider toxins cramped their muscles and dropped them writhing to the ground.

The wizarduke applied a healer's net of theriacal opals to Ripcat and then himself. They did not wait for the Charm to fully take effect. Against the spiders it could not, and it healed only their open wounds and did not counteract the toxins themselves. As they ran, their vision quaked with hallucinatory pain.

Two cacodemons descended before them, their muscular

ferocity broken into segments and planes in their preys' warped vision.

Drev fired into the forest awning. Clots of burning gossamer fell, spewing another swarm of spiders. Drev and Ripcat dodged the fiery torrent and barged through a shivering wall of snakegrass.

They hurled through the other side covered head to toe in green and brown spider-ticks. Drev set his weapon for rapid fire and, arms shaking with poison-tremors, he turned about, burning a circle of flames in the surrounding brush. Enclosed in fire, he yanked the knife from his gun's muzzle and began cutting at the ticks. Ripcat, too, scraped at his body with his assault knife.

The fire circle blazed hotly then died down as it spread to the ground Drev had already burned. When the wall of flames dimmed, no cacodemons were visible, and the fugitives hobbled through the charred trees away from the smoldering underbrush.

Thylia watched them in her emerald eye charm. She remained beside the charmway where she had entered the Spiderlands, unwilling to expose herself to the biting perils of the woods. With a gnashed curse, she kicked at an ashen clod and broke it to dust.

Behind her, through the charmway, Hu'dre Vra waited for her in Mirdath. She did not want to return without Drev's corpse. If she did, she knew she would suffer as he had made the Peers of Dorzen suffer.

A mite dangling on its filament from the rock promontory above bit her neck, and she smacked it and cursed again. For a moment, she considered summoning lightning again, but the pain and inaccuracy of that power dissuaded her, and she decided instead to use her Charm. The wizarduke was weak from the spiders' bites, and she was certain that her charmed strength could now overcome him.

She unclasped the dragonclaw hooks of hex-metal that secured her cincture of power wands. In the caked dust, she stood four of the wands on their ends, each an arm's length apart. Then she stepped back and rubbed two other wands together. Green sparks flew, and, with a chanted cry, she directed them in a flurry over the standing wands.

Charmlight unraveled like a leaking gas from the power wands in the ground, and human figures swirled up, spectral assassins with rusted claws, hacked faces carved from ruined skulls, stormbird wings, and squalid tatters of flesh.

Before their chrome eyes jellied as quicksilver, Thylia held the emerald eye charm and showed them the limping figures of Lord Drev and Ripcat. 'Kill them!'

The four revenants flashed away in a hellish blur, their hair of cobweb floss webbing them like things evoked out of a filthy dream.

The wizarduke saw them coming in his eye charms and warned Ripcat, 'The witch queen is in the Spiderlands. She's sent four Charm wraiths after us.'

Ripcat did not respond. He was looking around for caco-demons and seeing boiling wind and standing water floating in the air.

'They're fast things,' Drev said. 'Elusive. I don't think I can stop all four.'

He lifted his gaze from his eye charms. The thief was gone. The landscape of sharp trees and bramble shrubs seemed to veer and change color as the spider toxins took fire in his eyes. Before he could find where Ripcat had disappeared in the brush strewn with spider silks, the assassin wraiths whirled out of the treetops.

Drev got off one shot – a blue-white bolt that evaporated the specter it struck with an incendiary flash. Then another wraith snatched the firelock in its corroded claws. A third and fourth closed from opposite flanks.

The wizarduke drew the sword Taran and swung at the multiple images around him. His blow sliced through another wraith and reduced it to smoke. Then claws bit into his shoulders, and the sword toppled from his grasp. He felt the bite of a talon atop his clavicle and, with cold grim certainty, expected the lethal stroke that would tear out his windpipe.

An animal cry resounded from above, and Ripcat, shrouded in spider veils, dropped out of the canopy and pounced on to the wraith asaulting Drev. The thief's assault knife stabbed between the assassin's bent wings, and the thing shredded to mist and a hurt shriek.

The last of the wraiths circled madly, waving the firelock it grasped in its claws. Drev bent for his sword, and Ripcat dove to block the wraith's aim. It fired, and the green charmlight struck Ripcat in the chest and dropped him senseless to the ground.

Drev whirled the sword through the air and impaled the ghostly creature to a thorn tree. Screaming like torn wind, it dropped the firelock and wisped away.

At the charmway's rock portal, Thylia felt the deaths of her wraiths as physical blows. The first knocked her off her feet, and the others pummeled her to near-unconsciousness. She lay with her back against the cape of rock, her legs spraddled, black diamond eyes half lidded, mites crawling through her veils.

Drev bent over Ripcat, felt the intertwinings of the thief's lifeforce and the magic that had placed beastmarks upon him. In an instant, the beastmarks would fall away, and he would die for what he was, man or animal.

The wizarduke slapped on to the thief's burned chest a gold net of theriacal opals. Instantly, a breath heaved through the thief's body, and his spasming lids twitched and opened.

Ripcat put both hands to the aching lobes of his skull but could not find the strength to sit up.

Drev sheathed his sword, slung the firelock over his shoulder, and pulled Ripcat over his other shoulder. He staggered through the trees and adjusted his power wands for the strength to bear this extra burden.

Vision wobbling, he crossed a field where spiders large as cows and banded brown and white squatted.

The day had melted to magenta streaks, and the spiders sat inertly. One got to its feet and sidled closer, its cluster of black bead eyes aglint with twilight. Without lowering Ripcat, Drev drew his sword. Duskfire flashed off the blade, and the large spider moved away through the feathery grass.

Loops of starsmoke lay across the sky when Drev found the charmway he sought. It was no more than a sinkhole in the ashen ground among more thorn trees and their streamers of spider ribbons. But when he lowered Ripcat in and stepped down himself, everything changed.

The charmway opened in Sharna-Bambara on a pebbly stream. Grasses tossed under wind drifts with a fragrance of pollen and eroded rock.

By starlight, Drev examined Ripcat. He was whole but, like the wizarduke, scabrous with spider bites. His limbs floated lightly, and Drev held him down while he applied the theriacal opals to his wounds.

Dawn saw both men healed of their cuts, gouges and punctures. The toxins thinned in their veins, though colors still appeared burnished and lethargy weighted their muscles. They marched slowly all that day, bearing south, following the stream. To elude the Dark Lord's seekers, Drev periodically shaped charmed manikins and sent them drift-walking in different directions.

Nightfall took them to the river that the stream fed. Its stately breadth reflected the bright choirs of night, and they paused on its mossy bank.

'I must visit Tywi,' Drev announced. He breathed deeply and filled his lungs with a breeze of river scent and darkness. 'Will you watch over my body while I'm gone?'

'Can I wake you if there is trouble?'

Drev shook his head. 'You will be alone until I return. Use my eye charms to keep guard.'

'And if the cacodemons come?'

Drev threw a pebble on to the river, and it skipped several times, setting rings of ripples on the glossy surface, before splashing out of sight.

'Let's stay together,' Ripcat advised. Fear stained his heart.

'I'm a thief. I'm not a warrior like you. How can I protect you?'

'You have kept me alive longer than my own marshal was able to do,' the wizarduke observed sadly. 'And Leboc was the very best.'

'Then heed me and do not do this.'

'I must see that Tywi is still alive,' Drev answered. He stepped into the canes that clacked gently on a mudbank pocked with tracks of mice. 'I will hide here. If I take all my Charm with me, there will be nothing for the seekers to locate. If they find me at all, they will think I am in Nhat.'

Ripcat shivered. The spider poison still tainted him. 'Will you look for my partner?'

'Dogbrick?' Drev nodded. 'I will find him. Though it may be dangerous. There is a warlock who patrols the labor camp, and if he finds me, I may not return.'

'And then?' Ripcat queried, his green, slant eyes luminous in the dark.

'Take my sword and firelock,' Drev said evenly. 'Carry on the fight. If you can – free Tywi.'

'How will I find her?'

'The sword Taran,' Drev told him. 'It will point the way – if I do not return.'

'You *are* in love to risk so much.'

'Is it love?' the wizarduke asked, stepping deeper into the canes and becoming a part of the nightshadows. 'Or something wider?'

Ripcat slid down the moss bank to stand beside him. 'Are we going to talk of destiny again?'

'Our days pass like a fever.' Drev bent and came up with a tangle of river vines. 'Help me tie myself down with these.'

'What about vipers?'

'I'd be grateful if you'd keep them away.'

Ripcat took the vines and began knotting them. 'You ask a lot of vigilance from a stranger.'

'You are no stranger to me, Ripcat,' Drev spoke with certainty and unsheathed his sword.

'How can you say that?' The thief frowned. 'I am a stranger to myself. Who am I?'

'You are my ally. You have saved my life. And I have saved yours.' Drev clapped a hand on the thief's pelted shoulder. 'We are friends.'

Ripcat accepted the sword and firelock. 'You will return by dawn?'

'If I am not back by dawn, you must leave my body.' He wrapped the knotted vine about himself and lay down on a mat of trampled cane. 'Help me tie this off.'

The thief complied, and after Drev was secure, he grasped his hand and peered hard into his calm eyes. 'Be careful.'

Drev squeezed his hand and smiled calmly. 'I will return with news of Dogbrick and my Tywi.'

His hand relaxed, his eyes closed, and his body rose against the restraints of the binding vines. Lord Drev was gone.

Ripcat sat back and felt his soul stretch like a scream.

Daylight blew in through the torn walls of the sunken temple, and Poch watched Caval glide into trance. The aged sorcerer seemed to die upon his bones. His flesh shrunk as if suddenly deflated, and a mummied man sat erect in the breezy light of day.

A spicy, resinous scent hazed off his waxy flesh. In that fragrance unscrolled memories long forgotten. Poch breathed them in and partook of Caval's lost past as though retrieving his own occluded reaches of time.

Under a hoarfrost tree, a beardless Caval stood naked, no more than 6,500 days old, little more than Poch's current age. Yet even at that newfledged time of life, he possessed a Charmed countenance.

In the Brood of Assassins, Caval had been bred as a reconciler and he displayed the serenity and lucid thinking prized by the diplomatic corps. His people believed he was destined for service as a court functionary, and the brood had already made inquiries among the dominions, offering him for hire as a contracts expert and even a court manager. But young Caval's interests lay elsewhere.

A Charmed prodigy, he displayed a rare talent at retaining Charm in his own body without benefit of amulets. In his child hands, conjure-wire and witch-glass moved as if alive, shaping with their own elemental sentience clever amulets – egg-cookers, back-scratchers, bottle-sealers. Wizards traveled from distant realms to consult with him.

The Sisterhood offered the brood three times more for him than the highest bid from the dominions, and the Assassins reluctantly let him go – for the time being. Caval was too valuable to lose to the witches for a one-time payout when, with his bred managerial skills, he could be earning lifelong residuals for the brood from the dominions.

Eventually, several thousand days after his service to the Sisterhood began, his brood bought out his contract and installed him in Arwar Odawl as weapons master for a considerable payout – an unprecedented responsibility for one so young. But by then he was youthful in appearance only.

Naked under the hoarfrost tree, Caval had not dwelled on this memory in many thousand days, and he wondered what so distant a time had to do with Irth's peril.

He had begun his trance by nailing his attention to an inward image of Wrat, and he was startled to see that wedged face transform into this image of himself naked under the hoarfrost tree so very long ago.

Witches of angelic nudity circled him beneath a leaden sky. A bare plain of sere grass circled them in turn, and all were invisibly tethered to the white tree. They danced, braiding the hairs of silence.

Caval recalled this time in his early training. He had been with the Sisterhood 1,500 days by the time of this ritual called Climbing the Ladder of the Wind. He had amazed himself and his teachers with his facility with Charm, but none had expected what happened next.

The youth climbed the Ladder of the Wind above the sere

plain, higher than the icy marblings of the atmosphere, into the vacuum cold between worlds. Usually, neophytes such as himself visited Nemora. The bold ones went as far as Hellsgate. Few had gone beyond those near worlds and come back.

He remembered hanging there in the glittery dark with the Charmed worlds floating about him in the emptiness luminous as seashells. He began working his Charm with the crazy weave of amulets that he had devised for the occasion – and he vanished from the top rung of the Ladder.

Everyone, including himself, knew at once what had happened. He had fallen into the Gulf. He fell forever. He fell like a shadow out of the Empire of Light into eternal darkness. When his vision adjusted, he noticed cold worlds glittering among the clots of starsmoke that had formed them. His shadow brushed across their smoky faces.

*The Dark Shore*— He recognized, as serene as the brood had bred him to be.

He fell to a world of forests and aboriginal peoples. Among them, he wore a skin of light that covered his boyish frame with a bestial hulk of shaggy fur meant to intimidate the natives. He visited the tribes and spoke wisdom in their own tongues. He did what good he could for them while he prepared to create the amulets that would gather the Charm to help him climb the Ladder of the Wind back across the Gulf to Irth.

It had been done before, though the knowledge of this was occult. The uninitiates were not to suspect that the Dark Shore could be trespassed or many foolish lives would be forfeit.

Only those trained by the Sisterhood and the Sanctuary of Sages knew that Charm could be found anywhere in the Gulf and on the cold worlds beyond. But it was exceedingly tenuous and required tremendous cunning to devise amulets capable of culling that sheer substance. To the natives, he referred to it as alchemy, for it required ponderous equipment and produced a substance of concentrated Charm of golden luster in the tiniest dusty quantities.

To climb back to Irth, he would need his body's weight in alchemic gold.

He sought an assistant. From the peoples who lived in the cities outside the forests, he recruited a young, homeless man, who was sophisticated enough to comprehend his plight. His name was Reece, and he eagerly visited the forests where Caval worked and absorbed the young sorcerer's instructions.

In time, they became friends, and Caval invited Reece into his laboratory and later his abode. He told him of Irth and the Abiding Star. He taught him the laws of Charm.

With this knowledge, Reece became a potent sorcerer in his own world, wielding magic both in the wilderness and the city. He was able to gather for Caval everything he required for his alchemic laboratory, leaving Caval with the time to devise the amulets that would ultimately return him home.

For the final phase of the work, Caval needed a witch. Since none existed on the Dark Shore, he enlisted Reece's aid in creating one. They began with a female infant saved from flood waters. They named her Lara, and together they reared her in the forests in the manner of the Sisterhood, two men mimicking the ways of the Goddess. Very early they taught her the power dances so that she quickly grew strong enough to assist them in the arduous rituals of alchemy.

Nineteen summers she danced for them. They had trained her well, and her dances drew power to them from the terminals of the world. The work flourished. Until the late summer when the aboriginals killed her.

Caval was devastated. He remembered why he had not wanted to remember. Pain grasped his chest at the image of Lara's face rayed with her own blood.

She was dead – and young Caval had spun enough alchemic gold to finally climb again the Ladder of the Wind. He clambered back to Irth and left his sorrows behind on the Dark Shore.

Or so he had thought.

From his wider vantage in the Cloths of Heaven 38,500 days

later, he saw something that fused his spine to an icicle. After he had climbed the Ladder of the Wind, closed the Door in the Air, and returned to Irth and the astonishment of the Sisterhood – Reece had followed!

The trance nearly broke apart before Caval's shock, and only his fabled serenity retrieved the depthfulness necessary to see how this terrible thing had happened. Clearly, Reece had used the techniques Caval had taught him to work his own alchemy and climb the Ladder of the Wind after him. But the denizen of the Dark Shore did not know about the Door in the Air. Caval had never told him about that. The magic Caval had taught him opened the Door on its own. And Reece had left it standing open behind him.

*That is how Wrat brings his cacodemons to Irth!*

Caval woke dizzied from his trance. His eyes rolled about for a disoriented moment, and his arms swung sideways to steady himself before alertness yanked his stare into place.

His face looked hammered loose from rock, and he gazed at Poch as if paralyzed by a basilisk's venomous stare. From a great depth inside himself, he muttered, '*I* created the Dark Lord.'

## The Star Fallen

＊━＊

A star fell singing into the sea. Its fiery arc lit up the night sky, dimming constellations and brightening mushroom folds of clouds across the Reef Isles of Nhat. At the point on the horizon where the aerolite vanished, darkness bent backward over amethyst flames. A pale rose burned briefly there while a starsong blew in musical winds across the shoals.

Dogbrick and Tywi looked at each other across the sudden pastel dawn. They had been working separately for many days, the thief offshore in the waves and the waif raking the tideline. To avoid Whipcrow's ire, they kept apart. Exhausting nights and dreambound days used them up and left few opportunities to talk.

The starsong made them forget distance. They both heard dreamy beauty. To Tywi, the music called up a hopeful joy, like the tranquil amazement she knew in the Qaf after the beastfolk rescued her from the trolls and healed her with amulets. She had never felt so much Charm before, almost to the point of trance . . .

Dogbrick, too, experienced the precise hopefulness he had known in the desert when he carried his future in a brass-cornered trunk. He recalled the abundance of possibility he possessed with his fortune in Charm and how powerful he felt when he first gave Tywi a healing amulet and witnessed her change from pain to wonder. He remembered the words he had spoken to soothe her: *You are what lives after.*

So many days without Charm and then suddenly soaked in it again, Dogbrick and Tywi came to the same momentary happiness in their suffering. They saw each other across the bright air. Dogbrick waved, and Tywi dropped her rake and walked into the balmy music.

Others heard the starsong each in their own way. For the ogres, it burned like a scream. They ran from the beach and lay hidden in the marsh for long dark minutes after darkness smothered the song.

Whipcrow heard the same serenity as Dogbrick and Tywi, but it carried him to the tranquil loveliness of the warlock's gardens. The music lilted like the mesmermur breezes in the maze of blue and green glass at the Palace of Abominations, where the dead were kept awake. He thought of Ralli-Faj hung on his stick, watching everything with empty eyes. He decided then that he would retrieve this rare thing for his master.

Fog rolled in, soft, warm, and fragrant steam from where the star had burned out in the sea. Dogbrick and Tywi met each other on a sandbar as the sultry clouds encircled them in sea-stench and a tangy floral darkness.

'Follow the waves to shore,' Dogbrick advised. He unlatched his three-tined hook and tether from his trawl, and the net ballooned away in the smoky water. 'Can't see anything in this damn dragonsmoke. Let's go in.'

'Wait.' She stopped him by catching his massive arm, and his strength lifted her off her feet. 'I must speak with you. I think we can escape.'

He lowered her to the soggy sand and listened hard. Who might have heard her? *Escape!* Reaching into the velvet darkness, hearing the wild cries of others in the distance and someone laughing maniacally far out by the crashing surf, he speculated that Tywi was herself an illusion.

He missed his amulets and had to turn his face to the wind to catch the scent of her before he could dismiss his fear. She was real. She smelled like bruised fruit. She was starving. Yet she remained strong, hardened by her survival days in the factory lots.

Dogbrick relaxed. No one had overheard her. He sensed they were alone on the sandbar, two silhouettes, beastlike and frail shadows of each other.

'You are giddy from the starsong,' he warned and shouldered his coil of tether-line attached to a three-pronged hook. He lifted his head to listen, smell and look as far as he could into the incandescent blindness. The air smelled sweet and tepid, without a hint of threat. 'I feel it, too – the joy, the sense of possibility. We have been too long without Charm. The flash of the falling star has filled our hearts with hope.'

'No, there's more than just Charm.' Tywi stepped closer, and her voice softened to a whisper, 'Owl Oil told me not to tell you.'

'Owl Oil—' He dropped an unhappy laugh. 'The crone who believes hope is sour desire!'

'Yeah. She also said you're the strongest of us,' Tywi gently reminded him. 'You could help free us from this prison. That's why she used her opal to heal you.'

'You've seen her since?' he asked, distracted by a mournful yodel far off in the seething calm.

'Only afar. Sometimes at morning count. She works with a forage crew in the marsh.' Tywi leaned on his arm and confided, 'That energy Owl Oil helped me see in the dark – remember that? I know who it is.'

'She showed you the walking shade of Ralli-Faj,' he whispered back, suppressing a shudder of dread.

'She warned me about him. That's why I ain't tried to tell you sooner. But now—'

'It's the touch of Charm after so long without it,' he surmised and took her hand. 'Be careful what you say, Tywi. Silence listens, and we are Charmed but without amulets! Let's return to the beach.'

Again she would not budge. 'A Peer's been visiting, watching.' She spoke with breathy excitement. 'He came close to me once and we talked.'

'A Peer.' Dogbrick heard the gruff calls of ogres crawling among the dunes and whooping laughter mixed with grievous wails all up and down the beach from the blind scavengers. 'Ralli-Faj is a Peer.'

'Not the warlock.' She stood on her toetips to tell him. 'Some fugitive from the Dark Lord. One of his enemies.'

'Say no more to me.' He stepped back and released her hand. 'Without amulets, we can't know what is real and what an illusion.'

'Yeah, he warned me to tell nobody.' She followed him toward shore, into the deeper water of a tidal pool. 'Our enemies are cruel, he said.'

'The phantom is right.' He waded more surely toward the beach.

'Only this, Dog.' She stopped, the tepid water at her waist lapping in bioluminescent ripples. 'We got to get ready to escape.'

'To where?' He sniffed for danger. 'Ogres are excellent trackers.'

'We got a destiny,' she called after him.

He stopped and faced her small shadow. 'I don't like that word.' He squinted and saw the sincerity in her expression. 'Destiny. That is a clumsy thing. Hard to hold in one's hands. I prefer will. That's all in the hands.'

'We got to will it, then, Dogbrick.' Her voice was firm, and even without rat-star gems he received the impression that she spoke from conviction. 'This is evil. We got to stop it.'

He drifted toward her. 'Let us escape now.'

'What about the others?' They stood in a vacuole of the fog, seeing each other clearly. Dogbrick, bedraggled and hollowshanked, revealed the weight he had lost. Yet he still stood imposingly tall and broad of bone, and she told him, 'Owl Oil said you was the strongest. You got to help us all.'

'Me? I am a thief. I am not a warrior – and I do not serve the Peers.' He looked sadly upon the small animal before him. He had not attempted to flee by himself because he felt responsible for her. 'Look, this is our chance if you want to escape. In the fog, we can swim to another isle. I'll carry you. We will make our own destiny.'

She shook her head, her chop-cut hair plastered to her brow and cheeks. 'My destiny is right here.'

'With the phantom who visits you?' He leveled a cautionary stare. 'How do you know he is not Ralli-Faj? We are in his camp. This is a monstrous cruelty he works on you, Tywi.'

'No, Dog.' She took one hand of his in both of hers. 'This shade ain't evil. I felt him – with my heart.'

'Hmm. Your heart?' He patted her hands. 'You are in love with his handsome and powerful physique.'

She scowled at his mocking tone and the fear it touched in her that he was right, that the wizarduke come to save her was an illusion.

'He is handsome and powerful, isn't he?' Dogbrick snarled. 'Tywi, he is a skin of light – a deception projected by some malformed creature with a hungry soul. If not Ralli-Faj, some other dangerous servant of Wrat.'

A wet sucking cry swelled out of the waves, a ferment of many small cries surging shoreward in a tidal rush.

Dogbrick and Tywi grabbed at each other and shouted in unison: 'Seaworms!'

They splashed toward shore, Dogbrick huddling beside her with his arm over her shoulders. Whiplash shapes frothed in the misty water on all sides. A hive of seaworms had broken apart under the impact of the falling star, and the swarm frenzied through the waves and the soft sand.

A writhing coil tangled Tywi's legs, and she fell forward and jerked backward and down into wet darkness so rapidly no cry escaped her. Dogbrick jumped up, surprised, clutching her empty tunic.

Instantly, he spun about, grabbed his hook and heaved it forcefully at the sandbar behind him. The heavy prongs caught something living that pulled the hook out of sight. Dogbrick leaned his full weight on the taut line, and the sandbar split like a skin.

A tentacled maw rolled out – a writhing tube of glossy segmented worm thick as a treetrunk – and Tywi, mired naked in wet sand, struggled to free herself from a tangle of suctioned feelers. Where the suckers touched, scalding blisters mottled her flesh. The thing had already begun to digest her when the hook caught it behind the head. One prong emerged through the rubbery flesh beside a black staring squid eye.

Dogbrick pulled himself closer and twisted the hook with one hand while tearing away tentacles with the other. Tywi squirmed free and thrashed across the tide pool and into the fog. The thief tore loose his hook and pursued.

Seaworms snared his ankles but none large enough to hold him. He kicked and lurched across the pool and found Tywi struggling to pull herself out of the water. With one hand, he hoisted her on to the black lip of the shore. He draped her in her ragged tunic and scurried with her through the fog to the dry sand.

The ogres' driftwood fires shone like dark gems in the fog. Dogbrick mumbled about getting warm, but Tywi sat shivering in the sand and made no move to rise. Seaworm toxins sickened her. Numbness muted her limbs, and weariness swelled closer with the mist.

The thief caught her as she glided upward, shedding her mortal weight. He carried her to the nearest fire, where two ogres frowned at her hot wounds and called for a healer. Out of the gloom, a bent figure drifted.

Owl Oil knelt beside her, arms draped with coppery sheets of wet kelp. 'I'm tending burns up and down the beach,' she told the ogres and began placing the gelatinous ribbons on the young woman's blister stripes. 'A whole hive cluster is disturbed.'

'Can you help her?' Dogbrick peered anxiously at the woman's tired features, reading the rays of wrinkles for signs of what she saw in Tywi's limp and buoyant body.

'She's breathing without trouble,' Owl Oil said and brushed strands of hair from Tywi's sleeping face. 'Keep her Irthbound, and she'll sleep through the night. Dawn shall find her curled like a seed inside one thick husk of a headache.'

Dogbrick looked to see that the ogres were busy talking to each other and leaned closer to Owl Oil, gazing sternly at her from inside the hood of his mane, 'You are a witch.'

The crone tapped her leather vest with her thumb. 'Charmwright.'

'You talk like a witch,' the thief asserted quietly, glancing over his shoulder to be certain the ogres paid them no heed. 'The bosses call you a healer. And you happen to be here for Tywi. You always happen to be where she needs you. It smells of witchery.'

'I am watching over this young woman,' Owl Oil admitted. In the firelight, her caramel eyes gleamed with grandmotherly kindness. 'She has a destiny.'

'That word again!' He tilted his stare suspiciously. 'Then you *are* a witch?'

'No. I am no witch.' Owl Oil brushed the hair from Tywi's shut eyes, then looked at Dogbrick with grim candor. 'I am an enemy of the Dark Lord.'

'Hush!' Dogbrick flinched around and saw the ogres herding other scavengers to the fire. 'Silence listens.'

'Yes, smart Dog – but it cannot speak!' She giggled with silent mirth as she finished applying the kelp plaster. 'I am not afraid to speak so long as only silence listens.' She placed Tywi's wet tunic on an antler of driftwood within the thermal aura of the fire. 'Ralli-Faj is farther down the strand with Whipcrow. They are busy contemplating how to retrieve the fallen star. No one spies us – yet.'

'The warlock is a shade when he patrols.' Dogbrick stared into each underlit face as the scavengers came to the fire, recognizing them all, sensing no threat. 'How do you know where he is?'

'Never mind that.' Owl Oil smiled benevolently. 'The fallen star is an omen.'

'Omen. Destiny.' The thief pulled his head back. 'Woman, you speak like a witch.'

'Charm, Dogbrick.' She picked up a twig and stirred the flames expertly, luffing heat over Tywi where she slept in Dogbrick's arms. 'Nothing happens on Irth but for Charm. The star that fell returned Charm to a dominion that has lost too much of it since the Dark Lord erected his Palace of Abominations.'

He watched the ogreish profiles at the perimeter of darkness. 'Are you sure we can talk of these things?'

'You think I am one of them?' She tossed a disdainful look at the brutish silhouettes. 'Trust me, Dogbrick. We are allies.' She snapped her fingers, and a green spark winked in the air. For one instant it rotated like a big snowflake, revealing its lace of geometric angles, a perfect gem of light. Then she blew it, and it flurried before his startled face and disappeared through the velvet between his eyes.

A light went on inside Dogbrick. Improbable joy changed colors through all the small spaces of his body. It was a kiss of Charm.

'How did you do that?' Dogbrick gusted a big sigh, his body heavy, dark, and charmless again. 'You have amulets?'

Her tranquil smile widened. 'I have no amulets.'

'I felt Charm.'

'So may have Ralli–Faj,' Owl Oil said. 'Now I cannot linger. But I had to convince you, we are allies. We share a destiny.'

'And what is that?'

'To slay the Dark Lord and all his minions.'

'Slay?' A chill ran through him in the warm night, and he laughed unhappily. 'If you had said flee, I would have thought you mad. Now I know you must be a powerful sorceress. The only escape from the Dark Lord is death. But ours is more likely than his – unless you are a very powerful sorceress. Are you the one visiting Tywi in a skin of light?'

'That is no skin of light.' Owl Oil turned Tywi's tunic on its driftwood prop. 'It is a true shade. The shade of Lord Drev, wizarduke of Ux.'

'Drev? The regent?' Dogbrick blinked. 'I think not. If Wrat's most loathed foe is still alive, he must have crawled into a hole somewhere to hide from the cacodemons. And what would he want with a factory waif anyway?'

Owl Oil laid a hand of blessing on Tywi's brow. 'Destiny has joined them in this life.'

'I am a philosopher, Owl Oil,' Dogbrick said dryly. 'I believe every effect has its cause.'

'Then the cause is love.'

Dogbrick looked down with disbelief at the small woman in his arms. He did not find her attractive. She not only lacked beastmarks, she seemed too plain to elicit ardor in anyone. 'How can the regent of Ux, once the most powerful person on Irth, love a factory worker he's never met?'

Owl Oil clucked as if exasperated that anyone had to ask. 'They know each other from the Beginning.'

'Really?' Dogbrick rolled his eyes.

'You do not believe in the Beginning?'

'I told you. I'm a philosopher. I believe only in what I experience.'

Her smile flourished. 'Ah, but creation is so much larger than what we *can* experience.'

'I have my hands full dealing with what is at hand, Owl Oil.' He shifted himself so he was more comfortable under Tywi's airy weight. 'I don't need to be troubled with speculations about the unknowable.'

'The Beginning is unknown, perhaps, but not unknowable.' Her head twisted, and her tawny eyes rolled sideways. 'I must go. The warlock approaches.'

371

'Wait!' Dogbrick called, but she did not even glance back as she retreated into the hazy darkness beyond the firelight.

In his arms, Tywi twitched at Owl Oil's departure and then lay still. Her shade floated free of her body. She realized at once what had happened when she saw herself unconscious in the thief's embrace, her charmless body weightless, ready to drift away.

She turned so as not to have to watch herself, which frightened her, and looked at the red hands of fire scratching the darkness. The lit eyes of the scavengers gazed right through her when she passed in front of them, and she walked a slow circle about the big fire.

An ogre swung toward her, and she flinched as it stepped through her and stood drying its hands at the fire. She moved on quickly, back to where she had begun. Dogbrick sat with his heels dug into the sand, his thick arms crossed over her inert body. His beastlike face suffused with humanity studied the night and also the people and ogres the fire summoned.

She felt safe in his care and stood for a moment admiring the way attentiveness shone from him like an inner radiance, in which his gaze, turned low, noticed everything. Under the cascade of his mane, his long shoulders and muscular back shielded her from the night.

The sight of herself, naked, bony, painted in red kelp and elemental fireshadows, rekindled fear. She approached her salamandrine body, wanting to feel her way back inside herself. Then she saw him. He stood far behind Dogbrick at the edge of the fire circle, unmoving.

Lord Drev urgently motioned for her to stay still. He turned to observe something in the darkness, one hand extended to restrain her. She made herself look hard at the man, trying to discern if this were an illusion – if his sleek, placid nakedness disguised a horrid being. He seemed whole, a tall and strong physique perfectly proportioned by a lifetime of Charm, and when he beckoned her, she hurried to his side.

He led her under the scarp of a dune and pointed down the

beach. The sky had cleared, and she saw the planets and star trails and the fog feeling its way along the ground. Scavengers meandered legless through the low mist, obeying orders shouted by Whipcrow. Beside him, a transparency glinted, reflecting the cloudless sky. It turned, and its reflections gathered and burst like a star.

'Get down!' An electric iciness grabbed her arm where Drev touched her, and she crouched. 'It's Ralli-Faj.'

She spied the gleaming burnish of his transparent shade as it moved among the workers. 'Has he seen us?'

'No,' Drev answered, watching the clear shadow glint with night's shining darkness as it moved away. 'He is too intent on retrieving the fallen star. It would make a powerful amulet.'

Tywi stared at his profile. The harsh bonelines of his cheek, the ledged brow, bent nose, and long jaw lent him a fierce aspect. Yet, this close to him, she sensed his inward self, felt the resonance of warmth and friendship, and she realized: 'You called me out here – out of my body.'

'Yes.' His brow furrowed. 'You were in pain. I saw what happened. I thought perhaps you would like to see the night out here for a while with me.' He nodded toward Dogbrick's sturdy silhouette against the pulsing shadows of the fire. 'Your friend looks like he can be trusted to keep you Irthbound. Dogbrick is his name.'

'Yeah,' she said with surprise. 'How you know him?'

'I met his partner Ripcat in the woods of Bryse. We've become allies.'

'Ripcat—' Her features shifted quizzically. 'He saved me from trolls in the Qaf.'

'Yes, he's told me about that.' He sat with his back against the slipface of the dune, more relaxed as the warlock moved farther away. 'He is concerned about his friend Dogbrick and will be glad to hear that he is alive.'

'Is it your Charm that brought us all together?' Tywi asked and sat beside him. The ground felt solid yet buzzed with tiny vibrations, and her own luminous form seemed stronger, vivid, pure.

'No, Tywi.' A softness touched his harsh lineaments briefly. 'Something wider than Charm is at work here. Fate alone led me to Ripcat.'

'Dogbrick would be unhappy hearing that.' She pointed her smile at where the thief sat like a boulder. 'He don't believe in fate.'

'Fate continues anyway.'

'You followed it to me.' She lifted an inquisitive look at the wizarduke. 'I ain't sure yet I understand why.'

'You and I are something else, Tywi.' He smiled unevenly. 'Destiny led me to you.'

She liked how his broken smile canceled the severity of his features, and she dared ask, 'That ain't fate?'

'Destiny is the fate we see coming. Fate is hidden destiny.' His pale eyes widened, looking into her to see if she understood. 'I saw you in my earliest days, when I first learned to scry. You were there, in the timelight. You have always been there, because we have been together since the Beginning.'

She frowned. 'In the factories, ain't much talk of the Beginning.'

'I thought the Sisterhood had brought news of the Beginning to every dark corner on Irth, even the factories of Saxar.'

'The witches?' She shrugged. 'They was busy enough in the factories talking about the Origins. But I was hungry and sleepy. I listened only because, when they finished, they gave food and small amulets to the homeless.'

'There *is* a Beginning,' Drev spoke with conviction. 'It is the source of all time and all form. Everything we see has come from it.' He scanned the night as if he could read meaning in the patterns of the stars. 'The Abiding Star is the portal out of which pours all the energy of heaven. It radiates into the coldness of the void, where it chills and freezes to Charm, and light, and matter.'

'And fate?'

'It is the pattern in the energy that shapes all forms. All of time is woven in that pattern.'

'But what's this "will" Dogbrick talks about so much?' She straightened earnestly. 'What about our freedom?'

'No freedom from our freedom, the Scrolls tell us. Each of us *is* free – within the scope of our lives. And out here, between birth and death, that scope is very small.' He moved intimately closer. 'That is why we need others, to widen our freedom. That is the destiny that brings us together. You are the path of my freedom.'

'We can do together what we never could apart.' She echoed his sympathetic wisdom, yet pulled back from him, afraid of the feelings he stirred in her. 'That's true for me. Look! Here I am talking to *you*—' She jumped when he put his hand atop hers. 'Touching you – outside my body! You give me freedom. But what can I give to you?'

He withdrew his hand, and the air sparkled softly between them. 'Freedom is on the inside, too. I sensed you since I was a child, but I always turned away from you. I thought I had no time to find you. My youth was one continuous preparation for the regency that my forebears had created. And when I came of age, there was the regency. I was busy with the concerns of seven dominions – of all Irth! I could not think of myself without feeling selfish. I didn't have the freedom inside myself to seek you out.'

'But you're here.'

He lowered his face. 'Now. I should have come to you many days ago, when you were in Saxar.'

'How could you with all you got to do, all your responsibilities?'

'I was the regent.' He met her searching gaze boldly. 'I could have tracked you to Saxar. I didn't because I knew you were impoverished, nearly charmless. I could feel it. And I was afraid that if I came to you, even secretly, I would demean you.'

'Demean me?' Her stare swelled. 'I lived in trash bins.'

'I was afraid of demeaning your spirit,' he explained. 'I feel that, too. You *are* my other, my doublegoer. We share a spirit. It is solitary and proud. I feared that if I came to you, our differences, which are so great, would break that spirit.'

Tywi lowered her voice sadly. 'You mean, you thought I couldn't love you, because you're a Peer and I'm charmless.'

'I was as impoverished inside as you were outside.' He held up his right hand, and it shone with frosty luminance. 'The moment I lost the regency, I began my search for you. Now I can offer you what Charm I have left and the freedom of the outside – and, if you're still willing, you can give me my freedom inside.'

He offered his shining hand. When she took it, a current passed through her, and she shivered with bright clarity like a filament burning silently in its vacuum. Several precise moments lapsed in which she experienced the hard and familiar contours of her awareness before she realized she was not herself any more. She was Drev.

She knew his thoughts and silences. His consciousness flowed through her and into her own soulful depths, where she sensed him sensing her. Beings of light, they intermingled and shared the truth of each other.

*Flesh and thought make things small*, they thought, enlarged in their oneness, floating toward the starlanes above the watery layers of ocean ether.

Far below, Ralli-Faj sensed Charm among the dunes and moved up the beach. Ogres followed him toward the fire.

Drev and Tywi separated. Instantly, they found themselves again on Irth, human shapes of light. But they had changed. Tywi looked stronger, the cadaverous hollows of her skeletal frame had filled out, and Drev's stern countenance had gentled.

Their minds still rolled and surged from the union, and they reached for each other and then quickly stepped back from the burning cool sensuality that wanted to pull them back into each other again.

'You must go, quickly,' Drev whispered and pointed at the dunes in their sapphire fleece of starlit fog. The clear shadow of

Ralli-Faj shimmered with liquid reflections as he climbed the shore. In a moment, he would cross out of sight behind the nearest dunes before he came full upon them.

'I'd have loved you for yourself if you'd come to me in Saxar,' Tywi informed him with a shamefast and steady look.

Drev stared back with that same incandescent look, past sadness, healed of remorse by their contact. 'I know that now. That's why I had to risk everything to meet you like this, to know that. Now go!'

Tywi ignored the compulsion to hurry. That was his concern for her. Even separate, she shared enough awareness with him to partake of what he saw and judged. She knew exactly how long she had before the warlock came around the dunes. She paused and waved, and Drev cocked his head impatiently, telling her he would not move until she was safe.

*So hurry!*

His thought was palpable, a part of her that she took with him as she fled past tortured salt shrubs back to the fire. Her body received her easily, with a soft jolt like shrugging off a dream, and she opened her eyes and looked for him. Darkness swarmed through the starbright fog.

'So the crone was right after all,' Dogbrick mumbled. 'You're going to live. I wasn't sure. Your breathing got very thin.'

She unfolded from his lap, and he helped her stand. It was like stepping to solid ground after heaving days upon the sea. She staggered forward and down, and the thief held her upright while she retrieved her fire-dried tunic and put it on over the peeling kelp.

'You have a headache?' Dogbrick inquired. 'Owl Oil said you would.'

Her head felt flawless, but when she tried to say so, her mouth lolled open mutely.

'You need rest,' Dogbrick concluded. 'The seaworm toxin is still working on you.'

Before he could coax her to sit, Whipcrow strode into the fire circle clapping his hands. 'Back to work! The fog has lifted. Everyone back to work!'

A mask floated in the air behind him, an apparition of silvery-green ectoplasm, like an ancient mask of beaten copper and tin. The ogres quailed at the sight of it.

Whipcrow squinted at limp Tywi, appraising the numerous welts on her arms and legs. 'She's badly stung,' he observed coldly. 'Send her back to camp.' He would have gone with her himself, but with Ralli-Faj following behind, searching for something, he dared not. Instead, he confronted Dogbrick with a baleful scowl. 'Find your net. Get back into the waves. Dawn is hours away. Everyone back to work!'

An ogre took Tywi from Dogbrick, and the thief stepped back as the hollow mask floated by, sniffing after her. It veered away and circled the fire, clearing everyone out. Whipcrow regrouped the work crews and, with the spectral mask bobbing alongside, led them among the tumescent dunes.

Dogbrick followed the rest of the scavengers back to the sea. The flash of Charm from the falling star had worked a small but important magic in him, and he did not feel dismay but hope. Tywi was correct to demand that he save them all. He did not know how, but the enormity of the problem did not daunt him. Now that he was ready, the answer would discover him. The philosopher in him knew this was true. Only the thief needed to be convinced.

From that night on, he began talking with the others. Since his arrival, he had kept to himself, afraid of calling down Whipcrow's ire on anyone he befriended. Yet more than that, he had felt unworthy in the company of these particular scavengers. They had been rounded up by the ogres, because they were the leaders and workers of the society that the Dark Lord hated. They were people who owned homes, who had families, and who worked for their livelihoods. He was a thief.

These very people would have thrown him out of Saxar, exiled him to the Qaf if 100 Wheels or Crabhat had caught him. In society, he did not belong among them – but in this labor camp, fate had thrown him in with them and the falling star's music reminded him that he had something to offer. As a thief he had developed skills of deception and violence. And as a philosopher he had learned the patience to wait for the right time to use those skills.

Dogbrick sought out the most weary and despondent of the scavengers and spoke to them about the largeness of the human heart. He quoted The Gibbet Scrolls and added his own philosophy: 'Life is worth losing your heart to,' he counseled, 'but don't lose heart.' These platitudes he backed with action whenever he could, unobtrusively helping the weakest with their work, stealing more food for them, and assisting the healers with the sick.

Dogbrick's inspiration was Tywi. The falling star had changed her as well, and her transformation was the most mysterious renewal the thief had ever witnessed. From a withdrawn and mousy waif, she became overnight a presence infused with authority. She moved confidently among the scavengers, no longer a mere factory orphan but a woman with purpose and vision. Directed from within by the destinal part of her that belonged with Lord Drev, she knew as if instinctively who to approach, what to say, and how to cohere the disparate scavengers into a group that felt they shared a goal – to survive and eventually escape.

In a few days, the scavengers' sense of defeat and doom gave way to a quiet co-operation. The crews began to work more intently. They had a plan. With Tywi's and Dogbrick's gentle encouragement, they determined to defeat defeat, to grow stronger, and to be ready to take back the Irth. In time, the opportunity would come, and they would have to be ready.

Whipcrow had no notion of what galvanized the scavengers. The change occurred slowly over days and without any Charm; so Ralli-Faj, too, did not grasp what was happening. But the warlock, the manager, and even the ogres were pleased, because the crews worked more efficiently and increased the quantities of goods they dragged from the sea. Impressed by the profits earned from the sales of the tide's treasures to the crippled cities that needed raw goods, Ralli-Faj rewarded Whipcrow with more trance time in the gardens. In turn, the manager, who took full credit for the industry of his crews, increased the scavengers' rations.

With Whipcrow absent more often and the ogres no longer so bellicose now that they were earning extra dew-wine, the scavengers found their arduous lives less oppressive. Tywi and Dogbrick won the respect of the camp. Days on days passed in hopeful endeavor, waiting for a way out of slavery to open.

When none did and the extra rations began to seem customary, doubt set in. People argued, fights broke out. Crews scavenged less efficiently. Drownings occurred more frequently. Soon, Ralli-Faj noticed a decrease in his exports, and he curtailed Whipcrow's rapture time and sent him to oversee the camp more closely.

Less inebriated, the ogres patroled the camp and the strand with irascible vigor. Life became hard again for the prisoners. In despair, Tywi sought Drev but found him only in her dreams and then not real at all but an elusive figure. She had no answer for the perennial question of the camp: When would salvation come?

Dogbrick spoke for her, 'Fire burns, hope dwindles. Don't you see? We can't live on hope. Eventually it will exhaust itself and our strength will burn out. We have to live on each day and that alone. Who knows what love means? What is the sating of desire? These are questions we have to answer here. We don't need salvation for that. And if and when salvation does come, we will be stronger and ready for it.'

The philosopher's words, spoken softly to one or two individuals at a time, helped. All that had been achieved was not unraveled. A large core of workers recognized the benefits they had created for themselves from the greed of their overlords, and they strove to convince the others that Dogbrick spoke the truths that could keep them alive.

Nights and more nights of remorseless tidal work passed, and once again the crews brought in large yields. Whipcrow took his reward in the warlock's gardens, the ogres imbibed their dew-wine on the dunetops, and slavery became more bearable for the scavengers.

Dogbrick marveled that his words – his philosophy, which he had learned from Wise Fish on the streets of Saxar – had weight with the people who once would have loathed him. He had to turn his hard wisdom on himself to keep from bloating with pride.

*To survive, contain the counterflow,* he quoted from The Gibbet Scrolls whenever he felt himself becoming important. The flow of encouragement and philosophy into the camp was important, while the backwash of admiration and neediness from the others posed dangers as real on the strand as they were on the street. If the ogres ever took special notice of him, if Whipcrow ever found cause to act on his enmity, or if the warlock ever saw him behaving like a leader, he was dead.

The scavengers endured laborious nights and sleep-shackled days. Though Whipcrow and the ogres continually rearranged crews and sleeping quarters to discourage bonds of friendship and love, social groups gradually emerged in the camp and acquired stability: Lovers created families, families joined in clans. With this renewed order, efficiency increased to a higher level, because the clans devised ways to improve equipment and techniques. Less people died from injuries, and the new prisoners that the ogres delivered in their chattel carts adjusted more easily to enslavement and suffered fewer casualties. With no Charm and little hope, the camp endured.

And then the scavengers found the fallen star.

It was a fish-colored rock no larger than a woman's head, yet heavy as a boulder. The net that snagged it broke, and the star required seven men, among them Dogbrick, pulling on cables to haul it ashore. Five blackened stobs marked where its points had been burned off in its fall through the atmosphere, and the tarnished skin bore iridescent swirls and streaks where flames had jetted.

Owl Oil barged through the scavengers gathered about the fallen star and the watery trench it had dug as it was dragged on to the beach and announced, 'I'm a charmwright. I've worked with stars before. Get me a chisel. I can free its song. Hurry – before the ogres get here.'

The drunken ogres lolling on the dunes had not yet noticed what the scavengers had pulled out of the tide. But when Owl Oil used an awl as a makeshift chisel, the sharp, ringing tones alerted them. They came bawling and tumbling down the slipfaces of the dunes, weaving across the beach, swatting with torches.

The surface of the star broke away in glassy shards and exposed a face like a fist. Everyone pulled back from the terrible visage except the charmwright. She watched closely as the drilled-out eyes flashed open, pink with pinhole silver pupils.

Through those tiny apertures, the starcore interior emitted needle-thin rays that scanned the heavens from whence it had fallen. The face seemed surprised and pitiful. Then it noticed the charmwright and the others cringing behind her. The compressed features unclenched in the night air and became lovely with frightfulness.

Owl Oil met the radiant stare with her arms cocked at odd angles, her hands contorted in mudra-knots. For an instant, the starcore energy glazed over her and formed the green vaporshape of a younger woman with mild features and a distinctly regal mien.

The handful of scavengers close enough to view this clearly recognized that the body of the crone was a skin of light that disguised a Peer. Then she collapsed, and the star closed its eyes. Its glandular cheeks trembled, and a bewitched breath exuded from its tiny, ribbed mouth.

Music flared over the beach. A radiation of desire poisoned everyone. The scavengers leaped with shock, and danced, rolled in the wet sand, ran splashing into the sea.

Dogbrick dove into a tide pool, and the cold water broke the frenzy briefly. He climbed out and knelt on the gravel, staring amazed at the jubilantly frantic crowd thrashing in the sand. He saw Tywi among them, not dancing but clawing at the people in her way as she struggled wildly to reach Owl Oil.

Then the ogres came howling down the beach swinging their torches, their small faces clotted with rage. They jumped furiously on to the singing star and beat at it with their burning sticks.

Dogbrick sprang forward, bounding among the dancers until he reached Tywi. Opening a way for her with his imposing size, he guided her to Owl Oil, and together they carried her unconscious body out of the shadow of the enraged ogres. Not until they climbed into the salt grass did they dare look back.

The ogres continued pounding the star and had soon pummeled a crater into the sand. Yet the star still sang. Its music, undulant as water shadows, trembled in the air brighter for the beating, feeding off the furor of the ogres.

Black lightning uncoiled from the star-flung sky and blasted a gravel bar, spraying hot pebbles into the huddle of ogres. The roaring explosion and the gashing hurt of the flying rocks scattered the big hominids. They fled up the beach and bent around to behold with fear the arrival of Ralli-Faj.

Out of the momentary blackness of the shadowstroke, a bodiless mask floated. Fashioned into faceted flesh of dark amber and red epoxy, it gazed with empty sockets. Slowly, deliberately, moving with human speed and at a man's height over the water, it approached the crater where the fallen star lay.

A greenish vapor solidified to hands in the physical space where they belonged on the invisible body, and the warlock bent and picked up the star. The green hands raised the singing stone face-outward and turned it so that its glassy visage was visible to all on the beach.

The music changed in the warlock's grip. The star sang lower and more vesperal as if from the narrow confines of sleep.

Nobody danced. The energy of desire dimmed. With processional slowness, Ralli-Faj carried the raised star up the beach, past the cowering ogres and the dunes, and into the swamp tunnels that led toward the Palace of Abominations.

The power of the celestial stone filled the warlock with hungry excitement. This was the purest concentration of Charm he had ever experienced. But it was raw Charm unrefined by the mechanics of hex-gems or conjure-wire. It was his to shape, his to remake, and he carried it back to his gardens with joy.

On the way, he listened to its sidereal song. It sang like the wind, grabbing at everything, turning in mid-air like perfume. It sang of no ponderable thing but the distant lamps of the stars, the sparks of Charm running out of the Abiding Star and down into the darkness.

When the Palace of Abominations came into view with its skewed and tilted scaffolds crammed with cacodemons, the song of the fallen star changed again. The music grew sullen. It sang grimly of the door in the air that opened upon infinite spaces and silences – the portal through which the cacodemons had come to Irth.

Ralli-Faj tilted the star so that its music aimed at the roosting demons and laughed to watch them stir and fret. The starsong excited them with intimations of the chartless distances they had climbed to bask here in the fecund rays of the Abiding Star.

The warlock lowered the stone when the glaring pack began to sing along, more informed than he of the evil pleasures of the Dark Shore that caulked their ravenous hearts with nostalgia. The sound of their crying crawled through his blood like spiders searching for his heart.

He hurried into his maze garden, and the singing star changed its tune again. Among the blue and green glass walls and the topiary shrubs illuminated by crystal spheres, the music lilted serenely. The green hands lowered the fallen star to a bed of sand raked in annulate pastels. The hands disappeared, the floating mask turned to smoke and wisped away, chewed by the wind.

Ralli-Faj woke inside his own hung skin. Framed by boulders of chrysoprase, agate, and chalcedony, the fallen star sat in its bed of colored sand directly in his line of sight. Its tranquil music poured into the fragrant air thick as hot cane, surrounding him with a sugared heat that offered deeper raptures of trance.

But the warlock wanted something more than trance. The blue tongue in his mouth-hole sparked a command: 'S-see me!'

The singing stopped. Silence penetrated the garden like a bell's clarity. Then the fiercely alien face opened its pink eyes. Silver rays of coherent Charm shot from its pupils directly into the vacant sockets of Ralli-Faj's limp skin.

The warlock screamed, a vascular cry that sliced so sharply through the air it scattered the cacodemons from their high perches. The cutting shriek slashed distances, penetrating the marsh and crossing the dunes in a sudden rush of anguish that vanished over the sea without a single echo as if the dark had taken back what belonged.

The ogres cringed, and the scavengers gaped about with fright. 'What is that?' Dogbrick asked, hands over his ears.

'It is the warlock's cry,' Owl Oil answered. She sat in the salt grass, back propped against a sandy hummock of seagrape. Her tired face looked scalded glossy red where the fallen star's eyebeams had struck her. Even in the starglow, the burns showed crimson. 'He is hurting himself with Charm. Hurting himself stronger.'

After the frightful appearance of Ralli-Faj, many scavengers had panicked and fled, and the ogres and Whipcrow ranged up and down the strand collecting them and driving them back to work. No one had disturbed Tywi and Dogbrick yet, and they crouched protectively beside Owl Oil. She had just woken from her stupor and looked wrung.

'You all right?' Tywi asked, frowning, yet relieved to see her alert. 'What happened to you?'

The crone's head lolled backward, and Dogbrick offered her water from his flagon. She waved it away. 'I'm well,' she said, and her voice sounded vibrant. 'I took Charm from the fallen star. My body has not yet adjusted. But it will soon, and I'll be stronger than ever.'

'You took Charm?' Tywi asked, bewildered.

'This body is a skin of light, isn't it?' Dogbrick asked. 'We saw the shadow of your true self. You're a Peer.'

'Yes.' She rubbed her temples and blinked focus into her eyes. 'I am Rica the Conjurer.'

'Rica—' Dogbrick passed a look of awe to Tywi who frowned back with perplexity. 'She is the Ladyship of the Reef Isles!'

Tywi bowed her head. 'My lady—'

Rica stopped her with a firm hand to her shoulder. 'I must remain Owl Oil or my struggle against Wrat is forfeit.'

'Others saw you,' Dogbrick warned.

Rica sighed. 'It was a chance I had to take. I needed the Charm. There are so many who will suffer and die without it.'

'You have amulets to hold this Charm?' Dogbrick queried.

'I used my last hex-gem to heal you many days ago,' she replied. 'No. I don't require amulets to hold Charm. I am trained in the internal arts. I hold Charm in my body.'

'You got to run,' Tywi urged.

'Where would I go, child?' Rica shook her head firmly. 'This is my dominion. The only worthy escape open to me is death, and I am determined to stay alive long enough to see Wrat and his monsters destroyed.'

'But Charm don't work against them,' Tywi said with palpable fright. 'You got to run, my lady.'

'Charm is not our only weapon.' Rica nodded sagely to her two companions. 'Wrat's devils bleed at the bite of a sword.'

'Is this true?' Dogbrick asked, astonished.

'I have seen it in trance,' Rica assured him. 'Lord Drev and others across Irth are discovering this lethal truth. The fight has just begun.'

'I'm scared for you,' Tywi confessed. 'If Ralli-Faj finds you here with us . . .'

'Be afraid for us all,' Rica answered with sober alertness. 'The warlock has the fallen star.'

'What you mean?' Tywi asked. 'What is that thing?'

'It is not like the stars of the Gulf.' Dogbrick relayed what he knew. 'Those are giant spheres of burning gas. This entity is much smaller. It grew in the aura of the Abiding Star out of Charm and the void.'

'Dogbrick is right,' Rica said. 'It is a creature that lives in the ethers between Irth and the Abiding Star. It is a concentration of raw Charm. In the hands of a warlock such as Ralli-Faj, it can be the source of astonishing power. Listen! Listen to the strength it gives him.'

A bull-roar throbbed in the distance, a mournful lowing. It was Ralli-Faj absorbing the Charm of the fallen star. The twin beams of energy had filled the holes of his slack face with golden light, and he bellowed with the pain from the power that was expanding inside his shriveled form.

The human leather hung on its stick stirred as in a stiff breeze. Like an inflating balloon, the empty fingers plumped, the limbs swelled. Slowly, the warlock's empty body filled with Charm. His face of green fungus distended and jutted into skull-contours of cruel aspect. Swollen strength flared through his torso sculpting a wedge of taut muscle and grooved ribs solid as any living man.

The eyes of the fallen star closed, exhausted of Charm and song, and Ralli-Faj stood tall, his ebony skin, almost blue, stretched tightly to its human limits. His naked form stepped forward, and the stick that once propped him fell to the ground. The vitreous bulbs of his eyes recessed under browbone and epicanthic folds, and from their centers, inkdrops swirled and dilated and hardened abruptly to dark irises keen with malefic intelligence.

Whole again in every detail, the warlock raised his arms and released an exultant howl. The cacodemons on the soaring derricks replied with wild shrieks.

Ralli-Faj wiped the green fungus from his bald head and gazed down at the inert star and its glassy, off-human features. 'Rest,' he said in a dense voice. 'Later you will sing for me again.'

Giddy with his new freedom, the warlock marched through his garden with arms outstretched, touching the shrubs, fingering blossoms, running his hands over the cool glass walls. He broke into a run laughing with resonant glee as his bare feet gripped the grass and his legs powered him along the wending lanes.

Packed with Charm, there was no limit to his stamina, and when he came to the helical ladder that ascended to the torture tiers, he bounded up them. The ever-dying hung mutely in their amber cages. He pressed his giddy face up against each one, kissing their suffering with his joy. The juxtaposition of mortal opposites, of his vibrant well-being and their dismal suffering electrocuted him with desire.

*I live!* Over 200,000 days of life rejoiced in him. To his Charmed eyes, each day he knew on Irth watched him like a face in the crowd, and he remembered every one of them. They basked in his lurid health. Later, they would chant the choral memories that had sustained him all his many days, and great among them would be this day, when a piece of heaven came into his hands.

In the fallen star, he possessed sufficient Charm to live another 200,000 days. Or, should he choose to gamble, he might invest as much as half that power to depose Wrat – if he could find the man's vulnerability.

'*Everything made can be unmade,*' he sang as he hugged the pain-cage of Baron Fakel. The man watched him woefully from his contorted foetal embrace, his noble features a blear in the bloodsmoke. 'And somethings unmade – made again!'

With lavish laughter, Ralli-Faj shoved away and climbed spryly among the trestle rungs. He swung apelike along the scaffold struts to the tilted skyway ramps where the cacodemons watched him with reptile attentiveness.

He moved spryly into their midst. He breathed deeply of their dry sour musk and danced ecstatically among them. His hands touched their jaw-heavy grins and their talons like scythes. And he giggled like a child to think how well they would serve him if there were a way to usurp Wrat.

Starlight shone out from the warlock's tight pupils and touched the eel-lobed brows of the cacodemons, searching for knowledge of the Dark Lord. But all he saw were his own hot eyes staring back. They were, one and all, black mirrors.

If he angled his needle vision queerly, he could peer past the dark barrier, and he saw a shadowface, the same face in each demon skull staring out from behind the mask of fangs. By waving his charmlight, the warlock underlit that face and recognized the weasly features of Wrat.

Ralli-Faj dimmed his penetrating stare and looked away from Wrat's mocking sneer. Quickly, he made his way back through the raspy herd of cacodemons, not laughing, not touching them. On the open ramp, he hurried on without looking back.

The cacodemons grinned and watched after him with a cold fidelity.

## Strange Planet, Dying

❧❦❧

Emboldened by his previous successes in visiting Tywi, Drev again left his body among the river canes, watched over by Ripcat. Like a cloud blowing across empty sky, he sailed. Reef isles crawled below. Clots of stars reflected in the slick water between the dark land masses, and the islands appeared like strewn puzzle pieces.

He gazed upward into the unspeakable darkness among the stars, from whence the cacodemons came. They were born out of the forgotten. All that had fallen away from the light of Irth into the void had congealed in the eternal cold to these monsters. They were the living void.

The wizarduke's anxiety thickened further when the Cloths of Heaven appeared out of the foggy country. The broken sphinxes and the smashed crockery of temples evoked a stormy sorrow in him, and foreboding began like remote music.

Drev knew then he should turn about. In the transparency of time, he viewed the Palace of Abominations. The massive pyramid rose spectral white above the anarchy of the swamp. At its crest, a circular railpath hung like a vast medallion beneath an organic, vulval doorway that opened on darkness.

391

His vision penetrated. Within he saw Ralli-Faj, an empty skin strapped with cords and talismans to a pair of stilts.

*Tok. Tok. Tok.*

The stilts stepped closer, carrying the human pelt near enough for Drev to clearly discern the crisped flesh around the warlock's vacant sockets and the ghost fire in his woeful mouth.

Drev pulled away from this vision with a shudder that nearly broke his trance and returned him to his body. He rooted his attention on the terrain. Mangrove archipelagoes seeped fog whose tendrils reached across the spans of glossy water between the islands like strands of a snaring web.

Ill omens loomed everywhere in the star-steamed landscape, and he considered going back. But then the labor camp that held Tywi rose into sight. The pyramid of evil cacodemons seemed far away. It was a distant, pale wedge in the acrid darkness and appeared less threatening than he had feared. He soared down into the ramshackle camp, intent on finding Tywi and Ripcat's philosopher, Dogbrick.

The huts stood empty, the camp occupied only by the ill, two attending healers, and an ogre on patrol. The wizarduke flitted unseen among them, following the strand of Charm that bound him to his fateful double.

Skimming over a rutted path through a tunnel of hanging moss and mist, he spotted starlit dunes, white horizons of surf, and the diminutive figures of laborers toiling over the tide wrack. He accelerated, and at that very instant, the space ahead of him wobbled like a sheet in the wind – and Ralli-Faj on his stilts stepped out of nothing.

The warlock had sensed Drev when the wizarduke first came over the horizon. Chance alone had directed his searching gaze in that direction this night as he had paced the Dark Lord's adytum. The chamber atop the pyramid had only just been completed, and Ralli-Faj had carried himself there on his charmed stilts to inspect its construction. As he had peered out the slot doorway, admiring the view of the Cloths of Heaven, he spied the thin ray of an astral intruder.

Ralli-Faj had no notion who this intruder was until he floated down from the pyramid and confronted him in the swamp. The flimsy charmlight tried to elude him, wisping off like so much swamp haze.

The warlock raised the leg of one stilt. The black magic that Hu'dre Vra had installed in him made the sharp point of the stilt an irresistible destination, capturing from out of the air the tenuous ghost that had flitted into his camp.

Lord Drev veered away from the warlock, but an invisible hand gripped him and held him fast. Slowly, despite his fiercest efforts to break the spell of his trance and wake again in his body, Drev slid closer to the skin hung on its sharp stilts.

Suddenly, he was pulled very near to the cracked, reptilian flesh. He felt himself scrutinized by the eyeless face with its sunken nosehole and gaping mouth tongued in flame. Then recognition flared through the warlock, and the green fur of fungus that splotched his draped body glowed with astonishment.

'Wiz-z-zard of Hovernes-s-s!' The warlock's voice spit like hot oil.

*Ralli-Faj*, Drev greeted him with forced bravura. *I have sought you out to enlist your aid.*

A dark laugh gleamed from the warlock. 'I am no s-simpleton, Drev. You have come to s-spy out the Dark Lord's-s palace. And I have caught you!'

*I come to you as your fellow Peer*, Drev pleaded. *Surely by now you have heard, the cacodemons are not invulvernable. Swords cut them. Arrows can pierce their hide. We can fight them. Ralli-Faj, help us smash the claw of the invader.*

'Oh, the Dark Lord will be mos-st pleas-s-sed to hear your judgment of his-s flaws-s. Come, Drev. I mus-st get you in a container before you thin away to nothing.'

The warlock jerked forward and stab-walked down the marsh road, dragging Drev's wraith behind.

Drev could do nothing to extricate himself from the powerful grip of the alien magic. He helplessly watched the pale boles of swamp trees float by.

*With your help, we can rid Irth of these monsters,* he called out again.

'S-save your s-strength, wiz-z-zard,' Ralli-Faj advised coldly. 'After what your great-grandfather did to my dominion, I would s-sooner ally with hell than you.'

*You have, Ralli-Faj! Wrat is the living void. He will destroy everything.*

'And you will be there to s-see,' the warlock promised. 'I have created for you a s-special punish-shment to pleas-se my lord, Hu'dre Vra. The Pain Chain!'

Ralli-Faj surged with joy. On the pivot of this moment turned the promise of the fallen star. The Dark Lord would reward him richly for this prize. His future was assured and felt enormous. By that deep, shining lake of time, he strolled toward the gigantic pyramid with the doorway at its peak, long, indrawn and folded as a vaginal effigy.

Once within the watery glass walls of the lower enclosure, the warlock went directly to the rock garden where the fallen star sat in its bed of bright, ringed sand. The sad smoke of its song curled in the air.

'Behold, wiz-z-zard!' Ralli-Faj crowed and inhaled the Charm of the fallen star. His flaccid skin puffed up with charmwind so mightily that the straps fixing him to the crossbar burst and the stilts fell away.

The warlock dropped to his feet, whole and naked, a gleaming figure tan as burnished wood. His sockets blazed with heat and filled with a smoky swirl resembling eyes.

Drev stood immobilized by the warlock's magic, mind racing for routes of escape. Charm from the fallen star beat like the wind's vibration, and the entity's pink, fierce eyes peered directly at him, fully aware of his presence.

*Help me—* He appealed to the fallen being.

Ralli-Faj boomed laughter. He wrapped his muscled body in a scarlet robe, then spoke in a voice no longer frayed. 'This star cannot help itself. How then will it help you, wizard?' Laughter boomed again, and the warlock seized the misty shawl of Drev's ectoplasmic body in his charmed hand and dragged him out of the garden.

Up a wide curving rampway of stone, Ralli-Faj marched, waving Drev behind him like a victory banner.

Drev saw cells set into the stone walls and sealed in amber jolt past him as they climbed. Smeared human shadows floated within a swirling of lymph and bloodsmoke. Torn faces pressed against the brown glass, faces ripped almost to skulls.

The rampway spiraled upward to an enormous notch twenty yards high, where the night hung its chains of stars. They strode through that portal outside on to the brink of a walkway whose undressed stone plunged straight down the face of the pyramid toward a rusted winding engine and its train of corroded iron carriages.

Ralli-Faj stepped over the brink and, defiant of gravity, moved down that vertical path. 'I do wish we had more time to converse, cousin Drev, but as it is, your body of light grows dim. In here, the Dark Lord's magic will sustain you until your body arrives – and Hu'dre Vra himself comes to retrieve you.'

A blistered metal door squealed open in the metal carriage behind the winding engine, and the warlock hurled Drev's astral body into the black interior. The pain began even before the warped door slammed back into place and the engine shrieked into laborious motion.

Seamless as a flame, the hurt covered every sentient point of Drev's being. It ate like silence, voraciously and deep.

Lord Drev lost his mind at once but not his consciousness. He remained fully alert and exquisitely sensitive to the pure agony that owned him. Yet all power of reflection fled. Pain had become his being and awareness his overshadow.

Outside the grime-streaked portholes, the fixed stars and the tumult of the swamp flew by in turns as the Chain hurled around its clanking circuit, first up the face of the pyramid and then down. At the top of its climb, under the gate to Hu'dre Vra's adytum, the pain stopped. This proffered several moments of painless awareness in which to anticipate the plunging rush into irreconcilable pain. Randomly, the polarity of suffering and surcease alternated. The cycle was designed to baffle the wizard, to confuse all thought but the experience of hurt itself.

Drev screamed in various voices. His ghost-throat cried, painting the air in twenty colors of misery.

The warlock heard him and danced gleefully in the adytum, danced without stopping through the night and all the following day into the next night. He stopped only briefly, to dispatch a flock of cacodemons. Soon they returned with what the warlock had said they would find – the physical body of Lord Drev.

It had come floating up on the nocturnal tide above Nhat, bound for the Gulf, and the demons identified it and delivered it to the dancing warlock. He clasped the corpse like a lost brother and with a shout drove the rigor mortis from it.

Ralli-Faj escorted the wizardduke's soulless body through the colossal notch in the wall of the pyramid and down the vertical face of raw stone. At his gesture, the hurtling Chain slowed and eventually clattered to a stop so that its first carriage waited before him.

He yanked the door open and found Drev's soul like a broken wing on the tarnished floor. Deftly, the warlock plucked it up and jammed it into place in its own body.

Drev awoke, startled.

Colors throbbed. Sounds came in waves.

'The Dark Lord . . .' Ralli-Faj spoke in fragments, his rubbery face with its milky eyes pressed close, smelling of burned cloves: ' . . . comes this day to face you and . . . Peers become one with the dust of those whose days built the Cloths of . . . meanwhile, ride the Pain Chain . . . and so be gone!'

The rusted door clanged shut, and the metal hull shook with a desultory bong, then lurched forward, throwing him to the back of the carriage. A whistle pierced the loud metallic screams from the wheels and the rattling of the tracks, and the pain began again. Only this time, the hurt cut deeper, for it sliced into his living flesh.

Sprawled belly down on the buckled metal floor of the shaking carriage, impaled by black magic, he poured his suffering into a cry that spilled forth from him all at once and always.

With the growing blue of the skies, Ripcat worried for Drev. The wizarduke's body lay inert in the canes. No breath disturbed the fur at the back of the hand that the beastman held beneath the duke's nostrils. No pulse knocked in the duke's neck under his jaw.

Lord Drev of Ux, Duke of Dorzen, wizard of Hoverness, was dead.

Ripcat sat with the corpse all day, sorrow a mist in his ears, uncertainty a film on his heart. He felt sad for the dead man who had lost his life for love. He had shown the thief bravery, sorrow, deep caring and none of the arrogance the people on the warrens expected from Peers. Also, he took with him his passion to destroy Wrat. And that left the Cat pondering what he could hope to do without the wizard's expertise and direful rage.

Flies like black jewels mizzled the duke's face, and the thief brushed them away. He would at least have to continue on to Nhat, to free Dogbrick from the labor camp – and Tywi as well.

*But how?*

He unsheathed the sword Taran that the wizarduke had bequeathed him. Its lightness in his hand felt hopeless against the future's heavy odds.

Carrion eaters stood in the trees wrapped in their black wings, watching for him to abandon the corpse. A pack of hairless cadaver dogs with long heads and scorched faces prowled the riverbank, attracted by the carrion eaters. They fanned out through the cane, circling the dead thing.

Ripcat drove them off with flourishes of the gold sword. He moved lithely around the dead man in a slow protective dance until dusk and the tide of rising.

Drev's body floated off among the night's bright tinsels. Ripcat saluted it with the sword Taran. Silence was his prayer as the corpse lifted away, deep in the hand of space.

Ripcat sheathed the sword, strapped it to his back, slung the firelock over his shoulder, and went again his solitary way.

The power wand Leboc had given him repelled weariness and granted him the strength to avoid sleep. He journeyed south among the reef isles. Nourished by Charm and the wetland's bounty, he moved swiftly. By day, he crossed the islands, avoiding roads and villages, alert to presences. At night, when the tide withdrew and the coral bridges rose, he waded between the islands without benefit of lantern or torch, relying solely on night vision.

Unseen by any, he saw all. In the swamp, he slinked through the attic of the jungle, far above the boggy floor, attentive to the full compass of sky and terrain. When he doubted direction, he unsheathed the sword Taran.

'Show me the way to Tywi,' he intoned, evoking his memory of her from the Qaf.

The sword shimmered with blunt radiance and, by the intensity of its vibrancy in his hand, he fathomed direction. It guided him among the numerous isles to a feverish jungle of gigantic trees hunched under heavy manes of moss and bearded like teachers of sadness.

A charmless woman lay sprawled unconscious in one of these obscure alcoves. He would never have seen her in that slum of shadows and mossy veils if the sword had not taken him directly to her.

She wore an amulet tunic tattered almost to lace, and it was to this frayed web of conjure-wire and hex-circuits that the sword had been attracted. That and the firelock she hugged identified her as a Peer. Her features, bruised, streaked with swamp mud and swollen from insect bites, offered only a mask of despair.

Ripcat tapped her vine-lashed shoes with the sword, but she did not rouse. He stabbed the sword into the peaty ground and bent close enough to discern that she was alive, then removed the power wand from his waistband and placed it in her hand.

It did nothing. She was too weak – dying.

The thief examined the tarnished mesh of her tunic and found contacts for the power wand in the collar. He attached the amber rod and again nothing happened.

He poured rain water from his flagon and began washing her face, looking for wounds his cursory examination had missed. The swollen features twitched alert when the dripping water activated contact with the power wand and Charm coursed into her febrile body.

She jolted alert and swung her firelock to bear on the beastman crouching over her.

Ripcat retreated behind the sword Taran, hands raised defensively. 'I am a friend,' he said in an indigo voice that helped the wand's Charm soothe the frightened woman. 'I used my power wand to bring you around. You were dying.'

The woman put a hand to her collar and lowered the firelock, her puffed face already beginning to deflate. 'You saved my life.' She spoke softly, distractedly, as if listening to a riff of dreaming. 'But my brother – Poch. Have you seen him? I lost him in the jungle.'

He shook his head. 'Only you.'

She peered in the niello eye charm dangling from her left shoulder, found it dead, tried the other. It, too, remained opaque and no fiddling with the net of conjure-wire helped.

'I must find him,' she mumbled blearily, then caught herself as Charm came on stronger, having finished its work with her vital organs. Her gaze sharpened. 'Who are you?'

'Ripcat,' he answered, standing up from his crouch. 'But I didn't save you. It was the duke's sword that found you. I'm only its unhappy heir.'

She sat up taller and rose to her knees, looking both at the beastman and the sword standing in the ground before him. 'That is the sword Taran.'

'Yes.'

'*Heir?*' She rose to her feet, consciousness firming to clarity. 'If you are heir to his sword, then you must be an ally of Lord Drev.'

'I was his ally,' he replied. 'Lord Drev is dead.'

The woman sagged, but the mounting Charm in her tunic caught her. Despair at this grim news sharpened to an edge of determination: *This nightmare must end!*

She offered her hand to Ripcat. 'I am Jyoti, margravess of Odawl. I owe you a life–debt, Ripcat. So now you must tell me: Are we both allies against the same enemy?'

He marveled at the effectiveness of her amulet tunic as it distributed Charm vitally throughout her body, healing and cleansing her even as he watched. He took her hand and gazed into a pale, freckled countenance of rage without cruelty. She was a fury, a virtue of violence, controlled by a wider purpose. He liked her at once.

She returned his respect, clasping his hand strongly, when he acknowledged: 'Lord Drev's enemies are mine.'

Under the beards of the forest giants, they sat and told their stories.

While he spoke, she was grateful for the Charm he had given her, for it helped her hide the surprised fascination she felt at his physical appearance. All her life in Arwar Odawl she had had contact with beastfolk, from childhood playmates to her palace guards. But none had ever intrigued her as immediately and engrossingly as did this feline man. As she learned about his amnesia, his plaintive features seemed to emerge from a human depth deeper than his bestial traits, and she wanted to help him remember himself.

He mentioned Dogbrick, and she recalled the voluble philosopher, the thoughtful Dog who had escorted them out of Saxar so very long ago it seemed. Charm stitched their fates. And in this she found hope, a famished expectation that survival and even a just end to this nightmare were possible.

*I'm drunk on Charm*, she allowed and grew more sober with the realization, *I should be dead.*

The strong feelings this stranger had begun to stir in her, she decided, were no more than the rush of Charm into her starved body. When her turn came to recount her history of stupendous loss, she related it matter-of-factly.

Ripcat began to wonder as he listened if perhaps the sword Taran had led him to this woman: Perhaps while searching for the dead duke's Tywi, the magical blade had instead located his own soul double in Jyoti. He wanted to believe that. Her creaturely presence and her ardor attracted him. She looked not at all like the sable-tressed woman of his dreams, yet she inspired the same unanimous desire in him.

*How can that be?* he asked himself and searched for common traits. He found precious few and decided that she displayed the same spirit as his dream lover amd was worthy of respect, because in her actuality and mortality, Jyoti was his eternal soul's shadow. When he then learned that she had been trained as a warrior, he understood that the sword had found her to fill Drev's absence.

He unstrapped the scabbard from his back and placed it beside the sword Taran. 'Lord Drev's sword belongs to you.'

Jyoti stood and went to the sword. At this moment, her brother was somewhere in Nhat, alive or, just as likely, dead. Cacodemons haunted the Irth. All her past was ashes. These facts defeated the enthusiasm of Charm coursing again through her body, and, unenthralled by any hope that she could ever solve these problems yet grateful for the chance to try, she put her hand on the hilt and promised her life, her death, everything to the blade's cause.

She stared past the sword to Ripcat.

'I will go with you,' the beastman said. 'If you will allow.'

The joy she felt looking at him, lithe, blue-furred, empty of

Charm, full of animal divinity, was her magnificent astonishment at finding herself alive once again and Charmed. She would not refuse herself to this sword or to the graceful messenger who had brought it to her.

'Let's find my brother.'

Ralli-Faj stood in the hot daylight, feeling the Charm leaking out of his pores with a chill radiance. Slowly, as the Abiding Star crossed the sky, his physical body deflated while his mind rode the updraft of Charm far above the day sky.

Atop the buffeting atmosphere, in the Charmflow from the Abiding Star, the warlock knew rapture and emptiness. His message to the Dark Lord announcing the capture of Drev had yet to be answered, and he spent this interval of waiting disengaged from Irth.

When Hu'dre Vra's call came, little had changed down below: On the bright, triangular face of the Palace of Abominations, the Pain Chain still clanked along its endless track bearing Drev's ponderous freight of suffering. The camp's prisoners still slept in their huts, resting for the labors of the coming night. And the cacodemons came and went from the flues of the pyramid, completing their construction chores.

Only Ralli-Faj's body had changed. Fully deflated, it lay draped like a flesh rag over a supporting stick. He gazed out from his empty sockets with his Charmed eyes and saw an apparition of the Dark Lord before him.

Hu'dre Vra's imposing ebony armor floated translucently, imprinted over the garden's raked sand and the boulders of agate. His voice vibrated like a storm's tremor. 'You have done very well, Ralli-Faj. Oh, you have done very well indeed. I shall be in Nhat at first light tomorrow to inspect your prisoner – to reward you.'

The image slanted into sunlight and vanished.

In his heightened, Charmed state, Ralli-Faj's awareness reached deeper than the Dark Lord's phantom voice. The warlock saw the Dark Lord in Mirdath. His armor fell away like dead petals, and the famished nakedness of Wrat emerged.

Webs of mist from the cascades blew through the air on to the balcony where Hu'dreVra had stood to project his message to the warlock in Nhat. With a shiver, Wrat turned his back on the chill, vibrant air of the open portico with its panoramic vista of the Falls of Mirdath.

'The hunt is over,' he announced to Thylia, who awaited his pleasure among silken bolsters and squabs. 'That skin without bones found him last night sneaking around the ogres' camp.'

'Now that he is in hand,' Thylia beckoned with her body from where she lay, her black diamond eyes gazing at him down the length of her valiant nakedness, 'tarry with me. I have only begun to thank you for saving me from the Spiderlands – and for forgiving me after losing your prey.'

'My prey is in a cage of pain this moment,' Wrat leered. 'He suffers even as I steep myself in your exquisite and Charming expertise, witch.'

He stepped down into a round chamber hung with diaphanous veils of indigo. This was the pleasure altar in the palace of the sorceress Lyna, Countessa of Mirdath. Every 222 days, her witches and sages copulated on this dais in a sacred ritual of Charmed trance, a tantric rite with origins lost in pretalismanic times. It delighted the irreverent Dark Lord to take his pleasure here, and with the witch *queen*, no less!

As for Lyna – her corpulence, her dominion's perverse icon of beauty, quivered in hiding somewhere among the mud villages on the paddies below. His cacodemons were closing in. Since the savage and total destruction of the City in the Falls, the people had lost hope of salvation from the Peers, and informants abounded throughout Mirdath.

'Why do you think Drev was there?' Wrat asked as he climbed toward her over lustrous pillows and cushions.

'To spy on you,' she whispered and drew him closer. 'He sought you where you would most logically be – were it not for me.'

The telepathic voyeurism of Ralli-Faj wrinkled away as the witch's arms enclosed Wrat. Physical exigencies disgusted him. That was why he had sacrificed his viscera, burned it all away in a rapture of Charm, hollowed himself to a husk with celestial pleasures.

*Who needs the darkness of flesh*, he moaned to himself, *when one is a portion of light, a blazing star, a mind? Only the weak.*

With his own apparition, he summoned a cacodemon to set his flayed flesh upon his stilts. The tentacles worked far more deftly than any of his human slaves, and he quickly found himself standing upright.

*Tok. Tok. Tok.*

He stepped over to the sand garden where the fallen star sat in its bed of colorful silica. It slept, and he chose not to wake it. He wanted to avoid calling attention to it. Perhaps the Dark Lord would ignore it entirely, and he could keep it for his own raptures and strategies.

*Tok. Tok. Tok.*

He walked up the spiral rampway, checking the amber cells of prisoners along the way. The neon pink of the bloodsmoke swirling about their embalmed bodies informed him that still they lived, still they suffered.

Satisfied, he hurried on his way upward to the vast notch that exited the pyramid near its top. *Tok. Tok. Tok.* He stab-walked down the face of the pyramid, held in place by the same black magic that spun the winding engine and its carriages on their impossible arc.

Ralli-Faj knew well the reputation of the wizarduke as a Charmaster in the Lazor tradition. That was a pragmatic school of wizardry that the warlock did not underestimate, for he had been trained in it himself – over 150,000 days ago, as one of Lazor's own disciples. He had to be certain that Drev remained enthralled and had not devised an escape.

From the observation ramp, he watched the Chain slash past on its demonic rush toward nowhere. In the first carriage, Drev stood plastered against the long window, his hair like rays, his swarthy face smeared upon the glass in a slug-mouthed howl of mad, unbearable suffering.

The warlock smiled. His leather face did not move, but the blue flame flickered brighter in its mouthhole. He had designed the carriage so that his victims were forced to display their anguish: The only wild hope of minimizing the chaotic inevitability of pain was against the pane.

*Tok. Tok. Tok.*

The warlock staggered away, reeling with giddiness. He returned to where the fallen star slept and considered waking it. He wanted to puff up himself on its Charm and celebrate – but a chill shadowed through him. Someone approached his garden.

He sensed the unctuous anxiety of Whipcrow and pronounced the intonation that unmazed the glass walls surrounding his private garden. In the few moments that Whipcrow required to find his way among the pollarded fruit trees and sinuously espaliered vines, the warlock saw into his simple soul.

*Ah – another prize!* Ralli-Faj flared happily when he received the news that several informers among the scavengers had seen the healer Owl Oil drop her skin of light. The Ladyship of Sorcery, Rica, Duchess of Nhat, was already in his grasp!

Whipcrow skipped into the garden. 'My lord warlock, I have news—'

'I have already dispatched a cacodemon to bring Rica to us,' Ralli-Faj silenced his manager. 'Your presence affirms your loyalty to our Dark Lord. So come, Whipcrow – come with me to behold how our enemies journey to zero, so slowly, so very slowly.'

Whipcrow blinked and closed his mouth in a haze of awe.

*Tok. Tok. Tok.*

The warlock climbed again the wide, stone spiral. Whipcrow accompanied him proudly, disguising his horror at the sight of the embalmed Peers swimming blindly in their scarlet effluvia.

Halfway up, a screaming came. Moments later, a cacodemon flew by, dragging Rica in its claws and tendrils. The demon faces in the beast's thorax chewed at her, and as she whipped past, her face bleated a cry of hurt.

The warlock hurried his pace, and Whipcrow had to run to keep up, the sleeves of his black cowl flapping like wings. A mammoth portal swung into view, and the manager's run slowed to a procession of astonishment. Outside, thermal clouds soared over swampland and the afternoon lay sprawled across alluvial plains of golden waterways.

Rica lay in a puddle of her torn garments, her limbs drained of rigor, her slack face pressed to one cheek against the polished stone. Beside the enormous pylon, she was a mote, and the cacodemon hovering above her a bigger speck.

*Tok. Tok. Tok.*

Ralli-Faj walked his stilts to the brink and over. Whipcrow stopped to see him disappear beyond the edge. The cacodemon collected Rica, and she thrashed alert but could not extricate herself from its hooked and suctioned clasp. With a baleful wail, she disappeared as the demon dragged her through the giant doorway.

Whipcrow edged himself to the brink and gazed down at stilted Ralli-Faj and the viperous cacodemon dragging Rica into the face of gravity – toward the Pain Chain that he had watched from afar writing its zeroes at the top corner of the pyramid.

The Chain slowed with a metallic yowl. The draft of the gliding carriages lifted the empty arms of Ralli-Faj. As the first carriage drifted past, Whipcrow saw a man with a face of reckless fright pressed against the oblong window.

The manager pulled away, startled to behold such a paroxysm of torment gazing at him beseechingly. His chest burned hot, his heart igniting with desire in the presence of such power and powerlessness together.

He swung his gaze far across the immense span of the vault and dizzied. A metal door clanged shut with a doomful echo.

When he looked back, two carriages of the Pain Chain had faces smashed against their windows. Their shining distress energized him with unanswerable desire.

Then the Chain squealed and jerked into motion. He rose quickly to his feet and stepped over the threshold, eager to stand in the embrace of the Dark Lord's magic and watch the Chain drag its souls up out of hell and back again.

Predawn clouds piled up in a maritime wind that carried rain on to the beach and battered the ogres' bonfires atop the dunes. Several left their posts early to return to the camp, and only two ogres and Whipcrow remained behind to escort the scavengers back to their huts.

Whipcrow used the power wand of his staff to lash small windspouts off the incoming tide and drive the weary net-crews faster to shore. Since witnessing the torture of Rica and the wizarduke on the warlock's Pain Chain, he felt driven to work the scavengers harder and increase the treasures dragged from the sea.

Everywhere lurked informers. Rica's capture emphasized that truth, and Whipcrow determined to display before them his abject servitude to his masters. He prodded laggard workers with his staff, sparking them sufficient jolts of Charmed pain to make them scurry faster out of the water and up the tidal scarp.

As ever, Dogbrick slogged to the beach last, hauling the nets for two other workers. A windspout Whipcrow had set in motion swept over the beastman and submerged him. He surfaced spitting seawater and missing one of the nets.

'Find it, you muttwit!' Whipcrow shouted against the booming breakers.

Dogbrick dipped under but came up without the lost net. He pushed to shore, too tired to search any further.

Whipcrow's staff met him as he clambered to the beach and jolted him so severely that Dogbrick's fur rose in wet hackles and he howled with wrung hurt.

'Stop it!' Tywi yelled, running from where she had been securing rakes and dragging hooks to the last utility wagon.

Whipcrow saw that the ogres had moved up the beach, herding the laborers. Sure they were not observing him, he touched Tywi with his staff and sent a shock of Charm through her that sat her down stupefied in the wet sand.

Dogbrick snarled, and Whipcrow waved the luminous amber staff before him. 'Come on, muttwit,' the cowled manager challenged. 'Attack me. Go ahead. The ogres will strap you to a hornet hive after you wake up from my blow!'

The thief kept his wrathful yellow eyes on Whipcrow and bent over Tywi. Dogbrick helped her to stand, and she leaned heavily on him until she caught her breath and sensation tingled back into her limbs.

Up the beach they shuffled to the utility cart. Dogbrick helped Tywi into the back among the coils of net and sifting equipment, and he fitted himself to the harness.

'She walks,' Whipcrow demanded. 'Like all the others. No. Better. She pulls!' He yanked her out of the cart and shoved her to the front. Ralli-Faj was too busy with his Pain Chain to care any more what befell any of the prisoners, Whipcrow believed, and he felt less compunction to restrain himself with this scrawny woman who time and again had refused to satisfy him.

The rain came down in sheets as Dogbrick and Tywi pulled the utility cart among the dunes. Whipcrow followed, waving his luminescent staff like a lantern in the starless dark, signaling to the ogres ahead that all went well at the rear.

In the tunnel of swamp trees that led to the camp, the rain had washed out the dirt path, and two pelf wagons loaded with heavy kraken bones had sunk to their axles.

'Leave wagons!' the ogres commanded and waved the scavengers on through the driving rain.

A flash of lightning illuminated the arboreal tunnel so brightly that colors leaped from the foliage: Jade leaves, saffron moss, and scarlet air blossoms appeared out of the gloom, and an ogre fell to its back in the mud. Its small face in its big woolly head scowled in a locked grimace, and a startled moment passed before the second ogre realized its partner had been shot.

Another blue-white dazzle of lightning, and the standing ogre bounded into the air and crashed into the underbrush where it did not move.

'Charmfire!' Whipcrow cried in alarm.

Dogbrick roared to drown out the manager's warning and threw off the cart's harness. Seizing a fallen branch, he confronted Whipcrow, knocked the power staff from his hand, and punched him between the eyes. The blow kicked back the manager's cowl and splashed his spiked hair in a wide fan before he collapsed unconscious.

Tywi untied herself from the harness and squinted into the dark, driving rain. She had been hoping for liberation from the first, yet she had not expected it at this time. Drev's wraith had not returned, and she had begun doubting he ever would. A dream had visited her more than once that he was a human star stretched out in the fiery dark, burning and screaming.

When that nightmare threw her awake, she had peeked through the hut's withes at the radiant white pyramid that rose higher than the swamp. Near its top, she could see a circular façade like the face of a huge clock without hands. Later, when Whipcrow told the camp that this was the Pain Chain Ralli-Faj had built to torment Peers and that it carried Rica and the wizarduke himself, the pain of her dreams sharpened into the waking world.

*Who wields lightning to save us?* Tywi peered into the slashing rain startled, knowing that this was not her Drev who had come to save them.

From out of the dark, twin green eyes sparked and a slender beastface emerged streaked with rainwater. It was Dogbrick's partner, the mysterious thief who had saved her from the trolls in the Qaf. Behind him came the Peer she had helped to escape Saxar, pale, freckled Jyoti. They both carried firelocks, and Jyoti had a long sword strapped to her back.

Most of the scavengers had fled toward the camp after the first ogre fell. Those that remained scattered at the sight of the armed couple. Tywi called after them, 'These are friends!' But the taking of Rica by a cacodemon had stoked fear in all their hearts, and no one returned.

Dogbrick let loose a curving howl of glee at the sight of his partner.

'Silence, Dog!' Jyoti berated. 'We're not away yet.'

Ripcat embraced his friend, and Jyoti hissed for them to hurry away. Approaching the camp had been very difficult, for the ogres had rigged numerous booby traps and alarms throughout the surrounding marsh. Only slow, diligent use of Charm and Ripcat's uncanny senses had enabled them to penetrate the area undetected.

With Ripcat leading, they entered the swamp and moved swiftly over the path they had laid down coming in through the teeming ferns and mangroves. And Jyoti was right to hurry them. Moments later, a dozen ogres swarmed across the flooded path and into the fen.

Darkness and rain impeded pursuit, and the escapees crossed log bridges and then toppled the soft wood into the morass behind them. By the time the cacodemons arrived to continue the search, Ripcat had led them by footfalls light as breaths into a maze of glades where not even an army of demons could find them.

Dawn filtered through the storm clouds with a hyacinth hue, and they paused in a fern holt under a broad awning so dense only a few cold notes of rain came through. From a hummock perch, they scanned the terrain, searching for cacodemons in the violet sky and along the waterpaths and lily-lanes that crossed the swamp in giddy zigzags.

No one followed, though in the far distance they could discern tossing treecrowns where ogres beat the brush.

Jyoti unsheathed the sword Taran. In the soft haze of rain, its gold blade lit the dark cove. She handed the sword to Tywi, who was quavering with exhaustion.

The touch of Charm immediately revived the bedraggled waif.

Ripcat passed his power wand to Dogbrick. Not much charge remained in the wand, yet Dogbrick glowed with gratitude to feel again the warm, effervescent touch of Charm.

Without the sword, Jyoti veered toward despondency. After much difficult labor, she and Ripcat had succeeded in freeing his friend and Lord Drev's Charmed double, but Poch remained missing. All that remained of her family, he had to be found, alive or dead.

The waif Tywi hugged the sword Taran to her breast and gazed up at floating ferns and air plants that dangled like marionettes. The flush of Charm also carried with it Jyoti's contact, and Tywi felt her worry for her brother. At the core of incandescent health and well-being that was Charm resided a telepathic echo to Jyoti's calling. It came clearer to Tywi because she was not looking for it.

'Your brother—' Her mind reached toward where she sensed the boy calling back in reply to his sister. And she glimpsed again the plaintive, worried face she remembered from their meeting on the sooty streets of Saxar. She stood up and pointed the gold sword at a tangled wall of lianas. 'Poch is alive.'

With the blade she parted a curtain of hanging vines and revealed again the mazy waterways – and beyond them, a scrap of order in the tumult of misty swampland: Several pillars mounted by stone sphinxes with broken wings showed the way to the Cloths of Heaven.

'Poch is alive,' Tywi repeated in a voice that sang with certainty. 'And he's in there.'

Ralli-Faj learned of the escape of two prisoners from his labor camp at the same time that the Dark Lord arrived in Nhat. The cacodemons inside the Palace of Abominations sensed the approach of their master, and they began to chitter in singsong rhythms from their perches among the girders of the pyramid.

Their mesmermuric music sifted through the warlock's

gardens and burned him with fright. His hung flesh stood unmoving upon its stilts, and his eyeholes gazed emptily at the cacodemon who had intruded on his rapture to bring him the frightful news. In stunned silence, his mind refused to work.

The slinky demon wavered slowly. It danced to the chant of the others whispering in the silver air. It thought that the warlock might not have heard it the first time, and it repeated the message: 'Two prisoners escaped the camp.'

The raspy voice shredded the warlock's numb shock to raw fear. 'Es-scaped?' his fiery tongue spit. 'Who? How?'

'The thief Dogbrick,' the demon answered, its smaller thoracic faces humming the mounting chant of its brethren, grinning with a crazed bliss. 'And a female factory worker, Tywi. Two intruders with firecharms stunned the ogres and Whipcrow.'

'Intruders-s?' Ralli-Faj fought back panic. 'What intruders-s dare defy our Dark Lord? How many?'

'Two . . .'

'Two!' The warlock's shout cracked from his mouthhole in a spurt of flame. 'How could two overcome the ogres-s?'

'The rain drove most of the ogres to camp,' the cacodemon explained and swayed to the soft singing of its belly mouths. 'The intruders were swift.'

'Who?' Ralli-Faj's voice gusted with fear. 'Who are they?'

'The ogres and Whipcrow remain unconscious. I came at once.'

'Wake them!' The warlock gazed in dismay at the dancing cacodemon. 'Damn the ogres-s dis-s-like for rain – put magic on them! Find out who dared. But do not report here. I mus-s-t meet our lord now. Await me in the camp. Go at once!'

The demon slithered away through the air.

'Wait!' Ralli-Faj called, his mind sprinting to catch up with events. He cursed himself for the complacency that had allowed him to indulge again in rapture after his triumphant seizures of Drev and Rica. 'Find the es-s-caped pris-s-oners-s.'

*Wait again!* He stopped himself, realizing that the Dark Lord would know at once something was amiss if too many of his cacodemons were away. 'Take what demons-s are already on patrol. Find the es-s-caped pris-s-oners-s!'

With the demon gone, Ralli-Faj sank deeper into his shock. Sooner or later, the Dark Lord would learn of this.

*Better later*, he decided, *after the prisoners are recovered and punished.*

The cacodemons' chant shrilled, and by that the warlock knew that Hu'dreVra was moments away. He wanted to receive his lord at the top of the pyramid, in the opulent adytum that he had designed for the master of all Irth.

Using the Charm in his stilts, Ralli-Faj flew through his gardens and up the stone spiral. He glanced only briefly to his sides, to be certain that his prisoners remained immersed in their bloodsmoke. Their scalded faces gazed back blindly from within their transparent crypts.

He arrived at the summit to see the rainy dawn's mint colors streaked with flights of cacodemons. Out of their viperous writhings descended the Dark Lord in his jagged armor with his consort Thylia aflutter in her witch veils.

They lighted upon the curved lip of the vulval gateway, and even Hu'dreVra looked diminutive before the titanic portal with its towering folds of stone. The organic grandeur of the design melded anatomical motifs of labia, ovarian lobes, sphincters, and uteral convolutions to the pure, straight-line geometry of the pyramid and created within its vertex an immense, crystal womb.

The Dark Lord stood unmoving for a lengthy moment, appreciating what he beheld. The adytum's interior shone with a sonorous, watery glow, illuminating languid contours of bare-walled emptiness, curving and folding inward toward a secret candescent core. From there, serene mesmermur music sifted through the chitterings of the demons.

'The interior des-s-ign I leave to your own tas-s-te, my lord,' Ralli-Faj greeted Hu'dreVra. 'I pray this-s pleas-s-es-s you.'

THE DARK SHORE

'I am well pleased,' he conceded, though in fact he preferred the human dimensions of the palaces he had occupied on his tour. Yet he had to admit that this imposing and frightfully bizarre monument was precisely the structure from which he wanted to preside over the dismantling of Irth.

'What do you think of it, my dear?' the Dark Lord queried Thylia.

The witch queen sneered at the obscene architecture. 'I like it not.'

Hu'dre Vra boomed with laughter. 'Of course. It impales the female genitalia, the symbol of fertility, of life, upon the impersonal point of a pyramid, an abstract *thing*. It is a most apt symbol for what I am doing to this world. Job well done, Ralli-Faj!'

'Thank you, my lord.'

'Now show me our prize,' Hu'dre Vra gloated. 'Show me the wizarduke, Lord Drev.'

*Tok. Tok. Tok.*

The warlock on his stilts walked past the Dark Lord and the witch queen, across the labial threshold, and downward, perpendicular to gravity, toward the circular track, the cloacal emblem of all that the Dark Lord intended to eliminate.

The rusty Chain screamed to a halt at the approach of Hu'dre Vra. Thylia stayed behind in the giant vaginal frame of the doorway, gazing with fascination when the doors of the Chain cried open.

She loathed Lord Drev and his entire brood through the enmity that his ancestors had inspired in her people by their brutal insistence on unifying the dominions. And yet – at the sight of him, his flesh greenish white, his haunted eyes staring mindlessly from their sockets – she knew pity.

Her only consolation was that she had kept her silence. As witch queen she was privy to all the secrets of the sages in their sanctuaries and the witches in their covens. She knew from the first how the cacodemons had come to Irth. She knew the secret

414

of the Dark Shore. And she had breathed not a clue of it to Wrat. Amorous distractions, the most vulgar and pruriently simple pleasures, were sufficient to keep him preoccupied. Not once yet had he questioned the blind god Chance who had brought him back to Irth or wondered what roles were played by that god's two companions, Death and Justice.

His sturdy laughter rose up to her from where he confronted his enemy. She watched as he dropped his armor to face Drev as Wrat.

'How long I have anticipated this moment, my lord Drev,' the conqueror spoke with a proud joy. 'At last our roles are reversed. You taste defeat. I triumph!'

Drev knelt with exhaustion, gazing numbly. The Dark Lord infused him with sufficient magic to heal his torn soul. Sentience sharpened again in the wizardduke's features.

'Speak to me, Drev,' Wrat beckoned. 'Tell me exactly how you feel.'

Drev pulled himself upright and stared down at the man, until Wrat made himself taller.

'S-speak to your mas-s-ter,' Ralli-Faj commanded from where he stood looking on.

Drev took a moment to relish the absence of pain. He lifted his face to the chill rain and tasted the sky. Light shafts from broken clouds touched the swamp and ignited cusps of mist. He took in the beauty of the land, the mirror-sheen of the waterways, the muted colors and mulchy fragrances of the wet morning.

Then he looked into Wrat's malicious, close-set eyes and said calmly, 'You are a deformed man. And everything you do is deformed.'

'Ha!' Wrat pushed his sharp face closer. 'And who was it deformed me? The Peers! So that they could dwell comfortably in their floating cities, I lived as a scavenger right here in these reef isles. You and your kind deformed me!'

'No, Wrat.' Drev smiled knowingly. 'That is just your excuse to justify the murder that kindles your heart. Even as a Peer you would have been deformed. Regard your slave, Ralli-Faj, a Peer of as noble a lineage as my own.'

Wrat shook his head and showed his wet brown teeth. 'This is far better than I had hoped, my lord Drev. Remember when I killed your sister, Mevea?' His grin widened to see the wizarduke flinch at that memory. 'Recall how I skewered her through the womb with my sword and how she died screaming her curses at me? It was an ugly death.'

Drev reached for Wrat, but tentacles snared his hands and throat and threw him back into the corroded interior of the Pain Chain. The cacodemon who had seized him coiled atop the car and hung its gruesome head down to watch him with its tiny spider eyes.

'And what of those curses from Mevea?' Wrat asked, leering derisively. 'They did not stop me. Here I am. And there you are.'

Wrat laughed when the door slammed shut and Drev flung himself to the window anticipating the pain.

'Have the Chain make several circuits without hurting him,' the Dark Lord commanded. 'I think I should like to play with him for a while.'


Ralli-Faj left Hu'dreVra at the Pain Chain laughing and chortling at the sufferings of Lord Drev. Begging pardon to attend to the business of running the Palace of Abominations, the warlock made his way swiftly to the labor camp.

He floated out of the swamp mists on his stilts and toured the huts. With his faceskin of hollow eyesockets, he peered in at the frightened prisoners. They cowered and gawked back at him with shrill eyes.

Then he drifted to the central courtyard and planted himself at its muddy center.

The camp was so still that he could hear the fine rain sizzling atop the frond roofs and sighing from the marsh where the ogres hid. Afraid to show themselves, they pretended to search the fen trails and bog paths.

Only Whipcrow came forward, leaning heavily on his tall amber staff. He hurried out of the swamp tunnel where the abduction had occurred. Anxiously, he had been waiting for the return of the handful of cacodemons who had fanned out from there across the slough. At the height of his panic, he had actually *prayed* to the Nameless that the demons return with the fugitives in their tentacles before the warlock arrived. Now, as he scurried toward the flayed skin stretched upon its twin talisman poles, he ground between his teeth a curse on the Nameless.

The manager folded back his cowl and lifted his two bruised eyes to Ralli-Faj. 'Oh, powerful warlock, take pity on this pathetic Crow.'

'Who es-s-caped?'

'That mangy philosopher, Dogbrick!' Whipcrow answered with startled repugnance. 'And his servant girl, Tywi.'

'Tell me about them.'

Whipcrow pulled his shoulders to his ears and peered upward at the human hide with a pitiable perplexity. 'He was a thief in Saxar. She was a factory waif. They are gutter lives, my lord. They are unimportant.'

'They are important enough to s-someone for them to be freed at great ris-sk.' A blue spark spat from the warlock and danced briefly in the air. *Somehow*, he knew, *this touches upon Drev's arrival here. Yet how?* 'Who took them?'

'I don't know,' the manager whimpered. 'It was dark. Dogbrick struck me between the eyes.'

The stretched skin offered the silence of an inert thing. Within, Ralli-Faj quivered with rage and fright. Something terrible was amiss, of that he was certain. *But what?* His unknowing infuriated him, even as he coldly dreaded the fury he would face when this incident became known to mad Wrat.

*If I am to be undone by the blunders of ogres and beastmen*, the warlock intoned to himself, peering ragefully down at cowering Whipcrow, *then this sniveling dolt will precede me to hell!*

417

Whipcrow read Ralli-Faj's silence accurately, and he lifted his trembling hand and staff above his woeful face, his blackened eyes sparkling with tears. 'Please, great warlock, take pity on this frightened Crow.'

'In this-s world of cacodemons-s you cry for pity?' The splotches of green fungus on the boneless face of Ralli-Faj darkened to an ominous hue. 'You are not worthy of the humanity to which you pretend, beastman!'

'No!' Whipcrow screamed, sensing what was about to occur. He swung his staff at the warlock on his stilts, and the large power wand splashed to muddy water on contact with the black magic that infused Ralli-Faj.

The manager retreated three paces, shocked by the power to transform Charm into bilge water. With abject terror, he stared at the entity before him and opened his mouth to plead again for his life. But his palate held a bird's tongue and out jumped a bird's raucous cry.

Whipcrow spun about to run away, and the legs beneath him splayed at their ends to claws. His arms erupted to wings. His torso winced tighter. And his head shrank to the stabbing face of a crow.

The bird flew to the edge of the camp and lighted upon a rubbertree bough. From the side of its head, its ebony eyedrop watched the warlock warily. Then it cawed loudly, triumphantly, and spread its wings.

As the crow lifted into flight, the glossy leaves of the rubbertree exploded, and a carrion monkey snatched the bird on the wing. Its greedy claws bit deeper as the nightwings thrashed violently to escape. Then the fierce simian face shrieked fangs and tore apart the screaming bird, dropping loose feathers and gouts of gluey flesh.

Satisfied, Ralli-Faj turned his attention upon the ogres. From out of his naked pelt seeped a green mist. It pooled below him, where the sharp points of his stilts sank in the mud. Viscous bubbles blistered its surface and frothed to ichorous suds.

The warlock fed his wrath into the effluvia puddling below him, and out of that he shaped wraiths. They rose bent as monkeys with arms dangling streamers of paralyzing tendrils. Spectral faces pale and ripped as old bridal veils bared needleteeth and muscular, unhinged jaws that blurred like smoke as they raved.

After the wraiths had grown to the size of ogres, Ralli-Faj let them loose. They charged into the swamp on vaporous limbs of mealy wetness. They did not seem substantial enough to stay long intact, yet the foliage shredded before them.

It was the warlock's vehemence that powered them. In moments, the first desperate shrieks began. Minutes later, the hacked parts of an ogre emerged from the underbrush and crawled over the mud to the center of the courtyard as if hoisted by legions of army ants. A bloody haunch, both severed arms, and a huge keg-head with a woolly mane and ferociously condensed face, wide-eyed in death, crept into the muddy courtyard on wisps of ectoplasm. The wisps evaporated and left the butchered cuts steaming in the gentle rain.

The wraiths killed three ogres among the swamp coves as well as the two who had fallen unconscious before the firecharms. They lay groggily recovering in their treehouses when the murderous wraiths set upon them, and their screams reached like siren wails across the bogland. After the chopped sections of their bodies fell from the trees and came sliding into the camp on snails of green smoke, the warlock stopped the killing. His rage had exhausted him – and, besides, he needed the others to run the camp.

He turned his back on the filthy dismemberment and stalked out of the bamboo gates and on to the swamp track where the escape had taken place. A cacodemon rose from the congested verdure at the side of the path.

'Water holds no tracks,' it informed him. 'The land is too vast. We need more brethren.'

'No, no more brethren,' Ralli-Faj insisted urgently. He needed time to assess what was transpiring out there in the marshes. Since it in some way involved the wizarduke, he felt compelled to inform Hu'dre Vra immediately, before he learned of this from the cacodemons. Yet he hesitated.

In his long sight, Ralli-Faj saw that the Pain Chain moved by fits and starts. He could almost hear the cries of Drev and Rica curdling to echoes. Wrat was happy.

*Why disturb the Dark Lord now?* the warlock reasoned. *While he takes his pleasure, I will stalk his enemies. I will find Dogbrick and Tywi and those who freed them. I will turn this threat to my advantage.*

He would keep the few cacodemons involved in the search occupied with missions farther afield, he decided, strolling back to the camp. As for the ogres, none of them would dare betray him after today's punishment.

Flies hazed about the chopped corpses, and the warlock moved swiftly through the camp's crude gate. On the fen road that led to the palace, he heard the metallic screeching of the Chain's winding engine as it turned faster in pursuit of itself. He looked up at the pyramid, and a wash of pride soaked him at the grandiosity of its terror.

*Tok. Tok. Tok.*

Under the murmuring cypress bower, his stilts found the pavement that went directly to his gardens. Thylia stood at the sandbed of colored rings, gazing down at the sleeping star.

Ralli-Faj stopped with a startled jolt that wagged his limp arms. He had sensed no one in here. A moment later, he understood why. She looked at him through her crisscrossed veils of gray transparency and faded away.

A cold wind sliced through him. There would be no secrets from the Dark Lord.

All around Caval and Poch, the Cloths of Heaven breathed light as clouds flew past the Abiding Star. Rain dripped in. Mists rose. Shafts of lucid daylight penetrated the depths of the foggy ruins like narrow passages into a realm of lost souls.

Caval sat immobilized with shock in one of those blue rays of dayshine. Charm spilled out of him in ectoplasmic vapors and mixed with the rising rainsmoke.

Squatting before him, Poch, too, did not move. The viscous Charm wafted over him, sustaining his telepathic bond with the sorcerer. He experienced the man's scalding remorse. 'I have unleashed death and anguish upon many thousands! I have destroyed Arwar Odawl – your brood – your father, who trusted me—'

'You didn't know.'

'I didn't know – I didn't know anything at all . . .' He closed his leathery eyelids to face his own darkness. 'The blind gods used me.'

'They use us all, master Caval.' Poch spoke soothingly, grateful for the energizing Charm laving over him from the sorcerer. 'That's what the sages and witches teach, isn't that so?'

Caval recalled his own lifelong ambition to live as a sage and a self-mocking smile hooked one corner of his sad mouth. 'Chance flung me to the Dark Shore. Death cut me free of that cold world, most cruelly. And now Justice, yes, Justice has taken me into her blind hands.' His eyes snapped open, and he gazed forth unblinking as if he himself had become sightless. 'The destruction! The suffering! It's all my doing – all of it set in motion by me alone. Me alone. Alone of all on Irth . . .'

Poch feared for the sorcerer's sanity. He feared that the one man who might be able to save them was going mad. In a fright, he reached out and clutched the blue tinsel windings that wrapped the emaciated man and shook him. 'Stop it, Caval!'

'The mystery of our lives depends on the dance of the three blind gods,' the sorcerer mumbled, still staring with crazed attentiveness at the truth of an invisible world.

'Stop it now!' Poch shook the old man hard, flinging tufts of Charm into the air like torn fleece. 'Stop it! Stop it!'

The old man's face blurred with the ferocity of Poch's assault, and he saw then the terror in the boy and calmed down. He gripped Poch's wrists firmly and gently freed himself.

'Thank you,' he spoke earnestly and met the youth's apprehensive expression with a placid smile. 'I'm sorry. I lost myself. I'm better now.'

The sorcerer's Charm had steadied to a suffused radiance, an azure dusting aswirl about him, the pollen of an impossible flower. Poch understood that Caval's very bones had become a carrier of Charm. His body was a living amulet.

Though telepathy had vanished, Poch saw the imprint of profound sorrow in Caval's cracked clay face and knew the old man's pain could not be healed by Charm.

'Can you stop Wrat?' Poch asked, his voice edged with desperation. 'Can you stop him now that you remember?'

Caval shook his hoary head. 'I cannot stop him. The magic of the cacodemons is the magic of the Dark Shore.' He stood, and his aura of Charm dimmed – yet his large eyes grew brighter. 'I cannot stop him – but Reece can.'

'Where is he?'

'I don't know.' The elder put a quavery hand to his brow, where veins clustered like kelp. 'I must find out if he is still here on Irth. If he still lives.'

Poch shivered. In the diminishing shine of Charm from the sorcerer, he felt the damp chill of the rainy swamp. His breath painted the air with frail smoke, and he noticed he was panting. He strove to steady himself against the doubts and imagined fears that haunted him again in the absence of amulets. Though the sorcerer had restored the lad's amulet tunic, the hex-gems still held no Charm.

'If Reece is alive,' he asked, seeking hope, 'what can he do against Hu'dre Vra?'

'He could start by killing him,' Caval replied and walked to the edge of the ashen circle.

'Reece could do that?'

The sorcerer rubbed the air with his open palms, feeling

outward into the world. He was too feeble to sense much of anything beyond, and he gave up with a frustrated sigh. All his Charm had focused within. He would have to search from there.

He shot an annoyed look at the boy and wished he had the strength to keep him in telepathic bondage so he would stop asking questions and let him think about all he had just learned.

'You shared my memories of the Dark Shore,' Caval said. 'You know I chose Reece to help me with very difficult work. I did not choose a weak man.'

'But what about the cacodemons?'

'They are phantoms to him,' the sorcerer explained and returned to stand at the center of the scorched circle. 'He is a denizen of the Dark Shore where cacodemons are psychic entities, not physical creatures. They can't touch him.'

Excited, Poch pushed to his feet from where he had been huddling in the cold rainlight. 'Then we must find out if he is alive.'

'Precisely, young master.' Caval sat, face tucked in, veiled by his white hair and florid beard. 'Now if you will keep your silence for a while, my lord, I will search for him with a strong eye. But, mind you, my Charm is weak. The trance used me up. I will need some time. Will you stand back, out of the circle, and watch over me?'

'Of course,' Poch agreed and quickly exited the cleared area. 'Seek him at once.'

Unlike the erect and powerful old sorcerer who had guided him here with his Charm, Caval looked slumped over and simply unconscious when he entered trance. *He could be dead*. But Poch knew he was not, and he paced among the rubble anxiously, searching for vipers among the smashed plates of paving and chunks of masonry.

From around a broken slab of the tilted floor, a cacodemon glided. It had entered the Cloths of Heaven searching for the fugitives from the labor camp and had heard from afar the disturbed gravel of Poch's nervous pacing.

In the embroidered silence of dripping rain and muted bird

calls, it floated, watching its prey. The gaunt old one looked dead. No body light shone about him and no scent of heat tinged the chill morning from his inert body.

The boy it recognized from hive memory – Poch, the stripling whose sister Jyoti maimed Ss-o and Ys-o. That memory kept the cacodemon wary, alert for the presence of the margravess. Only after it had circled through the fallen girders and become convinced that no others lurked nearby did it swoop in to seize him.

A scream split from Poch at the sucking evil sound of the cacodemon's attack. He did not see the monster until the hooked tentacles snared him and yanked him violently away. Then he was pulled up against the tusked faces in the demon's thorax.

The mouths tore at his body, and the hideous jaws gnashing inches from his eyes widened in amazement at the rapid intensity of his shrieks. Its laugh laved him with its carnivorous breath, and then it chewed on his face.

Poch's frantic cries jarred Caval from his renewed trance and spilled Charm like holy dust, driving shadows away. He jumped to his feet in a whirlwind of light.

The boy was gone.

Caval saw him high in the bright attic of the ruined temple, thrashing in the cacodemon's coiling grasp. The eelish monster slithered through a hole in the tower wall that opened on the rainy sky and climbed rapidly away.

Under a wild cry, the sorcerer collapsed. Madness swooped in. It arrived as emptiness. Cabochons of raindrops on the ground so close to his eye appeared like polished scry crystals – and the future he saw in them was empty. As magnifying mirrors, they reflected his staring eye and the ramshackle interior of the Cloths of Heaven. And the ruins were empty of all but him.

He felt powerless before the curse of himself. He did not want to move. It was time to lie there and die. The evil he had loosed upon Irth had at last broken him.

A deep drumbeat sounded within the throb of his heart. It reverberated like the evocation drum the witches used to summon divine presences. His gray eye flexed and changed focus from the very close raindrops to the surrounding debris of silt-stained rocks.

Out of the rain mist rose three monolithic shadows. The blind gods.

Caval blinked.

The gods remained. Woolly as smoke, they leaned forward to include him in their confidence.

Jyoti soothed her comrades with a mesmermur song she had learned as a child from her father. It quieted the glade. Even the lizards did not stir, and when Jyoti was done, Tywi slept in Dogbrick's arms.

The margravess reached over and gently removed the sword Taran from Tywi's crossed arms. The waif stirred in her sleep and muttered incoherently.

'Sometimes she walks out of her body,' Dogbrick revealed. 'I think she learned how from Owl Oil – her Ladyship Rica.' His animal features tightened. 'The cacodemons took her – snatched her right off the beach.'

Jyoti sheathed the sword and secured the scabbard to her back. 'My brother is out here somewhere. I want to find him before the cacodemons do. So I'm going to the Cloths of Heaven. A sibyl told me the sorcerer Caval is there. Perhaps he can help me track down Poch.'

'We dare not linger here long,' Dogbrick worried. 'We must get out of the Reef Isles before the cacodemons organize a wider search.'

'The demons could be here any minute or not for days,' Jyoti said. 'But Tywi is not ready to travel. You both need to rest.'

Dogbrick nodded and leaned back against the mossy hummock. 'Morning is a good time to sleep. Go with her, Ripcat. Find the sorcerer the sibyl spoke of and bring him here if you can.'

Ripcat agreed and left his firelock with his friend. He moved lighter without it and scouted for Jyoti far ahead into the marshland. He skimmed as a fleet shadow through the swales, stopping at intervals to be sure Jyoti followed. From treecrests he searched out hazards and more easily identified coral bridges among the isles. Before noon, they reached the Cloths of Heaven.

Jyoti used the sword Taran to feel for Caval's presence in the rambling ruins, and the gold blade directed her to a fallen tower. Ripcat crawled nimbly over the toppled stone blocks and descended into a deep well where daylight burned at the bottom in rags of mist. An old man lay there face down in his beard, one eye cocked to stare at the ground.

Ripcat rolled the elder on to his back and felt life stir in him. His pulse feathered softly, and his breathing was thin and irregular. He gazed upward with blind eyes until Jyoti arrived and laid the sword Taran upon his withered frame.

'He is my brood's weapons master.' Jyoti recognized him. 'But so much more aged!'

Caval sat up, shaken yet alert. Down in his soul the gods continued their conference, but he could no longer hear them. The well-being of Charm drowned them out with the renewed vigor of his heartbeat. Even so, he well remembered their purpose with him, and he fixed his gaze upon the freckled woman with Lord Keon's broad jaw: 'Margravess—' The skeletal man struggled to sit up.

'Take the sword, Caval.' Jyoti urged it upon him.

Caval received the Charmed weapon and pressed his brow against its blade. Pulling Charm directly into his brain, he purged the madness that had seized him only minutes earlier. The black hues of his despondency brightened to gray transparencies very like witch veils. He saw through them to the shimmery depths of his soul. There stood three monolithic shadows, three pieces of elemental darkness that would not go away.

'I must tell you at once—' he croaked, then pressed the sword to his throat, to find the strength to speak: 'Poch has been seized. By a cacodemon. Just this hour. He was not killed outright. We must assume he is taken to the Palace of Abominations – to Wrat.'

Jyoti, without Charm to soften this news, felt her knees weaken to think of her brother's terror. She knelt and faced her weapons master with a glare of urgency. 'What can we do?'

'Not we.' He motioned for Ripcat to help him rise and seized the beastman's arm. 'Him. He will slay Wrat.'

Ripcat looked with surprise into the wizened sorcerer's demented scowl.

'Do you remember me, Reece?' Caval touched the sword to Ripcat's skull. 'Do you remember *Lara*?'

At the sound of her name, Ripcat plunged into trance. The sorcerer caught his body as he fell. He held the limp man in one arm and with the sword ripped from him the skin of light that had been his form in this world for over five hundred days.

The skin of light shredded to mist, and a young man with pale hair and rose-white nakedness rolled unconscious to the ground. He lay on his back, his softly-bearded face troubled, dream-wrought.

'He's so young,' Jyoti observed. 'He can't be more than 10,000 days.'

'I worked with him many years,' Caval remembered wistfully. 'But we worked in a laboratory where years are as days upon the Dark Shore.'

'What has happened to him?'

'He is remembering. Look.' Caval swept the sword across the supine body and charmsmoke lifted to images.

Together they watched Reece climb the Ladder of the Wind out of an abyss of darkness. He emerged in the bright air among the glassy spheres of Hellsgate and Nemora. The stars around him sharpened their spikes, and Lara called to him.

The dark music of her soul's shadow whispered from the eternity packed whole in the radiance of the Abiding Star. And the fool from the Dark Shore climbed toward it.

Between the Gulf and the Abiding Star lay Irth. Reece collided with that world so forcefully, he lost consciousness. His Charm and his body of cold matter protected him from outright extinction, and he survived to wake stunned on the wild planetary shore of his longing.

Lara's shadow sang from out of the sun. Only this was no sun that baked the anvil rocks and salt pans. It was the compact face of God. It was silence listening. It was all that Caval had foretold to him: The floodgate of eternity, the hot fire of time spilling upon vastness, and all the worlds of creation going down into its smoldering sunset billions of years deep.

Lara's shadow sang.

Quietly as pain, her dark song chilled him. At first, he could not find her, though her soul's shadow lay all about him. Not until he looked up did he see that her music sang down to him from the first sun. She had soared into the Abiding Star shining fiercely above him and lay forever and infinitely beyond his reach.

Reece raged with a delirious grief. He dashed across the blasted terrain, wanting to lift away and rise toward her. He ran until he had spent almost all his strength. Then he collapsed and lay upon this strange planet, dying.

In his madness, he spun a skin of light to protect himself so that he could go on and somehow find a way to the Beginning and to Lara. He shielded his blistered head and shoulders with cool blue fur. In the totemic style of the forest aborigines where Caval had trained him, he used the last of his magic to condense his strength into feline contours, amplifying his humanity with bestial powers.

And because he did this mad, desperate to survive, he used all his magic to create his new self. He invested everything he had of his old being – including the power of his memories.

Caval's charmsmoke lifted away from the comatose man, and Jyoti and Caval exchanged somber looks.

'Even without his beastmarks, he looks dangerous,' Jyoti said, glancing down nervously at the lithe, athletic youth marked discreetly yet clearly at his power points with small ritual scars and arcane tattoos. 'Will he help us when he wakes?'

Caval held her gaze gently. 'No, Jyoti. It is we who will have to help him.'

## The Stars Under Our Feet

❖❖❖

Reece woke Charmless and fraught with memories of the Dark Shore. Rain dripped in sparks through the well of daylight. The Cloths of Heaven loomed above him with its confused shadows, flitting dragonflies, and heights of ruin.

*Irth!* he realized with awe. He had climbed to the first world of Creation, to the place where magic began.

He sat up and squinted at the old man and the freckled woman of Charmed beauty kneeling beside him – Jyoti to whom, as Ripcat, he had already lost his heart.

She gazed ardently back at him, willing him to remember the destinal bond that had united them over the sword Taran, united them to find her brother or die trying. The question in her gaze could only be answered with love.

A frown creased his blond brow, remembering his life as Ripcat.

But now he was Reece. And there was Lara.

*Lara. Where is she?*

He could not hear the dark music of her soul's shadow any more.

'You would have to climb the Calendar of Eyes to hear that

again,' Caval explained, his harrowed face a bearded skull in the smoky light.

Reece flinched, realizing that the old man and Jyoti could hear his thoughts. His mind floated in the charmsmoke peeling off him. As the blue vapors dissipated, so did the telepathy. With it went the certainty that this decrepit mummy in tinseled windings was his former master, the visitant from magical Irth who had come to the Dark Shore to purify his alchemic gold. He peered at the old man, trying to see the Caval he remembered.

The sorcerer helped him by waving the charmsmoke over himself into a skin of light that masked him with the image of a beardless, red-haired youth of imperious mien.

'You!'

'Yes, Reece.' Caval regarded him with a supercilious smirk, a disdainful hauteur that loosened Reece's jaw it so perfectly reminded him of his teacher. 'We are together again – after so very long.'

Reece's frown deepened. 'Where is Lara?'

'Dead,' Caval said, with a contemptuous flare of his nostrils. 'You know that. You drowned her soul yourself.'

'It had become deformed.' Reece felt he was talking out of his bones, from so deep in himself and the past. 'She would have suffered.'

'Of course.' Caval's strong, young voice spoke coolly. 'You did the correct thing.'

'No.' Reece's frown became a scowl. 'I didn't. That's why I'm here. You, too, I think. We did the *wrong* thing, Caval. We should never have made her a witch.'

'The sword of Justice cuts both ways, old friend,' Caval reminded him with a cavalier smile in his handsomely self-possessed face. 'Would Lara have been better left in the flood to drown as a helpless infant? Or should we have abandoned her only later when she was old enough to suffer a death summed of her own choices?'

'Enough!' Reece pressed his fists to his eyes.

'It is never enough!' Caval shouted, and his skin of light shredded to mist. Reduced again to a withered husk of his former self, the sorcerer continued in a fragile voice, 'It is never enough with the dead. Remember, I taught you that. You knew better than to look. You knew about the shadow of death. You knew that if you listened too closely you would lose your own soul. You even tried to remind me. You do remember that. I know you do. I was there.'

Reece lowered his hands and looked up sadly at Caval.

'Lara was an echo of a higher love.' The sorcerer gestured with a spidery hand to Jyoti. 'What do you feel in your heart for this woman, whose life you restored, whose soul touched yours? Surely you see? There is a charmbond between you. For she, too, is an echo of a higher love yet, beyond the portal of the Abiding Star.'

'Where Lara has gone,' Reece whispered, peering inward on himself with open eyes.

Caval put a caring hand on his student's shoulder. 'If you will let her go.'

'Lara is dead,' Jyoti spoke up impatiently. 'But my brother is still alive. And he is suffering in the Palace of Abominations while you sit here talking.'

Reece stood up and lifted Jyoti with him. Bare-chested in his black cord trousers and worn boots, he filled the same stature as Ripcat but wholly human and of a far more vulnerable appearance. 'Let's go get your brother.'

'Wait.' Caval struggled upright and clutched at Reece for support. 'You have no Charm.'

'And neither can Charm harm me.' Reece steadied the doddering sorcerer and addressed him gently, 'I remember all that you taught me, Caval. And I know where I am. On Irth, I am a different breed of man.'

Caval clutched at him apprehensively. 'Yet you are still vulnerable to physical injury. If you are not careful, you too can be made a corpse.'

Reece pulled himself away from the quavery old man. 'I'm no fool.'

Caval shuddered in a cold breeze of ill omen that reached to his marrows. 'The Palace of Abominations has horrors other than cacodemons.'

Jyoti brandished her weapon. 'We'll meet those horrors with my firelock.'

'Ralli-Faj protects Wrat.' Caval tugged fretfully at his beard. 'He is a ruthless warlock and with much power. I must go with you.'

'No.' Reece spoke decisively. 'Together we must fix what together we broke. I will end this defiling of Irth. And you will close the Door in the Air that I left open so that this horror will never happen again.'

'I don't have the strength to climb the Ladder of the Wind,' Caval confessed weakly.

'Find the strength, Caval,' Reece pressed him. 'Go to the Sisterhood if you must and get their help. Only you and I can locate that Door in the vastness. One of us must go and close it or there will be more cacodemons.'

Caval raised his hands, grasping for a compromise. 'After Wrat, we will go together.'

'No, old man.' The taut lines in Reece's young face set firmly. 'I will not follow your commands again. Not after Lara. I climbed up here to undo all that. This time, you will obey me.'

Caval blinked wearily. The young magician from the Dark Shore was right, he knew. The three blind gods had already made that clear to him. In his episode of mad grief at what he had done, he had finally seen the necessity of Justice.

Chance, that had taken him to the cold world of Reece and Lara, and Death, that had freed him, both had to be balanced now by Justice. And to him that meant he had to accept all the consequences of his visit to the Dark Shore.

'It is for the best,' Reece said, glad for the acceptance he read in his mentor's withdrawn demeanor. 'Think. If you fail, I will

432

climb the ladder and close the Door myself. And if you succeed and I fail to slay Wrat, then at least the Door will be closed and Hu'dre Vra can summon no more monsters. In time, the united dominions will defeat him and slay the last of his cacodemons.'

Pale Caval stood motionless and almost invisible among dusty rays of gray stormlight. 'And if we both fail?'

Reece smiled sadly, with foregone clarity. 'Then we will have paid in full the blood debt for Lara.'

Jyoti was already climbing toward the broken wall that exited the ruins, and he followed her without glancing back. He felt no remorse toward Caval, having seen him scorched by time. He only hoped that the old sorcerer still had the cunning to find a way to close the Door.

Without his Charmed body, climbing proved arduous. Reece struggled to clamber up the rubble mound to the high perch where Jyoti waited. Skidding on the shattered rocks, he missed his Cat reflexes.

Jyoti offered him a helping hand, and he seized it gladly. She pulled him to her side, and they stood together on the ruined parapet overlooking Nhat.

Before them, the jungle and its mists sprawled to a horizon dominated by the Palace of Abominations. The sight of the pyramid, with its obscene cartouche of female genitalia and its hidden vaults of suffering, inspired a silence that called alone upon their courage. No words, only deeds, could fill that silence.

Clasping hands, they went forward to find their way through the ruins toward a future with no memory.

In the Palace of Abominations, Hu'dre Vra celebrated. Mesmermur music flooded the immense adytum, and hosts of cacodemons floated in majestic wheels, tentacles waving, viper lengths coiling among each other, coupling in grotesque braids and slithering chains.

The Dark Lord sat on an onyx throne set in the pharaonic mouth of the adytum. From there, he commanded a lordly view of the Reef Isles where he had been born, the tidal flats that had enslaved him, and the Pain Chain that enslaved his enemies.

At his side sat the witch queen Thylia, her black diamond eyes averted from the copulating cacodemons and fixed haughtily on the distant weather above the swamp, at the afternoon's bruised edge.

*The storm ends,* she thought, glad as never before to see lances of light leaning among the thunderheads.

'Why are you smiling?' Hu'dre Vra inquired. Of late, her passion for him had waned, and he sensed a deathly resignation in her. He had begun to think it was at last necessary to kill her a few times – and then, she smiled.

'The storm is over,' she intoned demurely. 'And light sheds the darkness.'

'If we were not such intimates, sweet Thylia, I'd think you were speaking in symbols.' Wrat wiped away his mask and pulled aside the queen's veils so nothing came between their naked faces. 'Yesterday, you were all over me. Today, we're talking about the weather. Why have you changed?'

'Everything changes everything,' she muttered disconsolately and pulled her veils back into place.

'Quoting sacred screed again.' Wrat hissed in exasperation and pulled her tighter to him. 'You cannot hide from me inside, witch. I am the supreme lord of everything. Remember Romut!'

Her black eyes flashed fright – or menace – Wrat was not sure which. Before he could pry into her soul with his magic or again pull aside her veils and read her intentions from the lines of her face, the cacodemon who had captured Poch arrived.

'You see, Thylia!' Wrat stood up on his throne and pointed at the chewed body of Poch hanging slack and pink as a skinned animal. 'My enemies suffer and die – and then suffer some more!'

He raised his right hand, and his fist blazed with astral flames. When he extended his fingers, Poch thrashed awake with a pain-stricken cry. His wounds bleared away.

'Why would anyone want to be my enemy?' he asked Thylia, head canted inquisitively.

'For some it can never be possible to be your friend,' she answered dryly.

'Ah, true.' He grinned evilly at Poch. 'Do you know Lord Drev of Ux?'

Poch gaped in terror at the small man before him.

'Speak to me, boy!' Wrat stepped closer. 'Or I will hear you sing!'

'Lord Drev—' Poch's mouth trembled, fear vibrating in him unhindered by Charm. 'He is your enemy.'

'Oh, yes. My enemy.' Wrat's smile widened to show his brown teeth, and his deadly eyes tightened deadlier. 'My *defeated* enemy.'

'I am not your enemy,' Poch declared from where he hung in the tentacled grip of the floating demon. His pallid face gleamed with oily fear, and he repeated, 'I am not your enemy.'

'Are you not?' Wrat twisted his head from side to side, mock-studying the boy. 'I slayed your father. I slayed your entire brood!'

Poch hung speechless.

Wrat's smile slipped away. 'Now I'm going to kill you.' From the air, he plucked a black scythe and ran the razor edge under the boy's jaw, ear to ear, etching a burning line of blood.

Poch screamed.

Wrat smiled again. 'Our first voice – the scream! The salute to pain.'

Poch squeezed his eyes shut, and his breathing labored to calm himself.

'On the Dark Shore, pain is a god,' Wrat whispered, his voice barely audible above the droning mesmermur music flooding the adytum. 'On Irth, we pay it only superficial notice, for Charm heals all our ills – for those who can get it. But on the Dark Shore, pain is the first and most pervasive truth of life.'

'I never did anything to you!' Poch bawled. 'Why are you doing this to me?'

Wrat tossed the scythe into the air and it did not come down. 'Why not?'

Thylia finally rose from the onyx throne and approached the frightened boy. 'Let him down.'

'Down?' Wrat chortled, and his tight eyes widened with glee. 'The only place he's going is *around*! He's going to ride the Pain Chain.'

'He's a boy,' the witch pleaded.

Wrat crossed his arms and cocked an eyebrow. 'A boy with a secret.'

Thylia's jet eyes watched impassively from behind her gray veils.

'You know what I'm talking about.' Wrat cajoled her with a bent grin. 'Most witches would see it. The queen, certainly. That shadow in his bodylight.' He plucked at the air beside Poch's head, and the boy's aura vibrated visibly: flash orange striated with grainy shadowbands. 'What else can this be but a secret? Hmm? Don't you think, Thylia? Look at it. It's so secret, he would like to hide it from himself if he could.'

'Leave the child alone,' the witch queen urged. 'You are misconstruing his fear.'

'Am I?' Wrat pushed his pointy face close to Poch's, and the boy smelled the rancid heat of his breath. 'When you are ready to give me your secret whole and entire, boy – just stop screaming!' He flashed a delirious grin, then ordered the cacodemon: 'Take him to the Chain.'

Poch kept his silence out through the portal and down the sooty plane of the pyramid. Even the rusty Chain did not unnerve him with the otherworldly screech of its winding engine spewing hot-metal fumes. But when the carriages slowed and the dented doors pulled wide, the sight of Lord Drev and Ladyship Rica crawling in their vomit, raving in shattered voices almost soundlessly – that broke him.

'I can help you,' Poch called out, then cried again louder, 'I can help you!'

'Please do,' Wrat invited and signaled for the cacodemon to

release him. He took the boy by the elbow and helped steady him. 'Tell me what you know, Poch.'

'You must promise me you won't hurt my sister,' the trembling boy begged urgently.

Wrat beckoned, and a tentacle swung before Poch's startled face. 'Tell me now – or ride the Chain and tell me later.'

'My sister—'

'She will have to make her own arrangements with me, dear Poch.'

The demented glitter of Wrat's wicked eyes decided it for Poch, and he clamped his jaw and closed his lids tight. He swore he would say nothing. He thought he could swallow enough pain to kill himself, and he did not cry out when the tentacles seized him and hauled him away.

He did not cry out until the Chain started. And then the pain slashed away all semblance of reason, meaning and mind from him. One circuit later, the Chain stopped, the door screeched open, and tentacles hauled him out gibbering everything he knew about Caval's escapade on the Dark Shore, the witch Lara and her tragic death, and her mournful lover, Reece, who had come to Irth to find her – and who had left open behind him the Door in the Air.

When Wrat had wrung from Poch everything he knew, the warlord had the cacodemons fling the boy back into the Chain. It shrieked into motion, and its cry was the Dark Lord's own.

The gremlin inside his heart scratched painfully, and he thudded his fist against his chest. 'No, we are not leaving Irth! I will not release you to the Dark Shore again until I have destroyed all my enemies. That was our agreement!'

The searing chest pain abated, and Wrat breathed deeper and relaxed his fist.

From the lip of the adytum, Thylia watched him, her veiled body floating like a flame.

*And just as dangerous*, he thought. *Romut was right to warn me against the witches.*

He sensed that she knew as much or more than he had wrung from the timorous boy, but her bodylight remained clear and flawless as water. Whatever she hid, if anything at all, he had never reached deep enough to find it.

And that would have been sufficient reason to slay her at once – if not for her other witchy skills.

Wrat clapped, and the dancing cacodemons fled the adytum in a rasping tempest. They stampeded over the canopy of the jungle, casting a shadow across the land wide as a curtain of night.

Thylia fixed her attention on them until they receded to a black cloud scudding above the dim green of a star. Behind her veils, she smiled at Wrat when he came flying from the Chain toward the adytum clutching his chest.

The gremlin was unhappy. She knew why.

*It has felt the change in the weather.*

She curled her legs under her on the onyx throne, features obscured by her veils, quiet, detached, watching Wrat approach in a burning brown wind, a fetid steam billowing with panic. Even with her impeccable training, fear tainted her when she smelled that feculent miasma.

'Do you know?' he demanded gruffly.

'The boy's secret should be no surprise to you, my lord.' She lowered her face-veil to confront him with her serenity. 'How did you think you got back to Irth?'

'The Ladder of the Wind,' Wrat answered at once. 'The black magicians of the Dark Shore know the invocation for the Ladder of the Wind. I wrung it from them.'

'You really are still the scavenger you always were, aren't you, Wrat?' She allowed herself a thin smile at his ignorance. 'The invocation for the Ladder of the Wind is commonly known. Anyone can climb into the sky, fool. But to cross the Gulf, one must know the secret that unlocks the Door in the Air.'

'I unlocked it!'

'No. It was left open before you ever climbed to it. It is being shut now.' Her smile ended. 'There will be no more cacodemons arriving from the Dark Shore at your beckoning.'

Fear gusted like wind in him, yet he was not moved. His face locked in a frown as he reached inward for comprehension. 'You knew about the Door?'

Her weary expression spoke for her.

'You used my lust to hide from me!' Wrat realized. 'Sex was your weapon.'

'You knew I plied your desires to humor you.'

'Of course I knew!' he snapped, and a black string of smoke seeped from his nose. 'That's what makes it so good. You *have* to please me. But I thought – all along, I thought you were submitting to save yourself. You deceived me!'

'Nonsense.' She lifted her chin defiantly. 'I am *queen* of all witches. I serve the Sisterhood. And I submitted to you to serve them.'

'By deceiving me!' A sharp stink of pitch assailed the space around him. The palpable presence of his fright and fury trickled as tar fumes from the holes in his head. 'You knew a Door was open that let me through and I did not open it. You knew all along there is another.'

'He is on his way here this moment to kill you,' she told him frankly.

Wrat restrained himself from ripping her head from her shoulders. He needed more knowledge to meet this unexpected threat and to quell the fear that maddened the gremlin inside him. 'Who is Reece?'

'A magus from the Dark Shore,' she told him, almost bored. In moments, she would be dead. If she wanted, her soul could then return to the Brighter World beyond the gateway of the Abiding Star. Or she might choose to stay for another life in a new body, to enjoy Irth again without the annoyance of Wrat. She had perfected her internal arts to assure her of this choice. The deeds she had worked for the Sisterhood with those internal arts had made her queen to begin with, and she was impatient for the last deed that would free her once more.

'How can I stop this magus?' Wrat asked, smoldering in a haze of bituminous vapors.

'Can you kill a man with your bare hands?'

'A weapon! I need a weapon!' Wrat gathered the tarry smoke around him into belled shapes of ebony armor sticky with spikes. 'Ralli-Faj!'

The warlock appeared almost at once, a tiny figure rising into the colossal doorway and hurrying closer.

*Tok. Tok. Tok.*

Erect on his stilts, leather mask pulled taut, Ralli-Faj hung like a crude effigy bedecked in amulets. Behind him, the cacodemons returned, darkly gliding on the golden rays of the afternoon.

'A man is coming to kill me,' Hu'dreVra informed the warlock. 'He is a magus from the Dark Shore named Reece. How can I protect myself?'

Ralli-Faj's mouthful of blue fire dimmed at this shocking news. Before he could speak, the Dark Lord sent a moth of blue flame flitting into the warlock's empty eye socket and infused him with all that he had learned from Poch.

'I mus-s-t s-see the boy!' Ralli-Faj insisted at once.

Hu'dre Vra signed, and a cacodemon exited to retrieve Poch from the Pain Chain. 'Why?'

'I mus-s-t s-see what he has-s s-seen!' The warlock's fungal patches rippled in bioluminescent waves, signaling his distress. 'This-s is-s dangerous-s, my lord.'

'No, little men,' the witch queen said drolly. 'This is more than dangerous. This is where we die.'

The Dark Lord raised both of his hooked and tined arms above his horned helmet. 'You do not frighten me, witch.'

'If you don't realize you are frightened,' Thylia told him in a frigidly measured cadence, 'then you're too scared to think. The gremlin knows.'

Hu'dre Vra felt the gremlin like a stone in his chest. It took much of his concentration to keep it calm.

'It senses the magus who can slay it,' Thylia warned, her black diamond eyes shining. 'It felt him the moment he doffed his skin of light. You feel him, too.'

*Tok. Tok. Tok.*

'S-silence her, my lord!'

'And take off that ridiculous outfit you're wearing,' she mocked Hu'dreVra. 'It's just an illusion to him, anyway. You'll have to face him as who you are.'

The armor fell away as gluey smoke, and Wrat strode toward her, his face dark with anger.

'I *can* kill with my own hands!' he yelled and grabbed her by the throat. She felt frail in his rageful grasp and offered no resistance. Eyes closed, she leaned into his lethal embrace as if giving herself in desire. Within moments, her body convulsed once, and she was dead.

Immediately, the impulse seized him to call her back with his magic. He threw her furiously to the ground and stepped back, disgusted at his own weakness.

Poch entered in the coils of a cacodemon. He looked mad, his hair matted, his face bruised where he had smashed it against the carriage window.

Ralli-Faj washed the boy in Charm, cleansing him of his wounds and his fright, soothing his heart's small immensity with the rapturous power of the Abiding Star. Then he peered into him and saw Reece.

'The magus-s approaches-s,' Ralli-Faj announced and stepped back from the boy. Now that he had made the connection by seeing Reece's face, he no longer needed Poch. He could sense the magus in the swamp below.

'I will send cacodemons.'

'Us-seless-s.'

'They can stone him to death.'

'He is from the Dark Shore, my lord. They become phantoms in his charmless presence. Near him, they can't even pick up twigs.'

'But the ogres can!' Wrat cried. 'Send the ogres! And you! You can kill him, Ralli-Faj. Stop him and we will share together all the spoils of Irth!'

'I will win that pledge with his-s corps-se, my lord,' the warlock promised and hovered backward out through the giant portal into the golden afternoon.

Wrat looked with dismay at Thylia sprawled before the onyx throne, lifeless. He waved for her to go away, and a cacodemon dragged her corpse into the air and out through the towering door.

In an effort to stare down danger, Wrat gazed at Poch in the coils of a cacodemon and did not blink until the details of the boy's horrified features took on lucidity and significance.

'You think I am defeated, don't you?' Wrat asked dully, stepping closer. 'I can see it in your face. That's what you think. I know. You are a messenger of my destruction, because you come from Arwar Odawl, the first city I destroyed.'

'I'm no messenger,' Poch asserted sincerely, afraid of the crazed look in Wrat's pinched eyes.

'What you really are sinks deeper than your memory can follow,' the madman instructed. 'Yet I will show you, vengeful messenger. I will keep you alive to show you. I am not defeated. I cannot be defeated. For I am greater than the ashes of which we are made!'

The cacodemons could not see Reece from afar. They spotted Jyoti in the marsh's sprawling fog. She ran through the torn mists with the sword Taran drawn, its gold blade barbed with hot spikes of reflected sky.

At the fringe of the marsh, they swooped over her, and she danced a cutting path into their midst. Only close up did the demons confront the magus beside her. He waved his assault knife in a warding pattern, and a score of cacodemons drizzled away into cold fumes.

Jyoti and Reece sprinted across the grass verges into the pyramid's shadow. They entered a maze of thorn hedges bright with impaled butterflies, many still twitching where the wind had flung them.

Using the sword Taran as a seeker, Jyoti brought the presence of her brother to mind and let the vibrancy in the haft guide her. The thorn shrubs gave way to blossoming bushes and espaliered vines.

They entered a cul-de-sac – a wall of blue glass – and Reece knocked against the glass with his knife, repeating the warding rhythms he had learned as a magus. The wall fogged away, and they rushed on.

Dwarf fruit trees and unhewn boulders of chalcedony and agate filled a wide amphitheater. Terraces of miniature trees and flowering arbors enclosed a central plaza of colored sands raked in broad hex-circles. At its center, the fallen star lay on the ground, asleep.

Reece's warding magic had broken the spell of walls and light. The ceiling of crystal spheres had vanished. Above them loomed the colossal interior of the Palace of Abominations with its enormous, skewed girders and shafts echoing with the shrieks of cacodemons.

The sword Taran pointed to a spiral rampway that ascended into the dense upper storeys of nested crypts, vaults and truss beams. But Jyoti did not hurry to it. She paused before the fallen star.

'Free it from its suffering, Reece,' she called to her partner. 'The Dark Lord is using his black magic to keep this poor creature alive.'

Before Reece could reply, a harsh cry shouted from the terraces. Two ogres, Gryn and Gnawl, charged across the sward swinging clubs.

Jyoti unslung her firelock – and a tentacle from above snatched it out of her hands. She ducked. With a cold whistle, a whipstroke tail sliced through the air above her.

Reece ran to her side, cutting a sigil in the air with his knife. He sliced the attacking cacodemons to mist above the topiary garden, then spun to face the attacking ogres.

Jyoti held them off with a flourish of the sword Taran.

Gryn and Gnawl circled in opposite directions through the dwarf shrubs and blossom trees.

A flung club struck Reece in the chest and dropped him breathless. Jyoti jumped over him and drove off the ogre who had swept in to grab him.

From the other side, another thrown club hit Jyoti's arm, and the sword spun from her grip.

Gryn and Gnawl pounced. With slashing knives, their prey held them off. But only for the moment. Gryn retrieved the sword Taran and hacked at the air with it.

Jyoti shouted a command to the sword, and its Charm flashed and burned the ogre's hands. When he dropped it, she darted forward. But before she could snatch it, Gnawl caught her leg.

Reece jumped on to Gnawl and stabbed into the woolly mane. With a cracked roar, the ogre threw him off, and Reece splashed into a sand garden. He watched helpless from there as the two ogres closed on Jyoti. They moved with frightful swiftness, snagging her knife arm, seizing her shoulders and bending her head to snap her neck.

With a desperate cry, Reece chanted again the spell that had first shaped his skin of light when he lay dying in the cinders under the Abiding Star. Blue flames whirled up out of the Irth and flung him to his feet as Ripcat.

His roar froze the ogres, and he lunged toward them, fangs and knife bared.

They dropped Jyoti. Still, they were not fast enough to avert slicing wounds from Ripcat's blurred knife. Bawling their hurt, they backed swiftly away, searching for where the firelock had fallen.

Jyoti took the sword Taran in her grip and ran toward the ramp. 'Let's go, Cat!'

'No!' Ripcat pointed to where Gryn had found the firelock. 'Take cover!'

Rays of blue charmfire exploded boulders and ignited

shrubbery. Ripcat rolled, leaped, bounced, and slithered among the gusts of flame. Flying shrapnel cut sparkling tracks in the air and kept both ogres crouched low and blind to their targets.

Out of the tumbling smoke, Ripcat burst upon the inexpert marksman and threw his blade into the ogre's small face. The green steel, driven by Charm, cleaved the creature's skull and stood embedded in its spine.

Ripcat plucked the firelock from Gryn's dead arms and turned it on Gnawl's howling attack. A burst of blue-white Charmfire charred the ogre to a burning skeleton.

Jyoti saw that Ripcat was unharmed, and she turned and bolted up the rampway, following the insistent hum in the sword Taran. She passed stone crypts with yolky windows where tattered bodies bobbed.

Down the wide ramp seethed a crowd of cacodemons. Jyoti ducked into a tight corridor between the crypts, and the monstrous throng swirled past her. As soon as they passed, she put aside the quest for her brother and followed after them. Ripcat's body of light was vulnerable to their claws – and if they murdered him, the magus would also die.

Drastic screams echoed from ahead, and she pulled Charm into herself from the sword Taran and ran faster.

Rounding the last bend, she glimpsed charmfire exploding rock gardens and boulders, slaying the demons that had rushed into the amphitheater. She fell flat.

'Ripcat!' she called, and when he ceased fire she charged down the ramp toward the remaining two demons. At sword's length, she whirled and cut through tentacles and flared claws.

The wounded cacodemons hauled their screams upward into a ventilation chute and disappeared among bonging echoes.

Ripcat ran to her across the scorched gardens. 'You didn't have to come back.'

'You're Ripcat again.' She sheathed her sword and clutched the blue fur at the side of his face. 'You're vulnerable to the cacodemons – and the Dark Lord.'

'I couldn't fight the ogres as Reece.' He handed her the smoking firelock, his head bowed resignedly. 'I wasn't fast enough."

'But you can't face Wrat like this!' she despaired and pressed her hands to the cat-facets of his cheeks. 'Quickly, take off this skin of light.'

'I can't.' His whiskers twitched. 'I don't *remember* any of the magic. I know that I am Reece, disciple of Caval, a magus of the Dark Shore. I remember that – but I don't remember how to work the sorcery.'

'Then we have to get out of here right now and find Caval.' She took his arm, but he would not move.

'Not without your brother.' His jade eyes lifted toward the ghastly interior of the palace. 'Lord Drev and Ladyship Rica are in here. If we can free them, their sorcery can free me, and together we can end Wrat's days on Irth.'

*Tok. Tok. Tok.*

'Big plans-s,' Ralli-Faj hissed from the burned hedges. 'S-small means-s.'

Jyoti pulled the firelock from her shoulder and, even though she knew better, fired one tight burst at maximum.

The Dark Lord's magic protected Ralli-Faj, and the Charmburst erupted into a blowback of cold green phlegm. The warlock laughed like sizzling acid, blue flames dancing in every hole of his head.

Jyoti and Ripcat pulled the thick ectoplasm from their faces and hands.

'Save your brother,' Ripcat whispered and pushed away from her. He darted in a smudge of fluid motion across the blasted garden directly toward the warlock.

Ralli-Faj seized him easily, yet the effort required a moment's tight focus – and in that instant, Jyoti vanished up the curled ramp, into the Palace of Abominations.

*Tok. Tok. Tok.*

'S-small matter,' Ralli-Faj sighed and crossed the burned

ground to where a shivering Ripcat hung among razor-twisted strands of Charm. The boneless face with its flame-haunted hollows drew very close to the anguished beastman. 'S-small matter indeed – now that you have been delivered into the hands of the Dark Lord.'

Caval trudged through the swamp, chewing curses at each misstep among the hummocks that plunged him waist-deep in mire. Charm kept away leeches and biting insects and also made him invisible to the spidery-eyed cacodemons. But that took all his magical strength, and he had none left to help him through the marsh.

The bog rose in mossy banks to the sward surrounding the Palace of Abominations. Caval sat there in the tasselled shade of ribbon ferns, catching his breath. Again, he cursed himself, *You're an old fool, coming here!*

In the Cloths of Heaven, after Jyoti and Reece departed, he had almost let himself die. At least from those ruins his soul could have climbed to the Abiding Star and into heaven. Even the three blind gods could not have denied him that.

But he had not forsaken his chance to return to the Beginning for the gods. He had slogged through the morass for a wider truth. He had come back not to serve blindness but light. His personal darkness had brought Wrat and his demons from the Dark Shore. The light that could dispel these shadows was him.

*And so the gods are fulfilled* . . . Caval groaned as he stood and stared up at the stained pyramid. Its sides seeped brown leakages from the seams of its stone panels, and a stench of decay hung in a sulfurous pall over this place of torment.

Death for him in this sepulcher was certain and Chance alone would determine his fate thereafter. As for Justice, he had served that god by sacrificing his personal hope of heaven to undo what he had wrought of hell on Irth.

*And so the gods are fulfilled*, he repeated to himself and shuffled toward the palace. *But not in blindness. In light. Caval. In light.*

He entered the open base of the floating pyramid with its wide expanse of hedge-mazes and walked through charred rents in the shrubbery burned by charmfire. Two ogres lay lifeless among shattered boulders and scorched sand, one with its face knifed open, the other a tarry skeleton.

In the middle of the devastation, a fallen star slept. Caval knelt before it. This denizen of the bright air reminded him of his abandoned quest, and he regarded it sadly, a sibling of Charm, fallen to Irth, not too unlike himself.

If he had more Charm, he would have killed it. Such a creature did not belong on Irth. The corrosive air seared like acid. But there was no returning it to the bright air either. It had completed its life cycle just as he had. Its fall to Irth was as tragic as his. It belonged in the Gulf, where the void would burst it to charmdust and scatter its beauty among the cold worlds.

With his big-knuckled hands placed each upon a point, he drew Charm into himself from the star. Gently, at first. Then, when the energy flowed freely, more hungrily.

Its eyes cracked slits of dazzling star rays, and the sorcerer quickly removed his hands. The lids closed at once, though colors around the star still looked faded.

Caval had not been able to draw enough power to end the fallen star's misery, but now he was strong enough to glimpse the shadows of time, stressed and still wavering in this scene of recent violence. He saw the ogres' assault and Reece's despairing resort to the beastbody of Ripcat.

And he saw Ralli-Faj – and in that stretched veil of human fabric, the final veil, the shadow of death.

A single tone sounded from his soul. It was the resonant chime of his dying, echoing back to him from the near future. It would lead him to Ralli-Faj.

Caval rose from the sand bed and bowed to the fallen star. 'Thank you, cousin. You have given me the strength to have for myself what I cannot give you.'

The sorcerer, more nimble for the star's Charm, loped in the direction where he heard his death. Its crystal timbre guided him up a spiral rampway set among carbon skeletons of dwarf trees. Cacodemons flitted across the ramp, patroling the lanes between the stone crypts. But the demons did not see him any more than did the tortured souls afloat behind the long windows of the pus-vaults.

'You can hide from the cacodemons-s, Caval,' Ralli-Faj called from around a blind bend, 'yet I s-see you. Old fool, turn back and I'll not s-set the demons-s on you. Begone!'

Caval smiled grimly and did not slow his stride. Since childhood in the Brood of Assassins, he knew that in hand combat silence was power. *The first to speak is always the weakest*, he remembered the old teachers saying.

Of course, they quoted the pretalismanic warriors who had no notion of packing Charm in words. Ralli-Faj fought as a warlock facing a sorcerer. His words could kill. But Ralli-Faj the warlock was not prepared to meet Caval the assassin.

*Why should he?* The sorcerer spoke to himself to counter the drowsy effect of Ralli-Faj's Charmed words. *Why should he indeed? No assassin could survive against a warlock.* And he smiled, because he did not intend to survive.

The warlock came into view backed by a glistening black wall of cacodemons. In their snaky grasp hung torn and bleeding Ripcat.

Caval lurched into a full-out run, his beard split and long white hair streaked back with the Charmed speed of his attack. He pumped power into his churning legs and ran with his arms whirling.

Ralli-Faj spat a spark that flew to the feet of the charging wild man and smeared like grease.

With a shout, Caval's legs shot from under him and he fell in a tangle of limbs and tinsel windings.

Ralli-Faj laughed – and his 'haw' of delight came out soundless against the shout from Caval – a sharp cry that expanded to a roar. Its cutting force emptied him of all Charm and struck Ripcat so forcefully it tore his skin of light.

A blond human face screamed from behind the shredded mask of Ripcat, and Reece plunged into the greasy smoke that had been cacodemons.

Ralli-Faj stepped into the fleeing fumes, reaching with his black magic for the running man. The necrotic haze of the extinguished demons obscured his power, and he used the amulets tied to his stilts to stir a charmwind.

From behind, Caval staggered upright and laughed. 'Your time is done, Ralli-Faj! All hope for your precious future is gone up in smoke!'

The sorcerer pitched his laughter to distract Ralli-Faj, and sparks of nervous light spat from the holes in the warlock's leather as he strove in vain to focus his charmwind before Reece disappeared among the crypts.

'Too late!' Caval guffawed. 'His body is dark. It's invisible to the strong eye.' The sorcerer laughed with lavish joy.

*Tok.*

The laughter stopped abruptly. The steel tip of a stilt lanced Caval through his beard and stood crimson out the back of his neck.

Ralli-Faj shook the impaled sorcerer from his stilt and frantically ran up the curving rampway, searching with eyes of fire for the escaped magus.

*Tok – tok – tok – tok – tok – tok – tok—*

Caval laughed. His wraith flimmered in the relict body heat of his cooling corpse, and he stared down at his dead body with merriment.

*Small price to save Reece*, he thought, even though the icy draft of the Gulf already tugged at him. *Whether now he lives or dies matters not. I did not abandon him in darkness – as I did on the Dark Shore. I have brought light to the three blind gods!*

That thought filled him with such a profound fulfillment that he calmed enough to hear the torn souls of the other dead sucking toward the abyss. His laughter dimmed, and he looked at his spent body with a firmer sense of forever.

Listening for the future, he heard nothing. *Should there not be echoes if Reece is successful and the Dark Lord falls? Why are there no echoes?*

He wanted to follow Ralli-Faj and be certain that Reece escaped, but he lacked the Charm. Only the Abiding Star offered him the strength to kindle consciousness in the effluvia he had become and to cling, however tenuously, to Irth. At nightfall, the nocturnal tide would carry him away and a new life would open before him – a life begun in darkness.

Tywi felt the Dark Lord dying. Behind her closed eyes, in absolute darkness, wild beasts raged and roared.

'Wake up, small thing!' Dogbrick growled and tapped her gently with the muzzle of his firelock. They stood among feathery canes clicking in the wind. 'Where has he gone? Where do you see him now?'

Tywi opened her eyes. An apparition of Drev floated in the tule mists beyond the next gravel bank.

It was not truly the wizarduke, only a mirage she had created for herself. She had used it at first for comfort in the fern holt where Jyoti and Ripcat had left them. Then, when she could wait no more, she used it to convince Dogbrick to go with her to the Palace of Abominations – to rescue Lord Drev and Rica.

Dogbrick, too, had grown impatient waiting for cacodemons to swoop down on them, and he played along with Tywi's visions of Drev. He crossed the gravel bank at the point where she had said the wraith stood, and he stopped cold and motioned his bedraggled partner closer.

'Behold the tower of perfidy!' he gnashed. 'Lord Drev led us most accurately.'

They peeked through a blind of waxed fronds at the titanic pyramid floating above a burning parkland.

'This place stinks!' Tywi exhaled sharply, eyes darting about, constantly searching for cacodemons.

'There has been a firefight,' Dogbrick said, misreading the erratic pattern of scorched vegetation. 'A great battle has raged here.'

'Ripcat – Jyoti?'

'Wait here. I will scout ahead.' He bolted out of the screen of wax ferns and dashed across the sward, clutching the firelock across his chest.

Tywi followed.

'I said wait!' Dogbrick whispered hotly. 'There will be cacodemons.'

'Look, Dog!' Tywi pointed through the smudged air of smoldering grass to where the wraith of Lord Drev stood, his naked wounds visible to them both.

'It's the wizarduke!' Dogbrick leaped forward, and the wraith retreated.

The phantom flitted among torched shrubberies with the shapes of animals, and they ran after it. Above them hung the massive interior of the pyramid packed with chambers and bowelings of ducts.

'Gryn!' Tywi identified the dead ogre with the cleaved face.

Dogbrick put a moldered sandal on its chest and pulled the assault knife from the ogre's backbone. 'That large roast over there must be Gnawl.'

They looked for Drev's wraith and found him hovering beside the fallen star, wavery as a flame. Maroon with sores, he gazed at them with vibrant, pain-mad eyes.

'Circle around the star from the back,' Dogbrick advised, leading Tywi through a yard of smashed agates. Sand fused to glass in long chromatic threads crunched under their sandals. 'It's alive yet. Was it luck protected it from the crossfire that burned these gardens or its own Charm? We'd do best, I think, to stay well out of its line of sight. Nearly killed Rica.'

Tywi walked toward the wounded shade of Drev, and it wisped away. With her imagination, she called him back. In her mind, she saw her apparition, without wounds.

Thin filaments of charmsmoke gathered to a semblance of the maimed duke.

'I can feel him, Dog!' Tywi called out excitedly. 'Drev is alive!'

Dogbrick lifted the fallen star from behind by hooking his elbows under two of its points. It was heavy, and he could only barely lift it. 'It's almost dead,' he reasoned. 'It's heavy with the emptiness of Charm.'

Tywi advanced toward the wraith, it vanished, and she summoned it back. She repeated this until it led her to the helical ramp. 'Drev wants us to go this way.'

Dogbrick staggered toward her, carrying the fallen star. 'Can't – take this – with us,' he groaned and dropped the stone star. Its top point punched a hole in the ground, and it stood upside-down.

Suddenly, its pink face tightened like a fist.

Dogbrick snatched Tywi by her shoulders and hauled her away before the star's eyes opened. Their radiance blended shadows across the damaged park, and the air before its gaze shivered like silk.

The star's charmlight shone on a baobab, illuminating protozoan transparencies in the branches – the gelatinous ectoplasm of departed souls.

Caval stood there, too. Neither Dogbrick nor Tywi recognized the bearded skeleton. To them, he appeared as a cadaverous ghost, which was what he was. A cacodemon had found his punctured corpse on the rampway and dragged it down to the garden to devour it in private.

The shriveled ghost waved them away, pointing and gesticulating at the baobab. Then the fallen star closed its eyes again, and Caval's revenant vanished.

'He wants us to go to that stout tree,' Dogbrick said and strode toward it.

'No, Dog!' Tywi waved to call him back. 'The ghost warned us away!'

From around the broad-trunked tree, a cacodemon emerged dragging the scarlet ribcage and eyeless head of the carcass that was Caval.

Dogbrick jumped away and collided with Tywi. She tumbled over the stony ground, and he wrenched himself away to avoid crushing her.

A tentacle snared his leg, dragging him furiously through the rocky sand. He fired maniacally at the tusked jaws in the creature's underbelly grinning to eat him.

Charmlight washed futilely across the meshing red teeth and spiderbright eyes. Swiftly, his free hand drew the assault knife from his belt and hacked with ferocious vigor. He kicked and howled and swung knife and firelock until he broke free.

Tywi seized his arm as he sped past, and he lifted her off her feet. Clinging to his shoulder, she gazed back at the gashed cacodemon writhing black whipstrokes in the air, its blood smoking in watery billows like squid ink.

Dogbrick ran until the ground gave way under him, and they splashed into a bog pool. On the far bank, they pulled themselves out, and the thief ground his molars for soaking the firelock.

'It ain't chasing us,' Tywi announced hopefully, peering back at the pyramid on her hands and knees, ready to spring away. 'Don't panic.'

'I'm not in a panic,' Dogbrick huffed. He shook clots of pond scum from the firelock. 'I slipped on the mossy bank.'

'Sure.' Tywi stood taller to be sure nothing followed them out of the pyramid's shadow. 'We're all right now. Nobody's following. The place looks empty.'

'You see Drev?'

'No.' Tywi sat back on her haunches and scanned the chambers of the swamp. Pink cranes stood on a green sandbar eating crayfish.

'Now at least you know he still lives.' Dogbrick set the firelock at its lowest setting, and sparks sizzled from the clip contacts. 'I think we'd better find some place dry to clean this firelock, and you can seek Lord Drev with your trances before it gets dark.'

They followed a stream that ran over a red floor deeper into the marsh. Saw grass closed around them and they prodded their way among the brittle stalks to higher ground.

Atop a rampart of junipers on a bough of blue lichen, Dogbrick cannibalized the firelock and Tywi lay down in a rectangle of emerald daylight.

She stepped out of her body and flowed across the lawn, back into the shadowy parkland. At the baobab, the jellied geometries of souls clung trembling to the branches.

Drev was nowhere to be seen.

The ghost of the old, withered man sat on a rootledge near where his scalped skull had rolled. He pointed along a singed hedge to a field of rolling black fog – the smoke of dead cacodemons.

Warped cries leaped from that seething smoke.

Tywi heard the Dark Lord dying. Inside the black fog, the wind of his screams carried absolute darkness and the raging roars of wild beasts.

She woke with a start on the blue bough in the fen.

'Ghosts?' Dogbrick asked, preoccupied with the parts of his weapon.

'Almost.'

'Dung of the Drakes!' the thief swore in frustration. 'This weapon is ruined!'

Tywi stood on the flat bough and reached for a view of the pyramid. 'We got to go back,' she said in a hush of awe and caution.

'Did you hear me, woman?' He showed her the breech slathered in virid scum. 'The firelock is useless. I gummed it up in the pond.'

'Forget the firelock,' she whispered to him. 'We got to go back right away.'

'Why?'

'Have you looked at the pyramid?' She grabbed his furry shoulder and pulled him to his feet. 'See up there! See the smoke?'

Inky tendrils of smog greased the atmosphere around the

pyramid. Staring closely, he saw they leaked from the palace ducts.

'It's the blood of cacodemons!' she said excitedly. 'It's the same blood as the one you knifed.'

'That is all bloodsmoke of demons?' He went on his toetips in amazement.

When he glanced down at Tywi, he saw her face glowing through its mask of mud. 'They're dying by the hundreds!'

Rett. The Dog Dim. Grapes. Little Luc. Skull Face. Chetto. And Piper. All the Bold Ones who had fallen into the Gulf with Wrat and survived, all his former comrades on the Dark Shore, who had been ritually slain and fed to the gremlin and its hive, walked Irth as ghosts.

They stood in the slewed shadows of Wrat's adytum inside the pyramid's apex. Wrat saw them from where he slumped on his onyx throne, and he stared at them from under his brow, through quivery baubles of sweat.

The sacrificial blood of these seven enabled black magic in Wrat, the power to bind the demons of the Dark Shore to his own Irthly frame. His hand clutched the purple fabric of his tunic, knuckles pressing against the pain in his chest.

Poch hung in the writhing coils of a cacodemon, watching Wrat with the sparkling intensity of a caught creature. He did not see the ghosts.

'Don't look so concerned for me,' Wrat called to him. 'With your help—' He winced and sucked a sharp breath. 'With your help, I will soothe this discomfort.'

The seven ghosts milled closer to their perfidious comrade, eager to watch him die.

'I am not dying, you charmless fools!' Wrat's voice leaked through his locked teeth. 'I'm not dying! It's the idiot gremlin. It can't take the pain!'

The cacodemons that died hurt the gremlin vitally. It writhed with the suffering of its hive.

'The thing wants to break free!' He laughed like a shout. 'It can't live without me.' He grunted as the gremlin torqued inside him. 'Your deaths made sure of that. So go away! I'm not dying.' His jaw clacked convulsively, and he forced a smile. 'I'm teaching these ignorant demons how to thrive!'

*Take it back*, Chetto called from across a cold space. His ulcerous ghost still rippled with the crawlings of cacomaggots under his skin.

*Take the gremlin back to the Dark Shore*, Grapes ordered, shaking his droops of polyps.

*Back!* the Dog Dim barked at him.

*Use your magic to climb the Ladder of the Wind*, Rett told him, pointing with his scar-cleaved beard toward the massive aperture of the adytum, where the afternoon boiled golden thermal clouds.

*Jump into the Gulf*, Little Luc insisted, his short, tow-headed body vibrant with anger. *It's your only hope of escaping certain death. Jump!*

'I won't do it!' Wrat shouted. 'I am the Dark Lord! I have come to loose chaos on Irth!'

*Then don't jump back into the Gulf*, Skull Face said and stepped forward into daylight. His noseless and lipless face stenciled the brightness. *I want to see you die here on the Bright Shore!*

Piper – tall and pallid, his lustrous red hair spilling over regal shoulders – remained silent.

'You think I'm done?' Wrat spoke through clamped jaws. 'No. To jump into the Gulf is to live again my defeat at the hands of Drev. No! We are staying here on Irth to rule all above the Gulf, with the stars under our feet!'

The gremlin twisted, and Wrat screamed to his feet and sat down again, heavily.

The ghosts stepped closer to view his suffering and entered the cauterizing daylight. Their shadows disturbed the light briefly and vanished.

'I'm still alive!' he yelled and turned a bleary face toward Poch.

The boy watched in horror as the tunic over Wrat's chest throbbed.

'The gremlin wants to flee its pain,' Wrat explained to the wide-eyed boy. 'But if it breaks free, it will not live long without me.'

Poch closed his eyes and pressed his chin to his chest, shutting out the nightmare.

*Be still or die!* Wrat commanded the bestial intelligence he hosted in his body. 'Calm down,' he said aloud to himself. 'You are in a panic. Calm down and let's face our enemy. You must trust me.'

Wrat took his hand away from his palpitating chest and gripped the armrests of the onyx throne. He anchored himself against his pain, and he focused the gremlin's magic on the source of their anguish.

The strong eye showed them Reece: He ran wildly through the winding corridors among the torture crypts. When he surprised cacodemons, he motioned at them – and they immediately curdled to smoke.

The gremlin gnawed at Wrat's ribs, and he shrieked, 'Where is Ralli-Faj?'

The strong eye searched deeper down the pyramid and located the warlock in the charred ruins of his palatial gardens. He hung on his stilts before a fallen star that stood on its top point, upside-down.

The star's eyes opened in its furious face, and twin beams of blue-white Charm flooded the burned parkland. Ralli-Faj absorbed the Charm directly through his coriaceous skin and began to inflate.

Wrat watched with naked awe, impressed by the warlock's dexterity in handling such raw power. The Charmlight was so strong, it wizened purple at the crispy fringes of his dried pelt and pooled in the empty sockets, gelling to an inhuman semblance of eyes.

The awe of its host calmed the gremlin, and the knot in Wrat's chest relaxed.

'Yes, that's it,' Wrat encouraged. 'Calm down. Ralli-Faj shares our strong eye now. And he possesses the Charm to chase down Reece.'

The gremlin settled to an irritated ache behind Wrat's sternum.

'Now that you are settling down,' Wrat continued soothingly, 'I can show you why you can always trust me. This is my world. I know how to use it – for us.'

The Dark Lord moved the strong eye from Ralli-Faj back up into the pyramid. He directed it at a smaller source of hurt and saw Jyoti running amok through the palace, blasting walls, ducts and portals with her firelock at the first glimpse of cacodemons, slaying some and wounding many.

Wrat smiled, unconcerned.

Within him, the gremlin sensed his smugness yet continued to writhe fearfully.

'Stop fighting the margravess,' Wrat said to his attendant cacodemons. 'Open a way for her at once. Lead her here, directly to us.'

The gremlin trembled, but Wrat patted his chest with gentle assurance.

'She is already defeated,' he said and cocked his head toward Poch.

The fright scrawled on the boy's face pleased the gremlin, and it finally calmed down completely.

In the strong eye, Wrat smiled to watch the cacodemons slither away into the lanes among the crypts.

Jyoti continued firing anyway, singling out the obscene vaults carved as human orifices where the demons often lurked. Explosions marched ahead of her down the empty corridors, shattering lewd façades and carved niches that could hide clusters of demons.

She avoided hitting any of the crypts. Behind their yellow

viewports, Peers floated in liquid agony. She reserved her berserk rage for demonic vaults and the chutes and scaffolds that connected the levels. The acrid smoke of seared metal burned her throat, but she hurtled on, following the direction of the sword in her left hand.

A pummeling stream of blue charmbursts smashed a utility wall ahead of her. Pipes twisted apart, spewing steam, and stone blocks crashed atop themselves and erupted to rock dust and whirling shards.

She stepped through the smoke into the expansive top chamber of the pyramid – the Dark Lord's adytum.

Far across an expanse of polished black stone, Hu'dre Vra sat on an onyx throne before a sinuous doorway tall as the sky and filled with shining clouds. His massive, gleaming armor shone like night. In the air beside him, tangled in the barbed loops of a cacodemon, Poch hung, tremulous with fear.

'Put down your firelock and my sword,' the Dark Lord commanded. 'Then you may join your brother.'

Jyoti stared at Poch, who gaped back mutely, too afraid to speak.

In the sky-high portal, among the towering clouds, a black thunderhead of cacodemons swelled larger, swarming closer at their master's beckoning.

Jyoti dropped the firelock and with both hands placed the sword Taran upon the rubble of the wall she had punched through. She looked again to her brother, and he did not object.

Then, head high, she walked away from her weapons and into the power of the Dark Lord.

## A Flesh of Dreaming

❖—❖

Under the baobab in the charred gardens of the Palace of Abominations, souls huddled. Lacking both training in the internal arts and Charm, these souls had amorphous shapes and nebulous perceptions of the world around them.

*So many!*

Caval counted over a hundred before he stopped. They were mostly human souls from the camp, slain as panicky cacodemons frenzied among them. They cast a glum mood over the tree under which the sorcerer's carcass lay torn in bits.

He strolled the length of the tree's long shadow. At its end, Thylia stood, lean and radiant as a tapered flame.

'Why are you here, brother?' the witch queen's ghost asked in a distant voice.

The old man gestured toward the chewed and blackened grots of his body. 'Waiting for the night tide, Sister.'

'You are bound, then, for the Dark Shore?' She stepped three paces nearer and parted her veils to reveal a sad countenance. 'You are not among the Brotherhood?'

'Loose affiliations.' He tossed it off lightly, resigned already to his new venture beyond the Gulf. 'And you? The Dark Lord grew

461

weary of your amorous witchery?'

She replaced her veil demurely, yet her jet eyes still smirked. 'You know the heart's hungers better than that, Caval.'

'Then if you didn't bore him,' he said, plucking his frazzled beard, 'you must have crossed him.'

'Does it matter now?'

He cocked a wispy eyebrow. 'Why are *you* here, queen of the witches?'

'I saw you with these other lost souls.' She motioned at the boughs of jellied blobs. 'I don't understand. Why are you in this filthy place and not among the Brotherhood?'

'I *was* learning their mysteries . . .' Caval began, feebly.

'But you took your life into your own hands, didn't you?' She shook her head knowingly. 'The Sisterhood has its apostates, as well. Like you, they follow the Lone Road to the Beginning. Few arrive. Most turn out just as you have, poor Caval, a ghost on the killing floor, waiting for the wind to blow it away.'

'As you say.' Caval's stare showed no hint of shame and none smudged him. With concern he asked, 'And you? What becomes of your ghost, Thylia?'

'The Mysteries, Caval.'

'I've heard tell.' He pursed his lips, impressed at the genuine salvation that the covens and sanctuaries offered their most zealous devotees: 'You've enough internal Charm to reach one of the Sisterhood's crystal collectors. There your soul will be stored and nourished, rested, until you are ready again for another life on Irth. Is that it?'

'Yes.' Her voice softened dolorously. 'I will not be joining you on the Dark Shore.'

'Not just yet, Thylia.' He smiled and tilted his head sagely. 'All of brightness eventually falls to dark. The Gulf awaits all Irth.'

'All, sorcerer?' Her voice arched to express her awareness of his sagely ambition, punctured by Ralli–Faj's stilt. 'There are the few among us who find their way back to the Beginning.'

'The holy do,' Caval concurred with a humble sag of his shoulders. 'Only the holy.'

'Yes, it was your *shadow* that pulled you back from heaven, wasn't it, old mage?' She regarded him ruefully. 'That insubstantial thing, that shadow of a good man not good enough, has broken many lives. You have earned your place among the damned for what your ignorance inflicted on Irth, Caval. Yet you should depart knowing your sacrifice was not unnoticed – and not given in vain.'

Caval accepted this judgment with a skeptical frown. 'How can you be sure of that, witch?'

'You have set the mage of the Dark Shore upon Wrat,' she answered with glib assurance. 'The gremlin knows it is doomed. Only Wrat insists on keeping it here to play out the full blood rite.'

'Yet, look, Thylia—' Caval pointed to where Ralli-Faj had walked his stilts to the inverted star. Under the pressure of the warlock's furious will, its eyes opened, and Charm flowed as a particulate silver mist into the slack skin.

'Reece may need help,' Thylia acceded with a worried squint. 'I will pray on my way to the crystal abode of the Sisters. I will pray for the magus from the Dark Shore.'

'No!' Caval called to her insistently. 'We must do more than pray.'

'More?' Her laugh floated from far away. 'We are ghosts, Caval.'

'Stay with me,' he requested with ragged, outstretched arms. 'You can yet make a difference.'

'How?'

The sorcerer motioned to the fallen star. The warlock's stilts stood empty beside it. Ralli-Faj, swollen to manshape, his brown flesh glossed with Charm, marched away trailing an aura of diamond chips.

On the rampway, a cacodemon met him with a knifebelt, and the warlock cinched it about his waist, not breaking his stride as he bounded after his prey.

'Ralli-Faj is far older than most suspect,' Caval confided. 'His origins are not in sorcery, where he has found his longevity. No. He began life, as did I, in the Brood of Assassins. Like myself, he is trained in murder.' He opened his webby hands and looked at her beseechingly. 'Reece is no match for him, in magic or in killing.'

Thylia's gaze constricted. 'Why are you telling me this, sorcerer? What can we shades do against the living? Precious little.'

'Oh, precious little, indeed.' Caval agreed wholeheartedly, feeling emptiness crawling through him with the waning day. 'Yet here, at the very edge, very little things matter a great deal. You do understand?'

Thylia backed away, believing he was mad, his mind rancid from the experience of death.

'Wait, Sister. I will need your help.'

'There is no help for where you are bound, lost soul. Fare light, Caval.'

'Thylia – behold!' He gesticulated to the beastman and mud woman creeping into the roasted garden. But the witch queen was gone.

*Flighty witches!*

Caval approached Dogbrick and Tywi as close as he could, yet with so little Charm he could not make them see him. Even so, he jumped and waved and wagged his long beard.

'You *are* mad, Caval,' the witch queen called from above him. She perched in the baobab tree among the shivering souls clustered like amoebae.

'Come down from there,' he summoned her urgently. 'I need your help reaching them.'

'How did you know they were coming?' Thylia asked. 'Who are they?'

'Never mind!' Caval shouted impatiently. 'Dance with me, Thylia!'

The witch queen floated to his side and danced the cadaverous old man across the blackened lawn to the wary intruders.

Tywi stopped Dogbrick with a startled hand. 'It's the old man, again!' she cried. 'The corpse the cacodemon was eating! The ghost from my trance . . .'

'I see him, too!' Dogbrick yelped. 'He's a frightful, horrid thing. Let's move away, quickly.'

'No, no, Dog. See him waving. He's pointing to the fallen star. He wants us closer.'

'More reason to be farther. Let's away.'

'I think he wants us to pick it up.' Tywi strode closer.

Morosely, Dogbrick padded after her, looking up at the underside of the pyramid, searching the circuitry of ducts, silos and receding shafts for cacodemons.

'Listen!' Tywi cupped a hand to her ear. 'He's talking to us!'

The thief listened yet even with his acute ears heard nothing.

Tywi bent close to the desiccated ghost, and Dogbrick held her arm, ready to snatch her away. But the phantom simply whispered and smiled. Then he bowed to them, stepped away and slurred to daylight.

The excited woman repeated quietly to the thief what she had heard from the sorcerer, and the beastman's hackles rippled. He immediately stooped to pull the star from the ground. With a grunting effort, he lifted it and staggered after his partner. She waved him on and scampered to the spiral causeway.

'You are a clever killer, Caval,' the witch queen gloated as Dogbrick lurched away. 'I am glad you served on Irth rather than ruled. It is too sad that we must lose you now.'

'Not now, Thylia. There is time yet. Let us use your Charm to follow them. Let us be certain our work is done.'

'Our work is long done, old fool.' She smiled benignly at the doddering sorcerer. 'You were most cunning to find this way to reach the living again – and to such lethal effect, too. I trust in the events you have set in motion, Caval. You are redeemed in the eyes of the Sisterhood. The Goddess watches over you even as she takes you into her uteral darkness, into a new life among the cold worlds.'

'But I want to see our victory!' Caval called after her. 'What if they fail? What if Reece fails? I must know! Or I cannot die!'

'You are already dead, old fool,' she called from among the crooked shadows of the baobab. 'Already dead . . .'

'I want to see Wrat dead!' Caval bawled.

He heard himself and flinched coldly. He sounded as maniacal as the monster he loathed.

Searching for Thylia, he watched shadows creep longer. She had vanished into the orange and purple lightfall of late afternoon.

Head hung with weariness and worry, the dead sorcerer drifted toward the wide, spreading tree of souls.

From the strong eye of the Dark Lord, Ralli-Faj drew sight. He searched for Reece and found him loping down a corridor of smoked glass pipes and checkerwork mosaics. The warlock recognized the orange and yellow banded hallway as a conduit for effluent steam pipes from charmworks below. With the strong eye, he opened the valves.

Reece vanished in sulfurous billows and reappeared almost immediately, turning fast and gathering the steam in a spun spell of dark magic. He shouted and stamped his feet wide apart, arms stretched out, head high, a human star radiating black light. Hissing a serpent's song, the steam threaded back into the valves, pulling after it the ultraviolet hues of Reece's aura.

Deep in the pyramid's interior, thunder rolled. The ramp under Ralli-Faj shook violently, tumbling him off his feet, and rock dust flurried in sizzling streams from the grating plates of the pyramid's surface.

The warlock sat up startled. The magus he confronted could destroy the palace!

Ralli-Faj called again on the strong eye – and he felt Hu'dreVra go slack with weakness as he gave freely the power to counter Reece's magic. Propped on his onyx throne in catatonic trance, unable to move without disturbing his spell, the Dark Lord locked his magical will to his opponent's.

The warlock ran to the chute that led to Reece. Black magic had been canceled in the pyramid, and the strong eye faltered and went out. He did not need it any more.

The Charmed chute carried him higher into the palace and dropped him through an open duct into a checkerworked corridor where steam hissed.

Reece waited for him crouched in the vaporous shadows and pounced even before the warlock hit the floor.

Ralli-Faj took the full force of Reece's blow in a falling feint, pulling the magus after him. They tumbled, and the warlock rolled atop his prey, one taut hand squeezing off Reece's windpipe, the other unsheathing from his belt a green steel knife with a barbed tip.

A double-handed blow broke Ralli-Faj's chokehold, and Reece squirmed free – but only to find himself with his back to the curved checkerworked wall.

Passing the knife fluidly between his hands, Ralli-Faj grinned to see fear in his opponent. Reece was no more than another simian without his black magic. He watched the knife with wild eyes, frantic features jumping with each twitch of the blade destined to slit his belly sternum to groin. The warlock's chest flushed hotly as he moved in to place the blade.

A sturdy thump swiped his attention. Dogbrick had fallen out of the chute and landed on his rump with Tywi in his lap.

The warlock's angry scowl showed glassy shards of teeth, and his inhuman cry assured them they would die next. His knife wove an intricate killing pattern between his hands, mesmerizing the frightened magus.

Tywi shouted, 'I kill you, Ralli-Faj! For giving in to the darkness, I kill you with the light!' She hopped out of Dogbrick's lap and exposed the fallen star in the beastman's arms.

'No!' Ralli-Faj shrieked like a jungle monkey.

When the star's eyes opened, all color washed away. The warlock's figure stood locked in a posture of defiance as Charm poured into him. His body swelled to balloon limbs and a goggling visage of terror.

His eyes popped first, emitting twin rays of fiery Charm. Then, all the holes in his body gave out, and he stood lanced with light, expanding beyond the limits of human recognition.

With a dull boom, his taut, glossy skin exploded, splattering rags of leathery flesh down the corridor in a gasping rush of sour air.

Hu'dre Vra felt the warlock's death in his chest. The gremlin writhed. To calm it, he stared out at the tall day and spotted Nemora cocked in the sky, cold and blue.

The gremlin's claws vised his ribs, and the pain forced him to drop his armor. It fell away as ill-shapen peelings and rustled on the floor like trash restless in the wind.

Wrat regarded the hordes of cacodemons gathered in the cavernous adytum. Legions of screaming mute creatures packed the space around him, their sour stink calling to the gremlin scratching behind his breastbone. Embedded faces with diabolic grins mouthed mesmermur music through their tusks. Its vesperal tones filled the jammed arena with a crawling calm.

Jyoti and Poch hung on either side of Wrat's throne, prominently displayed among the eelish writhings and serrated spikes of the enclosing hosts. Fist to chest, Wrat sat sullenly, the sword Taran hanging idly in his left hand.

Out of the hole in a stone bulwark where Jyoti had blasted her way in, ghosts entered. The Dog Dim scurried through, followed by Little Luc, Skull Face, Chetto, Grapes, and Rett. Piper stood on the threshold of the rubble-strewn gap – smiling wanly.

The ghost held a pipe to his mouth and blew a single, frosty note.

Reece stepped through the ghost and staggered to a halt among the broken stones. The throngs of cacodemons in sleazy tiers watching him with their tiny heatless eyes chilled his blood. Their interlocked bodies formed a cathedral of pestilential blackness reaching to the very cope of the adytum.

At the writhing center of its base, Wrat sat casually, mockingly. He nodded to his victims on either side and motioned Reece closer.

Before the magus could move, Dogbrick and Tywi stumbled through the torn bulwark, eager to catch up with him. Tentacles plucked them into the air and lofted them toward the ebony heights of the stacked cacodemons.

Reece briskly flashed an elaborate warding mudra before realizing that his magic remained canceled. In this state, he would have to physically lay hands on each demon to slay it.

'I can have one or more of your people pulled apart in an instant,' Wrat threatened dully, sounding almost bored. 'But I won't kill them just yet. Because I want them to watch me hack you into small pieces.'

Wrat waved the sword Taran and sent slashes of reflected light sweeping across the polished floor.

Reece flicked a look around him, searching for a weapon.

'We are very much alike, you and I,' Wrat said. 'We are consumed with selfish desire. We are greedy for what we want. You for Lara – and me for power. But what you want is dead. And what I have is most alive – and something we can share.'

'I had power in my world,' Reece replied. 'It had a bitter aftertaste and I want no more of it.'

Wrat chewed his lower lip and wagged the sword. 'You don't want power. And your Lara is dead. So, why are you here? What are you going to do? Kill me? Is that why you rushed here, to slay the Dark Lord?' A laugh shouted from him. 'And how will you kill me? With your bare hands?' He flicked his thumb across the sword's fine edge and shook his head. 'You are a fool. I offer you power. And you grope for death.'

Reece straightened, his mind reaching for words, for time to decide what to do. 'You say we are alike, and in our greediness, this is so. That is why I am here. I have lusted, like you, for what is not mine.' He allowed himself a brittle smile at the desire that had led him to this fatal moment. 'But I at least loved a woman. You love yourself.'

Wrat leaned forward, sword standing point down before him, both hands crossed on the hilt. 'For all your love, look where your woman is now! Look at you, cowering, unprepared for our fateful encounter. And look at me! I am the Dark Lord!'

His dirt-colored eyes squinted with the effort of his will. Without magic. Without violence. By will alone, he had forced this so-called magus to submit. 'Bow before me!' Wrat yelled. 'Bow! Or I will kill the margravess and her brother.'

Reece stared with alarm at Jyoti, and she gazed back helplessly from her tentacled bondage.

The magus exhaled a heavy sigh of resignation and bowed. His long pale hair brushed the debris of the fallen wall, and a murderous thought snapped into place. When he rose, he came up with rocks in both fists.

Whipsawing his right arm, he flung the first rock through the phantom blurs of cacodemons that swooped to block it and struck Wrat squarely between his startled eyes. The impact of the second rock against his exposed larynx cut short his yelp of shock. Wrat's head snapped forward, and he slumped dead even as the sword Taran clanged to the floor.

Instantly, the towering ranges of cacodemons vanished to tarsmoke tilting in the afternoon breeze, and daylight gushed into the empty chamber.

Released from tentacles that had turned to coiled vapors, the prisoners clattered to the floor. They fell around the throne and lay stunned, staring eyelevel at Wrat's corpse. Its bruised and cockeyed face jerked spasmodically, and Poch cried and Dogbrick howled to see the dead man's purple tunic bulge and shred.

The gremlin, like a maudlin puppet varnished in blood, shoved free of Wrat's ripped carcass and ran squealing into the fiery daylight. It charged with rabid, mindless fury across the floor, striking aimlessly with scorpion-jointed arms, seeking another host among the terrified humans sprawled around it.

Tywi screamed and scuttled wildly, and the half-blind and blistered gremlin burst toward her.

The sword Taran lay on the floor near Poch. With an astonished shout, he seized it and swiped at the gremlin. The razor edge sliced through the imp's bulbous head even as it mounted Tywi, and, with a piercing shriek, the tiny monster dissolved to a curl of black smoke.

The Pain Chain lumbered to a metallic halt, groaning bestially from its weary rivets. The stink of death disembarked first.

Dogbrick ran out on to the face of the pyramid. Though the black magic that powered the winding engine was gone, Charm from amulet panels within the pyramid held the Chain in place and allowed the thief to dash along the rampway.

He wrenched open the sliding door of the second carriage and a noisome fetor gushed out with Rica's ghost.

The enchantress's body lay melted upon its bones, a waxen skeleton in a charmwright's leather vest. Her mad wraith pulsed in the warm, amber rays of the Abiding Star, then flapped out of sight, like torn fabric in a gust.

Tywi dashed to the lead carriage of the Chain and with her own strength jarred loose the rusty handle. Through her hands, and through the tangled light in the steamy air around her, she felt Drev alive. Nevertheless, she prepared herself to be shattered at the sight of his corpse.

She shoved the door aside, and the wizarduke tottered into the light. Dogbrick caught him as he reeled forward, and he fell a long way through the smell of fire.

Entranced by this sudden release from the interminable tenure of his agony, Drev's mind ranged timefree across space. He soared beyond the turning light of the horizon.

Night spread toward continental Irth, and he flew beyond, to the oceanic farside of the planet. The sea polished its sapphires under the Abiding Star – and the dark blue facets greened to emeralds as the water grew suddenly shallow.

Streaming ocean froth and cascades of kelp, the sunken continent of Gabagalus rose for another day under charmfire and tumbling clouds.

The wizarduke circled high enough above the hemisphere to see weather spirals knotting clouds to storm fronts across eroded peaks and coraline crags of ancient iron mountains. Seawater ran in vast riverworks across the slick continental shelves.

He peered intently into the blotched hues of mucilaginous flora that coated Gabagalus in a motley of beige, buff and glistering brown slimes. Among the mountainous ranges, benthic cities hid, often behind vast, smoking cataracts of foaming brine.

His orbit carried him too high to see any trace of the highways, the wort farms and the rocket pads that he knew were down there. Since the beginning of talismanic time, envoys from the dominions of Irth had been sent to this amphibious domain. Most did not return.

Those few that did reported a sophisticated civilization, a boisterous colony belonging to an interplanetary utopia that spanned bright worlds. The salamandrine denizens of Gabagalus invariably treated their guests with a supremely empathic respect – yet toward the Drylands, as they called the dominions, they held complete and relentless indifference.

Drev watched the slippery continent drift away as his orbit carried him into night. He swung along the brink of the Gulf and then curved in his flight to glide back toward the twilit edge of darkness and the blue marblings of dayside Irth.

Saffron drifts of an afternoon in the Reef Isles widened around him, and he dropped toward the smoldering pyramid, into the smell of fire, and a circle of haggard, triumphant faces grinning at him from all sides.

Dogbrick carried the shriveled wizarduke away from the mephitic stink of the Chain. Tywi kept close, using their destinal bond to hold his ghost in place. When she touched him, she felt the heavy stone of his body and how his soul had already disconnected.

Then Poch ran alongside and placed the sword Taran in Drev's limp hands, and its Charm began to heal him at once. Reece and

Jyoti sprinted ahead to see if they could find theriacal opals among the cacodemons' vaults.

In the adytum, Drev raised his head and saw Wrat's torn carcass where it lay staring up blindly through crooked lids. Only then did he relax enough so that, when he lowered his head, he slipped past trance into sleep.

Even Caval's ghost at the base of the baobab tree felt the arc of destiny that illuminated that Charmed moment. He gazed up at the emptiness of heaven between the clouds and thanked the Nameless.

*Death has become easy.*

He turned to the Abiding Star, the white light that had yet to cool to matter, and relaxed in its warmth. Slowly, the rays lengthened and ruddied toward night, and slowly the old sorcerer faded away.

When Reece came at dusk to find him, to tell him what he had learned of himself from the Dark Lord, what he remembered that he had forgotten deeper than his magic, Caval's soul was gone. It had drifted out on the night tide.

The magus departed that night as well. He slipped away without farewell while the others worked fervently to release the Peers from the pain vaults. He had completed his role for the blind gods on the Bright Shore and believed that he had earned the right to continue his search for the first woman he loved.

Lara's soul scented the distances of Irth with her music. It led him far away from the Reef Isles. He followed it by boat to Drymarch. A dew-wine cartel had erected a sky bund there, at the site where cacodemons had burned the old docks.

A dirigible carried him north to Dorzen in anonymity, and from that festive city he sailed a wind cruiser across the Sea to jubilant Keri. By glider, he traveled deep into the north mountains away from the celebratory frenzy of the dominions. Finally, on foot, he climbed to the frost-laced gravel heights of the Calendar of Eyes.

The air burned cold, but his magic warmed him. On all sides

glowed the ash of dusk. Lara's song glittered brighter than ever he had heard since he had drowned it in the cold waters of the Dark Shore.

Atop a windy spire rock, he sat in the dark listening to the soulful singing until dawn. He stood up under a striated emerald sky to greet the Abiding Star.

It rose on all sides of him. White radiance shone from the Beginning and enclosed him within a dazzling dome of serenity, a brute joy that opened the gates to the secret kingdom of himself.

And there he heard Lara's song in its proper setting, and at last he understood.

He climbed down the Calendar of Eyes. Along the way, he stopped to close the Door in the Air. Stars infested the sky dense as sand, yet the Door was easy enough to find once he knew that it was there. He clambered to its slender threshold and stood at the sightless edge of forever, gazing down across the Gulf to the Dark Shore.

'Caval!' he shouted.

After a while came the reply, 'I am here, Reece. And I see you – far away . . . on the limb of a star . . .'

'I found Lara!' Reece called. 'She has returned to the Abiding Star! To the Beginning!'

'Of course . . .' Caval's voice stretched to red shadows. 'She is a witch . . . She belongs with the Mother . . .'

'But how?' Reece yelled into the blind depths. 'She died on the Dark Shore!'

'I took her dead soul,' Caval answered in time, his words smeared with echoes. 'I took her soul out of the river as it came downstream . . . I carried her back to Irth with me . . . gave her to the Sisterhood . . . her soul was sturdy . . . from a cold world . . . hardy enough for the sisters to save . . . they wove her a body on Irth . . . she lived 35,000 days . . . a witch in Keri . . . before she climbed the Ladder of the Wind . . . to the Beginning!'

Reece stood dazed above the mist of stars and the yawing

darkness beyond. In the few years it had taken him to gather the Charm to climb to Irth, Lara had lived decades and fulfilled Caval's broken ambition. 'Why? You never told me you were taking her soul back to Irth!'

Silence swallowed his cry. Eventually, from a tiny place in the darkness he heard the smallest whisper, 'I was selfish . . . never thought to see you again . . . never have to answer your questions . . .'

'Caval!' Reece shouted with all his might, his body swaying from the jamb and nearly toppling him into the Gulf. 'Without you in the dark, I could not be here in the light! Master!'

No reply came.

Reece closed the Door in the Air and climbed down the Calendar of Eyes.

When the cacodemons prowling the streets of Dorzen withered suddenly to charcoal scrawls of smoke, Lady Von knew at once that the Dark Lord was dead. She was on the street herself when it happened, plying her witchcraft among Peers huddling in sewers and imprisoned in warehouses.

Since her installation by Hu'dreVra as ruler of Ux, she avoided the palace. She preferred to move announced through the city with only a few handmaids, witches themselves, helping whomever was needful. In that way, she did not have to oversee the torture programs and instead could do what was in her power to help Wrat's victims.

Tar streaks of melted cacodemons hazed the air as Lady Von sped back to the palace in her coach. She rushed immediately to the central garden, where songs of water and pebbles rose to an open and vividly blue sky.

A handsome man in a silk tunic sat on a moss bench throwing petals into a trickling rill and watching mutely as they whisked away between his bare feet.

'Romut?' she called, and her voice startled small bright birds from the walls of black ivy. They spilled through the fern-hung bays and flew over a boulevard where she could see people dancing as news of Wrat's death spread.

The handsome man with the fleecy yellow hair continued plucking petals and dropping them in the crinkled water.

Lady Von stared into him with eyes darker than shadows and found his mind blank. Once she ascertained that the demise of the Dark Lord did not allow for Romut's soul to return, she turned away and left him to his mindless pleasures.

She found a group of old witches gathered around the champagne marble altar at the center of the crystal court. They parted their veils at her arrival, and she recognized none of them.

'Thylia is dead,' a witch mother with flesh of varnished wood announced. 'The Sisterhood has chosen you to replace her as our queen.'

Lady Von stood speechless before these bent messengers and groped for a reply. 'I am but a veil dancer in the Sisterhood . . .'

'The witch queen is not an earned rank, as you well know, Von.' The witch mother inspected her with an aspect of concern. 'The role the Sisterhood offers you is an appointed service. Are you prepared to accept?'

The petite young woman glared numbly. 'I am not worthy of such responsibility.'

'Oh, on the contrary, my dear.' One of the group broke away and swept toward her in muttersome veils. 'You suffered Romut's sacrileges against your body and when he came into your power, you did not return his cruelty. Instead, you cared for him.'

'And you did not truckle to Wrat,' the varnished face spoke again. 'Nor did you act foolishly and defy him outright.'

'You adapted to all the necessities for survival,' the witch at her side stated proudly, 'without betraying your vows to the Sisterhood. And those are the flexible qualities we want in our queen. Will you serve us in that role, young Von? Will you be our queen?'

'And my husband, Baronet Fakel, and our children—?' The well in her heart filled with all the love that the Dark Lord had tried to drain from her, and no words could carry the sudden feelings that rose in her.

'They will join us at Andezé Crag,' the witch mother assured her. 'There is room there for everyone's happiness! Isn't that so, sisters?'

The witches closed around their new queen, laughing and talking excitedly. And even as they celebrated in Dorzen, far to the south, in the Palace of Abominations, Dogbrick and the liberated prisoners from the camp removed the queen's husband and children from the pain crypts with the other Peers. Bundled in theriacal wraps, they were carried by balloon out of the miasmal swamp and taken to a makeshift aid station established on the upland pastures.

The balloons, the opals and all the materials for the station came from the lading docks and construction yards that the cacodemons had built in a nearby sea cove. Under the leadership of Dogbrick, whom everyone in the camp recognized, all the torture victims in the pyramid were quickly removed.

The presence of numerous charmwrights among the prisoners provided the necessary expertise to devise amulets for this careful work. Using treasures found on the docks and by laboring through the night, the palace was emptied of all people by dawn.

Ogres watched enviously from within the marsh. With the cacodemons gone, the ogres' perpetual war with people could continue vigorously once again, and they mumbled among themselves strategies for stealing the hoard of construction supplies abandoned by their former masters and destroying their hex-gems.

But Dogbrick's alacrity in organizing the building materials into the infrastructure of an aid station for the Peers stymied the ogres' plans. With the help of clever charmwrights, the philosopher designed a tent community on the high fields of the reef isle, and it was built overnight.

At dawn, after the last Peer was removed from the Palace of Abominations, the charmwrights fitted the giant structure with numerous anchor and ballast amulets and sank the pyramid in the marsh.

Bog water churned brown waves leprous with vines, tendrils and rotted logs, and the spying ogres fled deeper into the marsh. When they climbed into the canopy to look back, the Palace of Abominations had disappeared. Where it had stood, black water boiled.

The charmwrights named the bubbling morass Blight Fen and set over it a swamp angel, a muddy wraith of seaweed hair and mossy wings, to ward off the curious. That frightened the ogres. Ever afterward they set themselves apart from this remote corner of Nhat where the ruined Cloths of Heaven touched the percolating black waters of the drowned pyramid.

With their absence, the aid station on the grassy pastures above Blight Fen flourished. Cities from every dominion sent amulets and charmwrights to aid in the recovery of their Peers, and within days, most of Wrat's victims looked whole and could laugh again.

At night, when the wounded Peers were asleep in their theriacal hammocks, after the galleys had been cleaned and the night crews set to work preparing for the next day's meals, Dogbrick took time from his chores to sit on the grassy bluffs with the scavengers who remained.

Most of the time they talked about their hopes for Blight Fen and for Irth in the new days. Individuals recounted their camp experiences and what it took to salve their damaged souls. Visitors, who had come to see for themselves the preserved camp and the simmering black fen, occasionally asked Dogbrick for what he had learned in his captivity.

'The Empty Screed is right,' he gladly pontificated whenever called upon. 'There is no freedom from our own freedom. You have to make it up as you go along. Each remorseless day.' He strode to the edge of the bluff, his maned shadow cut from the starry sky. Pointing down the far side to the ebbing Sea and the tidal flats, he added, 'In the camp we were forced to look into mystery's mirror. We were forced to see that most difficult truth.

That we are all just little more than ghosts.'

'Such littleness is life!' someone would almost invariably sigh or chant at this point, quoting the *Talismanic Odes*.

'We *are* little more than ghosts,' Dogbrick would agree. 'Ghosts measuring distances by stories, right to the edge of the world. What does it matter then if our story is Caval's or Wrat's? The edge cuts away such petty distinctions. Good against evil? What matters light or dark in the void? The Gulf swallowed the holy sorcerer as readily as it took back the monster Wrat.'

'Churlsbane!' Sometimes the audience would curse him for what sounded to them too like the Dark Lord's nihilism.

Dogbrick smiled a glint of fang. 'Are we not little more than illusions, all of us?' he accused the scavengers Charmed free of their scars and the visitors protected by their talismans. 'One moment we are whirlwinds of charmfire standing on Irth. And the next, we are fugitives to our own bodies. Pilgrims of the abyss. Nomads in the cold worlds.'

For a day Drev lay in Charmed sleep, swaddled in trance wrap and strapped with theriacal opals to a hammock under a chrome tent that filtered rays from the Abiding Star. While he rested, Tywi helped Dogbrick and the other volunteers at the aid station. She removed drained hex-gems on the amulet casts of the wounded and fetched replacements for the charmwrights.

During a break in her chores, she met Dogbrick on a hill of salt-bleached grass. To one side, the Sea fumed among highwater boulders and on the other, the tents and pavilions of the aid station caught the radiance of the Abiding Star with their conjure-cloths of chrome and dazzling gold.

'You kept me alive in the camp,' she said, sitting with him on a driftwood bough dragged to this crest, no doubt, by ogres. 'And Drev says it was me kept him from Rica's sorry fate. So, you saved him as well, you see, through me.'

Dogbrick turned away abashed and swept his gaze over the shiny fabrics of the makeshift settlement. 'Look at us here on

Irth, perched at the crumbling edge of the Gulf with its vacuum and dim lit cold below, waiting to swallow us whole. Sooner or later, we all fall . . .'

'Yeah, Dog. All but the holy—' Tywi put a hand on his furred arm. 'I got a question. It ain't about the holy or the damned. It's just about living.'

'Good! I am neither holy nor damned myself,' Dogbrick said and put both large hands on the crude harness of power wands and rat-star gems he had rigged for himself from wharf supplies. 'Like most people, I'll walk the Bright Shore until I drop my body and my light carries me into the darkness of the Gulf. That is what the talismanic doctors predict, and I doubt them not at all.'

Tywi nodded and fingered her amulet necklaces, glad for the soothing strength they offered. 'You think this is a life we can love?' she asked. 'I mean, Dog – we've seen so many die. And so horribly. "Amulets heal the body, Charm heals the soul." That's what witches say. And yet, the dead – they are gone. Their absence mocks me.'

'Mocks you?' A startled laugh jumped from him. 'Now you're sounding like a witch.'

'Mocks what I'm feeling. You know what I'm saying.' An urgent expression brightened her stare. 'Dog, I love Drev.'

'Love!' The philosopher inhaled to begin a discourse on the bewitching truths of *The Screed of Love* but restrained himself when he saw the concern in his ward's tawny face.

'All I really know of him is just a dream. Yet I love him anyway. We can love dreams, can't we, Dog?'

'Some philosophers would say all that we can love is dreams.'

The shadow vanished between her eyes, and her body relaxed. 'So it's all right? Me and Drev?'

' "Love is a question," ' Dogbrick recited from *Screed* and peered at her with a warm glint in his amber eyes. 'The answer lies not with me, my drear dear, but with Drev.'

They both turned their attention to the flashing tent tops of the station, thinking about the healing that remained and the work yet to be done. Dogbrick bade farewell and strode back to work with a lofty gait, proud that he had counseled his ward like a sage, without wordy oration.

*Love,* he thought. *That is all that heals us in this creation of broken worlds. Not words. Words are hollow. It is the love they carry that heals.*

The philosopher turned his face into the wind to taste the spindrift and continued speaking to himself from the quiet of his heart: *We are all, then, healers, are we not? For we need love as much as we need Charm. Ah, yes, everyone is a healer, for we are all wounded.*

He pondered this insight, measuring the losses in his own past that love would have to fill. Tugging at his beard, he spoke to fill that emptiness, his words creating for him a warmth like the radiance of a star in its solitude:

*Alone in the wind with her dance, humanity seems to me very much like an old healer on the sliding scree of a mountainside under the vacant swirl of the shoreless heavens . . . All of her soul hovers in her incantation.* He sighed. *To what shall we dedicate the palsy of this dance, Dogbrick? To what? I tell you, man, by this pain of unknowing, by trying to know and understand this grief of living, we learn the extremity of love.*

Tywi watched after him fondly, seeing him talking to himself and glad that he had kept his counsel to her so direct. She felt gratitude again for his friendship and touched the talisman beads around her neck that he had given her and that allowed tenderness to wake in her after so much hardship.

Presently, her thoughts returned to Drev, and she wondered what their life together would be like.

In a day, the wizarduke would wake whole, purged of the damage inflicted by the Pain Chain. But for the time being, he ranged far from his unconscious body. In fever flight, he circled the globe and looked again for Gabagalus. Night held the far side, and all he saw below was the shining Sea, glossy with planetlight and starsmoke.

On the day side, he cruised through windhair clouds over the sacred crag of Floating Stone. The scorched quilt of farmlands in the shadow of the suspended mountain already lay speckled green, enlivened once more by charmwater.

Grasslands swept by, and occasionally he spied a prairie village floating in the quiet flaxen sea of grain. The far distance glinted with razor lines of shoals, tide pools, and the Sea's horizon. Drymarch paraded past with its dew-wine vineyards, pastel bungalows, and a sky bund stacked into the clouds with trade dirigibles.

Old Shard, the colossal granite port on the headlands of Mirdath, had wasted no time in erecting scaffolds above their famous helical towers that the cacodemons had toppled. Drev did not linger to inspect the busy reconstruction, for he was eager to see his capital again.

Adrift above the convoluted jungle gorges and cloud forests of Ux, Dorzen spun daylight from its domed minarets and suspended ribbons of pavement. But before he could fly closer, a soft yet insistent voice summoned him.

'Drev—'

He woke to Tywi's mild smile. Her hands, weathered as rocks, clasped his. All the hues of pain, all its oily stains on his soul, had been washed away by Charm.

Yet he remembered.

The sky and ground rising and falling on his harrowing ride to hell continued far back in his mind, where the light of talismans could never shine.

He remembered. The way to hell was slow and with many detours into memory. Of course, the road needed repair, riddled as it was with potholes of empty desires and lost loves . . .

'Drev – wake up,' Tywi called with gentle urgency.

Clarity flickered in his weary face as he forced himself to his elbows and took in his surroundings. Dawnlight breathed in pearly billows through the trembling tent canvas. The conjure-cloths gathering the first Charm of day had roused him. His sleep was over. He had absorbed all the Charm his body could hold. From this point on the healing required his awareness; it could no longer be done *to* him.

Tywi helped him sit, and he stared at her a moment without recognizing her, surprised how Charm had transformed her. She was no longer the street mouse of his trances but an intimate stranger with a quiet beauty that had been hidden before by dirt and despair.

He searched out the traits he found familiar – her dimpled chin, rabbit pout, and bold eyebrows – and the recognition he felt placed him again at the center, at the pivot of his life, in touch again with the fulcrum that the sages called destiny. With Tywi at his side, he sensed peace and its measures of happiness stretching ahead of them. He felt he would scry it for certain if he closed his eyes. But he could not stop watching her until she pulled him hard against her.

'We must never part again,' he whispered into the softness of her hair.

'Never.'

He separated from her, stronger and all at once more clearheaded, and he put a palm against her cheek. 'We have suffered many little deaths apart, Tywi,' he said, searching her eyes, wanting to be sure he understood her beyond Charm. 'Do you really think it's possible that we can enjoy a long life together?'

Her embrace answered him beyond words.

Within the hour, they departed Blight Fen with arms around each other in a wind cruiser with no captain but himself. The fleet craft carried them high above the melodious isles and hills of Irth. Helm secured, the ship hove through a clear sky, and they stood together at the rail, faces glazed and narcotized before the wind.

On that placid flight, they shared in person all they knew and feared. And only after their lovelocked bodies unstuck and they had tacked into the dusk and turned to run hard before a scarlet night did they share what they feared to know.

'What brought us together?' Tywi asked, sitting beside him on the pilot's bench, their joined arms at rest on the helm. She wore a throat band of rat-star gems that polished the transparency of her mind. Under its influence, thoughts and words moved differently in her.

'Is it Charm?'

'No, not Charm,' Drev whispered dreamily, face upturned to the gold-thatched sky. 'Not Charm. Fate.'

'What is that?'

'I'm no Dogbrick,' he stated flatly and regarded her from the smiling corner of his eye. 'I have no real answers to questions like that.'

'What do you *think* it is, then?' she prodded him, and turned her cheek to the balmy breeze.

'A pattern in the light of the Abiding Star.' He glanced back at the following sky of vagrant twilight. 'Shadows of heaven – I don't know. What we were when we were light, I suppose, before we cooled to bodies and destinies.'

'Then we met in heaven.' She liked that and let him know with a kiss.

He squeezed her hand with savage tenderness. 'What I fear to know is what set us apart on Irth. Peer and street orphan. What breaks the light into privilege and poverty? No sage has ever explained that to my satisfaction.'

Tywi hesitated to voice the obvious: 'That flaw is in ourselves. "Peers whisper to Peers." Isn't that the old saying? The charmless never hear what they say. We keep ourselves apart from each other.'

'That can change with us.'

'You *are* in love.' She laughed briskly. 'Excuse my giggling! I've had almost all my dreams in a trash bin, Drev, so they're less shiny than yours.'

'You don't think we can end the Peerage?' He sat up and stiffened with mock surprise. 'My great-grandfather united the strong and weak realms into the Seven Dominions. My grandmother set the Gemstar above Irth and brought together near and far. But you and I, Tywi, we will do even better. We will join high and low and make heaven touch Irth.'

'Now you do sound like Dogbrick,' she said, with an amused grin. 'I hope we can bring Charm to all the warrens on Irth. I can play that dream by heart.'

'Well,' he admitted upon a moment's reflection, 'even if you are right and we don't succeed, Irth can never be the same again. We are closer now to the Dark Shore. All of us, even street orphans, are Peers above that abyss.'

Mention of the Gulf made them shudder, and they hugged wordlessly under the night's red branch. A long time, they held to each other, their hearts full of departures healed by Charm.

'Let's rise above the darkness,' Drev suggested.

They parted smiling with a shared understanding and walked down separate sides of the cruiser, angling the hex-vanes on the rails to catch the last red rays. When they met at the bow and held to each other again, the sails of conjure-silk filled taut with dusk. For the moment, time stood still as their vessel lifted toward brighter layers of sky above the shadow of the world.

Poch accompanied Jyoti when she presented herself to Lord Drev with the sword Taran. The wizarduke, just recovered from his Charmed sleep, looked thin as smoke and eager to be away from Nhat with his new bride. Yet, he dismissed his cortège of well-wishers and excused himself from his beloved Tywi to meet privately with Lord Keon's children in the silver shadows of his healing tent.

He consoled them again for their terrible losses and heard all that befell them after their paths crossed in the Qaf. At the time, he had never expected to see them again. And yet here they were – the wan brother and athletic margravess, lone orphans of Arwar Odawl, survivors of perilous paths.

In a solemn gesture that had as much to do with tenderness as justice, he bequeathed them the sword Taran to serve as an emblem that would mark their generation and the beginning of a new Brood of Odawl.

Poch thought it a dubious honor to receive the blade that created the evil that was Wrat. What grace in a sword that had led scavengers against Peers? To him, the brother of a margravess, this was a sinister legacy, this cutting edge that had severed the life of the wizarduke's own sister, the Duchess Mevea. The youth might have thought the sword a bane and not a trophy at all if not for his sister's triumphant pride in receiving it.

'You carry nothing with you but what you have lost,' the wizarduke said to them upon bestowing the weapon. 'Carry that lightly and this sword may help you carve a future out of your emptiness.'

Soon afterward, the wizarduke and his consort left by wind cruiser, and Jyoti and Poch sat on a knoll outside the camp with the sword standing in the ground between them like a blade of daylight.

'I'm not going back with you, Jyo.'

Jyoti simply watched her brother with an animal calm. 'We have a city to rebuild.'

'Leave Arwar in ruins.' He frowned at her, his anger charmed to annoyance by the profusion of amulets he wore. 'Don't ever rebuild it.'

'Why?'

'No Charm can really heal it,' he said, bitterly. 'It can never be the same.'

Her calm tightened to relaxed vigilance. She looked for insight into her brother from the shadows of expression that crossed his face and from the colors in his voice. Since the cacodemons turned to smoke, she had been trying to understand what had become of him in the Palace of Abominations. He would not speak of it and hid behind his amulets.

'I'm leaving on the first flight to Moödrun,' she told him in exasperation. 'Just like we talked about. I'm margravess . . .'

'Of ruins.' He mocked her with a cold smile and added gently, 'Leave it that way, Jyo.'

'The earl of Moödrun has already been in touch, you know

486

that. He's sending an escort.' She searched for her brother in his taut stare, trying to see through the depths of his days to the loud and happy child he once was. 'Elvre looks to us for leadership, Poch. We are Arwar Odawl now.'

'You are.'

'I want you to serve with me.' She reached over and took his hand. 'It's too much for me alone.'

'You won't be alone.' He squeezed her hand affectionately and a glint of mischief sharpened his stare. 'There's the earl and scores of other Peers throughout the dominion who will be eager to replace our fallen brood.'

'No one can ever replace them—'

Poch rolled his eyes and let her hand go.

'What are you going to do, then?' she asked, proud at least that Charm had restored him to the wide possibilities of his life.

'I'm staying here.'

'Here?' she asked derisively and swatted at a tuft of grass seed. 'This is just swamp and ruins. What are you going to do here, curate an atrocity museum?'

'I'm going to work in Blight Fen,' he informed her with a self-assured smile. 'Dogbrick says that these tents one day will be temples of healing. People will come from all the dominions to study the curative powers of Charm.'

'Dogbrick—' The last of her calm evaporated, and she scowled at him. 'He's a beastmarked thief! This clutter of bright tents is just a chance for him to create a tiny fiefdom of his own. Why do you want to serve him in this remote place when you have a legitimate role to play in the larger world?'

He laughed at her with familiar zeal and a brother's chiding humor. 'Do you hear yourself, Jyo? You sound like Father. "A *legitimate* role to play in the *larger* world!" ' He gibed her solemnity with a stiff face that shattered to a jeering grin. 'What happened to the Jyoti who used to let Grandfather Phaz throw her around like a silly tumble monkey? Where's my sister who used to sand sled with me?'

'She became margravess.'

He nodded with glum acceptance and patted her hand fondly. When he stood up, he took notice of the silvergold blade. 'The sword belongs with you. I don't want anything to do with it. It reminds me of Wrat.'

'Don't judge this too quickly.' Jyoti rose and put her hand to the helve, so that it opened for her grip. 'This sword is far more noble than any loveless lie Wrat could put on it.' She turned the blade gently between them, sidelighting their faces with its gleam.

'It's venerable!' she continued, excitedly. 'It belonged once to the Liberator, the tailor Taran. And before him, it served kings.' She gazed into it deeper, and its light made a music in her eyes. 'It was forged on Hellgate in the first talismanic days by Tars Kulkan, the blind smith who founded the dreaming school of sorcery . . .'

Poch tossed her a friendly wave and walked off. 'As I say, it's your sword.' He strode across a grass field shiny with wind, walking away from the station of prismatic tents.

'Where are you going?'

'I'm meeting Dogbrick,' he replied. 'He's organizing perimeter sentinels with eye charms, in case the ogres decide they can't resist the supplies in our stores.'

Jyoti saw then that he was determined to go his own way, and she sighed, as much releasing him as accepting him. 'Fine. I'll know where to find you when I need you,' she taunted in her best elder sister's tone. 'We'll stay in touch by aviso.'

'Sure, Jyo,' he called over his shoulder. 'Some day we'll sit across a table and negotiate trade routes between Arwar and Blight Fen.'

'Some day.'

He waved genially without looking back and walked on, not needing her any more. A smile gleamed in her, then blurred to sweet sadness.

Jyoti did not wait for the earl's escort to arrive from Elvre. The

A Flesh of Dreaming

following dawn, still under the heel of darkness, she rode a sky-barge out of Blight Fen. The tandem-lashed balloons, forty in all and with a spry crew of eighteen, were bound for Moödrun laden with the tide scavengers' latest harvest of kraken bones and sea dragon molts.

From the stern rail, she watched the swamp angel burning in the twilit wilderness, illuminating the simmering black pool that had drowned the Palace of Abominations. As the barge pulled farther away, the angel flickered dimmer among the jungle isles and the solvent hues of daybreak.

Morning rose blue among tall ranges of luminous clouds. The calm and powerful Sea swept below strewn with spindrift and the blowsmoke of Leviathan rising to their shadow.

Elvre's green plateaus and jungle massifs lifted above the horizon. Soon, the sky-barge slid off the maritime wind on to the Road of Clouds, the main trade passage through the realm. Silver trestles of sky-bunds glinted above the forest awning and collected black dirigibles in clusters where cities thrived below.

The barge navigator informed Jyoti when they reached the closest approach to Fallen Arwar. On a launch stage above the cargo holds, she strapped herself into a personal glider, and the navigator set the hex-canvas to catch the rays of the Abiding Star at the necessary angle to carry her to the ruins. When he released the tethers, she rose through a fog of cloud.

She burst clear into a flyway of undulant and colorful waterbirds. For most of that afternoon, she sailed above a vast wilderness interior. Wherever she looked, she surveyed the cinnamon sprawl of rivers and rainforest bunched in emerald horizons.

Fallen Arwar came into view under the slant rays of late afternoon. Dense jungle encircled the impact crater, a chancre of melted rock crusted at its center with the debris of the fallen city.

Steam still rose in tendrils from the rubble mountain of twisted pipes, broken slabs and goliath chunks of masonry. Backlit by the swollen Abiding Star, the mound resembled a bald

THE DARK SHORE

death's-head foul with decay, already splotched by the jungle's spongoid growths and anguished ganglia of creepers and vines.

Other gliders wheeled on the thermals above the ruins: gawkers, mourners, relations of the lost, and a vigilant patrol of well-armed air rangers that the earl of Moödrun had dispatched to stalk scavengers. When she crossed the horizon, the raptor-cowled rangers identified her with their eye charms as their margravess, and they escorted her, using green glow wands to light the way toward a cleared escarpment above a riotous gorge of fronds and mist.

From where she came down in the clearing, she could view the crash site in vermilion and crooked last light. An air ranger helped her unstrap, another introduced herself and the squad.

*New faces, new names – a new city – everything new.*

She nodded cursorily to each of the rangers, then gave her attention to the shattered metropolis she was intent on rebuilding. In the umber light and with intoxicating currents of forest haze rising on the night tide, she visualized New Arwar. It would be as modern as old Arwar had been classical. She would set it to drift in a wide elliptic trajectory through the dominion with this death's heap as one focus and lively Moödrun as the other.

She had plans. And the new faces and new names would help her to fulfill them. She turned to address them and saw a scuffle among the rangers farthest from her. Several guards struggled with someone among the bloodshot shadows at the fringe of the clearing and threw him to the ground.

'A charmless miscreant,' an air ranger whispered. 'Probably crazed. Says he knows the margravess and demands to see her.'

'Send him forward,' Jyoti commanded, curious to see who was so quickly aware of her return to Arwar Odawl.

A pale, half-naked man rose and strode through the gauntlet of hooded rangers. He wore no obvious amulets, only his soft-soled thieves' boots and black cord trousers. Thin as a cat, he lacked the physical symmetry and developed musculature of a mature Peer, and by this farouche appearance the rangers reasonably

490

concluded he was a charmless rogue.

'Reece!' She greeted him with genuine and open surprise.

'I knew you'd come back here,' he said quietly.

She dismissed the others and stared hard at the soft-bearded man. In the silver planetshine, he looked more familiar than she remembered. 'Have you lost your magic?' she queried. 'Why did you let my rangers restrain you?'

'I was sure you'd see me eventually,' he answered candidly. 'There was no need for magic.'

She stepped closer, studying him avidly. 'After you killed Wrat, you left so quickly. Poch and I – Lord Drev – we all want to thank you for what you did.'

'*Thank* me?' An anguished shadow darkened his features. 'No. I'm the one who left open the Door in the Air. And because I left it open, Wrat came through with his demons. It was my fault that Arwar fell.' He stared at the fuming crater and muttered, softer yet, 'My fault that thousands died – and with them, your family.' Touching chin to chest, he spoke his secret hope, 'I don't deserve your thanks – but I need your forgiveness.'

Jyoti reached out and lifted his face to meet her ardent gaze. 'Love led you here, Reece. You came to find Lara.'

'A ghost. And in seeking the dead, I brought death.'

She nodded, and her eyes narrowed, understanding him. 'You came back to rebuild. Just like me. That's how you knew I'd be here. And that's why you didn't use your dark magic. You want what no magic can find.'

'Yes,' Reece said with a hopeful catch in his voice. 'You have a city to make new. I have a soul that needs similar work. I thought maybe—' He looked into her face for acceptance, and when she smiled quietly, the fog in his bones lifted.

A laugh deepened in her to see his extravagant and relieved happiness, a laugh of recognition, and she took him gladly in her arms and rocked with him beneath the teeming star vapors and planetary phases of the Bright Shore.

491

# APPENDICES

## The Gibbet Scrolls

✦━✦

Key: (Parentheticals are apocrypha that have entered common usage.)

Scroll One (The Sacred Screed)

1. Silence listens.
2. Everything watches.
3. (There is) No mystery between human beings.
4. The past is always changed. (Always the past changes.)
5. (Each of us is) A ritual sacrifice, a blood offering, made by the eternal urgency of the dream to the mortal powers of the world.
6. Every (truly) sacred act is felt first in hell.
7. The holy walk the killing floor of creation (and are) indistinguishable from the damned.
8. (There are) No false stories on the killing floor.
9. Scared is Sacred. (Scared Sacred.)

## Scroll Two (The Empty Screed)

10. To the condemned there are no lies.
11. Everything changes everything.
12. It is big inside a human heart.
13. Each horizon is a knife.
14. Where do you think the sevens run when they break out of the circle?*
15. The Goddess provides. Life sucks.
16. (There is) No freedom from our freedom.
17. Music is the judge of silence.
18. Wisdom is not always wise.
19. In the ancient theater of the night, every story is true.
20. To survive, contain the counterflow.

## Scroll Three (The Temporal Screed)

21. Life shapes itself on the anvil of dreams – and the hammer is death.
22. For the holy and the damned, time weighs a little less.
23. Those who give light are received by darkness.
24. Truth is the most necessary fiction.
25. Does the stream own its water?
26. For the lost and the hunted, time weighs a little more.
27. Hope is sour desire.
28. This is our curse: For every yes, a no.

## Scroll Four (The Screed of Love)

29. Love makes a monkey out of a mirror.
30. Love can neither be created nor destroyed.
31. Love is its own justice.
32. Love is the fullness of lack.
33. Lovers await the tread of the Huntsman from whose hand they will feed.

34. Love, and you will have many helpers.
35. Love is a question.
36. Love. Will it fly?

Scroll Five (The Command Screed)

37. To hold the scales, refuse the journey.
38. Fulfill your limits.
39. Know everything.
40. All else is darkness.

* This adage arises from the perception that the 360° of the circle can be divided evenly by all integers from 1 through 10 except 7; thus, 7 is considered by pretalismanic witches and sages to 'break out of the circle,' because breaking the circle by 7 produces an irrational number, whose non-repeating decimal sequence runs to infinity.

## About *The Gibbet Scrolls*

+—+

The forty aphorisms collectively known as The Gibbet Scrolls originated in pretalismanic times. About 750,000 days before the Brood of Dorzen's One-Eyed Duke defeated the Fierce Realms and established the Seven Dominions of modern times, these adages were first collected. The original scrolls did not survive the razing of Keri during the Goblin Wars; however, numerous copies made over the ages assure that the version extant today agrees in every particular with the most ancient texts.

In the aboriginal Kingdom of the Dog, a region comprising portions of modern-day Mirdath and Bryse, criminals and political prisoners condemned to death were required to write a complete sentence to prove their literacy and their subsequent right to execution by hanging. (The illiterate and recalcitrant were brutally hacked to pieces in a gruesome sacrificial ritual that prolonged death for several days.) The thin wood slats upon which the condemned wrote their last words were nailed to the brows of their corpses and ascended with them on the nocturnal tide.

Turbulent air currents and frequent storms above the Falls scattered many of the corpses across the mountain ranges, where they often became ensnared in the briar on the taiga slopes. Nameless sages and witches gathered their remains and launched them once again into the night. Legend decrees that the sage All Clouds collected the slat wood tags from the brows of the dead and culled from them the inscriptions that have come down to us as The Gibbet Scrolls, though modern scholarship indicates that this collation was almost certainly an effort of no one individual but a sect.

Much research has gone into why these forty lines were selected and arranged in this specific sequence on five separate scrolls, and that will not be discussed here. More than five scrolls may well have existed in earlier times, and there are frequent claims throughout history of a sixth and even a seventh scroll being found. Yet none of these alleged discoveries has ever been corroborated.

Since pretalismanic times, The Gibbet Scrolls, also known as the Five Screeds, have been revered by numerous religious and sociopolitical groups. In modern times, the collection has fallen into disrepute among the Peers in favor of the *Talismanic Odes*, the compilation of the spiritual and sociological insights from the workers of sorcery.